Derailed

Neta Jackson
Dave Jackson

CASTLE
ROCK
CREATIVE
Evanston, Illinois 60202

Published in Evanston, Illinois. Castle Rock Creative.

Originally published in 2013 by Worthy Publishing, Brentwood, Tennessee.

Scripture quotations are taken from the following:

The Holy Bible, New International Version®. NIV®. Copyright © 1973, 1978, 1984, 2011 by International Bible Society. Used by permission of Zondervan Publishing House. All rights reserved.

The New American Standard Bible®. Copyright © 1960, 1962, 1963, 1968, 1971, 1972, 1973, 1975, 1977, 1995 by The Lockman Foundation. Used by permission. All rights reserved.

The Holy Bible, New Living Translation, copyright ©1996, 2004, 2007 by Tyndale House Foundation. Used by permission of Tyndale House Publishers, Inc., Carol Stream, Illinois 60188. All rights reserved.

Harry's prayer (chapter 17 and 41) beginning with "For food in a world . . ." is by Manfred Wester. Copyright 1985 by Gisela Wester.

Publisher's Note: This novel is a work of fiction. Names, characters, places, and incidents are either products of the authors' imaginations or used fictitiously. All characters are fictional, and any similarity to people living or dead is purely coincidental.

ISBN: 978-0-9820544-8-2

Cover Design: Dave Jackson

Cover Photos: Dave Jackson and Getty/Bigandt Photography (dog)

Windy City Stories
by Dave and Neta Jackson

For a complete listing of
books by Dave and Neta Jackson visit
www.daveneta.com and www.trailblazerbooks.com

Prologue

The tremor in Mattie Krakowski's fingertips increased as they brushed her thin, lined lips. Through the dusty curtain, the late-afternoon gloom of drifting snow glowed neon blue. She pulled back the lace veil and studied the puffy mounds strewn up and down Beecham Street like igloos. Not one car had moved all day. The snow that covered the sidewalk was free of footprints.

"My, oh my, Tom! So this is what you call 'global warming'?"

She was talking to WGN's renowned meteorologist who had been explaining why Chicago faced its heaviest snowfall for February 9 in more than 125 years.

"I just don't get it, Tom. I just don't get it."

Tom Skilling was Mattie's friend. So were Regis and Kelly and Oprah and anyone else who cared enough to talk to her from the moment she woke up until after she fell asleep in her tattered old rocker . . . only to rouse herself later just enough to shut off the late-night car commercials that always blasted twice as loud as her friends.

Mattie surveyed her street once more. The city trucks hadn't even tried to plow Beecham. Still, none of the snow mounds were big enough to cover the big pickup truck belonging to the man next door. He was very industrious. A Muslim or something. Maybe he was out somewhere plowing parking lots. Those drifts were high. Mattie noticed that one nearly covered the awful For Sale sign the bank had planted in her yard. If that weren't bad enough, they'd come along and tacked the word Foreclosure on top. It still showed above the snowdrift.

She shivered and let the curtain fall back into place, releasing a musty whiff of burned toast, rancid grease, and scorched coffee. The place needed cleaning, but ever since her second-floor tenant moved out over a year ago, she'd had no money for cleaning help.

1

She hadn't been able to make her mortgage payments either. Her son had remodeled the second floor, but still she hadn't been able to rent it. Now the bank was telling her she had to move out.

She waved her hand in front of her face to fan away the dust. She didn't like to think about the things she couldn't change and turned back toward the TV. "You didn't say it was gonna be this cold, Tom. Don'tcha think a little warning woulda been considerate?" Pulling an old blanket around her shoulders, she walked to the thermostat in the hallway, the ragged ends of the blanket dragging on the floor. Though she'd turned the dial up to seventy-five, the thermometer needle said the temperature had dropped to sixty-two. No wonder she felt so cold! She tapped on the little gizmo her son had installed a few years before to help her save money and turned the dial up to eighty . . . and listened. But there was no familiar rattling in the air ducts to assure her that the old furnace had come to life. She waited . . . still no rumble from the basement.

Land sakes alive, she'd have to give Donald a call. Maybe if he knew she was freezing, he'd drive in from Elgin to see her. But no, no . . . he couldn't do that in this storm, and she shouldn't make him feel guilty. She was trying not to do that anymore. Besides, he was much too busy with those grandchildren. Mattie wrinkled her brow and closed her eyes. What were their names, again? She could see their cute little faces . . . no, wait, they were teenagers now, all knees and elbows and loud, much too loud . . . or, maybe one was even married. She wasn't sure.

Regis was almost eighty, same age as she was, and he didn't seem so forgetful. Still pretty handsome too. And he was such a nice man.

Mattie drifted back toward the living room. She'd check with Tom to see how long this cold snap would last, because she needed some heat!

Suddenly, her hand shot up to pat her withered lips. What if . . . what if . . .? Had she paid her gas bill? "Oh Tom, Tom," she called toward her TV screen, "I have to go check on the gas. I'll be right back. Now don't go away, Tom!"

She made her way into the kitchen and turned on the front burner of the stove. It lit with a poof and settled into a nice circle of blue flame. She held her hands above it, enjoying the warmth until the fringe of her blanket nearly caught on fire. "No! No! No!" She slapped at the fringe. "Whew." She took a deep breath and turned off the stove. So it wasn't the gas! At least she'd figured that much out. A paper-thin smile stretched across her face. She hadn't yet lost it all.

When she got back to the living room, Tom was gone. Mattie picked up the remote. "I asked you to wait for me, Tom. Now I'll have to find some other weatherman." She surfed through the channels, stopping on channel seven, and a woman she didn't even recognize was talking about the storm. What was it Tom called himself, a "meteorologist"? This woman looked more like a floozy.

Mattie stood in the middle of the room, staring glassy-eyed as the floozy pointed to charts and maps and recited meaningless numbers while Mattie's mind drifted back to her inoperative old furnace. Then she turned, shuffled back through the kitchen and opened the door to the basement. She didn't like to go down there. The old wooden stairs creaked, some light bulbs were out, and the place was damp. It was also a cluttered mess, what with Fred's old tools, mildewed National Geographics, racks of empty canning jars—Mattie hadn't canned since Fred died, but maybe someday—and . . . and the cockroaches. They'd never been able to get rid of those nasty things! But the basement also housed the old furnace, and it was calling to her. She had to go see what it needed. She turned the knob on the antiquated light switch and clutched the blanket more tightly around her as she gripped the handrail and began her descent.

Three steps down, her left toe caught the torn hem of the old blanket, and a little cry escaped as she realized she was tripping.

It happened so slowly that for an instant she thought she could catch herself, but the railing was wrenched out of her hand with such force that her body twisted all the way around and bounced off the lower steps with a resounding craaack, a crack that in that instant reminded her of the first home run Donald had ever hit in Little League.

As she tumbled backwards, Mattie grabbed the edge of the canning rack, hoping to stop her fall, but instead it pulled away from the wall, dumping a cascade of Mason jars down on her just as her head thudded on the concrete floor.

Chapter 1

I'M USUALLY WILLING TO HELP OUT AT MANNA HOUSE, the shelter for homeless women where my wife works as a cook, but their idea of a Valentine's party is seldom as kick-back comfortable as watching the Super Bowl had been with my Yada Yada Brothers. So when my iPhone sounded its Law and Order ring, I welcomed the opportunity to leave my little plate of tasteless white cake—definitely not something Estelle had baked—and slip out into the lobby.

I didn't recognize the number on the screen, but it was a Chicago area code, so I answered with a roll of my eyes. "Yeah, Bentley." Estelle bugs me about my gruff greeting, but soundin' like the cop I once was has knocked more than one telemarketer off his game.

"Hey, bro. How's it goin'?" The nasal twang was definitely not that of a brotha, but it sounded familiar.

"Uh . . . Okay, I guess."

"Great! Roger Gilson here. Might have somethin' for ya." Gilson . . . Roger Gilson. Of course. "Ah, yes, Captain Gilson."

"But not with the CPD. Moved over to Amtrak."

"Amtrak . . . as in trains?"

"Oh yeah. I cover from here all the way to the West Coast . . . along with one other captain, that is. Can you believe it?"

"What happened to the CPD?"

"Ah, you know. Budget mess. The police pension fund doesn't look so secure anymore. But then you already know that, and that's why I called."

Gilson's Internal Affairs had helped me nail my corrupt boss about a year ago. But it's hard for any cop to like Internal Affairs, and I still wasn't sure I trusted Gilson. So I cautiously asked, "What's up?"

"Like I said, I'm at Amtrak now, and we're in a bit of a tussle with the TSA. They're all over us to tighten up security or they'll take over. But with the mess they've made of the airlines, nobody wants them running the nation's trains. Know what I mean?"

Sounded like Gilson had jumped from the frying pan into the fire. If the Transportation Security Administration took over security for Amtrak, Gilson might lose his job. "So . . . why'd you call me?"

"You had some trouble with your eyes, right? Went blind for a while?"

"Yeah, I had a problem." A problem that'd scared me spitless because it might've been permanent. Had surgeries, wore eye patches for a while, even had to remain face down 24/7 for two whole weeks. It was a horror movie from which God alone had rescued me—but I didn't want to get into all that with Gilson.

"Anyway, I'm lookin' for a few men I can trust to work under-cover. Know what I mean?"

He waited while I coughed off to the side to keep from laugh-ing at him continually saying, Know what I mean? "Yes, Gilson. I know what undercover is."

"Well, we place undercover officers just about anyplace—in a station restaurant having coffee, sitting next to other passengers on trains, or in bathrooms mopping up."

"Ha! So you're lookin' for a black man to work undercover as a janitor. I don't think so—"

"No, no, no. You don't understand. I was thinkin', with you having been blind . . . you can see now, though, can't ya?"

"Good enough." I could see just fine, but the man wasn't listen-ing, so why explain?

"Great! Then here's the deal: You could work undercover as a blind man, wander anywhere . . . even up and down the aisles of a train. I can see it now." I could imagine Gilson waving his hand through the air like he was painting a panorama. "You staring blankly here and there from behind a pair of wraparound shades, but actually seein' everything. Nobody would even notice you. Know what I mean?" He stopped.

The idea galled me. What was the civil rights movement about if it didn't include helping black people be noticed as valuable, contributing members of society? Finally, I said, "Yeah, I know what you mean, but like Jesse Jackson used to say, 'I Am Somebody!' But you want me to pose as a nobody."

"Ah, come on, Bentley. Don't play the race card on me now. We're talkin' undercover, and I'm tryin' to offer you something."

I snorted. "Gilson, you oughta be selling used cars, but this isn't for me." The doors from the shelter's multipurpose room swung open, and I was glad to see Estelle out of the corner of my eye. "Oops, here's the wife. Gotta go, Gilson. But thanks for thinkin' of me. You take care now!"

I didn't wait for his response. Just touched the red END bar on my phone. "Whew!" I turned to see Estelle's eyebrows arched high in question.

"Ah, just a guy from back in the day with the police department. Wanted me to come work for Amtrak."

"Hmph. Been askin' all over for you. But it's like the ladies don't even recognize you since you shaved your gray horseshoe beard."

"Whaddaya mean? Handsome black man, bald head, just about this tall, seen hangin' around here all too often, and they don't recognize me?"

"Well." She folded her arms and studied me dubiously. "With that little beard you got goin' on around your mouth there, they say you look more like Louis Gossett Jr."

"And that's bad? Come on, now . . . Della Reese!"

Now she laughed. "Hey, you know I can't sing like her."

"But you sure can touch me like an angel." I winked, big.

She grabbed my arm and gave me one of those light-up-my-life grins. "Oh, come on, you. We're outta here." She glanced back over her shoulder. "Let someone else clean up the kitchen for once—we still got groceries to get, remember?"

I sighed. But with snow still piled high after one of Chicago's heaviest snowstorms, I didn't want to chance her getting stuck.

"Yeah, I remember, babe. Let me get our coats."

Twenty minutes later we were in the Jewel, and I was driving the grocery cart behind Estelle. We were paused in the produce section while she carefully examined each item before putting it into the basket when my phone rang. Gilson again. I was tempted to send him straight to voice mail, but I'd learned not to burn my bridges. Couldn't keep the sarcasm out of my voice though.

"What now, Gilson?"

"Ah, good. Now don't hang up on me again, Harry! I'm just tryin' to get you on the team here. And I've come up with a better idea. You worked K-9 for a while, didn't you?"

I hesitated. "Yeah . . . I'm still certified, but that was before I joined Fagan's unit."

"Great, then you know how to handle dogs. We're trying to expand our K-9 unit. Had a young officer complete her training with the smartest dog I've ever seen, but now she's on maternity leave and not likely to return since her baby has severe birth defects. So we have a dog—cost us thousands—without a handler. How 'bout that?"

I frowned. "How 'bout what? You wanna team me with someone else's dog?"

"Corky's young and like I said, smart, very smart. She could make the transition."

"Wait a minute. Handlers are what? Officers? Sergeants? You'd bust me down from a detective?"

"Oh, c'mon. We can work somethin' out. Meet me halfway here, Harry. I'm tryin' to reel you in. I'm sure we could—"

"Gilson! Would you shut up a minute?" The man sounded like he was on too much Vicodin, and it felt good to tell him to shut up. I was a private citizen now who didn't have to kowtow to anyone.

There was silence . . . for five seconds. "Sorry, Harry. Just gettin' into my creative mode. I'm a creative guy, ya know? That's what I love about this job. But seriously, we'd like you to come on board . . . like all aboard." He laughed at his stupid joke. "It doesn't have to be K-9, but I'm puttin' together a team, and they have to have integrity. That's why I thought of you. You proved yourself when you stepped up to nail Fagan."

Matty Fagan had been my boss, corrupt as they come, shakin' down drug dealers and stealing their guns and dope to resell . . . until I blew the whistle on him.

"Hey," Gilson continued, "how much were you makin' before we asked you to take early retirement?"

"Doesn't matter. I'm not interested." Of course I could use the money, but . . . "Sorry, Gilson. Don't think I'm up to travelin' all over the country. I like trains and all, but I'm a family man now."

"Ah, but that's the thing! Sure, you go out on runs, but then you're home for several days where you can focus on—hey, I didn't know you were married! And kids too? Man, you work fast. But you'll actually get more time with the family. Plus the benefits are great, free rail privileges for you and the family. Think about that."

"Harry!" It was Estelle, twenty feet ahead of me with a gallon of milk in her hand. "What good's the cart if I gotta hold this?"

"Sorry, Gilson. But I really can't talk now. I'm in the store helpin' my wife with shopping. Like I said, family man!" I shut the phone off and hurried to catch up.

I can hoof it with the best of 'em when walkin' or even joggin', but slow shoppin' is worse than snow shovelin' as far as my back is concerned. So when we finally got home, I flopped down on the couch beside my thirteen-year-old grandson, DaShawn, who was celebrating no homework over a five-day weekend by watching nonstop TV. The holidays hadn't been triggered by the huge storm, but for the kids it was as good as a "snow week." Thursday they were off for staff development, Friday for Lincoln's Birthday, then the weekend, and Monday for President's Day. You'd think they could have combined Lincoln with the other presidents, but not in Illinois.

Estelle was standing at the kitchen counter opening mail. "Harry . . . here's one for you." She flipped an envelope my way, and I caught it like a Frisbee, glancing at the return address. From my son? Rodney's name was followed by a long inmate number and the address of the county jail on Memorial Drive in Atlanta. My shoulders sagged. How'd he get himself arrested again? I'd visited that gray-towered bastille on police business and knew it didn't qualify as anyone's "home away from home."

Swearing under my breath, I ripped the letter open and turned it away from DaShawn, glad for once that he was glued to American Idol. The boy didn't need to deal with his father being in jail again.

I'd been estranged from Rodney for over ten years until the Department of Children and Family Services brought me his son a couple of years ago—a grandson I didn't even know I had—while Rodney was in Cook County Jail. We'd managed a few contacts, and I'd lined up an attorney who got his case dismissed. Thought things were going better between us. Then he went down to Atlanta "to put his life back together." We texted a couple of times, and then he quit answering. Made me mad, so I quit trying.

I scanned his scrawl. He'd been picked up on a drug charge, but this time he wasn't claiming it was a bogus setup. "It was my mistake, Dad. I never should've—" Dad? He called me Dad? I sat up a little straighter and kept reading. Rodney said he'd completed a drug treatment program that qualified him for early release—middle of February—provided he had "suitable accommodations." Meaning he needed a place to stay. "But I don't really want to go back to staying where I was. I'm afraid I'd just get back into the old patterns. So, I'm wondering if I could come live with you guys for a while?"

I slapped the letter closed and looked around the room as if someone was going to catch me reading such an outrageous request. Slowly I opened the letter and reread the words: "So, I was wondering if I could come live with you guys for a while?"

No way was Rodney gonna insinuate himself into our happy family! Wasn't gonna happen! Outta the question!

I started to fold the letter and return it to its envelope when I realized there was a second sheet of paper, a printed form from the Criminal Court of DeKalb County. Rodney had already filled in his name and inmate number at the top. All it needed was my name, address, relationship to the inmate, and a dated signature to create a formal invitation.

Of all the nerve!

I put everything back into the envelope and stuffed it into my pocket just as Estelle called, "Y'all shut that trash off and come to the table now. The pizza's gettin' cold."

We held hands and I said a blessing, pretty much the same short prayer I usually prayed, but the thought of what we were doing struck me as I said, "Amen." We were a family, the kind of family

I'd never provided for Rodney. His resentment of my too-busy life while I'd been a Chicago cop had taken its toll, and when I was home, I drank too much.

God had given me a second chance to be the kind of a father to DaShawn I'd never been to Rodney, and I wasn't gonna risk that by . . .

I looked around the kitchen table. There was something wrong with this beautiful picture. I knew God had forgiven me, but that didn't mean the past didn't still hang heavy over my head.

"So," Estelle said in a voice meant to perk us all up as she poured Pepsi into our glasses from a two-liter bottle, "what'd Rodney have to say?"

"My dad? Did he call?" DaShawn's eyes went big as he tried to corral his mouth full of pizza.

I sighed and gave Estelle a thanks-a-lot look. "No, son, he didn't call. I got a letter from him today." I glared at Estelle, but she ignored my distress. "He's still in Atlanta, but—"

"But what?"

"He just wanted us to know he's okay, and he's thinkin' about us." What else could I say? "And . . . and he wishes he were here."

DaShawn nodded with the understanding of a boy who'd been disappointed too many times.

Chapter 2

Estelle's plus size bounced our bed as she flopped down beside me, half sitting up against the pillows. "So . . ." She waited until I looked up from reading my Michael Connelly novel. "What did Rodney's letter really say?"

"Ah, not much. He's still in Atlanta." I shrugged and turned back to see how Detective Harry Bosch was going to catch the bad guys in the pages of my novel. I liked Harry . . . especially his name.

"Harry Bentley, I'm a real person talkin' to you here, not ink on some dead trees. What did Rodney have to say? I know it wasn't good, 'cause I can read your body language better'n you can read that book."

I closed it reluctantly and sighed. "He's back in jail—"

"Oh no. Harry, I'm so sorry. How come?"

"Got busted for drugs, I guess. Says he's up for release. But this time . . ." Don't know why I felt the need to defend him, but I pressed on. "This time he's gone through a drug treatment program, and . . . and he even called me 'Dad.'"

"Really?" There was genuine wonderment in Estelle's voice.

"Yeah, and he signed it, 'Merry Christmas, Rodney.'"

She nodded slowly. "Well, that sounds hopeful—though he's a little late with the Merry Christmas." Estelle sighed like she'd just finished climbing the stairs to our little apartment. "I sure do hope he can turn it around this time—not just for his sake, but for DaShawn. But Harry . . ." She hesitated a moment. "I don't know how long it'll last unless he makes a clean break with his runnin' buddies. I had my doubts when he went down to Atlanta sayin' he was gonna hook up with some old friends." She shook her head. "He needs to get away from 'em—all of 'em, Harry!"

11

"I know." I nodded in agreement as Estelle tied a night scarf around her head to protect her 'do. "You're right. He needs help—" I grimaced. "—and that's the other reason he wrote. He, uh, asked if he could come stay with us. Actually, it's a requirement for his early release, someplace to go. He even included a form from the county he wants me to fill out." I watched Estelle's mouth slowly drop open. "But don't worry, babe. It ain't gonna happen."

She didn't speak for a long moment, and I wondered what she was thinking. Her fingers toyed with the edge of the sheet. "Well, that's right of course. We just don't have the room. He'd be all up in our business—I mean, we wouldn't have any privacy, not to mention we gotta think of DaShawn now."

"I know, I know! It's an outrageous idea. Out of the question." Estelle pulled the blankets up to her chin, staring blankly at the foot of our bed as she slowly nodded her head. I turned to look at the same nothingness and nodded my head in unison.

"Though . . . you know, Harry, sometimes I wish we did have a big enough place where Leroy could come. I really do."

Long-term sorrow filled Estelle's voice. Estelle had an adult son too, but Leroy was schizophrenic and had nearly died in a house fire when he was trying to live alone. His burns were still not fully healed.

"I know, babe. But you know he needs to be in an institution where he can get his whirlpool sessions and those pressure sleeves put on—"

"But it won't be that way forever. He's almost healed."

Her pain about Leroy was deep. "The burns are almost healed," I said softly, "but he still needs full-time care, Estelle."

"Oh, I know!" She waved her hand across her face as if brushing away a gnat. "But . . . what if he got better? We ain't got no place for him, even then."

To my way of thinking, the idea of Leroy staying with us was really out of the question. But I was smart enough not to say so, not while my wife was having one of her guilt waves over not being able to care for her son in the way she thought she ought to.

✦   ✦   ✦   ✦

Tuesday morning, after DaShawn had finally headed back to school, Estelle poured me a second cup of coffee and then sat down across the table from me. She blew briefly into her cup. "You know, Harry, I been thinkin' . . . we really do need more space. I mean, even for DaShawn. We're all on top of each other up in here."

That was obvious, especially with DaShawn—now a gangling thirteen-year-old—in the house for five days straight in the middle of winter. We hadn't planned to stay in my little apartment after getting married, but a whole year had gone by, and we were still stuck there.

"Guess you're right." I stroked my chin, feeling the small beard framing my mouth and chin. But wise is as wise does, and I had to admit, staying cramped in our little apartment didn't make much sense. Thinking out loud, I said, "You know, with the recession and all, it's a buyer's market out there. Maybe we oughta take a look—not for Rodney, that's a whole other thing, and, uh, not . . ." I wouldn't rub it in about Leroy. "Let's just say you're right. We need it for ourselves. Maybe I'll take a look tomorrow."

"Tomorrow? Harry Bentley, sometimes you go from zero to sixty before I can even catch my breath."

"What? Didn't you just say—"

"I mean, it's the middle of winter. We just had a record snowstorm. This is no time to move."

I shrugged. "Maybe, maybe not . . . but think about it. Anyone tryin' to sell now has got to be desperate, so it might be the very best time to buy."

She held up her hands. "Whatever."

I finished my coffee, then casually went over and flipped on the computer. By noon I'd found four places on the Internet that looked interesting, especially with their summertime photographs of green lawns, flowers, and blue sky. Estelle had the day off, and I persuaded her to at least do a drive-by with me. But she was kinda closed-mouthed about it all, and I realized it was hard to get a sense of what the houses were like when the sky was overcast and the ground was decorated with mounds of dirty snow.

I had Bible study that evening with a group of brothers—mostly husbands of Estelle's group of sisters that called themselves the

Yada Yada Prayer Group—and when I mentioned we'd been looking at houses, Peter Douglass leaned over to me. "Stick around afterwards, Harry, I want to talk to you about that."

I lifted an eyebrow. Peter was one of the smartest businessmen I knew.

As the other brothers were leaving, he took me aside. "You bank with Chicago Sheridan, same as me, don't you?"

I nodded.

"Well, I was talking to my banker today, and he was complaining about all the repossessions they're having to process. I'm not one to take advantage of someone else's misfortune, but—" He shrugged. "—once the bank pulls the plug on a place, I don't think there's any harm in picking up a good deal where you can. You should check it out."

Made sense. In fact, I kept thinking about what he'd said until I fell asleep that night.

After dropping Estelle at work the next day, I drove over to the bank to talk to the mortgage officer who handled repossessed properties. She gave me a binder to look through—dozens of single-family homes. While I was looking, she brought over another listing. "I know you weren't looking at two-flats, but here's one you might consider. I'm familiar with this place because we did everything we could to keep the old lady in it, but it just didn't work out. Neighborhood's great, and with the income from the second unit, you'd qualify, no problem."

I studied the listing she handed me. Classic Chicago greystone, two stories over a basement with a wide tower of bay windows up the front, giving the building a somewhat castle-like appearance. It reminded me of the apartment on the South Side where I'd grown up . . . and suddenly the thought crossed my mind that it might be possible to move my elderly mother into a place like that.

I flipped over the listing and checked the asking price. The bank had conveniently calculated the monthly payments for anyone with good credit. Whoa, not bad! With what we were paying for our apartment plus what Mom was paying for hers, we'd almost have it covered.

I got copies of the listing on the two-flat as well as a couple of other properties and thanked the banker. But as I left the parking lot, nearly getting high-centered on a pile of snow, reality started to set in. With my pension and Estelle's part-time wages from Manna House, it seemed risky to take on a mortgage. What if we ended up like all those other "risk takers" who'd gotten themselves in over their heads? Ha! We might find ourselves knocking on the doors of some shelter.

Still . . . Estelle was right. Sooner or later we were going to have to do something. I checked the address for the two-flat. Wasn't too far out of my way, so I swung by for a quick look.

The house was on Beecham, a block that dead-ended on the north at Saint Mark's Memorial Cemetery, which wrapped around behind the homes and the alley to the east. When I turned onto Beecham from Chase Avenue, my foot came off the gas and I slowed to a crawl. In spite of week-old snow, the little neighborhood of brick bungalows and two-flats was so typically Chicago, I immediately felt at home—until I noticed the new McMansion built at the north end of the block, one of those big new houses that looked like the manor house at the end of a plantation lane using the cul-de-sac as its private drive. I briefly wondered if it'd end up in some bank's repossession binder too . . . but that wasn't why I was there.

I bounced over icy ruts under large, leafless trees, imagining the cool shade their arching canopy would provide come summer. I smiled. Very copacetic! Halfway up the block on the left was the greystone. There were still enormous mounds of dirty snow encasing unmoved cars interspersed with parking spots residents had laboriously shoveled out and marked off for their private use with sawhorses and old lawn chairs.

More than once over the years interlopers had been shot when they dared to "steal" a cleared and claimed parking spot in Chicago, so I carefully checked up and down the block before nudging my RAV4 into an open space without knocking over the sawhorses on either end. I was only going to be a minute, and no one seemed to be watching. I jumped out, zipped up my Chicago Bears jacket, and pulled my flat hat a little lower. Even though the temperature was hovering around freezing, the wind still had a bite.

If there was a for-sale sign in front, it was buried in snow . . . no, there it was, the word Foreclosure poking out. The building was obviously vacant. The unshoveled walk to the door had only a few footprints, probably from the mail carrier. I walked around the side of the building, where there were more tracks, a beaten path that ended at the side door. Just beyond I noticed a basement window had been knocked out and wondered about squatters, but the tracks I'd followed were iced over as though no one had passed that way for a few days. I plowed on through virgin, knee-deep drifts that sometimes held my weight and sometimes caved in, until I got around to the back of the house. A large white-barked sycamore tree spread over most of the small yard, and farther back was a two-car garage, serviced by the alley beyond. But there were no tracks leading across the yard to the garage or the trash dumpsters along its side. More evidence that no one was living there. I looked back up at the building. The tuck-pointing appeared sound, and someone had installed new windows on both floors.

The place might be worth considering.

When I picked up Estelle from work that afternoon, I told her about my exploits, carefully broaching the idea of a two-flat we might share with my mom. Estelle was silent for several moments, and I glanced over to see her gazing out the side window. Finally, she gave a short little laugh and shook her head. "Harry, tryin' to keep up with you is like chasin' a squirrel! Here I am, just gettin' used to the idea of us buyin' a house, and now it's a two-flat and movin' your mom in!" She cut her eyes sideways at me. "But . . . there's somethin' that feels right about it. I know we gotta do somethin' about your mom, and it'd sure be convenient to have her so close. I'm gonna pray about it."

Estelle's eagerness to pray about the two-flat should've encouraged me, but instead it got under my skin—not because I didn't value prayer but because I'd forgotten to pray. How could I have forgotten? I'd been a Christian for four years now, but sometimes around Estelle, I felt like I was still in kindergarten.

Chapter 3

Ihad a hard time falling to sleep that night as I wrestled with Estelle's comment. But it wasn't her fault. She hadn't accused me of not praying about the two-flat. All she'd said was she was going to pray.

But it had showed me up.

Man! Most of the time marriage is great, but sometimes it felt like a catch-22. I tried to do the right thing—like looking for a better place for my family—but I still ended up doing it wrong. I could just hear Pastor Cobbs preachin' about the Apostle Paul making the same complaint: "What I want to do, I do not do, but what I hate, I do." That was me, all right.

I punched my pillow and turned over. Estelle's breathing was steady, just shy of a snore. How come she was able to sleep like a baby? I guess my reaction to Estelle's promise to pray said something about our relationship too. If I'd taken the time to pray, I'd probably have included her more. But I plowed on, doing it all on my own, without her and without God.

All right, all right, God. I get it! I'm sorry! I really don't want to do this without you. Please forgive me.

I let that soak in for a minute, staring into the darkness.

Wait . . . had God just been talkin' to me? Not in a big dramatic way, like that time I'd nearly heard his voice when I was going blind. Still . . . it felt like he'd been guiding my thoughts.

My skin prickled. Did God care that much? A hot tear collected at the corner of my eye, and I quickly wiped it way. Man, why was I getting so emotional these days? Was it a symptom of getting older?

I grinned at myself in the dark. I guess you either let things touch you or you get harder. Seemed like the more of life you see, the more you gotta go one way or the other.

17

I was shaving my head the next morning when I heard Estelle holler for the third time, "DaShawn! Get in here and eat your breakfast. I ain't callin' you again."

"Just make me a toast an' peanut butter sandwich to go."

"I already scrambled you some eggs. You, too, Harry. We're runnin' late this morning."

I wiped the shaving cream from around my ears and got to the table before DaShawn.

"If that boy misses his bus . . ."

I shrugged as I sprinkled pepper on my eggs. "Well, you know I ain't takin' him. He can catch the next one and be late, as far as I'm concerned. Teach him a lesson."

"DaShawn!" In spite of her threat, she called him one more time.

"Comin'!"

The boy appeared, wolfed down his eggs, and slurped his OJ, his skinny butt barely brushing the chair before he was up and running for the door.

"Don't forget your homework!" Estelle called after him.

When the door finally slammed, Estelle plopped down in her chair at the table and wiped the back of her hand across her forehead. "I declare, I feel like I've worked a whole day already, an' I still gotta feed thirty picky women at the shelter."

I stifled a chuckle and we ate in silence for a few moments. I figured Estelle was still stewing about DaShawn, but then she up and said, "You know, Harry, I've been thinkin'. Everything's already set up for lunch at Manna House—did the prep yesterday— so I don't have to be in till 'bout eleven. Maybe we should go look at that house you found."

"Uh . . . really? The two-flat?" I couldn't believe it. "Sure. But . . . maybe we oughta take some time to pray together about it first, like you said. You know, be sure we're on the same page and ask God to guide us. It's a big decision."

She dabbed a crumb from the corner of her mouth with a paper napkin and gazed straight at me without one hint of it's-about-time in her sincere nod.

Holding hands across the table, I asked God to open our eyes to what we were going to see. I told him we didn't want to make any mistakes, but we needed a good plan for Mom and DaShawn, and we wanted him to guide us.

Estelle gave me her light-up-the-world smile and squeezed my hand when I said amen. Man, did that feel good!

But when I phoned the bank's real estate agent, the guy seemed reluctant to open the building, saying the place wasn't ready to show yet. The bank had given the previous owner some grace in getting her things out, so the first floor was still filled with the old lady's belongings.

I had my iPhone on speaker, and Estelle mouthed silently to tell him it wouldn't matter to us. Took some talking, but the agent finally agreed to meet us there at ten. To tell the truth, when we got inside, it wasn't so easy to look past the mess. The first floor was filled with mismatched furniture, piles of old magazines and newspapers, even dirty dishes in the sink. I turned on the water, and nothing came out.

"The furnace isn't working," explained the agent, "so we shut off the water and drained the pipes to prevent them from bursting."

We went down to the basement. More clutter surrounded a monstrous old octopus gravity furnace that had been converted from coal to gas, probably back in the 1960s. It would have to be replaced, same with all the appliances we'd seen so far. And everything needed cleaning and painting.

As we came back up out of the basement, I started to feel depressed. Maybe this wasn't the right house. But the agent said, "Before we go up to the second floor, there's one more room back here you haven't seen yet." He opened the door to a sunroom addition on the back of the house filled with dead plants—potted tropical trees and hanging baskets with limp translucent leaves, shelves of African violets and Christmas cactuses, their bright flowers shriveled like pieces of wadded up crepe paper. But the room exploded with brilliance as the morning sun broke through the clouds. It may have been winter, but seeing this room, I could imagine spring coming. I could tell Estelle was impressed too.

That agent was smart. He'd showed us the worst first, and then took us up to the second floor. "Apparently, the son of the old lady who lived downstairs was trying to upgrade the second floor," the agent said as we climbed the stairs. "He hoped to attract a tenant, but it never worked out."

He unlocked the door—and talk about night and day. The second floor was a total contrast to the first floor. The remodeling was top quality. Floors had been refinished, all the rooms painted, and when I looked out back, I saw a new deck with a railing on top of the sunroom below. Most of it was covered by a foot of snow, but I gave Estelle a wink. Could just imagine us sitting out there on a summer evening.

My depression lifted. The second floor let me see what could be done with the place, and I fell in love. In the kitchen, Estelle kept running her hands over the new stainless steel appliances and the marble counters. "Nice . . . very nice. I think I could make you some lunch up in here, Harry."

I frowned at Estelle and put my finger to my lips when the agent looked away. No sense telegraphing our interest. If we were going to make an offer, it'd be better to remind the agent how dingy the first floor was and how much that reduced the building's value.

But once we were driving home, I asked, "So . . . whaddaya think?"

"Mmm. Sure do like that second floor, but I can't imagine puttin' Mother Bentley downstairs."

I took a deep breath. "What if we calculated redecorating the whole first floor into our offer, plus new furnaces and laundry facilities in the basement? I mean, we could take our time. Mom doesn't have to move in right now, ya know."

I could feel her eyes on me. "You think we could swing it, Harry?"

"All depends on what the bank will take for it, but . . . I dunno. Let's keep prayin'."

On Saturday, I got the agent to show us the building again and this time brought Mom and DaShawn along. Mom's eyes lit as we

explained that she'd be living close to us. But Estelle and I didn't
want to discourage her with how terrible it looked. So when she
came into the entryway, and we pointed up the stairs, she looked
at them for a long minute.

"Where's the elevator?"

"This building doesn't have one, Mom. You're gonna be on the
first floor, but we can't take you in there until they finish painting
and fixing it up. Here, let me help you up the steps this once so you
can see how nice it'll be for you."

"Just once, huh?" She eyed the steps again, and then attacked
them, shaking off my helping hand and pulling herself up by the
hand railing.

Estelle swatted my shoulder and stifled a laugh with her hand
over her mouth. "Mom, you could climb Mount Everest if you put
your mind to it."

Once we got up to the second floor, she walked from room
to room, muttering, "Where's the furniture? Cain't live in here
without no bed, no table and chairs. Where's my TV? I gotta have
my shows."

With remarkable patience, Estelle explained everything once
more.

"Hmm!" was all Mom said, but I could tell she liked the place.
While we were guiding her through the second floor, DaShawn was
exploring on his own—upstairs, first floor, basement, and out back.
After we took Mom back to her apartment, I turned my head and
eyed him in the back seat of the SUV. "Well, what'd you think?"

He raised his eyebrows and shrugged as he nodded his
approval. "There'd be room for Dad."

I glanced at Estelle. "Don't think so, son. We told you we're
looking for a better way to look after your great-grandma. Your
dad'll need to get his own place. Know what I'm sayin'?"

I took DaShawn's silence as hesitance to agree. But after a few
moments he bounced back. "Hey, think we could put up a hoop
behind the garage?"

Grateful to get off the subject of Rodney, I said, "I think that
alley would be a great place for a little one-on-one, if you don't
mind your old grandpa takin' you to school."

"Ha! In your dreams, Pops!"

I reached over and squeezed Estelle's hand, but she rolled her eyes. "Thumpety, thump, thump, thump at all hours, huh? I don't know if I could take that."

As Estelle and I prayed, the possibility just got stronger, and the next few days spun by like a whirlwind. We found a contractor to give us a ballpark estimate on the renovations for the first floor, managed to get a credit approval, and negotiated with the bank toward a price we could afford. We even shared the plan with our respective prayer groups—Estelle with the sisters on Sunday evening and me with the brothers on Tuesday.

Some of the guys had questions. Young Josh Baxter, who was learning the ins and outs of building management at the House of Hope, a six-flat connected to Manna House for homeless moms with kids, warned me to be sure and get multiple bids for the rehab work. "They can often vary by several thousand. And get references too!" In the end everyone encouraged us to move ahead cautiously, and both groups prayed a blessing on our final negotiations with the bank.

"I think it's the right place," Estelle said when I reported how the brothers had responded. "I think it's where God wants us, Harry."

I grinned at her. "I agree."

It sure felt different—and so good—to be on the same page with my wife, both of us confident God had his hand on our plans. Guess I was learning something about following God's lead and not trying to do things all on my own.

The next day, after a difficult meeting with the manager of our apartment building in which I finally convinced him to let us out of our lease without any penalty, I was going back upstairs when my cell rang.

"Yeah, Bentley."

"Dad?"

I froze on the second-floor landing. "That you, Rodney?"

"Hey, how's it goin'?"

"Can't complain. How 'bout yourself?"

"That's why I'm callin'. You got my letter, didn't you?"

"Yeah. Yeah I did, but . . ."

"I was wonderin' if you filled out that form for me."

What could I say? "Uh . . . no. Actually, I couldn't. Guess I should've written you back and told you, but there's no way we can invite you to stay with us."

A long silence hung on the other end of the line as I slowly climbed the stairs and entered the apartment. "This is a pretty small place," I added. "Just don't have room."

"Never been there, you know."

His words felt like a jab under my ribs—a reminder of ten years when I hadn't had any contact with him, didn't even know he had a son. I cleared my throat. "Yeah, it's only a small, two-bedroom place with no dining room or extra rooms. With DaShawn and Estelle . . . you know I got married, don't you?"

"Yeah, you wrote me."

"Anyway, we're pretty jammed up in here as it is. Wouldn't work to try and shoehorn someone else in. Fact is"—I knew I was scrambling for excuses—"building management might even object."

More silence. I felt as weak and shaky as if I had the flu.

Finally, Rodney said, "Dad, I really need this. Wouldn't be like I'd have to stay very long. I could crash on the couch for a few nights while I found something for myself. All I need is for you to send in that form. My hearing got postponed for a couple more weeks, but I really need that form to be in my file when I go before the parole board. Know what I'm sayin'?"

I coughed. "Uh, yeah. Well . . . okay, see what I can do."

"Thanks, Dad. See ya."

Chapter 4

Rodney's call left an awful sinking feeling in my gut. I dug
through the old mail in the basket on the little table at the end
of the couch until I found his letter, pulled out the court form, and
read it.

Could I sign it truthfully? Frustrated, I threw it on the table. I'd
have to tell Estelle about the call, and that I'd hinted to Rodney
we might let him stay a few nights. A few nights . . . yeah, right.
Wouldn't hurt to grease the wheels for that sticky conversation,
so I grabbed the baskets of laundry and hauled them down to the
basement to start the wash.

When I came back up, DaShawn was home from school and already on the computer. "Hey, Pops, I read that letter from my dad.
Is he comin' to live with us?"

Oh, man! I hadn't intended him to see that. "Uh, I doubt it,
DaShawn."

"But sounds like he's in jail and wants to get out."

"Yeah. Sorry to say, he got in trouble again. But maybe this time
things'll go better for him."

"Well, I'd let him stay in my room. We could get bunk beds or
somethin'."

Ah, the resilience of youth. I knew DaShawn's memories of his
father were only slightly better than those of his mother, who'd
been a cocaine addict and a whore. But there he was, ready to forgive just to have his dad back in his life.

I put my hand on his shoulder and pulled him to me. "We'll
see. We'll see. Estelle and I'll need to talk about it." I pointed to the
computer screen to change the subject. "Whatcha writin'?"

"Just somethin' on mummies."

"Mummies! You sure that's for school?"

24

"Yeah. For history—about Egypt."

That evening while DaShawn watched TV, I herded Estelle into the kitchen and told her about Rodney's call.

"Harry, you can't sign that paper unless we're willin' for him to come here. And we already agreed this place is too small. It wouldn't be the truth—"

"But Estelle, it's all a farce. The county just wants him out of the state, out of their hair. They can't legally banish him, so they offer him this. It's just a formality. We'd be doing exactly what they want just by signing it."

She looked genuinely puzzled. "What're you saying? I thought we talked about this and agreed we couldn't invite him to live with us?"

"Yeah, but . . ." I checked the form again. "You know, it don't say how long he has to 'live' here." I wiggled my fingers in the air like quote marks. "When he called, he said all he needed was a place to crash for a few days."

Estelle squinted at me out of the corner of her eyes. "You're gettin' soft in your old age, Harry."

"No, I ain't. I'm clear this can't be permanent—or even long term. But since the form doesn't specify the duration, we're not agreeing to any particular length of stay. We could sign it and let him use the couch a few nights."

She lifted an eyebrow. "Uh-huh. And I'm sure you're gonna be the one to put him out, too, when he hasn't found a place in a few days?" But I could tell she was softening.

"Of course." I winked. "I'm the man around here, aren't I?"

"Oh yeah. You da man, Harry! You da man!" She laughed with warm humor and handed me a pen. "I'm just here to make sure you don't become no mouse!"

A week after doing our walk-through of the building, we paid our earnest money and signed all the initial papers to buy 7318 Beecham with an unbelievably quick closing date of March 15, less than three weeks away. The bank seemed anxious to get rid of the place, and I felt uncomfortable signing documents acknowledging we were buying the property "as is" with no warranty concerning the soundness of any aspect of the building. When I asked about it, the banker shrugged. "That's why we're willing to make such a quick sale at below market value. If we wait much longer, the city could condemn the property, then there'd be a lot of expense and a mountain of red tape to reverse. This way, you get the building, and once you pull the permits for the rehab, they won't condemn it on you."

Our attorney agreed, but it still felt pretty scary.

Once we'd signed, the bank wasted no time arranging for the son of the previous owner to clear out the first floor. I dropped by on Saturday just as a big U-Haul truck rolled up. The driver was a tall, lanky white guy, probably in his early fifties, with just a little gray in his mustache and around the temples of his slate-colored hair. He looked about as awkward as I felt, but he came forward with his hand out and offered a firm, rough grip of someone who worked in the trades. "Hey. Don Krakowski."

"Harry Bentley. You here to clean the place out?"

"Yeah. Sorry about taking so long to get my mother's stuff, but it's been crazy ever since the storm."

"No problem. So this was your mom's place? I'm sorry she wasn't able to stay." At least I knew I should feel sorry for anyone who'd lost their home.

He gestured toward the second floor. "I was hoping to get some good tenants in there to stop the repossession, but it just took me too long to finish the work. Then she fell, and that was it."

"Fell?"

"Yeah. You didn't hear about that?"

I shook my head.

"Well," his eyebrows went up, "we nearly lost her. Happened the night of the storm. Furnace went out, and she tumbled down the basement steps trying to check on it. I knew she shouldn't be living here alone." He waved at the street. "Whole neighborhood's changed, and I don't think she knew anybody anymore. She lay at the bottom of those stairs all night, nearly froze to death before the kid next door heard her calling for help the next day."

"Phew. Sorry to hear that." My excitement over getting the building choked in my throat like a wad of cotton. A stranger's financial problems hadn't touched me very deeply, but the fact that an old woman—this man's mother—nearly died in the process . . . "I'm sorry. I'm really sorry," I mumbled. "She okay now?"

The man shrugged. "Comin' along, but you know how a broken hip can be for an older person. I finally got her into a nursing home out in Elgin, not too far from me. But I don't have any idea what I'm gonna do with all her stuff. Probably have to put it in one of those storage places. Sure don't want it in my garage."

The two guys who'd come with Krakowski looked Hispanic, one young and strongly built. The older fellow was pulling hard on a cigarette, his weathered face as lined as a crumpled-up lunch bag.

"Uh, could you guys use a hand?" It seemed like the least I could do. "I don't have anything else scheduled for the morning."

"Sure. I only got this one day off work, and it'll probably be long after dark before I get home."

"Whaddaya do?"

"Ah, we install home security systems." He pulled out his wallet and handed me a card. "It's kind of far, but my boss has done jobs here before, 'cause we can beat most any local price."

"Thanks. I'll keep it in mind." I stuffed the card in my shirt pocket, knowing it would probably end up on my dresser until Estelle nagged me to clean it off.

The movers didn't clear out any of the trash—magazines, boxes, old canning jars . . . the list went on and on. Couldn't really blame them, and I told Krakowski to forget it so long as he informed the bank he had no further claim on anything in the building.

When I told Estelle about the old lady falling down the basement stairs, she sat down in a chair and held her head in her hands, shaking it back and forth. I waited until she looked up at me with tears in her eyes. "Harry, how can we move in there after what happened? It's like . . . it's like her ghost would still be there."

"You believe in ghosts, Estelle?"

"No, but—"

"Well, then, she didn't die. So there's no ghost." And it was too late to back out now.

27

"Harry! That's not it. It just doesn't seem right to benefit from her accident."

"Yeah. I know. I felt that way too. But her son said he'd known for some time she shouldn't be living alone. Now he's finally got her in a good nursing home out in Elgin."

"Hmm." Estelle sat for several moments. "I've done a lot of in-home elder care, but sometimes a person needs more help than that. And a broken hip is probably one of those times, at least until she recovers her mobility . . . if she does." She looked up at me. "Sit down, Harry. Let's pray for her. Did you get her name?"

"Yeah, it's Mattie . . . I think. Mattie Krakowski. And her son's name is Don. He even gave me his business card." I dug it out of my shirt pocket. "Here."

Estelle looked at it a moment before I asked for it back. She frowned. "Don't go tossin' that card on your dresser. We might need his number some time."

But that's exactly where I intended to file it.

After Don Krakowski had cleared out all his mother's stuff, the bank was remarkably flexible in letting me into the building with contractors to plan and collect bids on the rehab. The only restriction was that no work could begin and no equipment or materials could be left on the premises until after the closing date.

Three contractors bid on the first-floor work, and I lined up a furnace company Denny Baxter from my men's group had recommended. We'd be converting to separate furnaces for each unit.

We closed Monday afternoon, March 15, without a hitch. As we left the title company, the overcast sky in the west began to break up, letting bright shafts of sunlight knife down to the earth.

Estelle grabbed my arm. "God is good, all the time!"

"And all the time, God is good!" I grinned at her. "Hey, let's go out for an early dinner to celebrate."

"What about DaShawn?"

"He's got basketball. Won't be home till later."

"Hmm, guess there's plenty of leftovers—"

"Oh, come on. He'll be fine. How about El Barco Mariscos?"

"El what?"

"You remember, that Mexican place you liked down on Ashland."

"Oh, yeah, Mexican seafood. That was good."

The restaurant seemed crowded for a Monday evening, but we were seated within ten minutes. Our salads had just been served when my iPhone sounded.

Estelle gave me a warning squint. "Don't answer."

I looked at the screen and nearly complied because I didn't recognize the number, but it was local, so I gave Estelle an apologetic smile and slid my finger across the slide to answer. "Yeah, Bentley."

"Mr. Harry Bentley? Is your mother Wanda Bentley?"

"Yes. Who's this?"

"Mr. Bentley, I'm sorry to have to call you, but your mother's here in the ER at Saint Francis Hospital, and it looks like she's had a stroke. She's—"

"What? My mother?"

"Yes. The paramedics brought her in about twenty minutes ago. We've got her stabilized for the time being, but . . . you should get here as soon as you can."

Chapter 5

I TURNED OFF MY PHONE and slid it into my pocket. "We gotta go!" I raised my hand to catch the attention of our waitress.

"Harry! What's goin' on? We just got here. Who called?"

I felt as if I was floating in a fog. "Saint Francis," I mumbled. "Saint Francis Hospital. They took Mom there. Said she's had a stroke."

Estelle clapped her hand over her mouth, stifling a gasp. "Oh no. No, no, no. O Lord, have mercy." She pushed her salad back. "Yes, let's go."

We stood up, and I pulled out my wallet, counting out three twenties. That ought to cover it with a hefty tip. Our actions had finally caught the attention of the waitress, and she came scurrying over, a big grin on her face.

"Is everything okay? Your salad? Can I get you . . . What? You aren't leaving, are you?"

"Yes, we have to go."

"Well, if there's anything we can—"

"Family emergency." I dropped the bills on the table. "There, we're good."

I helped Estelle get her arm in the sleeve of her coat, and I'm afraid we bumped a couple of tables as we bolted for the door, but I couldn't help it if other patrons misunderstood our haste for dislike of the food.

At the hospital we headed straight to the ER, and the nurse at the desk confirmed Wanda Bentley was still being evaluated. They let us in, but she wasn't in Bay Six where she was supposed to be.

"You looking for Ms. Bentley?"

I turned to face what looked like an exceptionally young intern. "Yeah, my mother, Wanda Bentley."

"They took her for an MRI. She should be back in a little while. Won't be too long."

"But how is she?"

"That's what we're trying to assess." He gave us a who-knows shrug. "They got her in here right away, apparently as soon as she began exhibiting symptoms. So that's good, and so far there's only slight impairment. But we won't know until we have more information." The intern turned and looked across the ward. "Excuse me. I have to attend to another patient. Why don't you folks pull up a couple of chairs and wait."

I touched his shoulder as he turned to leave. "Can't we go be with her while she has the scan?"

He shook his head. "No one can be in that room, but as soon as she's done, they'll bring her straight back here. Just have a seat."

Estelle shook her head as we sat down. "That machine'll scare her to death."

"Why? What's it do? Isn't it just a big X-ray?"

"Hmph! Don't know if it even uses rays! But they slide you in this narrow tube, and then the thing whirs and bangs like someone hitting the outside with a sledge hammer."

I winced. Mom had always been slightly claustrophobic.

We kept on waiting, our conversation petering off for lack of anything useful to say. Estelle caught my attention with her eyes and rubbed her forehead with a couple fingers. Her little signal to me that I was frowning again. But why not frown? My mom was in serious trouble, and there wasn't anything I could do.

Finally, a nurse peeked in and said if we wanted something to drink there was a pop machine out in the hall.

Wait," I said when she started to leave. "We've been here over forty minutes. What's goin' on? The doctor said my mother would be back right away. Is everything okay?"

"Oh, I'm sure it is. I'll check."

She came back to say Mom had been waiting for transport, but was on her way now.

Once the nurse had gone, Estelle sighed. "That probably means she was stranded out in the hall like she'd been forgotten."

When they finally wheeled her back into the bay, she lay on the gurney, covered by a thin sheet, eyes closed, mouth open. A tube fed oxygen to her nose, and an IV drip hung from a pole.

For an instant, I thought she was dead. Then I saw her chest rise slightly. I waited for a second breath to be sure. "Mom?"

I was never gladder to see her eyes open and track over until they finally focused on me. She raised her right hand in a limp wave.

Thank you Jesus; she was even conscious.

The nurse who'd gone to check on her busied herself tucking in the thin white blanket around her and adjusting her pillow. "There now, Ms. Bentley, does that feel better? Are you warm enough?"

Mom's eyes rolled up to look at the nurse, and a smile animated the right side of her face. But I noticed that the left side didn't seem to move.

"Can you lift your left hand, Mom?"

It moved no more than an inch.

I sucked in my breath as Estelle gripped my arm.

A doctor appeared and moved the curtain aside, asking if we'd mind stepping out for a few moments so we wouldn't distract Mom while he checked a few more things. I glanced at my mom. She was looking at me as if pleading for me not to leave.

"We'll be just outside, Mom. Don't worry, we'll be back."

The nurse followed us, and I took the opportunity to ask whether she knew anything about what had happened.

"According to the paramedics, your mother was at Walgreen's picking up a prescription when the pharmacist noticed her slurred speech and having trouble getting the money out of her wallet. He asked her a couple of simple questions, had her try to hold her arms up, and told her to smile at him. Apparently, she had enough trouble with all three tasks that he had her sit down immediately and called 9-1-1. So I think we got help to her about as quickly as possible. Which is good. Less chance of permanent damage." The nurse smiled. "Excuse me," she said, raising a finger as though she'd be back in a minute, and slipped away.

When the doctor finished, he came out and gave us his tentative prognosis.

Mom had apparently had an ischemic stroke, which he explained as a blood clot that had inhibited circulation to the right side of her brain. They planned to admit her and begin administering medication to dissolve the clot. They also needed to discover the source of the clot—he suspected her legs—and take steps to prevent new ones from forming. At that point they would assess how she was doing and design a plan for her rehabilitation. The doctor was hopeful for substantial recovery. "She still has a little movement on her left side, so that's good. And though there's some paralysis to the left side of her face, making it hard for her to speak clearly, the language centers of her brain don't seem to be damaged. But we won't know for sure until later."

Estelle looked at me as though she wanted me to ask something more, but then she turned to the doctor. "What kind of time frame are we talking about here?"

"Hmm . . . impossible to say. Barring complications, we'll probably begin rehab within forty-eight hours, and when she's out of acute care, we can talk about a rehabilitation center. That's usually most effective for the first two or three weeks. After that, if you can set her up in a supportive living environment, recovery can continue on an outpatient basis."

For the first time, the implications of Estelle's question hit me. "Are you saying she's got to go to some place like a nursing home?"

He nodded. "Weeks, undoubtedly, but beyond that, it's hard to say. There's no telling how fast her recovery will go or how complete it will be. But if and when she achieves a certain level of functioning, there are home-based programs."

He must have seen the shock on both our faces, because he raised both hands as though urging us to not go there. "Let's take it one step at a time. She seems like a spunky person, so let's just pray."

Pray? Oh yeah. St. Francis was a Catholic hospital.

"You can be sure we'll be praying," Estelle said, almost fiercely, "and we've got some strong prayer warriors to call on too."

We followed Mom when they transferred her to the critical-care ward and once the nurses had her settled, we went in and pulled up a couple of chairs to be near her. From somewhere—probably her big purse—Estelle pulled out hand lotion and began applying it to Mom's dry old hands.

She looked up at Estelle and gave her a crooked smile and then started making noises with her mouth. I got up and leaned in close as she mumbled the same thing several times, the left side of her mouth remaining still like someone who'd received too much Novocain from the dentist.

"That's okay, Mom," Estelle assured her, but Mom kept trying to compensate with exaggerated movements of the right side of her face.

She mumbled a long string of gibberish.

Finally, Estelle got it. "She's sayin' she thought they were trying to bury her!"

Mom's eyes lit up. "Eee-ya. Eee-ya!"

I hardly cared what she was saying . . . just that she was trying to communicate. It was like she was coming back to us.

Estelle patted her hand. "No one was tryin' to bury you, Mom. What are you talkin' about?"

Mom launched into trying to tell us with mumbled words and wild eye movements while she pointed with the arthritic gnarled finger of her right hand.

Just then the nurse came back in. "Your mother's getting a little agitated now. She needs her rest. Will you be back tomorrow?"

"Please, wait!" Estelle held up her hand. "She's tryin' to tell us somethin'. Mom, are you talkin' about that MRI? Is that it? That big machine they slid you into, and it went bang, bang, bang?"

Even with the paralysis on the left side, Mom's face expressed obvious relief as she sighed and closed her eyes.

"Well, you don't need to worry, dear. That was just a hospital test. No one's gonna bury you." Estelle patted her hand.

The nurse pushed forward with a strained smile on her face. "I really need to check her vitals now and give her a shot so she can rest."

I eyed her, trying to decide whether to be assertive or plaintive. Finally, I took a deep breath. "Couldn't I just stay with my mother overnight?"

"I'm sorry, sir. When she's in a regular room, yes, but not here in the critical-care unit."

I didn't see why not, but Estelle touched my arm to urge me to not make a fuss.

I leaned down, realizing as I did so that Mom wasn't hard of hearing—at least not any more so than usual. "We're goin' now, Mom. But we'll be back in the morning."

Eyes still closed, she gave us a crooked smile, and we left.

"Where y'all been?" DaShawn scolded as we came into the apartment. "There ain't nothin' to eat!"

I glanced at Estelle out of the corner of my eye. Had she also forgotten? Didn't matter. I'd forgotten, so there was good reason for the dark frown on my grandson's face. Man! Is that how I look when I frown? No wonder Estelle's been on me to break the habit.

I sighed and pulled my attention back to the situation at hand. "Now, just cool down, son. I'm sorry we didn't call. We should've, but we've had an emergency. Great-Grandma's in the hospital."

Shock wiped the frown from DaShawn's brow as his eyes got large. "Hospital! She okay?"

Estelle sighed and tossed her coat on the recliner. "No. She's not okay. That's why she's in the hospital. She had a stroke."

"What's that mean? She gonna die?"

"We don't think so. Least not now. But she's facin' a long road of recovery." Estelle was digging in the refrigerator as she answered DaShawn. "Whadda you mean, there ain't nothin' to eat? What's wrong with this leftover spaghetti?" She pulled out a big tub. "Serve yourselves what you want and nuke it. I'll throw together a little salad."

While we ate, we filled DaShawn in the best we could on what had happened to his great-grandma. He was sobered, and I realized how deeply he loved her. We'd become a tight family.

Later, as DaShawn watched TV, Estelle and I did the dishes and then sat back down at the table with fresh coffee. I hadn't had time to think about the implications of Mom's stroke, but it was starting to sink in. "If Mom's gonna be in a nursing home for . . . for maybe months, what's that mean about her living in our new place? We just bought ourselves a two-flat. Got a pretty hefty mortgage to meet!"

Estelle slowly nodded her head. "And she's likely to need fulltime support even if she does recover. We knew this would come someday, but . . ."

"But what?"

"Well, don't forget—before we got married, even before I started working at Manna House, I did in-home elder care. I'm a certified nurse assistant, ya know."

I'd totally forgotten Estelle was a CNA. "You sayin' you'd take care of Mom? What about your job?"

"It's not what I wanna do, Harry, but she's family. We do what family needs, not just what we want."

My wife's comments rocked me. I knew she loved my mom, but I hadn't realized how deeply she'd made "my people her people," or however Ruth had said that line in the Bible. I reached out and took Estelle's hand, trying to swallow the lump in my throat. "Uh, yeah. That'd be great, babe, but that's months in the future from what the doctor said. And not even certain then. Even if she did move in, I'm still not sure it'd crack our mortgage nut. I mean, we'd have Mom's housing money—like we planned—but we'd lose your Manna House income."

"Ha! It's hardly worth countin', Harry."

She was right about that, though every little bit helped. But something was troubling me. "I don't get it, Estelle. We went into this thinkin' God was leadin' us. We prayed. We asked all our friends to pray. Buying the two-flat so Mom could live independent but still be near us seemed like a solid plan. And there wasn't one person who suggested it was the wrong thing to do! Now I'm feelin' the whole plan's been derailed."

She leaned back in her chair and used both hands to draw her long, black hair with the attractive silver streaks away from her face. "We're not to follow our friends, Harry. We're supposed to follow the Lord."

"I know! I know, but . . . but aren't godly friends supposed to help us test whether we're hearin' him right?" She nodded, and I took a deep breath. "What else were we supposed to do? Maybe we didn't hear God right. But . . ." I thought for a moment. "Everything seemed to work out so smoothly. I mean, it was almost like he was doing little miracles on our behalf to help us to buy that place, and then—poof!"

"Now Harry, you know God ain't brought us this far to leave us." She began to hum, and then broke into the familiar chorus. "I don't feel no ways tired. . ." She hummed some more, and then sang the last line, "I don't believe He brought me this far to leave me."

The song hung in the air.

Well . . . maybe he hadn't left me, but that gut-wrenching feeling of abandonment gripped me again like it had a couple years ago when I thought I was going blind. God had finally brought me through that awful experience, but somehow, what I knew in my head didn't help how I felt right then. Like someone had cut my anchor and I was totally adrift.

Chapter 6

Estelle had to work Tuesday, so I spent most of the day with Mom. She slept a lot, and of course, we couldn't have a conversation even when she was awake, but I think it reassured her that I was there. In the afternoon when Estelle was due to get off work, I left to pick her up, promising Mom we'd be back later.

But Estelle insisted on replacing me for the evening. "I'll take that little CD player with some praise music. That'll perk her up. And I might do her nails for her. They looked a little ragged last night. I'll be fine. So don't worry."

Well, that was Estelle, always doin' for someone else, but I shook my head. "What am I supposed to do? Sit around the apartment all evening and worry?"

"No. You get yourself on over to Bible study. You need the brothers more'n ever tonight."

"But—"

"No buts about it. DaShawn'll be fine. He can do his homework, then watch TV."

After we ate supper, I ran Estelle up to the hospital and then drove over to Peter Douglass's apartment for the Bible study. Denny Baxter was out of town for a coaches' training event, and his son, Josh, was tied up with an emergency water heater replacement at the House of Hope, so there were just five of us: Peter; Carl Hickman, who worked at Peter's software company; Ben Garfield, a retired Jewish guy with six-year-old twins; Pastor Cobbs, from my church, who could only attend the Bible study occasionally; and myself.

We'd been going through the book of Psalms and were up to Psalm 27. I was pretty distracted, thinking about my mom, until we came to verse 11: "Teach me your way, O Lord; lead me in a

38

straight path." Some of the other translations said "right path" or "smooth path." But when Pastor Cobbs read "plain path" from his old King James Version, it grabbed me. That's exactly what I need-ed—a plain path—and frankly, I'd thought God had been showing us a plain path, buying the two-flat with all the affirming signs along the way. But suddenly we'd crashed, and it didn't seem like he'd been guiding us at all.

I wanted to talk about it, wanted to tell the brothers how confused I felt. I wanted to ask if any of them had sensed our decision was wrong, and if so, why hadn't they said so when I was asking for their wisdom weeks earlier?

But Peter was already reading the next verse. "'Do not turn me over to the desire of my foes, for false witnesses rise up against me, breathing out violence.'"

"Oh, that's me!" Ben Garfield snorted. "We got enemies, Ruth and me. And they've been lying about us." Everyone looked at him in shock. "That's right, lying enemies, and they want to get Havah and Isaac in trouble."

"The twins? What are you talkin' about, Ben?" Peter Douglass asked.

Ben tipped his head back, frowning at the ceiling as though expecting some kind of revelation to be written there. "Yeah, it's no secret, it's hard trying to keep up with two kids at our age. Ruth's fifty-six, and I'm nearly seventy. But they're no vilde chaya—they're not hooligans. Just kids, you know. But our neighbor called the police, accusing our Havah and Isaac of stealing his trash bin. Now I ask you, what would two six-year-olds want with a trash bin? Nothing! But he's lying to the police and to the neighbors. And for some, it's like a bandwagon. Now they're saying the kids make too much noise. And they run through their flowerbeds. It's barely spring, after all! So where are the flowers?" He threw his hands up. "What difference does it make?"

Ben went on and on, monopolizing our whole time together with this tale about his kids irritating a couple neighbors, as though real enemies were about to drive him and Ruth from their home. When it was time to gather up prayer requests, I told the brothers about my mom's stroke and asked prayer for her, but there wasn't time to get into how confusing the whole event was for me. Ticked me off . . . but maybe my issue would sound as trivial as Ben's. Stuff happens. Did God care about any of this stuff anyway?

Had to face it. We'd still purchased a building that needed immediate attention, especially functioning furnaces if we were going to move in on Saturday. I spent most of my time the next few days working with a heating contractor. He brought in three men who worked twelve-hour days to finish installing both furnaces and re-routing all the ductwork. I snuck away for short visits with Mom when I could.

They had moved her out of the critical-care unit and into a double room to begin her rehabilitation. The nurses said she was doing well, but I couldn't see any improvement other than the fact that she seemed calmer. That allowed me to come and go more freely to oversee the work on the two-flat without feeling so guilty.

At first Estelle had protested that we couldn't possibly move Saturday, given the crisis with Mom. But we'd negotiated that move-out date with our very reluctant apartment landlord, and I was afraid he'd slap us with a penalty if we extended it.

So Estelle put out a call to our church asking for volunteers. We'd both put in our time helping other people move, so we were hoping there'd be a generous turnout. She took the rest of that week off work and spent every minute she wasn't at the hospital packing.

It wasn't long before Estelle had the living room piled high with stuff.

"I put all the stuff on the top of your dresser into a box, but once we get moved, you've gotta sort through it. And I declare, Harry Bentley, you had more stuff hiding in that basement locker of ours than would fit in one of those big containers they load on ships. What're we gonna do with all this stuff?"

I was inclined to tell her to throw it all out, but she had my fishing tackle piled on there—Hey! Maybe I should take DaShawn fishing this spring!—and there were my dumbbells. Couldn't let those go. "What about these suitcases, Estelle? Why don't we just pack clothes in 'em? And these garden tools. We'll need them in our new place." I opened an old cardboard box. "Hey, my college yearbooks! Haven't looked at these forever."

Estelle snorted. "And this ain't the time. Don't you sit down, Harry Bentley. Just put 'em back in the box. You can dig 'em out this summer." DaShawn packed his stuff in one evening, but then he didn't have to deal with sheets and blankets, dishes and canned goods.

Seemed like the list would never end.

But . . . the furnaces were installed and functioning by Friday as promised, and by midnight we were more or less packed.

A whole crew of volunteers from SouledOut Community Church turned out on Saturday to give us a hand. In spite of gray clouds that spit snow off and on all day, by three in the afternoon, we were unloading the third and—thankfully—last load from the U-Haul, mostly stuff from the locker that was getting stored in our new garage. But I was pretty bushed, so the ring of my cell phone was a welcome interruption.

I flipped over a plastic bucket in the corner of the garage and sat down. "Yeah, Bentley."

"I'm here."

I froze. Rodney. What did he mean, "I'm here"? But just then young Josh Baxter came up right in front of me. "Where should we put this, Mr. Bentley?" He and another young man were carrying the box springs from my old single bed before Estelle and I got married.

I pushed the mute button on my phone. "Uh, just lean it over there against the wall, but try to put something under it to keep it up off the concrete. Didn't we have a sheet of plastic over it?"

The phone was making noise. I put it to my ear to hear Rodney say, "You still there?"

"Yeah, yeah . . ." I held the phone out and saw it was still on mute. "Sorry 'bout that. I was tryin' to give some instructions to people here. What was that you said?" I got up and walked out

41

into the alley, away from the moving truck and the people who were still unloading.

"I said, I'm here. Bus just got in, so what's the best way to get up to your place?"

"Ha! Funny you should ask. We hardly know where we live anymore. We just moved today. That's what you were hearing, a bunch of people helping us."

"You mean you're not in that same apartment? You still got DaShawn, don't you?"

"Of course we got DaShawn! I just meant I'm not sure how to tell you the best way to get here. Lessee . . . If you came up by 'L' on the Red Line, you could get off at Jarvis. Or if you wanna take the Metra train, you could get off at Rogers Park. Either way—"

"Just give me the address, Harry. I'll get there on my own."

So now it was "Harry" instead of "Dad"? I told him our address, and he hung up—and then it hit me. Rodney was coming. To stay with us. Man! He couldn't have picked a worse day. I sucked in a breath and blew it out. Figured I'd better go tell Estelle before I lost my nerve.

I found her putting away dishes in the kitchen. She stared at me. "He's what? He's coming this afternoon?"

"That's what he said."

"Lord have mercy. What're we gonna do?"

"Uh, guess we better go out to eat tonight. No way you can cook in here yet."

She rolled her eyes. "I mean, is he plannin' on stayin' with us?"

I shrugged. "I presume that's why he's here."

"But . . . but we're not even set up for ourselves."

"I know, babe. Didn't think it'd be this soon. But . . . he's on his way."

Estelle sank down into a kitchen chair, looking very tired. "Oh, Harry, I don't know. First your mom havin' a stroke, then all this movin', and now Rodney showin' up . . . it's all a bit much."

I snorted. "Tell me about it. Nothin's turnin' out."

We just looked at each other. Finally she said, "Well, it is what it is. Guess you better tell DaShawn. But we're clear it's just gonna be a few days, right?"

"Estelle, he's not even here yet, so don't be on my case to kick him out."

"I'm just sayin' . . ." She shook her head. "I'm just sayin', things have a way of takin' root, like weeds." Pushing herself up out of the chair, she went back to shoving dishes into the cupboards, a little harder than necessary, I thought.

I watched for a moment, letting my mind escape thoughts of Rodney. Sure was nice to have enough room for everything. The kitchen in the old apartment had only half this much space. Thank you, Jesus—

Wait a minute.

I knew we're supposed to thank God about everything—there's a Bible verse about that somewhere—but here we were suddenly facing another derailment.

It was no longer as simple as Rodney sleeping on our couch for a few nights. How was I going to insist he leave when we had an empty apartment downstairs?

Chapter 7

THE MOVERS HAD LEFT by the time the doorbell rang, but before either Estelle or I could respond, DaShawn came running out of his new room. "That's probably my dad!" He raced out the door and down the stairs.

I walked out on the landing where I could see the action below as DaShawn opened the front door. Rodney stood there in the porch light with a few errant snowflakes swirling around. He pulled his head back inside his hoodie in feigned surprise. "Who's this young man? I'm lookin' for an old dude by the name of Harry Bentley who's carin' for my son, a little kid 'bout so high"—he held his hand out even with his waist—"with an Afro so big he might'a blown away like dandelions on the wind."

"It's me." Suddenly DaShawn assumed a far more mature demeanor. "I ain't had no Afro for years, Dad. C'mon, you saw me after I got it cut."

Rodney opened his arms wide. "I know, son. You're growin' up, and I've been missin' out. But I'm here now. Know what I'm sayin'?" The hug was quick, and DaShawn pulled away first, talking excitedly about our new house. But the interaction I'd witnessed cut deep. There we were, three generations of Bentleys . . . but I hadn't been there to be the father Rodney deserved. And now it was Rodney who hadn't been there for DaShawn.

Two generations.

It had to stop. I'd stepped in and done my best with DaShawn, actually considered it an assignment from God. But had it been enough? Was there any way a substitute dad could take the place of a kid's real father?

Rodney glanced up at me as he neared the top of the steps. "Thanks, Harry."

He looked good, not like someone who'd ridden the bus all day. His hair was neatly trimmed and he sported a pencil-thin mustache that made him look downright dapper. The tiny scar above his right eye was hardly noticeable against his otherwise smooth dark skin. I'd passed on some pretty good genes.

"Uh, I know this is a trip," he said, "especially with you guys movin' into your new pad an' all. But anything's better than Atlanta's 'Gray Towers.'"

"No doubt. Come on in." I ushered him into our unit. "As you can see, nearly everything's still in boxes, and it'll be awhile before we get settled. But come on back here. I want you to meet my wife, Estelle."

Estelle was still arranging the cupboards, making herself extra busy, though I knew she'd heard us come in.

"Estelle? . . . Estelle, this is Rodney."

I don't know how hard she had to work up to it, but when she turned around, there was the warmest smile on her face I could've ever asked for. She reached out her hand. "So this is Rodney. I'm pleased to meet you." She waved a hand at the kitchen. "Sorry for the mess. We just moved in."

"No problem." Rodney did the look-around. "Yeah. You got yourself some sweet digs here. Everything's new."

"Harry, why don't you get Rodney to help you set up the beds and arrange some of the furniture? I tried to tell everyone where to put stuff, but we'll be lucky if they even got it in the right rooms."

"Uh, Estelle, Rodney just got in. He probably—"

"No, no. That's okay. I'm glad to help."

"And when you guys get done, I think we should go out to eat tonight. I won't have this kitchen up and runnin' in time to do any cookin'."

"Yeah, Pops." DaShawn started jumping up and down like a ten-year-old. "Can we go to Gulliver's for pizza like we did last time with Dad?"

The boy was at that age where he was a child one minute and all grown up the next—or at least, thinking he is. I looked at Rodney and raised my eyebrows in question.

"Sounds good to me. Haven't forgotten how awesome that pizza was—how long's it been? Two years? Bring it on, man. In fact, it's on me!"

Rodney said he still had some money when the county let him go, but I hesitated. What if it was drug money? Did I want to know? On the other hand, offering to do something nice for his son and for Estelle and me was commendable.

Decided I didn't want to know. If the State of Georgia hadn't confiscated it, well then . . .

The next morning Rodney slept in—meaning he stayed curled up on the couch with his back to the living room while the rest of us tiptoed around. It got on my nerves. We were the ones who'd exhausted ourselves with the move the day before. And now we were trying to go to church. If Rodney had turned over a new leaf like he claimed, a little church might do him good.

I went over and shook his shoulder. "Hey Rodney . . . Rodney! It's time to get up and get goin' for church."

He rolled over and looked at me as though he had no idea where he was. Finally, he sat up and leaned forward, elbows on his knees, running his hands back over his head a couple of times. "So, Harry, where'd you say we were goin'?"

"Church. It's Sunday morning. Now, come on, get up. Breakfast is get your own. Estelle set out some cold cereal and milk. But if you want anything else, your guess where to find it is as good as mine."

I was surprised to find Rodney ready to go when we left for church. He sat in the back seat of my old RAV4 with DaShawn, who kept up a running chatter about how great our new house was and how I'd promised to put up a hoop in the alley. "And Great-Grandma was gonna live downstairs, but she had a stroke and now she can't, so maybe you could live there, Dad. How 'bout it?"

I flinched and didn't dare look at Estelle. We'd told Rodney about his grandmother's stroke the evening before while we ate pizza, and promised that later today we'd all go by the hospital to visit her. But DaShawn . . . huh! Leave it to a kid to introduce an awkward subject. Estelle and I remained silent, and to his credit, Rodney didn't pursue the subject.

But that afternoon, after we'd returned from the hospital and Rodney and DaShawn were playing cards, Estelle pulled me aside. "Let's go for a walk."

"What? It's freezin' out there and windy too." I'd been thinking of catching some March Madness basketball on TV.

"That's what coats are for. Come on, Harry. We haven't even had a good look at our neighborhood yet."

I thought there was plenty of time to do that. But given how tense things were, I decided to humor her. When we got out to the sidewalk and turned north toward the cul-de-sac at the end of our street, Estelle grabbed my arm and pulled me tight as though she was already cold. Nobody else seemed to be out on the street on such a blustery afternoon.

I pointed at the yellow brick bungalow next door as we walked by. "Saw our neighbors yesterday as we were moving in. Sign on the side of his pickup says Farid's Total Yard Service. Might be Middle Eastern or something."

"Mmm, maybe."

I could tell her mind was someplace else. "Nice little house. Maybe we shoulda kept looking until we found a single-family place like theirs."

"What we better do is figure out what we're gonna do with what we've got. Harry, we gotta talk about Rodney! You heard what DaShawn said this mornin'. I keep wondering if that's God's answer to our downstairs apartment—"

"What? God's answer? Aw, I don't know, babe. We were so sure he led us to buy this place as a way to take care of Mom—and now look. Can't believe you're suggesting 'God's answer' might be for Rodney to live here. That was just DaShawn shootin' off his mouth."

"You didn't let me finish, Harry. I wasn't saying we should get sucked into it just because DaShawn threw out the idea. We need to talk and pray about it. If the answer is still no, we should make that clear before expectations gain momentum. The last thing we need is for DaShawn to get all revved up over the idea and then we have to shut him down. We do need God's answer here."

"Well, we need somethin', that's for sure. 'Cause we can't cover that mortgage on our own."

After passing another tidy bungalow with its drapes pulled—seemed like everyone's drapes or blinds were pulled—we came to the cul-de-sac. I stopped and swept my hand toward the big new house that took up the whole end of the street. "At least we don't have to pay his mortgage. Can you believe that thing?" All the other homes on our street were modest brick bungalows of one sort or another except for our greystone and a redbrick two-flat on the other side—classic Chicago neighborhood. "What possessed someone to build an enormous house at the head of the street? It's out of place. Doesn't fit."

"Who knows? Maybe he grew up here and got rich and just wanted to come back to the old neighborhood. Wouldn't that be better than fleeing to the 'burbs the minute they make it?" She pulled on my arm. "Come on. It's cold just standing here."

I looked back over my shoulder as we started down the other side of Beecham. "Yeah, but did you check out that big black Lincoln in his drive? Maybe he's a Lincoln Lawyer like the guy in Michael Connelly's novel."

"You and your detective books. We were talkin' about what we're going to do with our first-floor apartment. And I think . . . maybe we should consider Rodney—it could be temporary, at least until we know what's going to happen to your mom. He seems very cooperative. Except, what's with him callin' you Harry all the time? I thought he was callin' you Dad."

"Ah, don't mean nothin'. Just street talk." But I had to admit I'd liked it when at first he was calling me Dad.

"Well, if you say so. And you know, it might be good for DaShawn, havin' his dad around."

I gave her a skeptical look, but I knew what it meant when she started spreading her mother-hen wings. I drew in a deep breath. "Aw, I don't know, Estelle. Too many maybes. Yeah, he's clean—but how long is he going to stay that way? And what if Rodney doesn't get a job and can't pay his rent? Then we'd be stuck. We'd have to kick him out so we could get someone else in there. Could get real nasty." I shook my head. "Just wish we weren't dependent on that rent money."

She loosened her grip on my arm and moved away slightly so she could look at me. "So, what would we do if we didn't need his rent money? Just let him keep on livin' there without payin' rent? He might need some tough love, Harry. Whether we needed the money or not, he needs to take responsibility for himself."

I scratched my chin, thinking about what she said. "Well, you're right. But if we had to kick him out, it could make a world of difference why we did it. Would we be doing it for his sake because moochin' off people ain't right? Or because we're desperate for the money? Hear what I'm sayin'?"

"Well, yeah, but . . ." Her voice trailed off.

When we were halfway down the other side of the block and she still hadn't finished her sentence, I prodded, "But what?"

"Oh, I don't know."

"Estelle, think about it. Are you really open to him livin' below us?" I remembered what she'd said about family when she was talking about caring for Mom, but Rodney was a whole other ball of wax.

She heaved a sigh. "Well, you're right. If we end up squeezin' him because we're bein' squeezed, then it's not a good idea. But, Harry, maybe he just needs a second chance. He seems to have a decent attitude, better than how you've painted him in the past."

I cleared my throat in a conspicuous way. "More like third or fourth chance." But I felt guilty the moment I'd said it. After all, God had given me a second chance in so many ways—a second chance at love, a second chance to be a father to my grandson. Still. "I'd like to, Estelle. I really would, but has he really changed? Or just become a better con artist?"

"Well, you're the cop, Harry. Thought you could read cons from a block away."

I hunched my shoulders as the gusty wind picked up. "Yeah, but there's a reason doctors don't operate on family members. When people are too close, your vision gets blurry. Whadda they call that—myopia?"

49

We'd reached the end of the block. The cross street was one way going west. Kind of a pain navigating one-ways to get into your own block—especially one with a dead end. As we crossed Beecham and headed back up our side of the street, Estelle pulled me back into our conversation.

"What would we have to do so we could be more objective, so we aren't caught in the middle?"

"Financially?"

"Mm-hm. That seems to be where the rub is."

I thought for a moment. "I s'pose we could set up clear expectations for Rodney, and to protect us financially, guess I could go back to work. Maybe I could get my old doorman job back at Richmond Towers."

"Harry! You were bored silly at that job. Why not the Chicago Police Department?"

I shrugged. "Maybe. Might have to take a cut in pay, maybe even in rank, but mostly it'd depend on whether they're hiring right now. The whole city's pretty much under a budget freeze, ya know."

She sighed. "Well, let's pray, Harry. Let's pray about it."

"Right now? Out here in this?" I waved my hand at the bare trees creaking in the icy wind.

She giggled. "No. I'm freezin' to death. I mean tonight, before we go to sleep."

That was more like it. We stepped up our pace and were almost home, when Estelle gripped my arm and jerked me to a near stop.

"Don't look now, Harry, but that's the second time it's happened."

"Happened? What happened? What're you talkin' about?"

"The blinds. Everyone on this street has their blinds closed or their drapes pulled. But somebody in that house right there—our neighbor—was peekin' out watchin' us until I noticed 'em. Then they jerked the drapes closed."

"Estelle," I moaned, "so what? Someone watched us walking by and felt embarrassed that you noticed 'em and closed their drapes. What's the big deal?"

50

"Yeah, but that's the second time. It happened when we passed that house right over there." She pointed at the house directly across from ours. "It's creepy."

"What if their drapes were open and they just happened to watch us pass? Would that bother you?"

"Of course not. It's just that . . . they obviously didn't want me to see them watching."

"They're probably just curious—wondering about the new neighbors."

"Maybe . . ." We started walking again and turned onto the walk up to our house. "Then I know what I'll do. I'm gonna go around and meet everybody. Bible says if you want to have friends, you gotta show yourself friendly. So I'm gonna . . . I'm gonna bake cinnamon rolls for everyone on this block."

"Estelle, we're not even settled in yet."

"Well," she said, hustling up the stairs to our unit, "maybe not tomorrow, but I'm still gonna do it."

Yeah, I thought, Estelle feels creepy when people peek out at us, but I feel queasy over whether we can afford this place.

Had God really given us this house? If so, why were we suddenly in over our heads?

Chapter 8

I HAD ALMOST DRIFTED OFF TO SLEEP, having little half dreams about how to mount that basketball hoop on the back of our garage. But it just wasn't fitting together the way I wanted it to.

"Harry? Harry!"

I opened my eyes. "Huh?" Everything was turned around. The window should be at the foot of our bed, but the dim glow of a streetlight came through Venetian blinds at my side.

"Harry, you awake?"

"What...?" I raised myself up on my elbows and remembered we were in our new bedroom. I turned toward my wife's familiar shape, smelling faintly of soap and powder. "What's the matter?"

"Nothing's the matter, honey, but I was just thinking . . . several weeks ago, at the Manna House Valentine's party, didn't you say someone from Amtrak Police called and wanted you to come work for them?"

I sat all the way up. "Amtrak? Oh, yeah, Gilson called me, but—" I choked off my words and blew out a long breath. "It's the middle of the night, Estelle. What's the clock say?"

"Um . . . eleven-thirty, but I couldn't sleep, 'cause I been thinkin', if it would make a difference for us to have the money to cover the whole mortgage ourselves, maybe you should take that job. Better than bein' a doorman. You don't much like being retired, anyway. And then we wouldn't be caught between Rodney's behavior and the bank."

I flopped back onto the bed and yawned loudly. "Not so sure it'd be better than that doorman job. At least no one woke me up in the middle of the night. Now go to sleep, Estelle. We can talk about it tomorrow."

"Okay, okay. Just think about it." She turned over, and within minutes I heard her breathing transform into the steady slowness of a peaceful sleep.

But no such luck for me. My mind started skittering like static electricity . . .

Okay. The reason we needed someone to rent our downstairs apartment was because Mom couldn't move in. The image of her lying up there in the hospital giving me her crooked smile floated through my mind. Was she feeling lonely? I should visit her more. But how could I? We'd just bought a house that needed a lot of work, and I'd have even less time if I got a job.

Of course, she'd been living alone for years and never complained of being lonely. At least now she had a roommate and nurses on duty to help her. Had to admit, though, at almost ninety, she had to be approaching the end of her life. Her best friend, Ethel, had died right after Thanksgiving. I really needed to prepare myself for that. A physical ache pulled at my heart, thinking of her passing. Sure hoped some of us would be there to hold her hand and pray with her when she went home. It'd be terrible to be completely alone.

How stupid we'd been to base our whole plan for this building on her moving in! Which was why I didn't want to base our future on Rodney's performance, either. Not good!

I flopped over on my other side. I needed to get some sleep. What got me goin' here? Oh, yeah, Estelle asking about that call from Gilson. Maybe it wouldn't be so bad to work for Amtrak. We could sure use the money. And she was right; with more financial stability we could give Rodney a genuine second chance. Maybe this was the time. I wasn't really worried about him holding down a job as long as drugs were out of the picture. He'd been a good worker ever since I got him his first job at age twelve helping our building manager for thirty minutes a day, picking up trash, sweeping the back stairs, or washing the door windows.

It was the drugs that did him in, and I didn't want them under our roof. We had to think of DaShawn. He was getting to the age where it'd be a big enough temptation to him too.

I rolled the covers off me and went to the bathroom, got a drink of water, and shuffled back to the bedroom. Careful not to disturb Estelle, I crawled back into bed. She was turned away from me, so I spooned up behind her, resting my hand on the curve of her hip. I lightly kissed the back of her neck. Maybe a little lovin' would get my mind on something different . . . if not calmer. She moaned contentedly and wiggled a little, then sank back into the steady breathing of a sound sleep.

Hmm, maybe another time. But I was realizing it might not be as easy with a guest in the house.

Rodney . . . yeah, the drugs did it. That's when I knew I was losing Rodney. I had just transferred from the CPD's K-9 unit—where, of course, I did some drug interdiction with my dog—to the Special Ops Section. The elite SOS unit supposedly targeted drugs, the lifeblood of the gangs. I wanted to get the scumbags who'd stolen my son.

I'd given the SOS a hundred percent, and we were making a real difference too—a difference, that is, until my boss, Matty Fagan, got greedy. My thoughts drifted back to the mess he'd created and the day I'd finally decided to blow the whistle. It's not easy to cross that thin blue line, and, as with most officers who decide they must do it, it was a career ender for me. You don't go against your own—not even for a righteous cause—without paying a price. The first installment for me was being asked to take early retirement so I could be "put on ice" while Internal Affairs prepared the case against Fagan. But even when the court case was over and Fagan had been sentenced, I knew better than reapply to the CPD.

Now Gilson had reached out to me, inviting me join him at Amtrak.

Ahh! . . . this wasn't working. I was right back into the same loop. I'd never get to sleep at this rate.

I started to ponder those harebrained ideas Captain Gilson had spun to interest me. They might be a figment of his creative imagination, as he'd called it—but what if some kind of detective role were possible? Perhaps my career in law enforcement wasn't over, after all. If I could become a K-9 detective with a drug-interdiction dog that I brought home at the end of the day . . . oh man! I'd have our place covered. Neither Rodney nor DaShawn could get involved with drugs without me being immediately alerted.

Of course, the dogs weren't for personal crusades. In fact, there was probably some regulation against doing what I envisioned. But hey, if that dog just happened to draw down on a stash or even some weed in someone's pocket, well . . . And if that didn't happen—I surely prayed it wouldn't—at least I could sleep without worrying that something bad might be goin' down under my roof.

Yeah, I could sleep without worrying . . .

Estelle's steady breathing calmed me like small waves on a beach. It was all I could hear in this quiet neighborhood, so different from the noisy blocks around our old apartment. I was close to drifting off . . . but a cloud still hovered at the fringe of my consciousness. Even if Rodney and DaShawn were straight, even if the finances on the house got covered, something still felt wrong with my world, something that cast a shadow over every joy. What was it?

My mother. She was near the end. I didn't want her to go, but there wasn't anything I could do about it.

Monday morning, I walked DaShawn to the corner a couple blocks south to catch the city bus. He didn't want to be seen with me, but this was the first day going to school from our new address, and I wanted to make sure he caught the right bus. As the bus pulled away from the curb, I was startled to notice that The Office, a friendly neighborhood bar, was just three doors west of the bus stop. I'd gotten myself in trouble there more times that I could count. So why had its proximity completely slipped my mind when we were deciding to purchase a house not more than a five-minute walk away? Was my subconscious setting me up with temptation? I would not yield. I would tell my Yada Yada brothers and Estelle about it to get it out into the light so God could help me.

But when I got back to the house, I lost myself in the day's events. Rodney had gone out to find a phone store that could reactivate his phone. "Got to get a newspaper too, snag me a job," he'd told Estelle.

Sounded good, but I knew how hard it could be for anyone who'd been "inside" to get a job. He was going to have to find someone who had a connection and would take a chance on him. Maybe Peter Douglass needed help at Software Symphony. I'd check.

"Estelle, let me do those dishes. You're still trying to set up the kitchen."

Her eyes went wide. "And . . .?" We shared a lot of household chores, even in the kitchen, but it wasn't very often I volunteered out of the blue to do the dishes.

"And nothin'. Just thought we might talk about what you said last night."

"Uh . . . and what was that?"

I dumped the coffee grounds in the trash. "You know, the Amtrak idea."

"Oh! I was so sleepy, I nearly forgot."

Then why didn't you save it till this morning and let me sleep? I thought, but I didn't say it. I scraped the last of the bowls and put them into the dishwasher. "Well, being a cop isn't an easy job. In fact, maybe the only thing harder than being a cop is being the wife of a cop."

"Not a husband of one?"

I tossed her a grin. "That too, I guess." My old partner, Cindy Kaplan, had never married. Maybe she was smart. "Anyway, the Amtrak scene might be a little different, but . . . police work is police work. And"—Did I really want to say this?—"I basically lost my first marriage over it."

Estelle gave me the eye. "I thought it was because of your drinkin'."

"That too." I raised my hands. "I'm not blamin' my drinkin' on my job, but the stress of the job was certainly part of my home problems. I let the job come first. Wasn't there for Willa Mae, wasn't there for Rodney when they needed me most. Brought home all the tension—if I hadn't drowned it before I got there."

"Well, I don't want any of them apples, Harry Bentley. If that's how you'd end up at Amtrak, go back to the doorman job."

I finished loading the dishwasher, then poured myself the last of the coffee. "If those were my only choices, yeah. But maybe I ought to check out what Gilson has in mind. I've had enough experience, I think I can tell pretty quickly whether it'd be like workin' for the CPD. If so, you're right, I should give it a pass. But even in the CPD, not every assignment was the same. I mean, working the K-9 unit was a whole lot different than working Special Ops."

Estelle climbed down off the step stool she was using to reach the upper shelves of a cabinet. "K-9, that's with dogs, right? I like dogs—well, most dogs."

"Yeah, me too. And you can't push dogs around the way you do people. If you do, you mess 'em up, and then they're no good for anything."

Estelle looked at me curiously. "So what're you sayin', Harry?"

"Well, when Gilson talked to me, he mentioned the possibility of workin' K-9 again. Now, I don't know if he was just shinin' me on or what. But—"

"But you're thinkin' about it, right?" She shook her head. "I don't know, Harry. I know I was the one who brought up that Amtrak thing. Sounded good in the middle of the night. But if police work's like you say . . . well, we got a good thing goin' here. I don't want to push you into doing somethin' that'd put you or us at risk—"

"And I don't want that, either. But other things are different now too. C'mere, sit down a minute." I took her hand and pulled her over to the little kitchen table. "First of all, babe, I'm in a much different place with God, and that means a whole lot." In the back of my mind, I had to check myself on that statement. But I really did have a different relationship with him now, even if we still had a few details that needed working out. "And there's you too, babe. That's a big—"

"Wait a minute. You tellin' me I can somehow do for you what Willa Mae couldn't?"

I grinned at her. "Yeah, and you just demonstrated it. You don't let me get by with nothin'. She just boiled inside until she exploded, and I never knew why until we were in the middle of Armageddon."

"Hmm."

"But it's more than that, Estelle. You believe in me. You make me feel like I can become the man God created me to be. I know I got a long way to go, but now I've got a group of Christian brothers too, and AA."

"You don't go to AA meetings anymore, Harry."

"No, but they're there. My prayer group brothers keep me on the straight and narrow now, but if I needed AA, I wouldn't hesitate. What I'm tryin' to say is, some major things in my life are different. I think I've got the support and the experience to make it work if the Amtrak job is worth pursuin'." Whew, I surprised myself with my little speech, even before I knew whether I wanted that Amtrak job. But somewhere in the back of my mind, I knew I had left out a piece. I had forgotten to tell Estelle or my bothers that The Office was just a five-minute walk away. But why bring that up? I hadn't felt any desire to drop into that little bar, didn't even spend time thinking about it being so close.

Estelle pursed her lips and looked at the hand I was still holding, then stared me in the eyes for several moments like she was running some kind of a BS detector on me. Then she leaned in and planted a kiss on my lips. "Well . . . okay. Why don't you go see what he has to offer?"

"If he still has anything to offer."

"But promise me, any red flags and you quit. I don't care what the consequences are. You're no spring chicken—you done retired once already—so you ain't buildin' a career. If it works, it works. If not, that's it. Okay?"

With a chuckle, I nodded agreement. Yeah, I could buy that plan. If we couldn't crack our mortgage nut with a job with the APD, we'd do it some other way. I could be a doorman again, if that's what it took.

She grinned and reached out to grab my other hand. "But first, we pray."

Chapter 9

I HAD PLANNED TO DRIVE ESTELLE to work that morning, but she wouldn't have it. "If the bus was good enough for DaShawn, I can walk a couple of blocks and catch it too. Just zip right over to the 'L' and down to work. No problem."

"But it's windy and cold out there, Estelle."

She walked over to the window and looked out to the right and then to the left. "But it ain't snowin'. In fact, the clouds are breakin' up. It'll do me good. You go visit Mother Bentley."

The mere mention of my mom gave me a little stab. "Yeah, yeah. Sounds like a good idea. But if you need a ride home, give me a call, okay?"

"Quit fussin', Harry Bentley. Go on, now. Go visit your mom. Take her some more praise CDs, and be sure those nurses are playin' 'em to her. She don't need to be starin' at that TV all the time."

"That's what she did at home."

"But she wasn't sick at home. Now she needs to have her mind stayed on Jesus, get her spirit ready to cross on over in peace."

The truth of what Estelle said shook me. Was God trying to tell me something, get me ready for her passing? How could I know when I'd missed the signals about buying the house?

When I got to the hospital, my mother was indeed watching TV—with the sound turned off, no less. I glanced at the screen. A "silent" talk show? Had she lost it entirely? But she gave me a crooked smile and reached her right hand up toward me.

"How you doin', Mom?" I leaned down and kissed her. "Hey, I brought you a Richard Smallwood CD. You want to listen to it?"

She mumbled a sound I'd come to recognize as yes.

59

The CD player on the windowsill was covered with a folded blanket. Didn't look like it had been used much. Once I got it going, I turned to her. "You like that?"

She gave me a crooked smile and a slight move of her head. "You want the TV off?"

Her gibberish and a sideways wave of her right hand meant no. She lay there watching the silent talk show and listening to Richard Smallwood while I sat in the recliner and watched her, thinking about all the years she'd been there for me and all the years that had come before me. What had it been like growing up in the Jim Crow south and then moving north to Chicago during the war years?

My restless night caught up to me, and I drifted off.

When I woke up, Mom was asleep, the CD had finished playing, and the silent talk show had turned into a soap opera. There wasn't really any reason to stay longer, but I had a dread of leaving, wondering how many more times I'd see her, how many more hours we would have together. Would I regret not lingering another half hour now instead of rushing off?

I stood up and walked over to the window. I started thinking about the mortgage again, then made a sudden decision to call Gilson.

Checking to see that I had a good signal, I dialed the Amtrak captain. To my surprise, Gilson answered on the second ring.

"Uh, yeah. Captain Gilson, this is Harry Bentley. I wanted to follow up on your call to me a few weeks ago. Were you serious about looking for some new personnel?"

"Sure was, but I'm not ready to retire yet if you're thinkin' about snatchin' my position. Ha, ha!"

"Uh . . ." Gilson's sorry attempt at humor took me off guard. Could I stand to work for this guy on a day-to-day basis? "Look, I'm not interested in your job, Captain, but as I recall, you mentioned a couple other possibilities—undercover detective, K-9 unit."

"That's right. You lookin' to climb aboard?"

"I'd be interested in coming down to have a serious talk if you've still got anything open."

"Of course, of course. In fact, Harry, to snag you, I'd create a position. When can you get here? I'm available anytime . . . oops, don't want to give you the wrong impression. We keep civilized hours around here. That means I go home at night, unless there's something serious breakin'. So . . . this afternoon? Tomorrow? Oh, wait. Can't do it this afternoon. Got a meeting with the Chicago Commission for the Homeless. Got a lot of homeless people hangin' out in Union Station, you know. Especially when the weather's bad."

I knew that was a problem at the train station like it was all over the city, but was Gilson recruiting me to herd homeless people out of Union Station? If so, the job wasn't for me. Having volunteered at Manna House a few times, I had a much more sympathetic view of homeless people now than I used to. A lot of people end up on the streets through no fault of their own, and I wasn't about to become the person who chased them out of a warm place to sleep.

"You said something about the K-9 unit and drug interdiction—"

"That's right. Did I tell you about Sylvia Porter and her dog, Corky?"

"You mentioned something like that."

"Yeah, well, we're still stymied trying to team Corky with a handler. Hey, I'm just lookin' at my Daytimer here, and tomorrow morning looks clear. Can you make it?"

"What time?"

"How 'bout ten? Should have the morning's dust cleared off my desk by then."

"Ten it is. Thanks, Captain. See you then."

I ended the call before he could say anything more.

But what was I doing? Going down for an interview with a man who irritated me no end with his annoying way of talking and his crazy schemes. I stood staring out of Mom's hospital window. I would keep the appointment, but if the job required me to report directly to Gilson, maybe I'd take a pass. No way did I want to work for a man I couldn't respect.

❖ ❖ ❖ ❖

The contractors I'd hired showed up to start work on the first-floor kitchen, so I spent the rest of the day stripping walls in the front room. The old wallpaper must've been put up with horsehide glue. By the middle of the afternoon when Rodney came in and stood in the doorway inspecting my work, I'd only completed half of one wall.

"How'd the job search go?" I grunted, still scraping with only a cursory glance in his direction.

"Got an interview at Home Depot. Said they'll let me know in a couple of days. But I don't know, man. Everything's all screwed up. Must've made a dozen calls. Nobody's hiring."

"Figures. Guess that's what it means to be in the middle of a recession, no matter what the President says."

"Tell me about it." He stood there watching me.

"Hey," I stopped scraping and spoke through clenched teeth, "you wanna change your clothes and lend a hand here or somethin'?"

"Oh, well . . . sure. Need to grab a bite to eat, then I'll be right back down."

He wasn't right back down. And as the minutes passed, the muscles in my jaws clinched into a near cramp. Why couldn't he have offered? It should've been obvious I could use some help.

He finally arrived without an apology for taking so long. Other than the few words necessary to coordinate the job, we worked in silence for the next couple hours, completing one wall and starting on a second until I heard someone come in the front door.

"That you, DaShawn?" I hollered.

"No, it's me." Estelle came into the room, taking off her heavy winter coat and hat.

"You're home early. What time is it?"

"Almost four, same as usual. Wasn't bad by 'L' and bus." She looked around at the wall-and-a-half Rodney and I had stripped. "Hey, this looks great."

"Ha! Nearly wore our fingers to the bone. That old paper's a bear to get off."

"Where's DaShawn? He should be helpin' you two. I'll send him down."

"Don't think he's home. Didn't hear him anyway."

"Maybe he sneaked by so we wouldn't put him to work," Rodney said with a laugh as he scraped vigorously at a particularly stubborn strip of paper. "That's what I'd've done at his age."

"Ha! No doubt." Estelle went on upstairs, but in a few minutes she was back leaning in the doorway. "He's not up there. Did he have some afterschool thing goin' on today?"

"Don't think so. At least he didn't say anything to me."

"And he didn't phone?"

"Nope. Haven't heard a word." I'd walked him to the bus that morning to make sure he took the 290 rather than the 96, but it never crossed my mind that he'd have a problem getting home.

Using a clean rag to wipe flakes of wallpaper off my shaved head, I walked out to the little vestibule where Estelle was standing and lowered my voice. "Should we go out lookin' for him?"

Estelle rolled her eyes and pointed into the first-floor apartment, obviously meaning Rodney. Was she saying it was his problem? I shrugged.

"Rodney," I called, "whadda you think we should do?"

He came to the doorway with a scraper in his hand. "I dunno."

I gritted my teeth. He sounded like he had when he was fifteen—I dunno, I dunno—but then he said, "Ain't met any of his friends yet. But I'd think they'd be the first ones to call."

Good point. But as far as I knew, DaShawn hadn't made many friends at school. Part of the problem was he was going to a magnet school, and none of the kids in our old neighborhood went to his school. There were a few kids in the church youth group he sometimes hung out with, but I didn't know their phone numbers.

I scratched my head. "Suppose I could call Josh Baxter. He works with the youth at church. He might know if somethin's goin' on."

"Worth a try," Estelle said and climbed the stairs back up to our apartment.

I called Josh, but he didn't know of anything happening with the youth. He gave me a couple of numbers for kids from the church, and I called them too. No one had seen or heard from DaShawn today, but then none of them went to DaShawn's school.

I called the school and got nothing but the answering machine. It was after four-thirty, and school had been out since two-thirty. I was beginning to get worried.

"I think we better go look for him," I said to Rodney, feeling frustrated that he wasn't more concerned.

When DaShawn first came to live with me, I'd enrolled him at Bethune Elementary where Peter Douglass's wife, Avis, was the principal. But it only went up to the fifth grade, so we got him into Stone Scholastic Academy, one of the better magnet schools on Chicago's north side. It hadn't been that far from our old apartment, and it was still an easy bus ride from our new place. All DaShawn had to do was catch the 290 over to Western and then take the 49B down to Granville and walk a few blocks east. Less than thirty minutes. I had talked through the route with him, and he'd nodded as if he understood. Hadn't even hinted it might be a challenge.

Rodney and I jumped in the RAV4 and retraced DaShawn's route to and from school, driving so slowly people were honking at us to get out of the way. Searching for DaShawn put Rodney and me on the same side, and the earlier tension between us melted as we offered little suggestions to one another about where we might look—up this alley, in the windows of that McDonalds, among the guys playing a pickup game on a park basketball court.

But we didn't see DaShawn. As we parked out front of our new house, I was kicking myself that I hadn't driven DaShawn for the first couple of days just to point out the buses and the stops. But at thirteen years old, he'd been using public transportation for a year or more, at least during daylight hours. He knew his way around this part of the city, and had never had any trouble. So what had happened today?

Estelle met us at the door. "Did you find him?" she burst out the moment we came in.

I shook my head.

Now she seemed downright anxious. "Maybe we oughta call the police. It's gonna be dark out there pretty soon, and we have no idea what's happened to him."

"You think he split?" Rodney asked, a pained look on his face.

"You mean run away? Why'd he do that?" I shot back.

Rodney shrugged. "Well, I did it—more'n once."

"When?"

"What difference does it make? You never knew anyway."

Ouch! I looked at Estelle.

"I think we ought to call the police," she said again.

"They won't do anything this soon."

"Harry, can't you call in a favor or two from your old buddies and get some more eyes out there looking? I'm gonna call the church and get a prayer chain going." She headed up the stairs.

I sighed, but I was beginning to feel the panic as well. We had to do something!

Chapter 10

I SAT DOWN ON THE STAIRS leading to our apartment and called Cindy Kaplan, my old partner at CPD, feeling as foolish as a new recruit on the first day of boot camp. Cindy was a good detective. We'd worked the SOS antidrug and gang unit together. She supported me in going up against Fagan, even though she couldn't risk putting her own career on the line. I knew I was out of line going to her with my request for help finding DaShawn. Still, she was my closest contact in the department.

"Hey, Cindy, it's Harry. How you doin'?"

"Couldn't be better. And you?"

"Not bad. Say, you wouldn't happen to be on the North Side right now would you?"

"I'm home, Harry. It's my day off."

"Oh . . . sorry. I shouldn't be botherin' you."

"Nah, that's okay. What is it?"

"Ah, nothin'—"

"Don't tell me you called about nothing, Harry. I know you better'n that. Now what is it?"

I was sitting there, elbows on my knees, looking down at the three steps below me, when I heard a key turn in the front door, and it swung wide open with a swoosh.

There stood DaShawn, a big grin on his face.

"Ah . . . no problem, Cindy. Or perhaps, I should say, my problem just walked in the door." I stared storm clouds at DaShawn as I talked and watched his grin dissolve. "I can handle it from here. Get back to you later."

Rather than relief and gratefulness flooding me, my tension flipped to anger. I stood up, towering over the boy with all the intimidation I could muster. "So where have you been, young man?" I yelled. Out of the corner of my eye, I saw Rodney come to the doorway of the downstairs apartment, but I didn't care.

DaShawn's eyes widened. "What's the matter, Pops? I got in before the streetlights came on."

"That isn't what I asked. I asked you where you've been?"

"Just across the street." He tried to reignite the enthusiasm he'd burst in with. "I was at the Jaspers. They live right over there"—he pointed toward the north end of the block—"and the twins go to my school. I've known them all year, played with Tavis at school sometimes, but I had no idea they lived on this street. It's really cool, Pops. They were ridin' the same bus home, and we figured out we now live on the same block."

I'd never heard of any Tavis, yet something told me to cool it, that this was one of the things I'd been hoping for. But I had a head of steam built up that needed blowing. "So you think that gives you an excuse to be over two hours late coming home from—"

"But the street lights aren't even on yet." DaShawn looked past me up the stairs, and I realized Estelle had descended part way to join our family summit. "Isn't that the rule, Ms. Estelle, come home when the streetlights come on? I beat 'em." When there was no answer from behind me, DaShawn looked over at his dad, standing in the doorway, appealing for an ally.

The fact that no one intervened bled off my remaining steam. I wouldn't have to fight this one on multiple fronts. I sighed deeply and came down off the steps to meet DaShawn on his own level. "Look, son, I'm glad you met some friends, and I'm glad . . . in fact, I'm delighted they live on this block if they're good people. But I don't think it would've cramped your style any to check in at home before going over to their house. In fact, the streetlight rule is for outside summer play when we know where you are. And besides—" I put my hands on my hips and leaned forward. "—you're never supposed to be in anyone else's house unless a parent is home and we've given permission."

"But their older brother was there, and—"

"Older brother doesn't count, not unless we give permission. Understand?"

"Yes sir." He dropped his head, and I knew it was over.

I glanced up the stairs at Estelle and could see the relief in her face. I turned back. "One more thing, DaShawn. You need to know we were all very worried. Your dad and I even retraced your route from here to school and back—"

"You did?" His eyes got big.

"Yeah, we did. And I called the school, called Josh Baxter at church, and . . . and when you came in, I was talking to my old partner at the CPD because we were about ready to file an official request for police help."

I could see the shock spread across DaShawn's face. He got it. No need to rub it in any more.

I again looked up the stairs at Estelle. "When do you want us for supper?"

A small crinkle at the corners of her eyes told me she approved of how I'd handled things. "If DaShawn will come up and help me set the table, we can eat in about ten minutes."

Lost a little more sleep that night, just coming down off the anxiety trip of worrying about DaShawn. But the next morning I caught the Metra train at the Rogers Park stop and headed down to the West Loop for my meeting with Captain Gilson. Entering Union Station from Adam Street, I might've missed the offices for the Amtrak Police if two uniforms hadn't been standing just outside. I was about to ask for directions when I noticed the APD sign on the glass doors behind them. A secretary led me through a dingy labyrinth to a small windowless office that seemed far too cramped for a captain.

Gilson stood up quickly from his desk, thin and a little shorter than I'd remembered. His moderately spiked brown hair didn't conceal that it was thinning and he was pushing fifty. With eyes wide and a rubber-face grin, he offered me his hand. "Phyllis, could you bring us a couple of cups of coffee? Cream, sugar, Harry?"

"Just black."

Gilson came around his desk and hurriedly unloaded a stack of files off an old chrome tubing chair. "Sorry 'bout that," he said. "Can't wait until we get our new offices. They're gonna be beautiful, over on the other side of the Great Hall. Here, sit down."

Instead of sitting back down behind his desk, he dragged his chair around to sit with me in front of it. I was surprised by this unusually egalitarian gesture.

Gilson took a deep breath. "I'm so glad you called me back, Harry. Now, what can I do to entice you to join us?"

I was tempted to tell him two hundred grand a year would be a good start. But instead I said, "Well, I got to thinking about your earlier call and realized I might be ready to get back into law enforcement under the right conditions. Wanted to hear what you had in mind."

The secretary delivered our coffees, and after Gilson took his first sip, he set his cup down and leaned forward. "I'm trying to put together a quality team here, Harry. I'm convinced passenger trains will play a much larger role in this country's transportation. We can't keep adding more highways and cars. Think of the environmental issues and our dependence on foreign oil. And the airlines are already feeling the stress of congestion. High-speed rails are comin'. Last fall I went to China and rode the MagLev train out of Shanghai—268 miles per hour. Can you believe that?"

Where was Gilson going with this? In spite of the president's vision, U.S. trains were lucky to exceed a hundred miles an hour on a few short stretches. It'd be a long time before we had super trains.

But Gilson pressed on. "Progress requires consumer demand. Demand depends on consumer satisfaction. And that's where we come in. It's our job to make train travel safe and pleasant for the public. So, we have to stay ahead of any crime wave that frightens and threatens riders."

"You talkin' about terrorists?"

"Well, sure, that's the big thing now in the media, but it's only part of it. I'm lookin' at the whole picture, and that's why I want the best team in the country based here in Chicago. See what I'm sayin'?"

I frowned. "And you think I might fit in . . . how?"

"You're a quality officer, Bentley. That's why I want you."

"To do what, exactly?"

"Well, I'm flexible. Like I said, it's the team that's most important. Then we make sure everyone's doing what he or she can do best. I've been thinkin' about your potential with the K-9 unit. Did you enjoy workin' K-9?"

I thought for a moment and then nodded. I really had liked K-9 and might've stayed with it if I hadn't felt the need to focus more aggressively on drug and gang intervention.

"Well . . ." Gilson took another sip of his coffee and leaned back in his chair. ". . . we have a spot for you there."

I stared at him, using an old interview technique of simply remaining silent until the other person filled the vacuum with more information.

"I think you asked me what rank you'd start at since you were a detective, but most dog handlers are just officers or occasionally a sergeant."

"Yeah, that's a question I'd have."

"We can be creative here, Harry. I also asked you about workin' undercover, remember?" He got up, went behind his desk, and rummaged through some files on a shelf. "I'm always lookin' for innovative solutions." He held up a thin folder and waved it toward me. "I think I found a creative precedent the brass did in Philadelphia. Remember how I suggested you might use your experience of being blind to work undercover? Well, that isn't what they did in Philadelphia, but . . . tell me, what do you think of when you think of a blind person?"

Think of? All I could think of was the horror I'd gone through when I'd had to wear patches on both eyes for days at a time. "Uh . . . don't know. Guess I felt I was too old to adjust to losin' my sight." I shrugged, embarrassed at how low the ordeal had taken me. In fact, at one point I thought I'd rather be dead—but I wasn't going to tell Gilson that.

"No, no, no. I'm not talking about how you felt about your own situation. I wanna know, when you see a blind person on the street, how do you know he's blind?" From behind his desk, Gilson beckoned at me with both hands.

"Uh, red and white cane, dark sunglasses . . ."

"And? What else might you see if they're out in public?"

Why was he playing this game with me? "I dunno . . . seeing-eye dog?"

"There you go! A service dog! Blind people often have a service dog, and they can go anywhere with 'em. The ADA guarantees it—walkin' down the street, into restaurants, even on trains. In fact, we have special accommodations for 'em. And they can go anywhere on the train, no questions asked. You see what I'm getting at?"

Suddenly, it all clicked, and Gilson's "creativity" didn't seem so farfetched. "You want me to be an undercover agent posing as a blind person with a service dog that is actually a bomb-detecting dog?"

"Almost." Gilson returned to the chair in front of his desk and leaned forward again with an eager expression. "We've got explosive-detection dogs, even vapor-wake dogs that can smell explosives on a suicide bomber just by walking past the person. Those dogs are amazing, better than any of the scanners the TSA uses at airports. But Sylvia Porter's dog, Corky, is trained for drug interdiction. The DEA has been claiming more and more drugs are moving on the trains, and they're probably right too."

"Look, Gilson. How long do you think it'd take for the gangs or the drug cartels to learn that the blind man who spends every day all day wandering around Union Station in Chicago is really a narc?"

"Well, around the station, I think you'd mostly work in uniform, but on the trains you'd be undercover. Different days, different trains, you might not be back on the same train for a couple of weeks, not very likely you'd get made."

It made sense, but I waved him off with my hands. "Like I told you before, I'm a family man now. Traveling across the country by train doesn't fit with my position in life. You need to find some single person where being gone for several days doesn't matter."

"Yeah but, like I told you, it wouldn't be that way. You know how many trains we could put you on for a day trip, there and back, and have you home in time for supper at night?"

"Ha, ha. I have no idea, but that promise is only as good as the on-time schedule of the trains. Right?"

"But we're getting better!" Gilson laughed with me. "Seriously, Chicago's a hub. Say we think dope's coming in from New Orleans, you don't have to go all the way to the Gulf to intercept it. We could send you down to Carbondale in the evening, and you could catch the City of New Orleans and be back by morning."

"I'd be gone all night?"

Gilson shrugged and made a no-problem frown. "That's just an example. What I'm trying to say is there're ways to manage a civilized schedule. Sure, there'd be the occasional longer runs, but we'd try to keep those at a minimum and give you comp time when they came up. You know we can't run the dogs twenty-four/seven."

"Yeah, dogs have it better than us humans sometimes."

Gilson laughed. "How about it, Harry? If you worked undercover, I could bring you in as a detective."

Gilson's web had nearly caught me. We talked about salary, and even that was relatively sweet.

Finally, I raised the stickler. "So who would I report to?"

He leaned back and stroked his chin, a far-away look in his eyes. "Well, now, that's a little complicated. Detectives normally report to me, but technically the K-9 handlers are under Inspector Larson out of Washington, DC. But Larson's focus is on detecting explosives, preventing a tragedy before it happens."

Hmm. So what did that mean? Who'd really be my supervisor? Sounded like it might be Gilson. Had to admit, his whole plan sounded a lot more practical than his first pitch over the phone, and he hadn't spent the morning feeding me off-the-wall ideas or too many smart remarks. So . . . could I work for him?

Standing up and shaking hands with the captain, I assured him I'd give him my answer the next day.

"One more thing before you leave, Bentley. I want you to come meet Corky. You'll fall in love with her."

The captain led me out and through the hallway to a room much larger than Gilson's office. Three uncaged dogs rested on the open floor of the large kennel. The two German shepherds looked up, but then put their heads back down once they saw I wasn't someone they were expecting. But the black Lab jumped up and ambled over, tale wagging, open mouth grinning as though asking if I had something for her.

"That's Corky." Gilson stood back as I let her sniff the back of my hand, and then kneeled down to greet the dog. I gave her a few pats and a little rub below her ears. She kept looking from me to the door until I asked the attendant who was sitting behind a desk, "She need to go out?"

"No, she's just been out. She's just bored. Thinks you might take her out to play."

"Sorry," Gilson said. "Harry, this is Creston. We have three attendants, so someone's always here with the dogs. Creston, meet Harry Bentley. He's worked K-9 before."

I stood up and stepped over to shake Creston's hand.

"Well, I gotta get back to the office," Gilson said. "But feel free to stick around and spend a little more time with Corky."

I stayed for another ten minutes getting acquainted with Corky. She had a rich black coat with a tiny white diamond in the middle of her chest. And she still had an hourglass waist with no fat—not yet, anyway. Had to watch that with Labs. She looked me in the eye, holding my gaze without being intimidated. She was calm, but eager. I liked that, as though we were carrying on a wordless conversation, agreeing we could get along, maybe even be good for each other.

"What's Corky's alert signal?" I asked Creston.

"She's trained just like the explosive detection dogs. We don't want them pawing into a bomb and blowin' it up. So, she'll sit down and point, eyes on the target, until you release her."

"Tail straight like a pointer?"

"Nah. Tail don't count with her. Could be goin' or could be still. Just watch her eyes. It's all in her focus. When she's found something, she won't budge until you release her. The word's 'Free.' Free, Corky!"

The dog jerked up and looked at Creston with a what's-going-on tilt of the head, puckered eyebrows, and a slight lift of her ears.

"Sorry, girl. It's okay," Creston said. He came over and gave her a pat. "I won't confuse her by saying her start word, but it's s-e-e-k." He spelled it slowly, with enough time between each letter so it wouldn't sound like the command.

"Gotcha." I stood up and Corky started panting and whipping that heavy old tail around as if to say, "We gonna go play now?" Work to her, of course, was just play. But she accepted my "No" signal and sat back down while I looked around the kennel. Nice place, institutional carpeting on the floor, eight separate cages. "They usually lie around out here unless one of them's not feelin' well," Creston said. Each dog had separate food and water pans, and there were a few chew toys as well as a couple of plastic couches for the handlers.

Finally, I said good-bye and headed home, recalling the eager look in Corky's eyes. She was very different than Zorro, the German shepherd who'd been my partner years before. Zorro was good, always had my back. But he was also kind of aloof, as though he didn't really need me. Corky, on the other hand, was definitely looking for a partner.

I took a deep breath. Slow down, Harry, I told myself. I still needed to review the whole thing with Estelle so we could pray about it.

Praying about a decision should bring a person peace. That's what the Bible seemed to say. But had to admit as I rode home on the Metra, praying about this job possibility made me as nervous as working for Gilson. Could I trust God leading us to do the right thing? Sometimes I wished for a little handwriting on the wall.

Chapter 11

THE DAY HAD TURNED BREEZY, sunny, and the temperature was climbing into the mid-fifties—an early break from Chicago's winter—by the time I got home from my meeting with Gilson. As I walked up to our new house, I noticed the yard for the first time since it had been covered with snow and ice. Tall yellow grass, all matted down like an old cow pasture, probably hadn't been mowed since last summer. Soggy, brown leaves packed in the corners beside the stoop and piled up under the bushes. I was tempted to spend the rest of the afternoon working outside, but I shook it off. Had to finish rehabbing the first floor. The contractors had been busy, but there was stuff I needed to do. Once that was done, we could concentrate on the outside.

As I walked into the first-floor apartment, I was amazed at how much Rodney had gotten done. "Hey, Rodney, you here? This looks great. We ready to paint?"

"Soon as that primer's dry." He came in from the kitchen where he'd been washing out the paint pan and roller. "The kitchen guy came by to take the final measurements for the counters and cabinets. Said they can't get the floor tile you ordered, but he'll be back tomorrow to discuss an alternative. Wants you to call him with the model numbers for the fridge, dishwasher, stove, and microwave so they can be sure of the sizes."

"Okay. Thanks."

By the time I'd changed my clothes, the primer had dried, and we began rolling the final coat. And by the time Estelle got home, we'd finished painting the living room.

That evening after we ate supper, DaShawn disappeared to his room, supposedly to do homework, and Rodney retired to the living room, which had pretty much become his domain, and switched on the TV. I put the last of the dishes into the dishwasher and stepped up behind Estelle, who was wiping down the stovetop. Slipping my arms around her waist, I pulled her close. She tipped her head to the side with a contented Mmm while I leaned down and kissed her neck. But when my hands drifted up, she slapped them away. "Harry!" she whispered and broke free from my embrace. She turned with a frown on her face and nodded toward the living room.

I turned to look, but we weren't in Rodney's line of sight and the TV was loud enough he couldn't have heard anything. "What's the matter? He can't see us."

"No, but he's still in there," she said, all hush-hush.

"So? DaShawn's always been in the house ever since we got married."

"That's different. He's still a kid, and besides, he has his own room. I . . . I just don't feel free with Rodney up in here like this."

"Well, let's go into our bedroom then." I grasped her hand and took a step to draw her after me.

She balked. "Harry, that's too obvious. We can't," she stage-whispered.

I sighed. We'd been in our new house no more than three days, and our love life was already taking a hit. I looked Estelle in the eyes. They had a dark pleading look in them that assured me she wasn't upset at me. I just needed to figure out how to reach through to her. "Then . . . let's go for a walk." A puzzled look came over her face. "And just talk," I assured her with a grin.

"So it's come to that, huh?" Her voice was teasing. "Have to go on walks just to have a private conversation."

"Hey, walks are good exercise. We should take one every day. Besides, I need to tell you about my meeting with Captain Gilson." Her eyes brightened. "Oh, yeah, your interview. Let me get my coat."

After letting Rodney and DaShawn know we were going for a walk, I motioned to Estelle and headed out the back way to the alley.

She followed but hesitated at the back gate. "What're we doin' out here?"

"Goin' for an explore, I guess. Come on." Taking her hand, I led her up the alley, past the last two houses on our side of the street and around behind the McMansion at the end of the block.

"Aha!" I pointed at a gate that led into the cemetery. "I thought I saw a gate in that fence the other day when I drove around this way. Come on. That'll be a nice quiet place to walk."

The gate was latched, but there was no lock on it. Cemeteries weren't public parks, but we'd be respectful and not disturb anything. Closing the gate behind us, we made our way to the access road that wound in a meandering loop through the whole cemetery. "I'm sorry I put you off back there, Harry. But I just feel so self-conscious with Rodney in the house. I don't know . . . married people are obviously supposed to have a married life, and we've had a great one, but we need a little more privacy."

"Yeah, I know. I wasn't really intendin' to . . . you know."

She cut her eyes at me sideways. "Maybe not, but I don't like to shut down a good thing once we get goin'."

As we strolled on, I prayed silently—in spite of my doubts—that God would show us what to do. I glanced at Estelle. Bundled up in her heavy coat with a thick brown hat she'd knitted herself pulled down over her head, she looked like a Russian babushka. But under it all, I knew she was the flamboyant love of my life. "Maybe we oughta go ahead and ask Rodney to move downstairs," I offered. "It'd only take us a couple days to get one of the bedrooms painted, and we got my old bed out in the garage."

"We could . . ." she murmured, then turned to look at me. "But would that make it harder to ask him to leave?"

I shrugged. "Well, we talked about that. But it'd also make a statement. Can't quite ask rent from a guest in your own house, but if he's in the apartment for which we need to receive rent, he needs to get on with his job search."

"Yeah, but . . . wouldn't that put us in the position you wanted to avoid—of us having to depend on his rent to meet our mortgage payment?"

"Lettin' him sleep in one of the downstairs bedrooms isn't the same as renting the apartment to him. Let's not get ahead of ourselves here."

"I know, I know, but it's just . . . we gotta be clear. We've kinda been going back and forth on what to do."

I wanted to tell her the back and forth thing wasn't my idea. We had a clear plan until God . . . oh, well. "Look, I hear ya. I'll make it clear we're not offering him the apartment, at least not until he has a job that can cover it. And speaking of jobs . . ."

"Right. You were going to tell me about your interview."

I pointed toward a bench. We sat and I replayed the whole interview and how—apart from a few smart remarks—Gilson's ideas seemed more reasonable when put into perspective. "At first I thought he was just throwing out exotic options like a salesman trying to snag a customer. But he was serious. I think he really wants me and is trying to create the role that would fit me best. I've never had an employer do that before."

"But . . ." Estelle turned and looked at me with a puzzled expression on her face. "A dog? What would you do with him at night? Leave him down there all alone?"

"Well, there's a caretaker always on duty at the kennel. And it's a really nice kennel—more homelike than just a bunch of cages. But the kennel's mostly for when the dogs need a break during the day . . . though I suppose I could occasionally leave Corky there."

"What? Corky? As in a cork bobbing round at sea? Ha! Ha!" It was her unrestrained laugh that had endeared me to Estelle from the very first. "I don't want no bouncy dog yappin' and jumpin' up on me."

Her laugh was so infectious we both had to lean against each other on the bench for support. Finally I said. "I don't think Corky's a yapper. She's a black Lab."

"She?" Her eyes got big. "Another woman, no less." We laughed some more until Estelle suddenly sobered. "You said occasionally you might leave the dog in the Amtrak kennel. What about the rest of the time?"

"Well, you know, usually she'd come home with me. Dogs and their handlers need to bond, become like family."

Estelle straightened her neck, raising her head high. "So not only are ya gonna take up with another female, but you think you're gonna bring her on up into my house? I don't think so, Harry Bentley!"

"Hey, hey, hey." I raised both hands in surrender.

She relaxed. "I'm serious, though. A dog? We've got DaShawn, and now Rodney. And you want to bring a dog into our life? Harry Bentley, I—"

I stopped her by raising my finger. "That's why we're talkin' about it, Estelle. I won't take the job unless we both agree it's the right thing. As for bringing a dog up into our house, I think you might just end up lovin' her. A Lab is one of the calmest, most well-behaved dogs there is. And how about that Hero Dog that was at Manna House for a while? What was his name—Dandy? Didn't you like Dandy?"

"Hmph! That's what I'm sayin'! Dandy was nice enough—okay, I admit it, he was real sweet—but dogs are dogs, and he was all the time sneakin' into my kitchen, stealin' chicken bones out of the trash. It's just what dogs do."

I shrugged. "Gotta train 'em."

"Uh-huh. But who'd walk her and clean up after her? And what about dog hair and mud?"

"Ah yes, there's that." We sat in silence, staring straight ahead for several moments. Chickadees flitted in and out of the bare trees. "I'd walk her, do all the caretakin'. It's part of the job." I hesitated. "But there's another plus side to bringin' a dog like Corky into the house. Gilson had mentioned the K-9 idea earlier when he phoned me, though he hadn't put it all together with the detective piece. But I got to thinkin' the other night when I couldn't sleep. One of the things that's concerned me 'bout bringin' Rodney back into the family is his influence on DaShawn. Right now, he seems to be doing pretty good—"

"Now that's an answer to prayer," Estelle said.

I paused for a moment. Yes, it was an answer to prayer. So maybe God was listening, even though he'd seemed kind of distant lately. "Anyway," I went on, "this dog is trained to detect drugs. She can smell 'em under any circumstances. With Corky in the house, we'd always know whether or not Rodney was clean—or even DaShawn or any friends he brings home, for that matter. Because, let's face it, he's gettin' to the age where he'll be tempted."

"Lord, have mercy," Estelle murmured.

"Think about it, Estelle. Most parents are between a rock an' a hard place these days when it comes to drugs. They can't be naïve about what their kids might be experimenting with, but on the other hand, no one can build a good relationship if they're constantly suspicious."

She turned to me with a frown. "You sayin' Corky would solve that problem?"

"No question. We'd always know our house was clean . . . or the moment someone tried to bring in a controlled substance."

"But wouldn't that be kinda sneaky, like we're spying on 'em?—almost like diggin' through their dresser drawers or eavesdropping on phone calls." She slowly shook her head. "I don't know, Harry. That could destroy trust."

I felt a little frustrated. Couldn't she see the benefit? "No, it wouldn't be sneaky. I'd explain everything right up front—that Corky is a drug detection dog, part of my job. I'd even demonstrate what she can do and tell 'em to never invite anyone home who might have drugs on 'em because Corky will detect even the slightest amount. Everything would be up front, don'tcha see? That's not sneakin' around."

She seemed to ponder that. "I guess not, but . . . I'd like us to pray about it."

"Well, sure!" I looked at my watch. "Oh no! It's seven-thirty, and I missed Bible study with the guys."

"Oh! I'm sorry, Harry. You could still go and get in on most of it."

"No . . . no, it's okay. We need some time to just pray together."

I was thinking we'd do that at home, maybe before bedtime, but Estelle took my hand and started praying right there. As she asked God to show us what to do about this job offer, I felt something stir inside me. Could I really put this decision into God's hands with confidence he'd work it all out? Could I believe he wouldn't jerk us around again? But what other choice did I have?

When we were done praying, I still wasn't sure about the job, but I did feel settled in my spirit about Rodney. I let out a deep breath. "Estelle, I think we should ask Rodney to move downstairs, just as soon as we can get a room set up for him. I don't think it'll complicate how long he stays with us. But even if it does, we can deal with that when the time comes. Right now, we need our apartment."

She threw her arms around my neck and planted a big kiss on my lips. "Amen to that! Don't mind if he still eats with us, but I agree, we should set him up downstairs." She stood up and shivered. "Brrr! I'm cold. Let's get on back to the house." Then she winked at me. "Maybe tonight I'll cash in my rain check on that little ol' fire you had goin' on in the kitchen."

Chapter 12

GREAT NEWS, BENTLEY! That's great news! Say, would it be possible for you to come on down this morning so we can start getting the paperwork and all the testing out of the way?" I could just imagine Gilson leaning back and putting his feet up on his desk. "Uh . . . testing?" By this morning, both Estelle and I felt I should tell Gilson I was interested. But . . .

"Yeah, you know, I'll sign off on the formal interview and the written test based on me knowing you at CPD, but HR insists on havin' a current medical and drug screening, polygraph and psychological exam—liability concerns, you know. But I'll try to expedite everything, and maybe we can get you sworn in tomorrow afternoon."

It'd been so long since I'd gone through a formal job application that for a moment all the red tape threw me. Gilson seemed to be doing his best to cut that tape, for which I should be grateful. But was he the captain precisely because he was the can-do guy who didn't fiddle around when he thought all the lights were green—or was he going helter-skelter on me again?

When I didn't answer right away, he prodded, "So, think you can make it?"

"Well, yeah. Guess I could." It was already nine-thirty.

"Hey, I'm not tryin' to squeeze a free day out of you. We'll count this as your first day on the job. And between all that rigmarole, we'll get you some more face time with Corky too. Okay?"

I shrugged, forgetting for a moment he couldn't see me over the phone. "Guess if Corky and I are gonna be partners, we better get to know one another. I've got a couple things to button up here first. Could probably make it by about noon, though. Will that do?"

"Whatever works. Oh, and Bentley, can you bring in your K-9 certification papers? And you had a degree in law enforcement, right?"

"Yeah, Northwestern Center for Public Safety."

"That's what I thought. You know, I checked you out pretty thoroughly when you dropped the hammer on Fagan. Had to know where you were comin' from before we prosecuted the guy. Anyway, bring your degree and documentation for any other training, citations, whatever. We'll photocopy what we need to satisfy the bureaucrats in HR and make this thing work. Okay?"

My mind scrambled to visualize where those records might be in the stacks of boxes we hadn't yet opened. "I'll see what I can do. We just moved, ya know, but I think I can dig up most of that stuff. See you 'bout noon."

"Outstanding! Oh, and I'll have to check with the motor pool, but I think Sylvia Porter's vehicle is good to go. Hopefully by the time we get you sworn in tomorrow, we'll have some wheels for you."

Sworn in tomorrow . . . My head was spinning.

I ended the call with Gilson, slid the phone into my pocket, and took a deep breath. That sly fox had played me, interspersing things he wanted out of me—stuff a little above and beyond—with incentives to reward my extra effort. Not many people get paid for the time they spend applying for a job. And a vehicle too? I'd just assumed since it was a train job there'd be no vehicle even though I'd be coming on as a detective.

It was all good—or at least seemed that way—but it was happening so fast. The night before, after getting back from my walk with Estelle, I'd joined Rodney watching March Madness as Kentucky trounced Indiana. When the final buzzer sounded, I said, "Hey, can we talk a minute?"

"Yo!" He clicked off the widescreen. "So what's up?"

I tried to ignore the fact that he'd commandeered the controller and carefully suggested that our next project downstairs ought to be a bedroom so he could have a space for himself.

"For sure, man." He patted the cushion of the couch beside him. "To tell you the truth, Harry, I appreciate your hospitality and all, but I don't sleep all that well on this here thing. A night or two, that's cool, but my back's killin' me when I get up in the mornings."

"Well, I got an old bed out in the garage that did me just fine for several years. We can bring it in for you. Should do until you can get your own place."

Not much gets by Rodney. He picked up on my meaning and gazed at me for several moments, his expression unreadable, then he shrugged. "Well, yeah, if that's where your head's at."

What did he think I wanted? Somehow I hadn't said it right. I tried to fix it by explaining, it was great having him around and good for DaShawn, but we needed to rent the unit as soon as possible to meet our budget, and it'd probably be too much for him, surely more house than he needed.

We'd gone back and forth and pretty much smoothed things over, though I think he still suspected we wanted him out of our lives altogether. Guess we'd have to work on that.

Then Estelle woke up this morning feeling confident the job with Amtrak was a godsend. She even mentioned the job when she blessed the bowls of cereal the four of us had for breakfast. By then I was feeling right about it too, so later the two of us prayed more seriously. Estelle told God we were going to take this first step in faith, and we were going to trust him to show us the next step. I still wasn't sure how much weight to put on the notion that we'd "heard from God." Maybe we should simply accept it as our best plan—given the options we faced—and hope he'd go along with the idea.

Gilson took all my documents and handed them to his secretary to photocopy. Then he turned me over to an HR person to walk me through the medical and psychological stuff—which lasted the rest of the day. So much for spending more time with Corky.

I didn't see Gilson again until Thursday morning when he personally took me to the motor pool. When he indicated an unmarked, slate-gray 2008 Dodge Durango, I thought, All riiight! This beats my RAV4 all to pieces. But then I opened the door. The darkly tinted back windows concealed a transport kennel that filled the entire back seat compartment. So much for replacing my RAV4.

The plush carrier included a thermostatically controlled fan, air conditioning ducts, water and food cups. I turned to Gilson. "Not bad. Back in the day, we carried our dogs around in the back of a slick back. Then, about the time I transferred out, they got SUVs with cages in the way back, but they were still marked vehicles, nothing like this."

"Well, you don't spend ten grand training a partner just to make 'em miserable. But these dogs earn it. Believe me, they do."

Back in Gilson's office, I signed a bunch of papers for the Durango, and he handed me the keys. "HR said they'd be finished with you by about two o'clock. Make sure they set you up with uniforms for when you work the station. Then when you're done, report back here, and we'll get you sworn in . . . unless you wash out." He grinned broadly. "Just kidding. I'll have a couple of Amtrak manuals you'll need to digest, and by then I should have your training schedule with the dog."

"Training? Will that be here?"

"Nah. Corky was trained at Lackland Air Force Base, of course, but for a brush-up like this, I thought we could use the CPD training center out in Des Plaines. I've signed you two up for a five-day refresher next week. But we can extend it if necessary. And then"—he held his arms out in front of him like a zombie and grinned—"the blind man cometh. But no rush."

No rush? Ha! I was beginning to feel like I was riding a roller coaster. "Tell me, Gilson—Captain Gilson, that is," I gave him a formal-looking face. "Are you aware of anyone who has actually disguised a drug detection K-9 as a guide dog?"

"Never heard of it. But that's its beauty, don't ya think? It'll take everyone by surprise."

"But can she do it? Corky, I mean. Can she do it?"

"Hey, you're the one who's worked dogs before. But why not? It's not like we're asking her to become a dual-career animal. She doesn't have to actually become a service dog, just look like one. Who'll know whether she's guidin' you or you're guidin' her? I mean, you're the key to the cover. If you look like a blind person, people'll assume Corky's your service dog. Right?"

"So I'm the actor, huh?"

"Well, yeah, but think of it this way, Harry, most people feel awkward around handicapped people and tend to avoid them. They expect them to be somewhat eccentric. All that favors your cover. Don'tcha see? You'll be fine."

Now I'm the eccentric actor? "Okay, but do you think Corky can work with that stiff guide handle on her?"

"Don't see why not. We're puttin' K-9s in bulletproof vests these days, when necessary, and it doesn't seem to hinder them. You gotta know I been thinkin' about this for a while. Even ordered one of those special harnesses with a stiff D-handle like blind people use. It's with Corky's gear, so don't forget to take it with you. C'mon, let's go see your partner."

I followed him to the kennel, and Corky recognized me the moment I came in the door and came bouncing over to me. I dropped down onto one knee and pulled her head into my chest, giving her a good rub and pat. It was really good to see that girl. But Gilson kept talking like there was nothing special going on. "Now my idea is, when you've identified a suspect, you make every effort to maintain your cover. Turn the case over to other Amtrak police, the locals, or the DEA and get the heck outta there. And we'll do our best to keep you outta court, too, to preserve your cover for as long as possible."

Yeah, well, we'd see. In my experience, police work's like war. Nothing ever goes the way you plan it.

I stood up, and Gilson held out his hand to me, conversation obviously over. "Get back over to my office about two or a little after, and bring Corky with you." He turned to the trainer who was sitting at his desk reading a magazine. "Hey, Creston, fill Bentley in on Corky's care—diet and anything else that she likes. Wanna make sure she's as comfortable as possible."

"Ah, there you are!" Captain Gilson got up from his desk when I came in. "And you've brought Corky. Great! She needs to be here for the ceremony."

"Ceremony?" Always the production master. I couldn't keep up with this guy.

"Of course a ceremony!" He flung his arms out to the side, eyebrows up, and eyes wide. "We heard from HR, they've signed off on you, so we can get you sworn in today." He collapsed his expansive stance and bent over to punch a button on his phone. "Phyllis, could you snag a couple of uniforms and come in here with them to witness this? And see if you can scare up a camera from somewhere. We need to document this too."

I had no idea why he thought this event needed documentation, but instead of questioning Gilson, I leaned down and gave Corky a good scratch on the rump. She responded with an enthusiastic tail wag and an eager look toward the door.

A few moments later the secretary knocked and came in with two Amtrak police officers. "Sorry, sir, but I couldn't find a camera." Gilson threw out his hands as though the absence of a camera aborted the whole plan. He stood there with such a blank look on his face, I almost felt sorry for the guy. I reached into my pocket.

"Uh, here. Use my iPhone. Is that good enough?"

Gilson dropped his hands. "Works for me. Give it to Phyllis, and let's get this thing done. Okay, Bentley, raise your right hand." He did the same. "And repeat after me."

Moments later, I was officially an Amtrak police detective. "Here's your shield and ID." He glanced at his secretary as he posed in the act of giving me my shield. "Take the picture, Phyllis. And here's Corky's shield too. Of course, she won't be wearing hers when you're undercover. And—" He handed me a pistol in a clip-on holster. "—is a SIG subcompact okay with you? I could probably scare up a revolver, if you'd prefer."

"No, no." I glanced at the piece—a P250. "No, this is fine." I clipped it on my belt, recalling the last time I'd worn a service weapon, when I'd been under Fagan's command. A weapon gives you a sense of personal power and protection, but it hadn't protected me from unintentionally contributing to Fagan's corrupt abuse of civic power. That's why I'd made the career-ending move of crossing the thin blue line. Certainly hoped I'd never have to face that choice again. I lifted a silent prayer, *God, protect me from ever havin' to use this SIG against any human being.*

Maintaining my cover sounded better and better to me.

"Maybe tomorrow you can grab a little time on the range." Gilson looked at the other people in his office. "Well, I think we're done here. Phyllis, get their witness signatures on those forms, and back to work, everyone."

When they'd filed out, he turned to me. "Harry, as far as I'm concerned, take Corky and head on home."

"But . . . I don't have anything set up for her yet." That's what I said, but what I was thinking was, Estelle is gonna to have a conniption fit if I walk in the house with this dog. We hadn't yet discussed the details, like where she'd stay, what were the house rules, how others should relate to her, all that kind of stuff. I stared at Gilson, hoping he couldn't see my panic. "Maybe it'd be better if—"

"No problem. Take whatever time you need tomorrow morning to get her squared away." He put his hand on my shoulder and gently ushered me toward the door. "Creston told you all about her feeding and care, didn't he?"

"Yeah. But—"

"Then you're set. See you tomorrow."

Corky already had her nose at the door, wagging her heavy tail against my leg as if to say, "Come on, partner. Let's get away from this crazy dude and have a little fun!"

Chapter 13

First day on the job, and I was on my way home in a smooth-running Dodge Durango SUV with a first-class K-9 carrier in the compartment behind me. The rush-hour traffic on Lake Shore Drive ground to a stop, and I glanced back through the grate. "Hey, Corky. How you doin', girl?"

Thump! Thump! Thump! went her heavy tail as she looked at me and panted her eagerness to get wherever we were going.

"Yeah, this traffic's a bi—I mean, it's a real mess, ain't it? But we'll make it. You just hold tight."

While we were stalled, I texted Estelle: B home sn. We crept forward two car lengths and stopped again. I laughed at myself. Perhaps I should've texted, B home when we get there.

It was six twenty before I turned onto Beecham Street, and immediately I heard Corky stand up, her hot breath on my neck as she whined a little woof. I looked back. How'd she know? Perhaps she sensed my anticipation.

I drove to the end of the block and did a U-turn in front of the McMansion so I could park on our side of the street. Corky was so excited when I clipped on her leash, she exploded out the door and hit the ground sniffing everything as she pulled me up the walk, catching my latent scent from who knows when. "Corky, heel." She immediately dropped back to my side, but she was nevertheless trembling with excitement. At least the snow was gone and I wouldn't have to clean off muddy feet.

I unlocked the front door and noticed the lights in the downstairs unit were off. Rodney must be done for the day. And then it hit me. I should've warned Estelle that I was bringing Corky home tonight.

I laid a hand on the dog's head as we ascended the stairs. "Calm down, girl. You gotta be on your best behavior. First impressions are lasting, ya know."

I opened the door to our unit. "Estelle, I'm home. And we've got company."

She peeked out of the kitchen wiping her hands on a dishtowel with a welcoming smile on her face. Always the gracious host, even if I was surprising her. And then her eyes dropped to the wagging, panting bundle of black happiness at my side. "The dog? You brought the dog home tonight? But . . . we don't have a place set up for her!"

"Yeah, I know. Gilson kind of pushed her on me, but she'll be all right. She can curl up on that little throw rug on the floor by our bed—"

"In our room? Can we talk about this, Harry Bentley?"

"Oh, sure. No problem. We can find another place if you—"

"I just want to talk about it."

"Yeah, of course."

Corky had sat down by my side and seemed content to wait patiently, sweeping the floor with her tail and smiling at Estelle, then up at me, like a child waiting for her parents to agree to take her to the movies.

Estelle stared at the dog for a moment. "What'd you say her name was?"

"Corky."

Immediately alert, Corky looked up for the next command. And then to my utter amazement, Estelle bent over, hands on her knees. "Come here, Corky."

Corky glanced at her, and then looked back at me. I dropped the leash and nodded. Up off her haunches, Corky approached Estelle with a sideways gait, head low in submission while her tail swirled circles.

Estelle patted her head as Corky leaned into her. "You're a good girl. Good girl, Corky." My wife glanced at me. "Gotta admit, she seems sweet enough."

I could hardly believe what I was seeing. Thank God for little miracles . . . or maybe it wasn't so little.

When DaShawn came in from playing with the kids across the street—with permission, this time—he immediately plopped down on the floor and gave Corky a royal welcome. Every boy should have a dog at some time in his life, though I realized it would be a little different with Corky, given the fact that she was a working dog and had to go with me every day.

Estelle headed back into the kitchen. "Where's Rodney?" I called after her.

"Asked him to go down to that little market on Touhy to pick up some milk and coffee, and bananas, if they've got any. Don't know how we ran out before shopping day, but we did."

Ten minutes later I heard his footsteps on the stairs, and Corky growled. "It's okay, girl. Just lie down." But when Rodney came in, Corky still watched me closely until I nodded. Then she got up and went over to greet him. I held my breath as Corky sniffed around.

"Well, well, what's this?" Rodney took his jacket off and tossed it onto the couch. "Didn't know we were gettin' a dog."

Corky was no longer interested in Rodney. She'd gone over to the couch, sat down, and was staring intently at Rodney's jacket, not three inches from her nose.

My heart sank. "Free, Corky."

She came back over to me and sat down, tail going wildly as she looked up, expecting a treat. I didn't have anything to give her, so I went into the kitchen and got a small corner of bread crust and rewarded Corky, using the moments to think what I should do.

As I turned back, it didn't appear as though anyone else had noticed what Corky had done, but I knew I had to take the bull by the horns.

I picked up a dining room chair and took it into the living room, turned it around backwards, and threw my leg over it as I sat down. "I don't know if you all noticed how Corky followed Rodney's jacket over to where he tossed it on the couch. Did you see that?"

"Yeah, what was that about?" Rodney asked.

"Good of you to ask. Corky's part of my new job—"

"So you got the job, Pops?" DaShawn said. "Awesome! Guess God answered your prayer, Miz Estelle."

91

"Yeah . . . I got the job. And the job I got," I looked over at Rodney as he sat down on the couch by his jacket, "is in drug interdiction. That's what Corky's all about. She's a drug detection dog." Rodney's face went blank as I continued. "She can smell the slightest amount of most illegal drugs, and when she does, she sits down and points with her nose to the place where it is. Nothin' gets past her."

"Oh, man, that's cool, Pops. I saw that on CSI once. This German shepherd found a whole car full of weed."

None of us said a word as the implications of our recent demonstration sank in. Rodney's blank face became steely hard. "You tryin' to tell me this bitch says I got drugs in my jacket?"

My heart was pounding hard. "That's what it looked like."

"All she did was come over here and sit down for a moment. Don't mean nothin'! Look, she's sittin' down by you now. Maybe she thinks you got drugs on you!"

"Not the same. See, she's lookin' all around, not signaling a thing. Just because she's sittin' here doesn't mean anything. Shall we try your jacket again?"

Rodney snorted. "What difference does it make? You obviously want me outta here. This is a bunch of bull, 'cause I'm clean. I haven't touched anything since I went to jail in Alanta. And that's the truth."

He stood up, grabbed his jacket, and started looking around as if to collect his stuff and clear out. "I was hopin' for a second chance, Dad!" He snarled the word with disdain. "But I see I ain't gonna get one around here."

DaShawn's eyes were darting form his dad to me. "What—?"

"Now just hold on a minute here," Estelle broke in. "You sit back down, Rodney. I believe God brought you here, and I believe God gave Harry this new job. We just gotta figure how the two go together."

"Not with him thinkin' I'm still dealin'. I'm determined to go straight, but can't do it if I'm bein' falsely accused."

Estelle's eyes were hopeful. "What about that Harry? Could Corky be making a mistake?"

"With a signal that clear? I don't think so."

Rodney was still glaring. "Whaddaya mean? She just wandered over here. Maybe she wanted to climb up here on the couch for a snooze and my jacket was in the way."

"We'll see about that!" Estelle marched over. "Gimme that jacket." She grabbed it before Rodney could object. "Turn that dog's head, Harry. Don't let her see where I'm going." She took the jacket through the dining room to the little alcove by the back door where there was a row of waist-high coat hooks on the wall and hung it on one. It was within sight of all of us. Estelle returned and said, "Okay, let her go."

I'd been gently facing Corky's head toward the front of the apartment so she couldn't see where Estelle had gone. I let go, and Corky looked up at me, smiling, tail wagging.

"See, she ain't doin' nothin'. This is a crock. I'm outta here."

"No, no. You wait right there. Harry, what's the deal?"

My mind was spinning like a wind-up top. I'd hoped beyond hope that my son was getting his life straightened out. And now this! Could I . . . should I press the point? Maybe I should let it go. Except . . . if he was still dealing or even using, we had an impossible situation on our hands. We couldn't keep him in our house where he'd undoubtedly influence DaShawn.

I bit the bullet. "Corky, seek!"

Corky jumped up and trotted around the room sniffing the furniture, the bookcase, the TV and the cabinet below it. Then she went to DaShawn, Estelle, and Rodney.

"See, I'm clean. She didn't do nothin'."

"Hold on. Let her work."

Corky trotted excitedly into the kitchen, and we all followed to watch as she sniffed at each cupboard door, under the refrigerator and under the stove and dishwasher. Satisfied, she came out and circled the dining room table, then went toward the back of the apartment, zigzagging the floor with her nose. Nothing of interest until she got to that back alcove and the coats. She immediately zeroed in on Rodney's coat. She sat down, tail still, nose and eyes as immovably focused on the jacket as if she were made of stone.

"She's doin' it!" DaShawn yelled, amazed by the demonstration.

"Oh no," his voice sagged. "She found it."

"No she hasn't!" Rodney's voice had lost its belligerence and was appealing, almost crying. "Ya gotta believe me, son. I'm done with that life. I'm clean. Ya gotta believe me. I haven't touched nothin' since before I was locked up in the Atlanta bastille."

"Corky, free." The dog looked up at me, expecting a reward, but I didn't have one. A more important thought had entered my mind. "Rodney, did you have this jacket when you were arrested in Atlanta?"

"No."

"So, how do you have it now?"

"Went by the apartment where I was stayin' and picked it up along with some other stuff I'd left."

"So it was with your friends the whole time you were in the joint? Well, it's dirty now." I grabbed it from the coat hook and took it to the dining room table, reversing each pocket. A gum wrapper, a crumpled up tissue, an 'L' ticket, a couple of fuzz balls, but nothing incriminating.

"Here, let me see that." Rodney grabbed it out of my hand and flipped it open to reveal an inside breast pocket I hadn't noticed. He zipped it open defiantly, dug his hand in, then slowly pulled out a crumpled joint. As soon as he saw it, he flicked it onto the table as though it were a hot coal. "Hey, that ain't mine. I never rolled filters in the end of my joints. I swear. Somebody else must have borrowed my jacket and left this in it, but this ain't mine."

Hmm. Good story. But how did I know he never rolled filters? How did any of us know?

"What were you arrested for in Atlanta?"

"A packet of crack. They don't bother you for a little weed."

I walked over to the back window and looked out without seeing. How I wanted to believe the best of Rodney. Wanted to believe he was straight now and would stay that way. It was a reasonable explanation, but . . . was I being naïve? Then the words came to me, "Love . . . always trusts, always hopes, always perseveres." We'd studied that passage in my men's Bible study, and the Bible was never naïve about sin, but the guys had shown me it also encouraged us to give one another the benefit of the doubt. Surely, if Rodney wasn't straight, we would discover it soon enough.

I turned back to my family and took a deep breath. "All right. But you saw what Corky can do. She's amazing, absolutely amazing. Let this be a lesson—no one, and I mean no one can enter this house with any drugs. She'll detect 'em. It's her job."

Rodney looked at me, his eyes betraying a mixture of relief and skepticism.

I picked up the joint. "I'm gonna flush this. Estelle, you think this jacket's washable?"

She checked the tag on the collar. "Says, 'Cold water wash. Tumble dry warm.'"

I handed it to Rodney. "Why don't you take it on down to the basement and put it in the washer, son. And when can we eat, Estelle?"

Estelle's smile seemed to stretch ear to ear. "As soon as DaShawn sets the table."

Chapter 14

RODNEY AND DASHAWN WERE ON DISH DUTY Wednesday evening, so after supper I used Corky as an excuse to slip out for a walk. The moment I was out the back door and hit the cold air, I sighed so deeply, it was as though I'd been holding my breath ever since I'd come home. "What have we gotten ourselves into, Corky?" I said once we were in the alley. She hunched up and backed into a bush. Her embarrassed eyes said she didn't want me to watch, so I looked away.

The door of the garage next to ours was open, light shining out into the alley, and from within came a loud banging. Once I'd bagged Corky's recyclable contribution and dropped it into our trash can, I wandered over and looked into the open garage.

The big lawn-service pickup was nosed into the garage and someone was underneath beating on the snowplow attached to the front. When the banging stopped, I said, "How's it goin'?"

"Not bad," came a strained voice. In a moment our neighbor scooted out from under his vehicle and stood up. He transferred a two-pound sledge from his right hand to his left and extended his hand to shake mine, then realized it was dirty and pulled it back.

I extended mine a little farther. "No problem, man. No problem. I'm Harry Bentley. Just moved in on Saturday."

"Farid Jalili." He gave my hand a good shake. "Yeah. Saw the truck and all those people. Sorry I couldn't help, but I had to go to work."

He had a slight accent, not Spanish or Indian, so I figured that my earlier guess of Middle Eastern was right. "Ah, that's okay," I said. "Had a bunch of folks from church helping us."

"Church, huh? What church?"

"SouledOut Community, over in the mall on the corner of Howard and Clark."

"Hmm." His eyebrows went up. "Didn't know there was a church in there."

"Yeah. It's a storefront, pretty big but tucked back in the corner." I'd seen his wife wearing one of those scarves over her head, so I didn't want to push the church thing too much and moved on to a safer subject. "I've seen your truck out front. You own your own business?"

"Oh yes. I got tired of working for other people, so I took the—how do you say it?—the plunge."

"Great. Bet you had lots of work with the storm."

"Ha! More than I could manage, and I hit a curb and bent the blade a little." He held up his hammer. "Unfortunately, this won't do it."

"Hey, I got a hydraulic jack somewhere. It might do the job if you can get an angle and find something to push against." I shrugged. "That's if I can find the thing."

"Oh no, no. I would not want to bother you. A jack's a good idea, but I can rent one from Home Depot."

"Hey, what are neighbors for?"

He nodded and smiled broadly. "Right now I have to go in the house. My wife has already come out twice to retrieve me to eat."

"Oh yeah? Well, see ya around, then."

I gave him a wave and walked on down the alley. "She's gonna retrieve him to eat, huh? Whaddaya think of that Corky?" But Corky was more interested in sniffing who had been down the alley before us.

The next morning I took Gilson's advice and stayed home long enough to go to PetSmart and outfit Corky with a nice bed, a couple of pans, some treats, and bags of food. Creston had told me that all the dogs were on a very strict diet. Estelle had complained about Dandy, that yellow dog at the shelter, stealing things out of the garbage in her kitchen, but I knew I'd have to watch that she didn't slip Corky treats here at home.

After I'd arranged everything for Corky in our apartment, I went downstairs to see how Rodney was doing with painting the bedroom, Corky following my every step.

"Hey, Harry," Rodney said when I stood at the door to the bedroom. "I should finish this today. You said there was a bed out in the garage?" His tone was cordial enough, but there was still a gulf between us.

"Yeah. Bed's out there. I can help you bring it in this evening, if you want."

"Nah, don't worry about it." He dismissed my offer with a wave of his hand. "I can manage. Or DaShawn can help when he gets home from school. I want to get everything set up so I can get back to the job hunt tomorrow, if that's okay with you."

"Sure. Best of luck." I started to leave but turned back. "Oh, that reminds me. I meant to speak to one of my Bible study buddies. He owns a business, could ask if he has any jobs open. I'll try to give him a call today. Hey, you oughta come with me next Tuesday. You might like it."

Rodney just nodded and went back to painting. I snapped my fingers for Corky and headed out the back way and stopped to inspect the kitchen. It was looking beautiful—counters and sink in, mosaic tile backsplash installed, ceramic floor down. "Hey Rodney," I called toward the bedroom, "those guys say when they'll be back to finish the kitchen?"

"This afternoon. They're pickin' up the appliances."

Wow! Those guys work fast.

Corky and I went on out to the SUV and headed down to the Loop. It took me an hour to get three uniforms from the store on Wabash, but I arrived at work in time to check in with Gilson just after he got back from a late lunch. I spent the rest of the day getting acquainted with the other APD officers and exploring the station with Corky. I didn't attempt the blind man cover but wore my shield prominently on my belt and kept Corky on a standard leash.

In the middle of the afternoon, Corky sat down and signaled one of the backpacks carried by three college-age kids who were sitting on the floor next to the wall in the boarding lounge. For a moment, I didn't know what I should do. Corky and I had at least a week of training before Gilson expected us to be on duty.

Wait a minute! Why was I hesitating? They were breaking the law. I flashed my shield. "Any of you carrying dope on you?"

"Who? Us? No way, man. We're clean."

"Corky here doesn't think so." When the guy started to get up, I held up my hand. "Stay put. And all of you keep your hands where I can see 'em." I studied all three—a long, lanky kid with blue eyes and dark-blond hair so limp it simply fell straight down from where it grew. At least it was neatly cut. One arm was through a strap of the backpack Corky was identifying as dirty. The two girls appeared younger and embarrassed, a flush rising up their necks like matching temperature gauges. Their intentionally ripped jeans were offset by a stylish pea jacket for one and a high-end ski jacket for the other that probably cost daddy over a grand.

"Where you headed?" I asked.

They looked at each other until the girl in the ski jacket said, "Urbana. Heading back to the university after spring break."

I glanced up at the board. "So you'd be taking the Illini, huh?" All three nodded.

"Well then, you got a little time here. Mind if I search your backpack?" I ask the guy.

"Huh?" He pulled it a little closer. "What for? You gotta have a warrant first, don'tcha?"

I gestured at Corky with my thumb. "She's my warrant. Law says I don't need a warrant for drugs in plain sight." I waited until he got a smug expression his face. "It also says that identification by a certified drug detection dog is the equivalent of seeing them in plain sight. Corky's got a badge. You want to see it?"

He didn't know whether to believe me or not.

"So, you gonna let me look in your pack?" We were attracting an audience. "Hurry up, man. Open it up before I take you into custody."

"Hey, I ain't got nothin' in there but a little packet of grass. I swear."

"You better hope that's all I find. Now unzip it and hand it up here to me. No, you stay on the floor." I reached down to touch my dog's head. "Corky, free." She took a step back, watching and wagging her tail vigorously as though she'd cornered a rabbit in its hole.

The kid unzipped his backpack and handed it up to me, a sour look on his face.

I fished around in the compartments until I found a packet of marijuana, just a baggy with an ounce or two in it. "Is this all?" I shielded it from the onlookers.

"Yeah, man. That's it. I'm tellin' ya."

I dug around a little more without finding anything else that appeared suspicious. "All right. Hang on a minute." I pulled out my radio and called for a couple of uniforms to come and help me.

"Hey, I thought you said if I opened my pack you wouldn't take us into custody."

"Just for questioning in the office . . . and to check out these girls' packs."

"I thought you said you needed a warrant unless the dog was doin' whatever she does."

"That's right. But she gets a second chance. She might have been distracted by your little stash."

"Hey, they're clean. I'm tellin' ya."

"We'll see, won't we?" My backup arrived. "You can get up now and follow this officer. I'll be right behind you."

All three started off, heads down like they were already part of a chain gang. But as we went through the station, the girls started complaining that they were going to miss their train. In the questioning room, I dumped everything out from the guy's backpack and patted him down while the girls stood off to the side with terrified looks on their faces. Probably the first time they'd been busted.

Nothing else incriminating turned up in the backpack. "All right, you can reload your pack, except for your baggy of weed. Ladies, would you put your backpacks on the floor, one there and one over there." Then I turned to my eager Lab. "Corky, seek!"

It was obvious that we'd placed the most suspicious items on the floor, but Corky first went to the girls and sniffed around them before checking out their backpacks. Very interesting, I thought. But nothing got signaled.

"Looks like you two were a little smarter than your friend here." I turned to the kid, who stood as tall as I did, though he carried himself with slightly stooped shoulders. "All right, tell you what we're gonna do. You pick up your little bag of weed and follow Officer Kramer down the hall to our own private restroom where he'll watch you flush it—all of it, every leaf—down the toilet and then rinse out the baggy and put it in the trash. When you're done, come back here and get your stuff. Then the three of you can go catch your train." I glanced at my watch. "Almost four o'clock. You got about five minutes before the Illini pulls out."

He grabbed the baggy and started pushing Kramer toward the door. Kramer planted his feet. "Hey, hey, hey, don't you be touchin' a police officer or I'll arrest you for assault and resisting."

"I ain't resistin' nothing. Come on, man, let's go."

The girls picked up their backpacks, and the one in the fancy ski jacket looked at me. All the embarrassment and fear were out of her face. "If you make us miss our train, I'm gonna file a complaint."

"Yeah, you do that, you little ingrate. Now get outta here."

Once the kids were gone, I looked at the two officers. "Thanks for the backup. Ha! Big deal for my first day on the job with Corky." I glanced at my watch again, as though I didn't already know what it said. "Nearly quittin' time. See y'all tomorrow."

As I drove home, I wondered if the day had been a foretaste of what my job would be like—penny-ante busts that would have no impact on the drug trade or the lifeblood of the gangs in Chicago. What was I doing?

Chapter 15

FRIDAY I WORE A UNIFORM—it had been a long time—and saw Gilson only briefly. He'd heard about Corky and me bustin' the college students, as had most of the other APD officers. It had become something of a joke, but Gilson said, "No, no. It was good. Shows you and Corky can work together just fine. Next week's your training out in Des Plaines. It'll be a good tune-up for the both of you. And by the way, they have a trainer out there who used to work with guide dogs. She'll be able to help you two with your cover. Pretty cool, huh?"

I just nodded. The more I thought about Gilson's undercover blind man idea, the more I had to admit it might work, so I held my peace and got the paperwork from Phyllis, along with the address of the CPD K-9 training center and the name of the person we were to report to on Monday morning.

When I got home that evening, Estelle was all in a rush to get us fed. "And then," she announced, "I want you to go shopping with me, Harry. I got a lot of baking to do this evening, and need you to help me pick up the supplies."

I mentally clicked through all the things I could remember—knowing I often forgot events Estelle scheduled—church, work, school. But I drew a blank. "Uh . . . what's up? It seems to have slipped my mind."

"I'm gonna bake cinnamon rolls for all our neighbors. Remember, 'if you want to have friends, you have to show yourself friendly'? It's in the Bible. Got my kitchen set up, so tonight's the night . . . and probably most of tomorrow too."

"And I'm supposed to do what?"

"Help me with the shopping. And tomorrow I want you to come with me to meet the neighbors. I don't like not knowing who's living around us."

"We didn't know everyone back in the apartment building, and . . . and I already met Farid next door. Seemed like a great guy. Oh, that reminds me, I need to find my hydraulic jack for him to use."

"Well, you can do that tomorrow while I finish up the baking."

There was no stopping Estelle when she got a bee in her hairdo. The next morning I found my jack, and though the smell of those fresh cinnamon rolls almost kept me housebound with the hope of a taste, I carried it to my neighbor's house.

A woman I assumed was his wife answered the door, smiled, and said Farid was out in the garage. I thanked her and headed around to the back. Should have tried the garage first.

"Farid?" I pushed the side door open. "You in here? I found my jack."

"Harry? Come on in. I never got over to Home Depot. Many thanks."

We spent the next hour rolling around on the floor of his garage, trying to position that jack so he'd have the right angle and a strong enough purchase to push his plow back into shape. Finally, we positioned the truck over an inch-high lip in the concrete floor and started jacking.

"I think that's got it. Look." Farid measured the two sides of his plow and they were identical. "Oh, man. I can't thank you enough. You're really a godsend."

"No problem. Glad I could help."

We crawled out from under the big pickup, and he rolled up the cord for his droplight. "Say, where was that church you said you went to?"

I told him again and watched as he nodded his head while he hung up the light. "It's been a long time since we've been to church. I don't know. Do you think . . . I mean, this is a Christian church, right?"

"Oh yeah, Christian. We believe in Jesus and follow the Bible." He shrugged. "We tried a couple of churches years ago when we first came to America, but I don't know . . ." He shrugged again. "So, you're Christians?"

"Yes, yes. That's why we left Iran."

"From Iran. Wow! You know, I don't think I remember your last name."

"Jalili . . . Farid and Lily Jalili. Yeah, we had to flee Iran after they firebombed my store."

"No way! What happened?"

"Well, I had this little boutique in Tehran—women's clothes, handbags, shoes. Police said it was because we were selling Western designer stuff." He shrugged again in his characteristic fashion. "But I know it was because we were Christians, 'cause that's what the guy yelled when he threw the Molotov cocktail through the window."

"Oh, man, so sorry to hear that. Musta been terrifying." I paused, thinking he might tell me more of his story, but instead he just thanked me for my help and told me to let him know any time he could return the favor. He seemed eager to get back in to his family, so I went on home to see how Estelle was doing.

I spent the next hour helping her package batches of six cinnamon rolls each in plastic wrap with a ribbon around them and a little tag with our name on it. Of course, we had to sample a cinnamon roll or two . . . with a good cup of coffee. When Estelle had warmed up my cup for the second time, I said, "Hey, you know that family next door? I thought they might be Muslim, but they're not."

"Oh?" She paused in the middle of pouring her own coffee.

"Their names are Farid and Lily Jalili, and they are from Iran, but Farid says they were forced to flee because of their Christian faith. They had a little store—women's clothes and stuff—that got torched by Islamic extremists."

"Oh no! How scary. When did all this happen?"

"I dunno." I thought for a moment. "Must've been quite awhile ago, 'cause he said something about not being able to find a good church when they first came to the States. But he said that was years ago." I shrugged.

Estelle finished pouring her coffee. "Well, it's nice to know there are other Christians in the neighborhood. Now we'll have to get acquainted for sure."

I grinned. "That's what I was doin'."

By midafternoon we were ready to set out with Estelle's "neighborhood warming" gifts. DaShawn was writing a report on the Civil War for school, and we were glad to escape his whining. He was supposed to be starting spring break, but he'd failed to turn in the report on time. His teacher had sent home a notice giving him one last chance. If he finished it over the weekend and put it in the mail, postmarked on Monday, she would accept it. Otherwise, he would receive an incomplete. Sounded like a generous deal to me, so I had no sympathy for his complaints.

When we got to the bottom of the stairs, I stuck my head into the apartment. "Hey Rodney," I called toward his new room, "we're goin' out for a while. DaShawn's upstairs doin' homework. Okay?"

"No problem."

We were barely out the front door when Estelle said, "What's he doin' in there? He doesn't even have a TV."

"I dunno. S'pose we could loan him that little one you had before we got married."

"Sure, if you want." She pushed me to the right when we got to the end of our walk. "Let's go this way. You already met the guy with the truck. And this woman in this house—she pointed to the bungalow to our south—was one of the people who yanked the drapes closed on me that day. We're goin' to her house first."

I laughed. "Remind me to never let you get on my case, babe, or you'll love me to death."

"Ha, ha! You better believe it." She hugged my arm close to her ample bosom. "I'll dog ya 'til I gotcha!"

The neat little house next door had a nice porch with a swing, though it was covered with dust as if it hadn't been used for ages. I reminded myself that spring had barely sprung. Who'd be porch sitting in a Chicago winter?

Estelle had to ring the bell twice before an elderly man opened the door a couple of inches. "Yes?"

"We're Estelle and Harry Bentley from next door." Estelle smiled warmly. "We just moved in last week and thought we'd say hello." She held out a package with a red ribbon and a little note with our names on it. "I made you some fresh-baked cinnamon rolls."

The man turned back stiffly as though the vertebrae in his neck were fused. "Eva, it's those people next door wanting to sell us something."

"No, no, no. They're a gift . . . get-acquainted gift."

"Eva!"

We waited in awkward silence, me wishing the guy would just take the bloomin' cinnamon rolls so we could get out of there. Finally he was joined by a thin woman with a little tremor that bobbled her head under a bubble of fuzzy gray hair. She wore a faded blue print dress, and I had to stifle myself remembering that as a kid I would have called her a classic "fuzz-print." At least she was more hospitable than her husband. "Oh, how nice. Won't you come in?"

"Only for a minute," said Estelle. "We just wanted to introduce ourselves and say hello."

We went in and all sat awkwardly on cheap French-provincial furniture that had never been intended for relaxing. "Well, we're Karl and Eva Molander," the woman offered. "Been here ever since this neighborhood was all Swedish and German—"

"Except for the Krakowskis—"

"Yes. They were Polish. But now . . . well, it's all changed, and we're the last ones—"

"Ever since you got Mattie's place," Karl said coldly. His comment made me squirm.

"What a shame. What a shame." The old woman closed her eyes and brought a clenched fist up to her lips. "That was frightening. Just frightening to think that she fell and no one knew a thing about—"

"Nobody knew. Of course, how could they? I mean, she's the only one we really knew on the whole block. And now—"

"In fact, we used to pray—" Eva glanced toward Karl as though she'd said too much, then shrugged. "—anyway we prayed for everyone when we knew 'em by name. Even after the Mexicans and all the others started moving in, we still prayed for a long time. But . . ."

Estelle took advantage of the first break in their tag-team spiel. "And that's why we wanted to say hello."

"Yeah," I added as I moved to the edge of my seat and glanced at Estelle, "and if there's anything we can do, just let us know. We'd be glad to help." But right then, I just wanted to get out of there.

"Well," said Karl, "Mattie sure needed lots of help, but she didn't get it from anybody around here. Of course, her son tried to help by remodeling the place so she could rent it, but . . ." He turned his stiff body a few degrees and looked out of the corner of his eye at his wife.

She nodded. "Then it got snatched right out from under her." She might as well have added, by you thieves!

That was too much for me. I stood up. "Well, it's been good to meet you." I touched Estelle's shoulder. "We better be goin' now. But like I said, if there's anything we can do, just let us know."

I couldn't wait to get out on the sidewalk.

"Whew!" said Estelle, glancing back over her shoulder as the Molanders' door closed behind us. "That was something."

"Yeah," I said, chuckling, "they used to pray for everyone. Does that mean another Christian family on the block."

"Ha! Lord have mercy! I'll just let him be the judge of that." She was silent for a moment. "You know, it's like they blame us for the old lady's accident."

"More like they're accusing us of takin' her house from her. But it wasn't us who did it. It was the bank."

The next family was Hispanic—David and Maria Morales and her brother Roberto Jimenez—and very gracious. If we'd run into someone else like the Molanders, I might have mutinied on Estelle.

As we approached the house on the corner, we met the family coming down their front steps—obviously Jewish, probably Orthodox, given the man's flat-brimmed black hat, long black overcoat, and untrimmed beard with ringlets hanging down by his ears. The woman wore a long black dress extending below her winter coat and had her hair tucked up under a black knit covering. They stopped long enough to exchange names and hellos. Isaac and Rebecca Horowitz had three children, a boy about seven with a yarmulke on his head and a younger girl. Rebecca was pushing a stroller with the third child—a grinning toddler cuddled under blankets. "Thank you so much," Rebecca said as she took the cinnamon rolls and hurried up on the porch where she deposited them in their mailbox.

"Yes, thank you," said Isaac. "I wish we could invite you in, but we are on our way to Shabbat services, and we're running a little behind."

"Oh," said Estelle, "is there a synagogue near here?"

Isaac told us where the nearest shul was. "We're barely just within the teḥum Shabbat—walking limitations, you know. If we lived next door . . ." he shrugged as he thumbed toward the Molanders' house, "we'd be too far."

We wished them well and crossed the street. When they were out of earshot, Estelle said, "You think she left the rolls in the mailbox because they can't have yeast in their house? The cinnamon rolls have yeast in them."

I shook my head. "I think that's only for Passover."

The family in the house on the other side of the street was from Congo. Three generations—a grandfather, a mother who worked at Abbott Laboratories, and a teenage boy.

Next to them lived a white family with two young children, a girl and a boy. And as soon as we introduced ourselves, the husband said, "Oh yeah, you're the people who got the old lady's house." It was beginning to sound like the whole neighborhood considered us opportunistic vultures, and I had to bite my tongue. Estelle graciously changed the subject and asked about the children, who the mother proudly announced were homeschooled. Soon they were demonstrating all the fascinating things they'd learned just that week.

Alejandro and Corina Alvarez lived in the only other two-flat on the block. They had three kids, and apparently several other family members or friends also lived in the building. I couldn't quite figure it all out, or perhaps they didn't want to be too specific about the relationships. Maybe some of them had immigration issues or something. That was none of my business, but it might explain a strange thing Alejandro said. After expressing how glad they were that we'd stopped by, he said, "We've lived here six years, and we don't know anybody on this block. People wave, but they don't talk to each other."

What was going on in this neighborhood?

No one was home at the next house, a fine-looking yellow brick bungalow with four leaded Prairie-style windows across the front divided by arched columns. And it was getting dark by the time we got to the little house where Estelle said the other person had "pulled the drapes" on her. No one was home there, either.

"Well, we better quit for today," Estelle said. "Wouldn't want to arrive at anyone's suppertime. I'll do the rest tomorrow afternoon."

"Yeah, well, only if you let me go with you to that McMansion at the end of the street. I want to know who lives in that big ol' thing."

Chapter 16

WE HADN'T VISITED MY MOM in several days, and I wanted to see her, but when we got home from church on Sunday, Estelle said she had to finish delivering the cinnamon rolls that afternoon or they'd get stale. "What would our neighbors think of us if we gave them stale rolls?"

"Ha! I'm not sure cinnamon rolls will either make or break us. Seems like most of 'em have already made up their minds. They may not know each other very well, but apparently that doesn't stop the gossip."

"Now, Harry we don't know that for sure. We haven't met everybody yet."

"Yeah, but how many made some kind of snide remark about us stealing 'the old lady's house'?"

"Harry, only the Molanders said anything like that. A couple of others may have said something about us moving into 'the old lady's house', but they didn't mean anything by it."

"I don't know. The Molanders may have been right about the relationships breakin' down in this neighborhood, but I'm beginning to think they've kept the gossip lines open." I rolled my eyes. Wouldn't have minded going with her to meet the rest of our neighbors—in fact, I was kind of curious—but had no idea how much of my time would be tied up next week training with Corky, so I really felt I should go to the hospital.

"Okay then. You go see Mom," Estelle said, "but you be sure and give her my love. Ya hear?"

I promised . . . provided Estelle would fill me in on what she found at that McMansion. She laughed. "I keep seeing these big ol' limousines drive up to that place. Very fancy people goin' in and out."

"Ah, maybe it's a private club or something." I waggled my eyebrows at her like Groucho Marx.

Rodney and DaShawn were willing to go with me to the hospital, which I knew would please Mom. And I wasn't disappointed. She was napping when we got there, but the nurse encouraged us to wake her up. "It's okay. She sleeps too much anyway."

Mom opened her eyes and smiled when I took her hand, looking from one to the other of us. Maybe it was wishful thinking, but her smile didn't seem as crooked as it had earlier, and the sparkle had returned to her eyes.

I realized I'd picked up her left hand. My heart skipped a beat. I couldn't recall whether the paralysis on her left side had also made her arm and hand numb. But at least this time she'd felt me touch her. It had awakened her. Was the rehab working? Was she getting better?

I patted her hand, but her hand didn't move or grip mine. Maybe she hadn't really been asleep and just heard us. But she did look pretty good, and she was definitely happy to see us.

We stayed a couple of hours, and I felt proud of DaShawn for how hard he worked to decipher what Mom tried to say. Sometimes he got it, and that delighted Mom no end. But the process also showed me she'd made very little progress in the speech department. And even though she was thrilled when DaShawn guessed what she meant, it was also terribly frustrating to her when he didn't, and the process wore her out.

"Hey, Mom, we're gonna go now. Estelle sends her love. We'll be back." I paused, wanting to tell her how much I really loved her—hadn't done that for who knows how long, and I wanted it to be more than the "Love ya" messages people often say to each other, but I couldn't put together the words.

Mom reached out with her right hand and her eyes got big, but when she tried to speak, she had to say it three times before I understand her moans: "When?" It broke my heart to realize how lonely she felt. It definitely was different than being alone in her apartment. There she was free to do for herself, get out to the market when she felt good enough, and she looked forward to us taking her to church. But in the hospital she was trapped among strangers in a body that made communication, let alone travel, difficult.

As we came out of the hospital, DaShawn claimed "Shotgun" and climbed into the front seat beside me while Rodney got into the back. We'd no sooner pulled out of the parking lot when Rodney's cell rang. "Yeah? . . . No, no. Can't! . . . Not now. . . . Why? . . . Don't give me that crap. . . . I'll get back to you." And then he hung up.

He didn't offer any explanation, and both he and DaShawn rode in silence, staring out their respective windows as my thoughts returned to Mom. It was time to put the last scraps of my dream for her quick recovery to rest. She wasn't going to be moving into our first-floor apartment anytime soon . . . probably not ever.

So, what does that mean, God? We need to get a paying renter into that unit.

Most of our family tension had eased now that Rodney had moved downstairs, but he didn't have a job and couldn't pay for the apartment. Even if he did find a job, it was unlikely to pay enough to cover a place of that size.

As I pulled my RAV4 into the garage beside Corky's Dodge Durango, Rodney turned to me. "Say, Harry, you think Miz Estelle would mind if I took DaShawn out to dinner this—"

"All right, Dad!" DaShawn exploded from his window-gazing reverie and turned around to face Rodney. "Where we gonna go?"

"Just hold on, now. I'm askin' your grandpa somethin'. Whaddaya think, Harry?"

I pushed the button to lower the garage door, and we all got out. "Well, let's go in and see. Unless she made some kind of a big meal, I can't think of any problem. With all the bakin' she's been doin' lately, I'll be lucky to get a bowl of soup."

"So where we goin', Dad? Huh? Where we goin'?"

"Baker's Square okay? We can walk there easy enough."

✦   ✦   ✦   ✦

Estelle had cooked—honey-baked lentils over rice. But it was the kind of meal that made great leftovers, so she had no problem with DaShawn and Rodney going out. After they left and we both sat down at the kitchen table, Estelle said, "What's up with those two?"

"I have no idea. While we were driving home, Rodney got this strange phone call, and then they were both as quiet as a couple of mannequins until we pulled into the garage. That's when Rodney asked DaShawn if he wanted to go out to eat."

"Hmm. Guess it's a good thing for a dad to be taking his son out." She wiped the corner of her mouth with a napkin. "So, how's Mom?"

I shrugged. "Guess she's doin' okay, but I don't think she's makin' any progress with her recovery, and she really hated to see us leave."

"Lord have mercy." She stared at her plate for a moment and then she looked up at me. "Doctor say anything more about home rehab?" I shook my head, but I was too depressed by Mom's situation to talk about it, so I asked Estelle how the rest of her neighborhood visits went.

She chuckled and took a deep breath as though she too was glad to change subjects. "They were great! Wish you could've joined me. Though there still wasn't anyone home at that yellow-brick place across the street. But next door to them lives a young single gal who's a professional singer, Christian, no less."

"Oh yeah? Someone we know about?"

"Grace Meredith." Estelle shrugged and took a drink of water. "Never heard of her myself, but she must be pretty good. She travels all over the country."

"White, black, what? She a gospel singer?"

"White girl. More like praise and worship—CCM, I think she called it, Contemporary Christian Music. Anyway, just to let you know, I invited her to supper Wednesday evening."

"Wednesday evening? Why?"

"Just trying to get to know our neighbors, and she seemed . . . I don't know . . . like she needed a friend."

"And that would be you, I suppose!"

Estelle grinned. "Maybe. We'll have to see."

"Yeah, but you remember, don'tcha, I got that training all next week? I have no idea when I'll get home."

"Oh . . ." She grabbed her chin with her hand. "Forgot. But they won't be holdin' you too late, will they? You said yourself they've got to consider the dogs."

"I wouldn't think so, but I just don't know." Estelle gave me a worried look. "Don't worry 'bout it, babe. Even if I'm a little late, it'll work out. So, who's next to her? Isn't that where DaShawn's friends from school live?"

"Yes, and I'm really glad I met them. They seem like a great family, and they're old-timers in the neighborhood too, in spite of what the Molanders said. Probably the first black family on the whole block."

"Well, there you go! If they were the first black family, then no matter how long ago they moved in, they'd still be interlopers as far as the Molanders are concerned."

"Come on, Harry. Give 'em a break."

"Oh, I would if they didn't claim to be Christians. Even Jesus couldn't abide hypocrites."

Estelle sighed. "Anyway, I was telling you about the Jaspers. It's Jared and Michelle. Now, let me see . . ." She counted on her fingers. "They've got an older boy and twins about DaShawn's age. Jared, the father, works as an air traffic controller at O'Hare, and he's a deacon at Northside Second Baptist. Michelle is a social worker and heads up the women's ministry at their church. Got the impression they're involved in everything that goes on at their church—Sunday school, youth, prayer meeting. I don't know how they do it with three teenagers."

"Hmm. They sound like church addicts."

"What?"

"Church addicts. You know, people so busy with church stuff they ain't got no time for other people."

"Harry Bentley, what's got into you? Why are you so cynical tonight?"

Her question gave me pause. Was I being cynical? It was tempting to defend myself, but I had to admit, I did feel all tied up inside. Maybe it was Mom. I just wasn't ready to see her life end this way. I shrugged away Estelle's question and got up. "I dunno. You want some more water while I'm up?"

"No, no thanks. But I'm tellin' you Harry, these Jaspers are good people, and we're blessed that their kids reached out to DaShawn. He needs good friends. Lord knows there are too many of the other kind."

I returned with my water and sat down while Estelle eyed me. I could tell she still thought something was bugging me, but she didn't push it and pretty soon picked up her tale of visiting the neighborhood.

"After the Jaspers, I went to the 'McMansion,' as you call it. And I declare, that's some place. If you think the outside is over the top, you oughta see the inside. The foyer is two stories high with a huge crystal chandelier, and beyond that there's this sweeping curved staircase that comes down. My, my, my." Estelle was shaking her head. "Anyway, this pretty young thing came to the door, but when I started tellin' her why I was there, she interrupted me and said she didn't really live there, but 'Mister Lincoln'—that's what she called him—'Mister Lincoln'—"

"What, that's not his name?"

"Hold on. Found out later his name's Lincoln Paddock, but she called him 'Mister Lincoln' and said he was busy. Just then this guy who looked like a movie star came down the stairs. He was barefoot, in jeans and a white T-shirt, and smiled real big at me. Guess he'd heard what I was trying to tell the girl, because he said, 'That's okay, Jill, I'll take it from here.' She nodded and blushed and went back up the stairs. I watched her for a moment—pants so tight, they looked painted on—and before she got to the top, two other girls came out and leaned over the bannister, one was this sista with long black extensions and the other looked like some blonde hooker. I tell you, Harry, don't you go down there without me along, ya hear?"

I put my hand up to cover my mouth.

"What . . . what are you laughin' about?"

"Nothin', nothin'. Go on."

"Well, I gave him the cinnamon rolls and told him who we were. And he said he'd been wonderin' who'd moved into the old lady's house—"

"Sounds to me like more gossip."

"I don't know, Harry, he didn't say it with an attitude. He was just making conversation. But I tell you, there was something funny about that place. While we were talkin', I heard a bunch of other people, upstairs and in other rooms downstairs. It was like they were having a party, and it was the middle of Sunday afternoon."

"Well, people do have parties on the weekend, you know."

"I know, but . . ."

I lowered my voice to a conspiratorial whisper. "Maybe it's a cathouse."

"Oh, Harry, quit bein' silly. I was worried since there were only six cinnamon rolls. Probably didn't take enough for everybody."

Ah, that was just like my Estelle. Even though she thought something funny was going on in that "cathouse" her warm heart was concerned that she hadn't delivered enough treats for all the "kittens."

When I finally I got control of myself, I said, "Estelle, don't worry about it. I'm sure your gesture was appreciated."

"Yeah, well, I still think somethin' isn't right in that place."

"And now who's bein' cynical?"

She took a deep breath and sat up straight. "Well, not me." She waved her hand across her face as though dismissing the subject. "Let's see . . . oh, yeah." She reached over to the counter and grabbed a scrap of paper. "Took some notes. Last house was the one at the end of the block on our side of the street."

"You mean on the other side of Farid?"

"Mm-hm. A young boy named Danny answered the door, looked about eight. Cute kid. Tow-headed, blue eyes. Haven't seen him around, but the weather's been cold until recently. Anyway, he called his dad to the door. Name was Tim Mercer. Tim was very gracious, and as soon as he heard who I was and why I was there, he said, 'This is great, let me call my husband. He'll want to meet you too.'" Estelle paused and gave me a look. "Another man came out of the kitchen wiping his hands on a dishtowel. Name is Scott . . . Scott Hanson. He's Danny's 'daddy'—"

"Wait a minute." I couldn't help interrupting. "I thought you said Tim was his dad." I held out both hands in a what-gives gesture. "That's right. Tim is Danny's dad and Scott is his daddy."

"Oh . . . oh . . ."

"Mm-hm. That's right. Kind of took me aback, too, but I can tell you they were some of the most grateful people on the whole block. They thanked me several times and kept apologizing for not having welcomed us first. Tim kept sayin', 'This is the way it should be, reachin' out to each other.' I tell ya, Harry . . ." Her voice drifted off. After a moment, she frowned like she'd remembered one other detail. "Scott said they moved here six years ago from a condo they owned down in Boystown. Said they'd been there forever but they wanted a yard for Danny. They thanked me again for comin' by, said no one had welcomed them when they moved in."

Well. God sure had planted us in an interesting neighborhood.

Chapter 17

ONDAY MORNING, CORKY AND I piled into her "chariot" and headed out to Des Plaines for our first day of training. I thought we were already working like a team, but I understood the need for recertification. We were supposed to check in at the training center at 8:00 a.m., but it took me a lot longer to get out there than I'd figured.

As I drove, I thought about Estelle's report on the neighbors she'd met. What struck me most was the response from the gay couple two doors north of us. Of all the people we'd visited, Estelle said they'd seemed the most grateful and gracious. No one else had apologized for not welcoming us. Were the two guys at the end of the block just friendlier by nature? Or had our other neighbors—even the Christian ones—simply avoided the subject because they felt embarrassed?

As a Chicago police officer, I'd gone through all the anti-bias seminars the city could throw at me, and certainly Chicago's gay community actively defended their civil rights, doing their best to make sure the cops treated them fairly. But I'd never really gotten to know a gay couple, certainly not a family with a child that lived a quiet and peaceful life like any other family.

It made my head swim! As a Christian, even just as their neighbor, how was I supposed to relate?

Whoa! I hit the brakes, almost sailing past the Canine Training Center. I wouldn't have noticed it if it hadn't been for the three blue-and-white Chicago police cars parked out front. My watch said two minutes after eight when I turned in and parked beside them.

Frankly, it looked like a junkyard with a high, barbed-wire-topped chain-link fence surrounding a low, rundown metal building with an old trailer house and a semitruck trailer on the sides.

But the sign said Chicago Police Department Canine Training Center. I turned off the engine and looked back at Corky. "Guess we're here, ol' girl."

"Woof!" She was up, tail wagging, ready for anything.

I clipped on her leash, grabbed my paperwork and headed for the door. Barking dogs from within the building assured us we were at the right place. When I pressed the doorbell, an officer opened it, glanced at Corky, and said, "Return your dog to your vehicle, then come back and check in."

Okaaaay. I led Corky back to her backseat kennel.

Once inside the training center, I was introduced to Sergeant Marie Sayers, an attractive young woman with long dark hair caught up in a ponytail, who did not look like a junkyard cop at all. Dressed in dark-blue slacks and T-shirt, her badge and the weapon clipped to her belt were the only things identifying her as a police officer. I was glad I'd worn civvies.

She looked over my papers. "Why don't I give you a tour before you bring in . . . Corky, is it?"

The center covered forty acres with buildings, kennels, obstacle courses, and small structures in which "perps" could hide while the dogs searched for them. There was even a row of old cars where the dogs could practice searching for fugitives or drugs.

Back at the office, Sergeant Sayers said, "All right. Let's see how Corky does. Why don't you go get her?"

I'd begun to feel very comfortable with Corky. She'd retrieve her KONG toy whenever I threw it for her, and she was well behaved, smart. We'd even busted those students. But suddenly, I felt nervous as I walked to the SUV. What if she freaked out in this new setting? What if she couldn't work a search pattern? What if she got distracted?

We spent the morning reviewing basic commands. Sometimes Sergeant Sayers had us repeat an exercise a dozen times even though Corky seemed to be doing it exactly right. When we broke for lunch, Corky was happy to flop down on the cool floor of one of the concrete kennels, panting, her tongue hanging out of the side of her mouth. In the afternoon, the sergeant wanted to watch her work search patterns to make sure she didn't cut corners and miss likely hiding places. For these, Corky searched for a rubber KONG with a treat inside.

Corky and I showed up at the training center two minutes before eight on Tuesday and had a great workout, but Sergeant Sayers wanted me to leave Corky at the kennel for a couple of nights to see how she did in a strange setting. I hated to leave her, but Tuesday night was my men's Bible study, so maybe it was just as well. Everyone wanted a report on how the new job was going. I told them I'd probably be working undercover, so couldn't tell 'em or I'd have to kill 'em. Everybody got a laugh out of that, and then I filled them in on everything—everything, that is, except Gilson's wacky idea for my cover—and asked for the guys' prayers. Prayers for protection, for God's purpose in the job. By the time I got home, I was bushed from the long day and glad I didn't have to walk Corky before going to bed.

Wednesday, it was also just as well Corky was still "sleepin' over," because as soon as I got home, Estelle needed my help finishing up supper for our guest, the single woman who lived across the street.

A half hour later, I'd just finished arranging the chairs around the dining room table when I heard DaShawn call, "Yo, Pops! The lady's here!" I usually didn't mind him calling me Pops—kinda nice, actually. But sometimes the way he threw the sentence together sounded too ghetto, and this was a white woman coming to dinner.

I hurried to the top of the stairs and put on my warmest smile. "You must be Grace. Estelle's been telling me about you." As she neared the top, I extended my hand, introduced myself, and invited her in to take a seat on the couch. She had medium-long dark hair, brown eyes, and was wearing black slacks, a turquoise knit top with some silver-and-turquoise jewelry—very attractive, I thought. But what did I expect for a singing celebrity?

I realized I'd been staring when Estelle rescued me by hustling in carrying a tray with several small glasses.

"There she is!" Estelle said. "No, no, don't get up, young lady. Would you like some cranberry juice? It's nice and cold, feels good on a warm day like this."

Estelle sent me downstairs to call DaShawn and Rodney, but when I introduced Rodney to our guest, he just mumbled, "How ya doin'?" followed by a quick handshake, and then sat on the edge of a chair as though he were about to leave. Even after Estelle called us to the table, Rodney didn't say a thing during the meal except to ask for the food to be passed or say thanks when someone handed him something.

When we were all seated, Estelle asked me to say the blessing and my mind went blank. What could I say that would be appropriate for a singing celebrity? And then it came to me. I cleared my throat as Estelle reached for the hands on either side of her. "Lord God, for food in a world where many walk in hunger, for faith in a world where many walk in fear, and for friends in a world where many walk alone, we give you thanks. Amen."

When I looked up, Estelle's eyes were wide. "Harry Bentley, where'd you get that prayer? Never heard you pray like that!"

I reached for the fried chicken. "Don't you remember? Last Thanksgiving, at the Manna House dinner, that Canadian pastor prayed it. When I looked around at all those women at the shelter, I thought, That says it all. Been bouncing around in my head ever since."

Estelle had outdone herself—chicken, ham, cornbread, green beans. Grace—she insisted we call her Grace instead of Miss Meredith—really seemed to enjoy the meal and complimented Estelle on it. "But you shouldn't have gone to so much trouble."

Kind of to get back at Estelle for acting so surprised at my prayer, I said, "Trouble? My wife lives to cook! She cooks for the Manna House Women's Shelter, you know."

"Is that why you married Miz Estelle, Grandpa?" DaShawn piped up. "So's you could eat good?"

I glanced at Estelle, not sure how far to carry this, but her expression was as peaceful as could be, so I pointed my fork at DaShawn. "Now there's a smart young man."

"So you cook for a women's shelter?" asked Grace, "I'd like to hear more about that."

Estelle shrugged. "Not much to tell. Stayed there myself for a time, till it burned down. Bunch of good sisters at SouledOut Community Church helped me get back on my feet, so I decided one way to give back was to volunteer at the shelter when it got up an' runnin' again, which turned into a job—"

I couldn't leave it alone. "'Cause they liked her cookin'."

"You . . . just eat." Estelle let me know I'd better drop the subject. "What I want to hear about is Grace's singin'. I'm just sorry we don't have a piano, 'cause I sure would love to hear you sing."

Grace flushed. "Well, I did bring one of my CDs as a gift for you. Mostly praise and worship music. Several are my own songs."

DaShawn's eyes got big. "You got a CD? Can I listen to it? I got my own CD player. An' I already got fifteen CDs. But Grandpa won't let me listen to—"

"DaShawn! You're interrupting," I said. "That's real nice of you, Miss Meredith. We'd love to hear it. My wife tells me you travel 'round the country giving concerts, said you just got back from someplace and got another trip comin' up this weekend."

That loosened her up a bit. She told us about her most recent tour in the Southeast states, an upcoming concert in St. Louis, followed by a ten-day tour on the West Coast. But I got this funny feeling there were some things she'd rather not talk about. Not surprised. It had to be a hard life for a young woman.

"What about you, Mr. Bentley?" she asked abruptly, like we were tossing a ball around the table and saying, "Catch!" At least she hadn't thrown the ball to Rodney. I told her I'd just taken a new job with Amtrak Police and was going to leave it at that, but DaShawn nearly blew my cover by saying, "Yeah, an' now we got a dog—"

I stopped him with a kick under the table, and Estelle changed the subject. "Rodney, you and DaShawn done? Why don't you two go in the living room and watch some TV. I'll call you back when it's time for dessert." As they left, she called after them, "And don't turn it up too loud, either."

Grace insisted on helping us clear the table and said how nice it must be to have our son and grandson living so close downstairs.

Had to explain that DaShawn lived with us, but Rodney's presence was temporary. "He's looking for a job so he can get a place of his own."

"That's right," Estelle added. "That's something you can help us pray for."

We cleared the table as Estelle started a pot of coffee. "So, tell us about this upcoming concert. How can we pray for you?"

Grace suddenly got tears in her eyes. "I—I'm sorry," she whispered. "I do need some prayer."

"Now, now," Estelle clucked, "you sit down there at the kitchen table, honey . . . that's it. Harry, hand her that tissue box. Now, tell us what needs some prayer."

Dabbing her eyes, Grace blurted out that her last tour had ended rough—she'd come down with a virus, lost her voice, and had to cancel some concerts. Sounded like the stress had gotten to her and she'd begun to fall apart.

"My agent added the St. Louis concert kind of last minute as a way to make up for the ones I had to cancel. But I—I'm having a hard time getting my confidence back. Was supposed to fly to Cincinnati for a concert last weekend, but . . ."

The tears returned, and I handed her another tissue.

"It's all right, baby, it's all right." Estelle patted her hand.

Grace shook her head and then let her shoulders sag as if she were releasing a great burden. "Okay, see, I . . . I had a pretty awful experience with airport security back in January coming home from the tour, and last weekend . . . well, guess the memory of my last experience was too fresh. I backed out at the last minute. So my assistant had to rent a car and drive us to Ohio. We're going to drive to St. Louis this weekend too."

"Well, now, that seems wise," Estelle said kindly.

"Except . . ." she sniffed, "the West Coast tour is coming up. Once the tour starts in Seattle, we'll have a tour bus. But I've got to get there first. I just—" She gritted her teeth. "—just don't want to fly anymore." She rolled her eyes apologetically and blew out a long breath. "So guess I could really use some prayer about that."

Estelle patted her hand again. "Well, we can sure pray about—"

"Why don't you take the train?" I said.

123

"What?" Grace looked at me as if I'd been speaking a foreign language.

"The train. They handle security a lot different on the trains. You hardly know they're there. Like I said, I just started workin' for Amtrak, but they've got trains goin' everywhere. I know, we think everybody flies these days, but that ain't the only way to get from here to there. In fact, they got trains runnin' several times a day to St. Louis. You could try it this weekend, see if you like it."

Grace stared at me like she was waking up from a long dream—or maybe a nightmare—to find the day wasn't so frightening after all.

Chapter 18

At noon on Thursday, Sergeant Sayers declared us ready for recertification. "So, let's spend the rest of our time seeing if you and Corky can play blind man and guide dog. Okay?"

"I know Captain Gilson had that wild idea for my cover, but it seems kind of crazy to me. Don't you think so?"

Shouldn't have asked a question, because that gave her the opportunity to tell me how creative she thought it was. She grinned at me. "Besides, that's part of what Amtrak contracted us for. If I skipped it, we might not get paid. So go out to your vehicle and get that harness with the D-handle."

We spent the rest of the day and all day Friday stopping at curbs and going up steps with me trying to scuff my feet as though I were "feeling" the surface. "But Corky's not guiding me," I protested. "She's just heelin' and obeyin' like she always does."

"You know that, and I might have noticed it because I used to train guide dogs. And of course blind people would know the difference, but most of them can't see well enough to notice. So just work with me here, Bentley."

"But can Corky go back and forth? Captain Gilson wants me undercover when I ride the trains, but there'll be a lot of days I'm in the station, in uniform. And Corky won't be on a D-handle."

"Shouldn't be a problem. When she's on a D-handle, she heels. When she's on a leash, she can roam a little. She's going back and forth around here. You'll be okay."

When we finished Friday evening, Sayers declared our ruse "passable," and handed me our recertification papers as we went out the gate. As I drove home and glanced at them sitting on the seat beside me, I realized that the student I'd busted in Union Station might've beaten the charge if I'd arrested him, because even though Corky and I were trained, our certification wasn't up to date.

Oh well, maybe the guy learned his lesson.

Corky and I got home Friday evening barely in time for me to go with Estelle to the Good Friday service at SouledOut. I was tired, and though the service was short, it was somber and kind of depressing. While we sang that old spiritual, "Were You There When They Crucified My Lord?" I kept replaying in my mind the gruesome scenes from Mel Gibson's movie, The Passion. But it helped me realize how much Jesus loves us. And at the conclusion of Pastor Cobbs's sermonette, he reminded us of our hope: "It's Friday, but Sunday's comin'!" And that's just what I needed.

I had Saturday off, so I helped Rodney finish painting the first-floor apartment—the sunroom and the back entrance. The bathroom was finished, and the appliance people had promised to have all the kitchen appliances installed by the coming Wednesday.

It was time to say something more to Rodney about finding a place of his own.

After I mentioned it to him, he continued to cut in the pale-yellow paint around the sunroom windows with the patience of an artist. "Hasn't been much time to look," he said between strokes.

"Oh, I know, I know. No rush. You've been a great help. Estelle and I are rock-solid grateful. But, you know . . ."

"Yeah. You're lookin' for me to move on."

"It's not that. We just want to make sure you have a place you can afford."

"And a job, right? But I've kinda had a job, ya know?"

"Exactly, and I'm not complaining. Believe me, son . . ." My voice drifted off. I didn't know how to take my foot out of my mouth, and I couldn't even imagine what to say anyway. I stood there with my mouth open.

"Look," Rodney said, "I know what you're sayin'. We're almost done here. Monday I'll start beatin' the streets for a job. If you can give me some time to find one and build up a little reserve, I'll move on as soon as I can."

That wasn't what I was trying to say, but I still couldn't think of a way to put it that didn't sound like we didn't want him around or didn't appreciate all his help.

Finally, I shrugged and looked down at all the tiny paint spatters on my hands. "That's good enough. Take your time. Find something good . . . in terms of a job and a place to live. DaShawn loves havin' you around."

"Yeah, I think he does." Rodney didn't say anything else, but I could almost hear his next phrase: But I'm not sure about you!

When would I ever get it right with my son?

My Law and Order ringtone woke me from a sound sleep in a room lit only by the glow of the iPhone's screen. My eyes were so blurry I couldn't see the caller ID, so I just answered, "Yeah, Bentley," realizing that my groggy voice didn't sound authoritative enough to deter even a rooky telemarketer.

It wasn't a telemarketer.

"Mr. Bentley, this is Saint Francis Hospital. I'm afraid your mother's taken a turn for the worse."

I came fully awake. "What happened?"

Estelle sat up in bed and switched on the reading lamp on her bedside table.

"That's why we're calling, Mr. Bentley. It's too soon to tell, but she's unconscious. It may have been another stroke."

"Another stroke? We'll be right there."

It took nearly twenty minutes for Estelle and me to throw on our clothes, get to the hospital, park, and find out where Mom was. To my surprise, she was still in her same room, lights dimmed, and only the slow beep of the monitor obscured the rasp of her labored breathing. "Why isn't she in ICU?" I whispered impatiently to the nurse who was adjusting the pillow under Mom's head.

Estelle went to the other side of the bed and picked up Mom's hand. She shook her head, and immediately fished some lotion from her large purse and began anointing Mom's hands.

The nurse answered in a normal voice, seemingly without concern for waking Mom. "We're doing everything we can for now. The doctor may order another MRI, but I kind of doubt it."

"Whaddaya mean, you doubt it?"

"Well, if it's a bleed . . ." She shrugged as though there was nothing to be done. "And if it's a clot, she's already on Heparin."

"Heparin . . . that's that blood thinner, right?"

"It dissolves clots."

I nodded, but . . . why were they giving her Heparin if there was a chance that she'd had a bleed? They probably had their reasons, so I postponed that question until later. "When did this happen?" I whispered even more softly.

"You don't really need to whisper."

"But . . .?"

"She's unconscious, Mr. Bentley. If we happened to wake her up, well, I guess you could consider that to be an encouragement."

Estelle stopped massaging Mom's hands. "You don't expect her to wake up?"

The nurse gave us a condescending smile. "Well, no one can say for sure, but in cases like this . . ."

"I don't receive that." Estelle straightened to her full height, squared her shoulders, and declared in a defiant voice, "Where there's life there's hope."

The nurse shrugged. "I suppose you're right, but—"

"Are you finished with whatever you're not doin', 'cause if you are, I think Harry and I can take over now."

Without another word, the nurse left.

I watched Mom, breathing steadily, but otherwise lying as still as stone. Would this be the end? I wasn't ready for it. We'd talked about her not being able to move into the apartment, but I hadn't seriously considered this her actual end. I'd never gotten around to telling her how much I loved her.

We just couldn't let her die yet!

I eyed Estelle. "What'll we do if we need that nurse again?" Estelle shrugged. "Press the button, I guess. But right now it's time to call on a higher power."

It wasn't like Estelle to talk like she was in an AA meeting, but I knew what she meant as she reached across the bed to grab one of my hands, laid her other hand on Mom's forehead, and began to pray.

Estelle prayed until I thought my back was going to break from leaning forward to hold her hand. She beseeched God to "Wake up Wanda Bentley, and grant her a little more time with her friends and family. Lord, we ain't ready to say good-bye." She reminded God of Mom's years of faithfulness and reminded him how he'd added time to King Hezekiah's life when he'd prayed a similar prayer.

The prayer went on, but my mind drifted to the story of Hezekiah. If I remembered correctly, God had granted him fifteen more years of life. Mom was already eighty-eight and rather infirm. Even if she did recover from her stroke, I doubted she'd be very happy with us if we signed her up for fifteen more years.

Finally, Estelle wrapped up her prayer. "Father, we need your resurrection power here, so I ask all these things in the mighty name of Jesus Christ, our risen Lord. Amen!"

She squeezed my hand, and I opened my eyes and stretched back to straighten my back. As I did, Mom coughed twice and opened her eyes. She smiled her crooked smile and then looked at Estelle and mumbled something.

"Oh!" Estelle squealed like a schoolgirl. "Praise you, Jesus! Thank you, Jesus." Estelle began clapping her hands, then grabbed the hand controller and pushed the call button. "That nurse has gotta get in here to see this right now."

I didn't care whether the nurse saw this or not. I leaned close to Mom's face and grasped her gnarly hand, softened by the cream Estelle had applied. Our eyes locked. "How ya doin', Mom?"

She mumbled something, and while I had no idea what she said, I could tell from the look in her eyes that she recognized me and knew where we were.

A shock went through me as though I'd grabbed a live wire. This was my time! "Mom? Mom! You know I love you, Mom. I . . . I haven't said that for a while, but I really do. I want to tell you, I love you. And . . . and I want to thank you for all you've done for me over the years, and . . ." I couldn't think what else to say.

Her eyebrows lifted in recognition and she smiled again, as peaceful as could be, then closed her eyes just as a nurse came in.

It was a different nurse.

"My mother just woke up and spoke to us!" I patted her hand. "Mom, Mom, the nurse is here. Mom . . .?"

"Maybe she went back to sleep," said Estelle. "But I saw her and heard her too. She's conscious."

"Hmm." The nurse hurried over to check the monitor and took Mom's other vitals. Then she looked at me with a skeptical expression on her face. "You say she actually spoke to you? What'd she say?"

I frowned and stuck out my lower lip. What difference did it make what she'd said? "Well, it was hard to make out, you know, 'cause her mouth doesn't work quite right, but she was lookin' me in the eye and talkin' right to me. No question about it."

Estelle, meanwhile, had gone back to praising the Lord, eyes closed and hands clasped as she thanked God over and over again under her breath for answering our prayer.

The nurse busied herself writing things on Mom's chart, then said in a flat, unconvinced voice, "Well, let us know if she wakes up again."

I wanted to shake her, make her acknowledge how big this was. "Oh, you bet we will. We'll ring you soon as she's done sleepin'. You can be sure of that!"

There were two recliners in Mom's room, and we sat up with her for the next couple hours as she slept peacefully. Every so often Estelle murmured, "Unbelievable! Absolutely unbelievable! God just did a resurrection miracle, and we got to witness it."

I felt the same and nodded in agreement, making brief responses as we marveled over what had happened. But finally, Estelle fell asleep, and my eyes also grew heavy watching Mom's still form in the bed as her monitor continued its hypnotic beep. Finally, my eyelids closed, and I slipped into a strange dream in which I knew I was dreaming, but everything was logical and as believable as if I'd been awake. Mom woke up again, but this time she sat up in her bed and spoke as clear as ever. "Where are my slippers, Harry? Where did they put 'em? And get me my clothes too. I'm ready to go home."

Her speech wasn't slurred and her smile wasn't contorted and she used both hands to steady herself as she swung her feet around onto the floor.

I was fixin' to get up and help her when Estelle began calling to me.

"Harry, Harry! You're snoring."

I jerked awake. "What? Oh, sorry. Did I wake up Mom?" I glanced over at her, but she was still asleep . . . and didn't need me to get her clothes.

"No, but you woke me up. Now turn on your side and put a pillow under your head before that nurse comes in here to see if you're trying to start a lawn mower."

I stared at Mom for a few moments. She wasn't smiling or talking or sitting up to go home. Nevertheless, that phrase—that she was "ready to go home"—stuck with me. Was she still counting on our downstairs unit, or was she thinking of her old apartment?

I raised my head and spoke in a hushed voice. "Hey Estelle, you asleep?"

Her head rose slowly, and my wife gave me a deadeye look. "Not . . . quite."

I laid my head back. "Sorry."

She sighed. "Wha'd you want, Harry?"

I sat back up. "Well, I was thinkin' that maybe we shouldn't rent out our lower unit. Maybe Mom will recover enough to come home. And it would be downright too bad if we hadn't saved it for her." I waited a moment. "Just sayin' . . ."

"Hmm. I was thinking the same thing. Wouldn't that be nice? But . . . let's just get some sleep, Harry. Tomorrow's Easter."

"Easter? We can't go to church. I mean, we need to be here with Mom . . . when she wakes up." The image of her asking for her slippers and clothes flitted through my mind. "She might need us."

Estelle waved her hand dismissively. "You can stay here if you want, Harry, but I'm going to church to thank the Lord for what happened here tonight."

"Mom's just had another stroke, and you want us to leave her?"

"You're thinking about the stroke, but I'm thinking about the miracle of God in wakin' her up out of a coma. God deserves some praise."

Estelle sat up in her chair and reached over to dig through her purse on the floor by her side until she retrieved her little Bible. She sighed deeply as she flipped through the pages. "Here it is in Psalm 107. 'Give thanks to the Lord, for he is good; his love endures forever.' Then it goes on reviewing all the great things God did. But in verse 31 it says, 'Let them give thanks to the Lord for his unfailing love and his wonderful deeds for men. Let them exalt him in the assembly of the people'—that's the church—'and praise him in the council of the elders.'" She closed her little Bible with a thump and dropped it back into her purse as if the matter were settled.

"And that means we have to go to church this morning?"

"Well, that's what I'm gonna do. I don't want to be like the nine lepers who went off without so much as a 'thank you, Jesus' after he healed 'em. I want to be the one who came back to thank him."

"Of course, we'll thank him when we're . . ." I stopped before saying, when we're done watchin' over her. "But that doesn't mean we have to go to church today. We'll tell everyone when the time's right."

"Well, for me this is the right time. It's a way to exercise my faith that Jesus has healed Mother Bentley. Isn't that what you want?"

"Of course, but . . ." Had Jesus really healed her? Maybe Estelle was right that we needed to exercise our faith so God could show us what was really going on. Suddenly, I had this vertigo feeling of being jerked around again, not knowing what was going on. Why didn't God just tell me straight—Buy a house. Get a job. Take your mom home. But could I have accepted such simple directions?

I looked at the clock. It was already six thirty. Too late to get more sleep and too early to get up. Mom was still breathing peacefully in her bed. But was she asleep or unconscious again? I wanted to know. I wanted to know more than I wanted to thank God for waking her up.

Suddenly, recognition struck me like the voice of God. He had awakened Mom just long enough for me to tell her that I loved her.

I hadn't even begun to unpack the implications of that possibility before a third nurse came in and took Mom's vitals, read her chart, and asked us if anything else had happened. Then turned Mom onto her side. Through it all, Mom did not wake up.

When the nurse left, I turned and stared at Estelle. It was Easter. What better time to praise God for a resurrection? Whether it was just a brief respite for me to say good-bye or a longer-term healing, I had no idea. But Estelle was right. God still deserved to be praised. "Okay. Let's go to church this morning."

A couple of hours later on our way to church, we stopped at McDonald's drive-through to pick up a couple Egg McMuffins and some tall coffees for breakfast. While we waited for the window person to collect our food, I turned to Estelle. "You think God brought Mom back so she could live in our first-floor apartment?"

"Perhaps . . ." She was quiet a moment. "But whatever, he has a purpose. I know that much."

"But . . . what if we can't figure it out?"

She got a pained look in her eye. "You know there are some things we may never understand this side of glory." I knew she was thinking of her own son, Leroy. And then her eyes brightened and she pointed me back toward the window. "Here's our food."

Chapter 19

IN SPITE OF OUR STOP AT MCDONALD'S, we arrived at church early and Estelle disappeared while I made my way to our usual seats near the front on the left-hand side.

I'd come to expect Easter at SouledOut—or Resurrection Sunday, as Mom called it—to be one of the most inspiring events of my year. And I was not disappointed. Estelle sat down beside me with an out-of-breath whoosh just as worship began with "Was It a Morning Like This?"—Jim Croegaert's powerful song made famous several years ago by Sandi Patty. We continued by singing "Christ the Lord Is Risen Today," and couldn't stop when the music group led us in Ron Kenoly's "Jesus Is Alive."

Once we'd quieted down a little, Sister Avis Douglass, our worship leader, said, "Last time we were together, Pastor Cobbs told us, 'It may be Friday, but Sunday's comin'!' Well, brothers and sisters, I'm here to tell you, Sunday's here, and Christ has risen!"

In a thunderous response that shook our building like we were inside a bass drum, the congregation responded in unison, "He is risen indeed!"

Then Sister Avis introduced our newly formed choir, which gave a heavy gospel rendition to Andrae Crouch's classic, "The Blood Will Never Lose Its Power." It was so powerful, a young sister started getting happy and the church Mothers had to gather around and fan her down. I was in the groove myself, thanking Jesus for his sacrifice, when the Holy Ghost pricked my heart with the words of the second verse, "It soothes my doubts and calms my fears . . ." Yes, yes. I'd been struggling with doubts and quaking with fears. I wasn't too proud to admit that now.

During all my years being a cop—facing drug dealers, getting shot at a couple times, careening through high-speed chases, and even doing that B-and-E on my old boss's house to get the evidence against him—the adrenalin had carried me through and I hadn't recognized fear . . . or maybe it was the alcohol I'd used to come down off of it that fogged my memory.

But lately, with all these changes in my life, I'd come to know doubts and fears with no adrenalin to hold them at bay. It humbled me. I knew I needed Jesus in a way that was deeper than I'd ever acknowledged. I didn't even try to wipe away the tears as I sang along, "'It will never lose its power!' Yes, yes! Thank you, Jesus. Oh, thank you again."

My eyes were still closed when I felt Estelle rise from the seat beside me. I looked up. Had Sister Avis asked us all to stand? No. It was just Estelle, and she was walking toward the front.

As she neared the low platform, Sister Avis said, "This is a Resurrection Morning in more than one way. Sister Estelle has a testimony she wants to share with us all."

When Estelle took the mike, I could see her hand shaking, but her voice was clear as she told about Mom being in a coma during the night but coming out of it when we prayed for her. I felt embarrassed that it had been Estelle who'd done the serious praying. I'd been too caught up in my own doubts and confusion to expect God to move on Mom's behalf.

The church broke into thunderous applause when Estelle finished her story, and Sister Avis encouraged everyone to speak out loud our thanksgiving to such a good God. After a few moments, Pastor Cobbs took the mike and spoke over the praise.

"Lord, we thank you on today for waking us up on this Resurrection Morning, clothed and in our right minds. We want to thank you for all you've done. You made a way outta no way. You showed up right on time. You were a doctor when we were sick. A lawyer when we were in trouble. You helped us pay the bills when we were down to our last dime. Oh, we thank you. We thank you."

How true it was. In spite of feeling derailed by all the things we'd been through, God had been there. I hadn't been alone.

✧ ✧ ✧ ✧

After church, we swung by the house. I was irritated that Rodney hadn't gotten himself and DaShawn to church, but Estelle was gracious and simply apologized that she hadn't been able to make Easter dinner. "In fact, Harry and I are heading back to the hospital right now to be with Mother Bentley. We'll probably grab something to eat in the cafeteria. But you guys can fix yourself something here. There's plenty in the fridge."

"Can I go?" It was hard to tell from his voice whether DaShawn wanted to spend the afternoon with his great-grandma or wanted to avoid the makeshift meal he and Rodney would have to throw together.

"Uh, I dunno. You got any homework?"

"Pops, what's the matter with you? I been on spring break all week!"

"Oh, yeah." Had I really been so distracted by work that I forgot DaShawn was off from school? "You know there's not much to do just sittin' in a hospital room. Great-Grandma's mostly asleep." I resisted letting myself fear that she might have slipped back into a coma.

"Hmm. Then can I go play with Tavis?"

"If one of his parents is home and says okay."

When we finally got to the hospital, Mom was awake—eyes open, lookin' around to give us a crooked smile when we came in. Her words still came out in gibberish, but she pointed with her good right hand toward the back of her head and mumbled the same thing.

"What, Mom? Does your head hurt?"

"Oooo." She shook her head slightly, clearly indicating no, and tried to verbalize her complaint again.

"She wants her head up," Estelle said. "Push that button that raises the back of her bed."

"Ahh. Ahh. Ahh!"

I hadn't seen Mom this animated since she came into the hospital. Obviously, the damage of the stroke still inhibited her movement and ability to speak, but her spirits were high.

When the nurse came in, she said Mom woke up from her morning nap shortly after we left for church.

Since it wasn't possible to carry on a conversation with Mom, we just sat with her watching TV. The second TV preacher of the afternoon was standing at the Wailing Wall in Jerusalem doing a "documentary" in how the fast-moving recent events in the Middle East proved Jesus would return just as soon as construction began on rebuilding the Temple on Mount Moriah. "All the plans are ready," he said, the wind stirring up a little dust and whistling in his mike, enhancing the on-site effect. "They could begin construction tomorrow if sufficient international pressure could be brought to bear on the government of Jordan, which controls this part of Jerusalem. But your donations to this ministry will help us bring that pressure and hasten the Lord's return. The Bible says we are to be 'looking for and hastening the coming of the day of God'—Second Peter three twelve—and this is how you can help. Write your check today or call the number on your screen with your credit card in hand."

In one form or another, Mom had been listening to similar charlatans for the last forty years. One more wouldn't hurt, so I closed my eyes and drifted off.

"Harry, Harry." Estelle's voice and her gentle shake of my shoulder woke me from my nap. "Mom's asleep again. Maybe we should go."

I looked toward the window and could see that it was late afternoon. The TV was still going, but the sound had been muted. "Yeah." I pushed the leg rest down on the recliner and stood up, my head feeling light for a moment. "Has the nurse been in?"

"About fifteen minutes ago. She thinks Mom's doing fine . . . considering."

We drove up the alley behind our house and parked in the garage when we got home. I had to take Corky out for a walk, and it looked like rain was coming, so I hustled up the back steps, and as I expected, Corky was all over me the moment I opened the door.

"Yeah, yeah, yeah, girl. Get down! Just wait a minute."

I was reaching for the leash when I heard a loud racket coming from outside at the front of the house, like a "cat fight" of the human variety. I walked through the dining room and into the living room, and saw that one of the front windows was up, probably because the day had been warm enough to enjoy the fresh air.

The sound was getting louder, like some ghetto witch yelling and screaming, parading her family business in the street for everyone to see and hear. I couldn't think of anyone on the block we'd met who'd behave that way.

"Corky, just hold on a minute. I gotta find out what's goin' on."

I slid up the window screen and leaned out. Rodney and DaShawn were standing on the front steps while a woman in tight pink shorts, platform heels, and a low-cut top stood in front of them screaming. She had one hand on her hip—a hip cocked so far to the side that it looked out of joint—while her other hand shook a finger at Rodney, all the time cursing and yelling.

Didn't take me long to recognize Donita—Donita Stevens, DaShawn's mother and Rodney's ex. Last time I'd seen the woman was two years ago when she'd been living with her pimp, Hector, and I'd managed to obtain custody of DaShawn.

"What you doin' wit my boy up in there with that thievin' ol' cop, anyway?" she was yelling. "You ain't got no right!"

I watched a few moments more, amazed at how Rodney kept his cool. DaShawn, on the other hand, was obviously upset. He stayed close to his dad, but kept moving nervously like he was afraid of what was about to happen.

"Come on, Corky. I've seen enough."

Corky was down the front stairs before I'd taken four steps, panting at the front door, her tail wagging her whole rear end. When I let her out, she shot past DaShawn and around to the side bushes to pee. I stepped out onto the porch and between Rodney and Donita. "What're you doin' here?"

"Dad, I'm handlin'—"

"No! This is my house, and you're not welcome here, Donita. You need to go."

She arched her back and shook that finger at me. "I don't give a flyin' fig what you think! I'm here to get my boy, and you ain't gonna stop me, not this time, you, you—" And she called me both the F-and N-words. "And you're not free to use that kind of language around here, either!"

"Huh! This here's a free country, and I'll say whatever I want to say . . . you—" More N-bombs.

"Dad, let me—"

I ignored him. "Corky." I pointed at Donita. The dog sniffed— and sat down suddenly, stock-still, nose pointed at our "guest."

"Get that dog away from me! Get her away! What's she doin'? Get her away, I tell ya!"

I pulled out my iPhone and made a show of turning it on. "What Corky's doin' is identifying you as someone who's holdin' drugs. And what I'm doin' is dialin' 9-1-1."

"What? What you talkin' 'bout?"

"You heard me. I'm dialin' 9-1-1." I made a show of punching the 9, with its little beep. "Ya see, Corky's a certified drug detection dog, and I'm an Amtrak police detective. I could arrest you myself, but it'll be less paperwork if a Chicago cop does it. So . . ." I made another show of punching the first 1—beep.

"Wait a minute! You ain't got nothin' on me. I'm clean."

I pointed at Corky, who remained sitting a foot away from Donita, nose pointed unflinchingly at the woman. "Dog says otherwise, and she knows. Should I finish dialing?" I raised my finger.

Donita glared. "Any cop has to have probable cause to search me. I know my rights."

"Sure you do. And Corky just provided that probable cause. What she smells with her nose is just as good as if you were twirling a baggy full of rock in plain sight."

"You lie."

"Shall we see?" I started bringing my finger down on my phone.

"Wait . . . wait a minute." She raised both hands. "I don't want no hassles."

I backed off and lowered my phone. "Okay. Here's the deal. You don't show up here unannounced ever again. Phone first—"

"I did! I phoned this fool the other day."

I turned to Rodney. "Is that true? When was that?"

139

"Dunno. Week ago, when we were comin' back from the hospital."

Oh, yeah. I remembered that cryptic call when he was riding in the backseat. "That?" I turned to Donita. "That don't count. You want to come to my house, you get my permission. I'm the one who has custody of DaShawn—and you'll need a good reason too. And another thing, if you ever show up here again with drugs on you—even the smallest amount—I will have you arrested." Now I was the one shaking a finger in her face. "Don't test me, woman. I'd as soon see you in prison as not."

Suddenly, the rain that had been threatening for the last half hour began to fall in huge drops as it can only do in the Midwest.

"Oh, sh—!" she cursed so loudly I was sure all the neighbors could hear. "Now look whatcha done!"

But did I care? Ha! I was glad to see her running down the street in those platform spikes, holding onto her copper-colored wig as the rain beat it down around her ears.

Rodney stepped back up under the porch roof out of the rain, wagging his head. I thought it was at Donita, but maybe it was at me. DaShawn looked pained, almost like he might cry. I put my arm around his shoulder. "Come on, son. Let's go in."

Chapter 20

ᴅᴀSʜᴀᴡɴ ʜᴏʟʟᴇʀᴇᴅ, "Bʏᴇ!" and thundered down the stairs the next morning, eager to get back to school after his boring spring break. I clipped the leash on Corky, ready to head out the back door to work when my iPhone rang.

It was Captain Gilson. "Hey Bentley, we got a tip from the DEA that there's a load of grass comin' in on the California Zephyr. They don't know who's carrying it, but it's supposed to be a substantial amount. So bring whatever you and Corky need for an overnight. I'm sending you out to meet it in Lincoln, Nebraska."

"What?"

"You'll take the westbound Zephyr this afternoon. It gets into Lincoln about midnight, plenty of time for you to get off and catch the eastbound coming back through Lincoln about three hours later."

"Three in the morning? You want me to catch a train at three in the morning? Man, that's above my pay grade."

"Hey, that's why detectives are salaried. You're not on the clock. Remember?"

"Yeah, but—"

"Look, have a second cup of coffee and get your stuff together. Train doesn't leave until two this afternoon, but get here no later than eleven. We got plans to make."

"Yeah, and we need to talk. See ya when I get there."

"Oh, and Bentley. Don't forget a pair of wraparound shades and . . . and bring some kinda cool hat, maybe one of those flat caps like golfers wear, something to give you a little character. Go buy yourself one. We can expense it. Know what I mean?"

I pressed end and slipped my phone into my pocket. Something to give me a little character, huh? Like I don't have any character?

141

Yeah, well, I had an old plaid flat cap, so beat up it looked like Corky had used it for a chew toy. I'd take it just to spite Gilson for wanting me to play the ol' blind man routine. I'd need to stop at a Walgreens to pick up a pair of wraparound shades.

I hung up the leash, much to Corky's disappointment. "Estelle?" Guess she was still in the bathroom. "Estelle, I'm not goin' in till a bit later. Tell you about it when you come out." I knew she wouldn't like me being gone overnight any more than I did. We'd planned to see Mom.

I went into the bedroom and sat on the edge of the bed, head bowed. Corky came up and laid her muzzle on my knee, her sad eyes looking at me and then off to the side as if to say, "What's the matter, Boss? Why ain't we goin'?"

I gave her a scratch under the ears. "All right, girl. We'll go." I got up and pulled my overnight satchel out of the closet and began packing. But a lump rose in my throat that a dog seemed to understand me so well without a hint of judgment.

"Ah, Harry. Glad you're here." Gilson looked at his watch. "Hey, not too early for lunch. Let's go up to the food court and get some Chinese."

I gulped. Fast-food Chinese was about as authentic as a reality show. Not the way to start a train trip, in my opinion. But Gilson was the captain.

We dropped Corky at the kennel, and ten minutes later got ourselves seated with plastic plates piled high with fried rice, General Tso's chicken, and chow mein.

"Okay, here's the skinny," Gilson said. "The DEA claims they got a solid tip on a large shipment of marijuana being moved from Reno, Nevada, to Chicago on the Zephyr, but they didn't get their people to the station in Reno before the train pulled out—"

"Ha! Shoddy police work. That's on them."

"Now hold on a minute."

I knew I'd spoken too soon, trigger-happy from being on edge about this whole charade.

"It's not that simple," Gilson explained. "The Union Pacific Club just had its eighty-sixth annual convention in Reno, and the Zephyr had to add two cars to accommodate all the people heading home. A hundred sixty-two people got on in Reno. Allegedly, one of them's a mule, but most are happy conventioneers who support the railroad. We don't want to make 'em angry by questioning everyone who boarded in Reno, and we'd be accused of profiling if we only looked at the other passengers."

"So how am I supposed to do what the DEA can't?"

"Ah, that's the thing. This is the perfect test for you and Corky. You catch the train coming this way in Lincoln, and you'll have nearly twelve hours to find our man—"

"You're sure it's a man?"

"Just a figure of speech. Anyway, you'll have access to the whole train without disturbing any conventioneers or anyone else until you identify our mule. Then, bingo, give the DEA a call and have him picked up at the next stop."

"How much weed is he supposed to be movin'?"

"DEA says over forty pounds. Could be worth two hundred thousand dollars on the street. Not bad for a start if you can catch him, Bentley."

I could feel the hook set. When you put a challenge in front of me, I can't resist. "Okay. What's next?"

Gilson shrugged. "You brought Corky's harness, didn't you?"

"Yeah."

"Good. Got your tickets down in the office. Pick 'em up and get your disguise on. Then I guess you can hang out in the Metropolitan Lounge till train time. It's for first-class passengers, so there's coffee and comfortable chairs. A little before two, someone'll give you a ride to your sleeping car. You're booked in a handicapped compartment, but don't hide out there. You got a bad guy to catch!"

He looked down at my plate and frowned. "Hey, you've hardly eaten a thing. Don't you like Chinese?"

"Oh, I love Chinese, but . . ." I pushed the plate a couple of inches away. "Since you booked me first class, I get free meals on the train, right? Think I'll stick with Amtrak cuisine."

143

"Mr. Bentley, the California Zephyr will be departing in about thirty minutes. If you'd take my arm, I'll be glad to escort you to Track 8. I have an electric cart there that can take you to your sleeping car."

"Oh, that's not neces—. . . I mean, that's good of you." I stood up, realizing that I'd almost dismissed the offer of help. "Thank you. My bag's right here by me." I reached out and took the elbow of the young woman who walked me out of the first-class lounge, Corky coming along obediently at my other side. She helped me onto a seat on the cart and I moved over to make room for Corky at my feet. We waited while an elderly couple got on in the seat in front of me, and then we hummed along the walkway beside the rumbling engines to the sleeping cars. The couple was let off at the first sleeper, and I was taken to the second.

"Here you are, Mr. Bentley. The car number is zero five three two. You'll want to remember that. I think Chuck Murphy's your attendant, but uh . . . doesn't look like he's here yet. I'm sure he'll be along in a few moments. But if you'd like, I can help you get situated."

"I think I can manage." Whoops! I was going to blow my cover if I didn't remember that I can't manage. "That is, if you'll just tell me where my compartment is, I can probably find it. I'm supposed to have an accessibility compartment."

"And you do. It's right up the steps here—just two steps. The first one is a stool, and the next step puts you in the train. Your compartment is to the right at the end of the short hall, right here on the first level."

Corky and I made it into the vestibule.

"Oh, here's Murphy. I'll let him take over. Have a good trip, Mr. Bentley."

"Don't forget my bag."

"I've got it, sir," said a deep voice from behind me, accented like a man of my color. "Straight ahead a few more feet, and you'll be in your compartment. I'll help you get situated."

144

I made it into my compartment with what I hoped was convincing awkwardness and sat down while Murphy described where things were in the room. He was going into such detail that I finally said, "That's okay. I can see a little bit, enough to get around . . . with Corky's help, of course. I can make out the sink, the toilet, the windows and door. I'm not gonna smash into the wall or anything."

"Well, that's good. Now, I can bring your meals to you if you'll give me your order—"

"No. That's okay. I can make my way to the dining car. Just tell me what direction it is. I'll get the waiter to tell me what's on the menu. I like getting to know people."

"Yeah, but . . . what about your service dog?"

"Corky can sit on the floor under the table. She'll take up the floor space beside me, but two people can still sit across from us."

"I don't know, sir. What if they don't want a dog down by their feet while they eat?"

"Lot of people like dogs. We'll find some. Now which way?"

Through my shades I saw him shrug like he couldn't believe I wanted to wander around the train, but that's exactly what I planned to do. "Well, sir, you go out your door and down the little hall with bathrooms on both sides, across the vestibule to another short hall. On your right, you'll find a stairway up to the upper level. When you get to the top, turn to your right, heading toward the rear of the train. The diner's the second car." He paused, and then as though he had decided to tell me everything, he added, "Beyond that is the observation/lounge car. Snack bar's downstairs. All the cars beyond that are coaches."

"Thanks. That's very helpful." Then I thought of something. "Oh, and when I'm coming back, how will I know that I've arrived at my car, what'd she say it was, zero five three two?"

"Yes, five thirty-two. Uh . . . well, we've got braille on the walls for most things, but the car numbers change. I guess . . . I guess you just have to count. It's the second car forward from the diner."

"Good enough. Thanks, Murphy."

"Anything else I can do for you now? If not, I've got more passengers coming."

"I'm fine. See you around." I gritted my teeth. Oh well, it was just a figure of speech.

He started to leave, then turned back. "If you need anything, you can push this call button right here by the toilet. There's another at your seat, on the wall just behind your head."

Once Murphy closed the door behind him, I watched the other passengers streaming past my window, headed to their compartments and coaches. "Well, Corky, for better or worse, here we go."

The westbound California Zephyr was only three minutes late departing Union Station. Not bad. I stared out the window at Chicago's underbelly slipping by . . . the Lower West Side . . . South Lawndale, just a few blocks north of Cook County Jail . . . Cicero, the train picking up speed as it zipped on out to the burbs.

"Guess we better practice navigating this thing, Corky."

She was ready to go in a moment. I, on the other hand, was concerned whether we'd be able to make our way through the narrow hallways. I put on my shades and gripped Corky's harness handle.

When we got to the stairs, there was nothing to do but let her go first. Wasn't like the wide steps we'd practiced on at the training center, but I figured that was okay. Even when going ahead, a service dog would help a blind person with balance and indicate when they'd arrived at the top. We turned right like Murphy had said. It wasn't the width of the halls that provided the biggest challenge. It was the swaying of the train. I couldn't rock back and forth like a drunken sailor on the deck of a rolling ship. I had to stay to a narrow lane on the right side so Corky would have room to walk at my left side. But when the train lurched, I nearly tripped over her body. It took us a while to get the hang of it, but we made it through the next sleeper and then through the dining car with the waiters watching me like they feared I'd end up falling across one of the tables.

Frankly, that was my worry too.

When we got to the observation car, I found the first empty seat just to take a break from our ruse. If the tracks were smoother, it wouldn't be nearly so challenging.

I'd been sitting there several minutes, attempting to stare straight ahead through my mirrored wrap-around shades as though I was unable to see the sights other people watched zip past like fans at a Ping-Pong match, when I realized Corky was on point. She was sitting—not lying at my feet—pointing her nose at the smartly-dressed woman in the lounge chair to my right.

From behind my shades, I surveyed her carefully. An attractive white woman with short brown hair and perfect makeup, definitely under forty, legs crossed, relaxed—perhaps a businesswoman from Naperville heading home after a short day at the office in Chicago's Loop, but if that was the case, why hadn't she taken the much cheaper Metra commuter train? There was an attaché case on the floor not far from her feet. Unless someone else had left it there, it was most likely hers. It was large enough to carry some significant drugs, but Corky wasn't indicating it. She was steadfastly indicating the woman. Her tailored black pantsuit didn't appear to have any pockets in which she could conceal drugs. In her lap, along with a small purse, was a paperback copy of . . . the cover flipped up when she turned the page—The Shack.

The Shack? One of the hottest-selling Christian novels of the last few years? Well, appearances can be deceiving, and Corky was saying she was dirty.

Chapter 21

CORKY HELD STEADY, INDICATING A HIT on the woman while I tried to figure out what to do. First of all, she wasn't my target! I had bigger fish to fry on the return train. But to attempt some kind of an interdiction now would blow my cover, and Gilson wanted me to maintain it as much as possible. Second, even if the woman did have some drugs on her, the quantity was probably minimal— a few joints, maybe some crack or designer drugs . . . or perhaps they were just her own prescription drugs.

The woman kept glancing at Corky as if she were afraid Corky was going to throw up on her. I almost laughed, because when Corky was indicating, she sat with her head low and extended as she stared, dead-eyed at the point she believed smelled of drugs.

The woman shot me a do-something expression, then realized I was blind. "Hey, mister, what's with your dog? Looks like she's . . ."

"Sorry," I said and stood up. "Corky, free." I felt around for her handle, then led her farther down the car to a seat where I could keep an eye on the woman. What if Corky had been mistaken?

This whole program was based on the confidence that a certified drug detection dog wouldn't give me false positives. We'd nailed that student in Union Station, and I'd worked with her for a week at the training center and saw her deliver flawlessly. And yet, it was a possibility that nagged me.

When we stopped at Naperville, I got the answer to one of my questions. The woman didn't get off, which explained why she hadn't ridden the Metra commuter train. She was going at least as far as Princeton, the next Amtrak stop, halfway across the state.

A little over an hour later as we slowed for the Princeton stop, the woman got up, picked up her attaché case, and came past us

148

through the doors into the coach cars. Corky didn't even flinch as she passed. Hmm. When the train stopped, I watched furtively out the window. The woman detrained and walked smartly toward the parking lot. As the train began to move again, I got up and returned to the seat the woman had vacated. Without me giving Corky any instruction, she spontaneously sat and indicated the seat where the woman had been. Ah-ha! It wasn't the woman but the seat that Corky had indicated. Someone who'd been sitting there before her probably spilled a few flakes of marijuana into the chair.

It was a good reminder for me. Corky might be accurate, but there were other factors that could screw up a hit. Having been off the job for two years, I was rusty and needed to watch myself. The woman wouldn't have been a threat, but a mistake like I'd almost made could get a guy shot in a business like this.

"Estelle?" Lightning flashed and thunder rumbled like a jet fighter breaking the sound barrier as I ducked under the portico that projected along the trackside of the big old Lincoln Station.

"Uh? That you, Harry? Where are you? Somethin' wrong?"

"No, no. Everything's okay. Just got in, and it's storming here. But I thought I'd give you a call."

I heard her groan and huff. "It's midnight, Harry."

"Were you asleep? Just wanted to check in."

"No, but I was in bed!" She paused. "Ah, it's okay, Harry. I was still reading. Glad you called. How's it goin'?"

"Okay, I guess. Hardly anybody here. A few other people got off with me, but they're long gone. Just started raining, so I'm gonna go wait in the station after I walk Corky a little."

"When did you say you pick up the return train?"

"It's due in about three twenty, but they say it's runnin' about forty minutes late."

"Well, I'll pray that everything goes okay, but Harry, don't call me when you get on unless there's some problem."

"I won't. Good night, Estelle . . . hey, you go see Mom?"

149

"Not yet. I went over and prayed with that young woman—Grace Meredith, you know, about her upcomin' tour. Gonna see Mom tomorrow after work. She might not understand why you aren't with me. Don't want to worry her, but I don't think she understands the difference between you being a Chicago cop and you working for Amtrak."

"Yeah, well, she was always worried about me when I was on the streets."

"And it's different now, right?"

"Yeah, it's different. Good night, babe. Love ya."

"Love ya more."

I pocketed my cell and cautiously looked around. Family or friends had picked up all the people who detrained with me, and the station area was completely deserted.

I relaxed my blind-man act a little and walked along the huge building toward a lighted Amtrak sign at the far end. Lincoln Station was a classic three-story building of brick and limestone. All the doors of the main building were closed and locked, but through a window I could see the ornate great hall, dimly lit by night-lights and exit signs. Streamers hung from the chandeliers as if in anticipation of some gala banquet. It didn't look like the building was used any longer as a train station. A little farther along, I came to a bronze plaque attached to the outside wall explaining that the building had been constructed in 1926 as one of the largest stations the Burlington Railroad ever built. It was now part of Lincoln's Haymarket District.

At the far north end of the building, I went through the door under the Amtrak sign into a one-story add-on structure. A maintenance man was mopping the floor of the utilitarian waiting room. He glanced at me with a nod, and I nearly responded. Then from behind the thick glass of the ticket window along the side, a middle-aged female clerk with fuzzy gray hair called, "Hey, you can't bring that dog in here. No pets allowed."

"I'm sorry, ma'am. This is a service animal—"

"Don't care what breed he is. No dogs in the station."

I drew closer, somewhat tentatively, as if not quite sure of her location. "Corky's a she, and a service animal's not the breed. She's a trained seeing-eye dog. Surely you're familiar with the Americans with Disabilities Act? She's permitted, by law, to accompany me into any public place."

"Well, I don't know anything about no act. I'm just goin' by the sign on the door. Says No Pets Allowed. And we don't allow no loitering, either. You got a ticket?"

I was tempted to swing my jacket open to display my weapon, shake her up a little. Lincoln's a nice city, but this woman talked like she just got in from the cornfields. Figured she must be new on the job. Probably why she'd drawn the graveyard shift. I pulled my ticket from my inside pocket and waved it at her as Corky and I passed her and sat down in the seats.

"Ain't no train through here for another three hours," she called out.

I nodded. "And I'll be waitin' for it."

"Well . . ." She said it as if she was running out of objections. "Where'd you come from, anyway?"

"Just got off the California Zephyr."

"From Chicago?"

"That's the one."

"And you're headed right back there?" She obviously didn't have enough to do, stuck there in the middle of the night.

"You got it." I stood up and muttered in a voice just loud enough to be heard, "Come on, Corky. Bet even an ol' blind man can find a bench outside that's out of the rain—and out of the hassle."

I did find a bench deep under the portico, up against the old building, but gusts from the northwest swirled mist in on us so that I longed for my winter coat. Sensing my chill, Corky sat right on my feet, leaning her body up against my legs. I hugged my small overnight bag to my chest to keep off some of the damp. Gilson hadn't commented on how raggedy my plaid flat hat was, but now I was paying for it. Should have bought a new wool one, maybe one with fold-down earflaps.

In spite of the cold, I drifted off to sleep and awoke only when the bell and screech of the Zephyr engine rumbled past us and brought the train to a stop. It was scheduled for a short stop—only five or six minutes—so I got up and started moving down the platform toward the forward cars, Corky at my side.

"Can I help you, sir?"

"Yes, please." I held out my ticket in not quite the right direction for the train attendant.

He glanced at it. "Six thirty-one . . . uh, your car is the last car on the train. Sleepers are back there on this run. Don't know why. Do you have anyone with you to help you board?"

"No. I'm traveling alone . . . except for Corky here." I turned awkwardly and started to move toward the back of the train."

"Wait. I'll walk you down."

Gilson—or probably Phyllis—had again booked me in the accessibility compartment on the lower level of the sleeper, just as before. "Your berth's all made up for you, Mr. Bentley," said Angelina, my new attendant. "Is there anything I can get for you?"

"No, thank you. Don't think so. Oh, one question. Where's the lounge car?"

"Fifth car forward. There are two more sleepers, then the dining car, and after that the lounge car. But the bar closed about eleven last evening."

I wanted to establish an excuse to wander around the train in the middle of the night. "Oh, that's okay. I might sit in one of those lounge seats if I can't sleep."

"All right, then. Just be careful, especially going between cars. Have a good night. You know where the call buttons are. Just push one if you need me."

"Thank you."

Once she closed the door, I lay down on my berth. As Gilson had noted, I'd have nearly twelve hours to find my mark before we got to Chicago—presuming that was his destination. No need to go manic searching now. I decided to catch a little shuteye first.

The annoying trill of my iPhone alarm woke me at five. Ack! Oughta change that alarm tone, maybe to a blues riff. Then I realized the train wasn't moving. The station sign outside my window said Omaha, Nebraska. According to the printed schedule, we'd be here fifteen minutes. Most stops were no more than a few minutes, just enough time for passengers to detrain or board. No time for smokers to satisfy their craving or service dogs to relieve themselves.

"Come on, Corky. You need a walk. Could be your last chance." We came out of the compartment and stood in the vestibule. Trying not to appear too independent, I called, "Miss Angelina," out into the space above her head. She was only a few feet from the door.

"Yes, Mr. Bentley."

"How long are we going to be stopped? Can I walk my dog?"

She took me to the dog run and promised to make sure I got safely back before the train departed.

Once the train was underway again, I showered and shaved—amazing how much they can tuck into these compartments—and headed off with Corky to hunt for the mule. I thought it'd be easier to make my way through the cars while most people were still asleep.

That was true. Once on the upper level, I didn't have to negotiate passing people with Corky. But I hadn't even gotten out of our sleeping car before it struck me: if the mule was traveling in one of the larger sleeping compartments, it might be impossible for Corky to catch the scent of the dope.

A dog's sense of smell is amazing, ten thousand times more sensitive than humans by some estimates. But smell still travels on air currents, and if the smell's floating the other way, even a trained dog won't catch it.

If we didn't find our mule anywhere else in the train, I might have to think how to access closed compartments. But that posed a prosecution problem. If Corky couldn't smell it from outside, I would need a warrant to enter the space, and of course there was no way to get one en route.

I pressed the panel of the connecting door to the next car and it wheezed open. We had a lot of train to explore before I needed to worry about closed compartments. When no one was around to see us, Corky and I moved forward with ease, not groping for the vertical handrails to maintain balance as we passed between cars, or trying to find the pressure plate that opened the doors. I tried to watch Corky to see if she picked up anything suspicious.

In the dining car, the waiters were putting the final preparations on the tables for breakfast.

"Sir, sir. We're not open yet. Come back at six, and it'll be first come, first served."

"That's okay, I'm just going through."

There were only a half dozen passengers in the observation car. Some were curled up in the seats, obviously having spent some of the night sleeping there. But a couple were awake, mesmerized by the silvery mists floating above the newly sprouted corn in the predawn fields of Iowa. Corky stopped at the "dirty" seat again. No one was sitting there this time, and I released her to continue her search.

Most people in the coach cars were still sleeping, making it easy for Corky to take her time as we made our way down the aisle. I tried to remember Sergeant Sayers' advice: "Relax, civilians won't know how a service dog would lead her handler down a train aisle. A blind person might know, but probably can't see. And how often are you likely to encounter a trainer on a train?"

I paused to let a little boy greet Corky when he insisted on petting "the doggy" while his mother, who was nursing a baby, fumbled to control him. Though I could see all this through my shades, I tried to keep my head up as though I saw nothing.

First coach car, no hits. Second coach car, Corky wanted to go down the steps to the lower level. I followed her, but when she didn't show any interest in entering the section usually reserved for the elderly or handicapped, I hesitated for fear it might startle passengers if they awoke to find a dog's nose at their elbow.

Third coach, nothing. I was beginning to worry. Had we received a false tip from the DEA? But with the added coaches for the returning conventioneers, this was a long train, so we continued on, all the way to the front, where only a baggage car separated us from the engines.

Still no drugs . . . or at least none that I'd found.

Chapter 22

Corky and I turned around and faced a coach full of passengers, some beginning to wake up, some already nodding in time to earbuds in their ears, kids whining, other people with hoodies and blankets pulled over their heads trying to catch a few more winks.

I held my head straight ahead as I surveyed them all through my mirrored shades. Who was the mule? Probably not the mother with three small children. And not the three elderly couples scattered in different parts of the coach. And how likely was it that one of those conventioneers with the Union Pacific Club logos on their sweatshirts or caps was carrying forty pounds of marijuana?

Admittedly, I was profiling. But every good cop does it. That's what it means to have good street instincts. You just don't do it in an obvious or offensive way.

There was a lot more of this train to search. I'd only cruised through the easy part. I needed to search the lower compartments.

When I got near the center of the front coach, I spoke out to the air. "Excuse me. Is the bathroom downstairs?"

"Yeah," said a man nearby. "They've got some downstairs. But they're kinda small." When I started to move tentatively forward, he said, "That's right. That's right. Just one more seat, and then the steps are on your left."

"Thank you."

Corky and I made our way downstairs and entered the compartment with six pairs of seats, three on each side. The space was sometimes reserved for families or handicapped people because there was extra space at the front to store a wheelchair, walker, or even a power chair. But I walked blankly down the aisle between the seats while those who were awake eyed me curiously. When I reached the back, I intentionally bumped into the wall. "Uh, are there bathrooms down here?"

"Back the other way."

"Thank you." I turned and passed everyone without noting a response from Corky. Crossing the vestibule, I opened the door to one of the toilets.

That was a mistake. What was I supposed to do with Corky? We couldn't both fit into that little closet, but I knew people were watching me from behind to see how I'd do it.

"Stay, Corky. Sit. Stay."

She obeyed, and I went in and took a few minutes to do what Corky couldn't do on the train. Then I came out, retrieved my dog, and went back upstairs.

I followed the same routine in the next four cars without Corky identifying anything suspicious. But in the lower level of the last coach car, we got a hit.

As we entered, Corky immediately sat down, indicating a young man spread across two seats at the front of the compartment. Stubborn cuss—how'd he manage to keep two seats for himself on such a full train? The guy was sleeping, his head cushioned against the window by a folded up jacket. A shaved head and a spiral tattoo snaking up his thick neck sure fit the stereotype. In the extra space at his feet—the space that might've accommodated a wheelchair or walker—were two suitcases and a backpack. Corky's nose was pointing straight at the suitcases, and they were plenty big enough to hold forty pounds of marijuana.

Beside the suitcases was a pile of trash from at least two large McDonald's bags. Hmm. Looked like the guy hadn't been eating food from the diner or snack bar. Probably didn't want to leave his seat . . . or more likely, the treasure at his feet.

It all fit. I had my mule!

Above his seat, secured with a small clip on the wall was a blue card with "Naperville" written on it in black marker by the conductor to indicate the passenger's destination so he wouldn't let him sleep through his stop.

"Free, Corky," I muttered, and then in a slightly louder voice, but not one intended to wake my mark, I said, "Is the bathroom down here?"

Another helpful passenger directed me back beyond the stairs.

It was tempting to forget the ruse and go up the stairs and back to my compartment. But I carried it through.

Ten minutes later, back in my own room, I flopped down in my seat and gave Corky a pat. "We did it, girl. We got him. We got him!" I took off my shades and looked out the window at the Iowa countryside zipping by. "We got him!"

I pulled out my cell, checked whether I had a signal, and called Gilson. "Hey, Captain. Wasn't sure you'd be in the office yet."

"Whaddaya mean? It's almost ten o'clock. How's it goin'?"

"Got my man. Or at least I've got him identified. He's getting off in Naperville."

"Naperville? Why Naperville?"

"Business is probably better out there in the 'burbs with all those rich kids."

"But you're sure it's him."

"Sure as I can be without actually arresting him. So, how you want to play this?"

"Your cover still good?"

"Well, he sure doesn't know me. He was sleeping when I identified him."

"How 'bout everyone else?"

"I think I'm good."

"Great! See, it's workin', Bentley. You were the skeptic, but now you proved it's possible. We're gonna make a hero of you yet. Hold on."

The phone went silent for a few moments, and then Gilson came back on the line. "I'm gonna have to call you back with the plan. A lot of different agencies probably want to stick their finger in this pie. But we got some time. Just make sure he doesn't detrain early."

"How am I supposed to do that?"

"Ha! Just tackle him if he tries to jump the train! I'll be back to you."

I'll admit, I was kind of geeked myself. I'd already spent twenty hours on this trip as a blind man, and as far as I could tell, no one suspected that Corky and I weren't authentic. Maybe Gilson was right. If they played it right and didn't apprehend the guy until after he'd gotten off the train, there was a good chance no one would know they'd been riding with a drug dealer. It was a good plan: get your man without frightening the citizens.

I thought about Grace Meredith and the awful experience she'd had with airport security. She'd have been comfortable on this trip, I was sure of it, even though law enforcement collared a bad guy right under her nose. I tried to recall the conversation following the meal she'd had with us in our home. I didn't think I'd actually told her I was a cop, just that I worked for Amtrak. I couldn't mention that I worked undercover, but I might let her know some time that I was an Amtrak police officer and ask if she'd felt safe traveling by train.

I got out my phone and dialed. "Estelle, hey did you ever talk to that young woman across the street after she went to St. Louis? Did she take the train like I suggested?"

"Yeah, she took it."

"How'd it go?"

"Actually, she came over to thank you for suggesting it. Said it was very restful."

"She gonna do it again?"

"Harry, how should I know? I'm at work. You okay? What's goin' on?"

"Nothin'. Everything's fine. Be home this evening, early I hope."

"That'll be nice. Missing you."

"Me too. Did you visit Mom yet?"

"No, Harry. I told you. I plan to go today right after work."

Bam! Bam! Bam!

Corky growled—the first time I'd ever heard her do that. "Hey, gotta go. Someone's at the door."

"Okay. Bye."

"Bye."

I'd ended the call and was reaching for my shades before I realized I hadn't told Estelle I loved her. Never wanted to miss that.

"Yeah," I called toward the door as I put on my shades and glanced at Corky. She was standing stiff-legged in the middle of the room, facing the door with her hackles up. "It's okay, girl."

The door opened slowly, and there stood the drug mule . . . with what looked like a Ruger SR9 in his hand.

Chapter 23

Iarrested my reflex to grab my service weapon, and apparently the guy didn't notice my flinch, because his gun remained aimed more at Corky than me. "Call off your dog." His voice was low and threatening as he glanced quickly around my compartment.

A low growl rumbled in Corky's throat. "I said, call your dog off."

"Corky, down. It's okay, girl." I reached out slowly and patted her head, intentionally missing with the first wave of my fingers. "You don't have to worry 'bout her none. She's just my guide dog. She won't hurt nobody." I was trying to think fast. "What's the matter, anyway?" I swung my head back and forth a few degrees as if trying to fix my intruder's position. "You the conductor?"

The guy just stood there trying, I hoped, to decide whether I was a threat. "Were you just in my compartment?"

"Well, I . . . I don't know." I kept watching for an opportunity to take him out. But in all my years as a cop, I'd never had to kill anyone, and didn't want this idiot to be my first. "I . . . I don't know. I went for a walk, but . . ." I tried to sound bewildered while keeping all the fear out of my voice.

"Your dog. They said you came down into my compartment, and your dog was sniffing my stuff."

"Down? Oh, yeah. We were takin' a walk and I had to use the bathroom. Went downstairs, but guess I kinda got turned around a little. Easy to do, ya know, when you're going 'round those spiral stairs."

I could see he was weighing whether to believe me or not. "Yeah, well I was asleep."

"Ah gee, man, I'm sorry. Didn't mean to wake you up."

159

"You didn't, but what was your dog doin'?"

"Corky? Ah, she don't mean nothin'." Then I remembered the McDonald's bags. "She . . . she was probably just sniffing around for food. Haven't fed her yet this morning."

He stood there silently. Did I need to spell it out? "She'll eat anything, ya know . . . old French fries . . . anything." Slowly his head started to nod, and then he widened his stance and slowly raised his gun, held steady with both hands until it pointed right at me.

I thought I was a goner until Corky started to growl.

The guy looked down at her and lowered his gun, tucking it back in his pants. "You better feed your dog—and keep her away from me."

He turned and left, leaving my door open to slide back and forth with the sway of the train.

I waited for a few moments and then closed my door and fed Corky. My hands shook so much half of the food spilled on the floor, but Corky didn't mind.

While I sat and watched her eat, I dialed Gilson.

"Hey Captain, a change in the situation here. The guy's armed, and I'd judge him to be highly dangerous."

Corky and I had made our way to the last coach car as the train slowed. We were half way down the stairs as the Naperville sign slid past the window. Hopefully, my mule was preparing to de-train. I'd convinced Gilson to let me position myself where I could quickly move in behind the mule and block the door to prevent his jumping back on the train should something spook him. We didn't need him escaping on down the line or worse, taking a bunch of passengers hostage.

With a squeal of the brakes and a slight lurch, the train stopped, and I looked out at the station. On the far side of the building, extending above its roof, the masts of a mobile TV truck extended into the air. The dish on top read, WGN Channel 9. Had someone tipped off the media? Stupid, stupid! Or maybe they had just intercepted police radio chatter and come on their own. In either case, if my mule saw that mast . . .

The police seemed to have cleared the train station of passengers. Two men who looked like electricians were adjusting a ladder leaning against a light pole at one end of the station, and another man was sweeping the sidewalk at the other end. I hoped they all were backup. "No, no. I got it." It was his voice, just around the corner at the bottom of the stairs. The train door opened and cooler air rolled in as luggage rolled across the vestibule. "Watch your step," said the attendant.

I followed but hung back in the relative darkness of the vestibule as our guy stepped toward the station, his large suitcase rolling behind him while he carried the other by hand. Two other passengers who had detrained were coming this way when one of the "electricians" intercepted them and directed them around the other side of the building. I thought he overdid it a little, pointing to the top of the light pole and waving them away from any falling hazard. But the platform got cleared.

So far, no one had moved on the mule as he headed for the breezeway along this side of the station. The whistle blew, and the attendant shut the door, toggling the heavy handles tight as the train pulled away.

"Oh, sir, you weren't getting off . . . I didn't see you."

"No ma'am. I'm fine, just a little turned around, I think. Can you tell me where car six thirty-one is?"

"Oh yes. It's toward the front of the train. Back up the stairs and turn right. Then I think it's five cars . . . no—"

"Don't worry ma'am. I'll ask someone if I don't recognize it. How much longer before we get into Chicago?"

"Oh, won't be long. Last I heard, we should be arriving at about three thirty."

"Thanks." I climbed the stairs and began making my way forward, Corky dutifully leading me up the aisle. Once I was back in my compartment with the door closed, I dialed Gilson's cell.

It rang five times and then went to voice mail. "It's Bentley. What happened?" The perp was off the train, and we were safely underway, but had they arrested the guy?

Fifteen nervous minutes later Gilson called back to say that they got their man.

"Yeah, but I didn't like seeing that media truck there. Who tipped 'em off?"

"What difference does it make? Everything went smoothly, no shots fired, no civilians around when they busted the guy. Gotta hand it to you, Bentley. You did good!"

"Thanks, Captain. So I've been thinkin', this is gonna generate a mountain of paperwork. But since everything's buttoned up, do you think I can put the report off until tomorrow? I'd like to get home early to see my wife."

"I don't know, Bentley. It's gonna be more than paperwork. DEA'll wanna interview you."

"Tell 'em tomorrow. Don't forget my mom is in the hospital." Finally, he relented and promised to cover for me. "But don't you be late tomorrow morning. If I promise them you'll be available first thing, you better be there."

I got home just after Estelle returned from visiting Mom. DaShawn had gone with Tavis to shoot hoops at Pottawattomie Park. "He phoned for permission," said Estelle, "but I'll be glad when you put up that hoop on the garage. Who knows who he's hangin' with over there in that park."

"I thought you didn't want a ball thumping at all hours behind our house."

"Well, I don't, but it beats not knowing where my grandson is."

I smiled and gave her a big hug. I think it was the first time she'd called DaShawn her grandson. It warmed my heart. Kissing her cheek, I let her go and plopped down on the sofa. "So, how's Mom?"

"About the same, I guess. I didn't try to explain why you weren't with me."

"Hmm. S'pose I oughta go see her myself this evening, but I hate missing my Bible study."

"You could probably wait till tomorrow morning."

"Nah. Gilson wants me to be in early."

"Early? Where's this promise of comp time when you have an overnight run?"

"It's because we got the perp, and there are reports and paperwork and interviews I've gotta follow up on."

"You got him? Why didn't you tell me? I'd've thought you'd be beatin' a drum the moment you walked in the door."

"Yeah, well, it wasn't that big a deal." No way was I gonna tell her about the guy facing me down with a gun.

"But big enough that you've gotta go in to work early tomorrow."

"Comes with the territory, babe. Comes with the territory. Hey, what's for supper?" I stood up. "I'll help you cook."

"You're on, mister. I was just gonna make some rice and fry up a couple catfish fillets. But one of your awesome salads would go really well with that."

A few minutes later, when the catfish was sizzling in the pan and I was preparing the lettuce on my cutting board, I asked, "What's the latest with Rodney?"

"Oh, I dunno. He lit outta here this morning before I even went to work. Didn't say a thing about where he was goin' or when he'd be back."

"Well, if he misses dinner, he's gonna be the loser. That fish smells great."

Before I started mixing a dressing for my salad, I called Denny Baxter and told him I wouldn't be able to make it to study because I needed to visit my mom. I asked him to have the guys pray for her. "You got it," he said.

Rodney showed up just in time for dinner and said he'd been hunting for a job all day. I nodded, pleased. "Sooner or later that'll pay off," I said as we sat down to eat. I wanted to give him some more encouragement, but during the meal all DaShawn was interested in was hearing me tell how I'd caught "the bad guy."

At first, I hemmed and hawed, unsure what I could reveal. I finally decided I could tell about the woman in the observation car and then how Corky identified the sleeping drug mule. In neither instance did I have to describe my cover as a blind man, and I definitely left out the scene where the drug dealer confronted me in my compartment.

I was glad to have an excuse to leave the table so I could get to the hospital. When I got to Mom's room, a nurse was helping her eat. It was kind of late for supper, I thought, but even from the door I could see she was using her right hand to spoon food up to her mouth. The paralysis on the left side of her face, however, meant that it frequently slipped out and down her chin. The nurse was patiently catching it and cleaning off her face.

When Mom noticed I'd entered the room, she became animated, waving her hand and talking in her garbled way. I finally figured out that she didn't want to eat in front of me. There was still quite a bit of food on her tray, so I told her I was going down to the cafeteria for some coffee and would be back later. The nurse nodded her approval.

When I got back, Mom had finished eating and was cleaned up, watching TV. She waved me close, and I gave her a kiss, then pulled up the recliner and sat by her, holding her hand as we both watched TV.

By nine o'clock, Mom had fallen asleep, and I switched to channel 9 to catch the early news, remembering the media truck I'd seen in Naperville had been from WGN. The broadcast kept teasing viewers with short clips about a "special eyewitness report" on a major drug bust in the western suburbs, but I had to wait through everything except the weather and sports before they got to their little three-minute feature.

Finally, the anchor introduced the report.

"Combined efforts of the Drug Enforcement Administration, the Illinois State Police, and the DuPage County Sheriff resulted today in the arrest of Antonio Quintero, nineteen, of Oakland, California, for possession of nearly forty-five pounds of what appears to be high-grade marijuana with an estimated street value of as much as two hundred twenty-five thousand dollars."

The video switched from the "talking head" of the anchor to a short clip showing a handcuffed Quintero being led away from the Naperville Amtrak station by two burly officers who tucked him into a DuPage County Sherriff's car.

"The arrest was made in Naperville shortly after two thirty this afternoon when Quintero stepped off the eastbound Amtrak California Zephyr train with his cache of drugs."

In the video, Quintero kept his head ducked and his face away from the camera.

"According to authorities," continued the reporter, "the DEA had been investigating Quintero since he purchased a ticket in California two days ago but only confirmed that his luggage was filled with an illegal substance when a DEA K-9 unit identified it after Quintero detrained."

A new video clip showed a beautiful German shepherd standing at attention by a DEA agent.

"'At no time,' said a DEA official, 'were train passengers or the public in any danger during the arrest.'"

That was it. The "special eyewitness report" was over.

I flipped off the TV and stood up to kiss Mom's forehead before I left.

As I walked down the hospital hall toward the elevator, I shook my head. Gilson had done a good job keeping me undercover. But I didn't like the attention paid to the DEA's K-9 agent. What if Quintero saw the clip? Would it be enough to get him thinking about the other dog that had been sniffing around him? What if he put two and two together and had enough juice to put a hit out on me?

Wasn't very likely. And such risks are always part of police work. So why did it bug me so much? Maybe I was just disgruntled at being denied my share of the credit. I'd worked hard to ID that guy and had to look down the barrel of his Ruger SR9 to do it. Didn't like all the credit going to someone else, even if it was for my own safety.

Chapter 24

Captain Gilson was ecstatic the next morning when I knocked on his office door. He ushered me in, Corky following right at my heel. Gilson sat down behind his desk, leaving me standing there in my smartly pressed uniform like I was a kid in the principal's office.

"It worked, Bentley! It worked! And did you watch the news last night? There wasn't even a hint of your involvement. Your cover's secure." He pushed some papers around on his desk for no apparent reason. "The DEA's gonna be here within the hour. They want to interview you, but I don't think it'll be any big deal. I asked them yesterday to keep you outta court if possible, and I think they'll be able to do it.

Elbows on his desk, he folded his hands in front of his face. "Now, when they're done with you—"

"Captain, I'll at least have to give a deposition to show probable cause for their arresting that guy."

"No, no, no! That's the beauty of it. They brought their own dog. All they have to say is that their dog identified the contraband, which I'm sure he did."

That bitter taste rose in my mouth again, but what could I say?

"Sit down. Sit down and relax." But as soon as I pulled up a chair and sat down, Gilson got up and went to his wall map of Amtrak's Midwest routes. "When the DEA's done with you, I want you to plan some more trips. I want us to make some busts without having to rely on DEA tips. I want us to find the stuff entirely on our own."

He started tapping the map with his finger. "Our routes meet in Chicago like spokes of a wheel converging on the hub. And Chicago's a big drug market, dope's coming in from the south and

166

west every day, but some of it goes out to the north and east too. So I want you to start riding the rails and nailin' those guys!"

When he stopped to catch his breath, or maybe it was to see if I was tracking with him, I decided to lighten things up a little. "First you want me to play the ol' blind man, and now you want me to act the hobo? I don't know, Captain. Are you typecastin' me?"

"What do you mean, hobo? I didn't say anything about a hobo."

"It's just . . . you know, hobos used to ride the rails? Forget it. Look, I don't mind bein' undercover. I'm just concerned whether this ruse'll continue to work. But go ahead with what you were sayin'."

"Well, what I meant was, I don't think you'll need to go very far on most routes, you know, just like down to Galesburg or Champaign, and then catch the return train coming back. You only gotta be on long enough to search with your dog."

With his mention of Corky, I glanced down. She was lying on the floor, chin resting on her crossed front paws. She looked up at me and over at the captain, causing the tufts of fur above her eyes to waggle like curious eyebrows. I reached down and scratched her behind the ear to assure her, This too shall pass.

Gilson carried on, "Out by the ticket counter you'll find printed schedules for each of the routes. Use them to plan your trips for the next month. Some you ought to be able to do as day trips, but some'll require overnights."

I stood and took a step toward the map, Corky rising to support me. "Look, Captain, before we get too far into this, I think we need to arrive at an understanding. When I took this job, you portrayed overnights and multi-day trips as rarities, and you even said there'd be comp time. I think we need to arrive at some mutual expectations here. Know what I mean?" I used his phrase.

I was kicking myself for not hammering all this out in writing before I took the job. From the very beginning, Gilson had done plenty to let me see how over the top with wild ideas he was. I should've paid more attention to my hesitations.

"Harry, of course. Comp time. Hey, didn't I tell you to go home early yesterday? I don't want to burn you out. In fact, I'm suggesting you write your own ticket here. You make your schedule. Just bring it back to me for review. The only time we can't be flexible is if we get a call from the outside—the DEA, TSA, or some other law enforcement agency that needs our help. Then we've gotta step up. But you go see what you can come up with on your own. Okay?"

"But just to set some parameters," I persisted, "any time I'm gone overnight, I earn a full comp day, right? And I never work on Sunday—"

"Now, now, Harry, never say never! You know emergencies come up in law enforcement. I won't put you out there on a Sunday if you don't wanna go . . . unless, of course, it's absolutely necessary. Isn't that good enough for you? I think it is. Now you go work on a plan for your next month and get back to me later this afternoon." He put his arm out as though he was going to pat my shoulder and walk me to the door. "Okay?"

Fortunately, his desk phone rang and he detoured. "Yeah?" Then he covered the receiver. "The DEA's here. Go give 'em a pound of flesh. See ya later."

Yeah, right. But after I was done with the DEA, better believe I was gonna write myself a reasonable ticket.

After the interview, which didn't last more than an hour, I dropped Corky off at the kennel—don't think she really wanted to stay there—and returned to my office with the route schedules.

I soon discovered that most major trains out of Chicago ran once a day, but it wasn't that simple. For instance, one Empire Builder left Chicago about two fifteen each afternoon, headed for Seattle. At 3:55 p.m., a returning Empire Builder was expected to arrive. But because the trip took some forty-three hours each way—if they were on time—two more trains passed each other in Montana that same afternoon, having left their starting cities the day before, while a fifth train was about to pull out of the Seattle station heading east.

I didn't want to ride the Empire Builder all the way to Montana just to catch an eastbound train to bring me home. That'd eat up two full days. I frowned. Of course, I could get off earlier, but all I'd gain would be a longer wait in a station to catch that returning train.

Had to be a better way.

I picked up the schedule for the Hiawatha train. It was more of a commuter service, running between Chicago and Milwaukee five times a day. Hmm. I could ride the Empire Builder as far as Milwaukee, then catch the 5:45 p.m. Hiawatha back to Chicago. Or take a morning Hiawatha out if I wanted to ride an Empire Builder back that same afternoon.

Bingo, my first day trip! But could I check a whole train in an hour and forty minutes? Corky and I'd have to hustle.

I tried to put together similar combinations between long-run trains and shorter commuters for the California Zephyr, the Southwest Chief, the Texas Eagle, the City of New Orleans, the Cardinal down through Indianapolis, the Capital Limited, and the Wolverine up through Michigan.

Unfortunately, out of those eight "spokes," I was only able to arrange day trips on half of them. The others would be overnighters. But there were also shorter-run trains I could cover with day trips: the Illinois Zephyr, Carl Sandburg, Lincoln, Saluki, and the Illini. None of them were likely major drug avenues into Chicago, but perhaps they distributed drugs out to smaller cities.

By three o'clock I'd put a trip plan on the captain's desk for the month. He scanned over it, his head nodding slower and slower as he read, then he looked up at me with a frown on his face. "Where's the Southwest Chief? You gotta know there's a reason it's nicknamed 'The Drug Train' comin' this way and 'The Money Train' goin' west. After all, it comes from LA and travels through towns in Arizona and New Mexico not that far from the border. I mean, we've got a detective stationed in Albuquerque for that very reason, but we can't put him on the train. He's too busy in New Mexico."

I held up both hands. "No problem. It's just a day run. I can put it in anywhere. I'll take the morning Carl Sandburg down to Galesburg, then catch the returning Chief that afternoon. Be home by three fifteen."

Gilson frowned and stroked his chin. "Three hours isn't bad, but for your first run on that particular train, I'd like you to spend a little more time and ride it both ways. Why don't you make it an overnighter by taking it all the way to Kansas City, sleeping over, and coming back the next day?"

"Okay. Why don't I swap out the . . . the Texas Eagle run. I think I had it down for next week, April 14, wasn't it?" I pointed to the forms in his hand. "However . . ." I took a deep breath. ". . . as you can see, I've scheduled no more than two trips per week, one day trip plus one overnighter. Could do two-day trips but not two over-nighters. The rest of my time's here in the station, not undercover. Those are my limits, Captain. Unless there's specific intelligence tip on a major case like you mentioned, we stick to that load."

Gilson leaned back in his chair and pursed his lips. But I plunged on, saying what I had to say. "We gotta come to an understand-ing here, Captain. Ya know, I don't need this job. You came to me. We're trying an experiment with this undercover K-9 thing. And that's good. I'm willing to keep workin' it to see how it pays off, but if a schedule like what I've drawn up isn't something you can work with, then perhaps you need a different undercover man."

My heart was pounding as I tried to control my breathing. I'd never laid it on the line with a boss like that before . . . or wait a minute. Yes I had. I'd confronted Fagan—even pleaded with him several times—to clean up his act before I went to Internal Affairs. Definitely a bigger deal than this.

Gilson stared up at me with an I-can't-believe-this expression on his face. I should've paid more attention to what I was getting into before I signed on, but he also should've known what I was like when he hired me.

Seconds crept by like hours as my breathing slowed, and I reas-sured myself that we had to get this straight. Yeah, I needed a job to cover our mortgage, but I didn't need this job. I could get a secu-rity job or even go back to being a doorman if I had to. I wasn't too proud for that. Of course, I'd miss Corky. In just two weeks she'd become my partner. No, more than that. I loved that dog. If I had to quit, maybe I could buy her from Amtrak . . . oh, yeah. For how much? Twenty grand?

"Well," said Gilson, handing my schedule papers back to me, "swap the Texas Eagle for the Southwest Chief, then have Phyllis photocopy the schedule for me. Otherwise, looks like a good start. But speaking of the Southwest Chief, sometime I want you to get all the way out to Albuquerque to meet Detective Conway. He's a good man, about as hardnosed as you." A slight smile crinkled the corners of his eyes.

"Absolutely. I'd be glad to meet him." I gave the papers a shake in the air. "I'll have Phyllis make you a copy. See ya tomorrow."

Out in the hall, I blinked. What just happened? Had Gilson accepted the parameters I'd put on my job? Seemed like it. But would he remember them tomorrow or the next day? I had to admit he'd never gone back on anything—he just went forward, forward so fast you had to scramble to keep up. Ha, ha! Well, I'd scramble. In fact, from now on, I'd keep ahead of him.

"Got some things straightened out with Gilson, today," I announced to Estelle as I hung Corky's leash on the hook and watched the dog go check her food dish.

Estelle wiped her hands on her apron and turned from the pot she'd been stirring on the stove. "That's good, hon. Come on over here and give me some sugar."

We kissed. "Mmm." She rolled her eyes, a little smirk on her face. "That's a pretty good start . . ." She turned back to the pot. "So, what's this about your boss?"

I explained how there might be occasional longer trips if the Feds got involved, but otherwise I'd laid down the law, no more than one overnight per week.

"Every week? Harry, I don't want you—"

I raised my hands. "Hold on, now. Yeah, probably every week, but he also agreed to give me a full day's compensation for every overnight. I even wrote up my own schedule for the next month. That means a four-day workweek most weeks. I'm gonna take Fridays off, but we can switch that around sometimes if you want."

"Hmph! I'll believe it when I see it." She added some salt to what she was cooking. "But . . . does that mean you're gonna be free this Friday?"

"Yep. I already put in my overnight this week when I went out to Lincoln to catch that dude with the weed. Why? You want us to do somethin' special this Friday?"

"Unfortunately, it's not me. Gotta work. I've been thinking of askin' Grace Meredith, that young woman who came to dinner, if she'll come with me to the shelter this Friday for a visit. But we got a call today from that Don Krakowski. Remember, he's the son of the woman who used to own this place."

"Yeah. I remember. Met him when he came by to pick up her stuff."

"That's the thing. He said she left a box here, some legal papers and old mementos that are real important to her. Doesn't seem to be with the stuff they put in storage, so she's been beggin' him to bring her by to look for it. He's got this Friday off, so he wants to come then. I tried to tell him we'd both be workin', but he was very insistent. Wanted to know if anyone else would be home. Of course, there's Rodney, but I had no idea what he's got planned. Anyway, I told this Don fellow we'd call him back."

"I don't know about any box with that kind of stuff in it. Do you?"

"No, and I tried to tell him that, but he said his mother won't give him any rest until she's had a look for herself."

"Sounds like that fall down the stairs left her a little . . ." I twirled my finger by my ear.

"Harry! That's not polite."

"Well, I'm just sayin'."

"Actually, I did ask how she was doin', and he said she's doin' pretty well, but she really misses her old home. Seems like the least we can do is invite her to see how nicely you've fixed it up, especially if you're gonna be home Friday."

I shrugged. "Sure, I guess."

"Then would you make the call? Number's on that slip of paper pinned to the board by the phone."

I guessed it wouldn't hurt for the old lady to come look, though it might feel kind of weird, guiding her through her old place after we've been making changes to it. Kinda wished Estelle was going to be here. She was better at this kind of thing than I was.

Chapter 25

ISPENT A COUPLE HOURS WITH MOM Friday morning. No change that I could tell, but she seemed to appreciate me playing some of the praise CDs Estelle had sent. Don't think any of the nurses bothered to play them for her. But then, that's not their job.

I put on the CD that Grace Meredith had given us. Figured if Estelle was making friends with her, the least I could do was listen to a little of her music. Just hoped it wasn't too "contemporary" for Mom. But it was nice, and the woman certainly had a fantastic voice. I could see why she traveled all over the country giving concerts. I'd hate to be on the road that much . . . Wait a minute! That's exactly what I'd gotten myself into. I thought Mom had drifted off, but at the last song, Mom's eyes came open and a crooked smile brightened her face. She raised her right hand and began keeping time with the music with her index as though she were directing a choir. As it played, I recognized the old spiritual. Perhaps I'd even heard Mom sing it in church sometime back in the day.

I listened more closely.

> *Give me Jesus,*
> *Give me Jesus*
> *You may have all the world,*
> *Give me Jesus.*
> *When the waves of trouble rise,*
> *When the waves of trouble rise,*
> *When the waves of trouble rise,*
> *Give me Jesus.*

"Waves of trouble," huh? Sure felt like I'd been through my share of waves lately, more like a storm! Tossed one way and then another over so many things. But Grace's crystal-clear voice drew me on.

> *And when I come to die,*
> *And when I come to die,*
> *And when I come to die,*
> *Give me Jesus.*

Was she singing to Mom? Whether or not this was my mother's time, it wouldn't be long till she crossed over. The rhythm she kept with her finger, though it moved only a couple inches at a time, affirmed her sincere request, "Give me Jesus. You may have all the world, give me Jesus."

Could I say the same?

> *Now hear the voice that calls,*
> *Now hear the voice that calls,*
> *Now hear the voice that calls,*
> *Come to Jesus.*
> *Come to Jesus,*
> *Come to Jesus.*
> *For Him give up all the world,*
> *Come to Jesus.*

As the mellow notes of Grace's voice drifted away, I just sat there. I'd already come to Jesus. I believed. I knew that when my number was up, I'd follow Mom in passin' over to be with Jesus. I'd turned away from the booze and had embraced the second chance God had given me to have a new family, to become a father like God to my grandson and receive God as my father. I'd thrown myself on Jesus' mercy when I'd been losing the sight in my left eye, and He'd spoken to me and healed me. We had a relationship.

So why was that simple old spiritual bringing tears to my eyes?

I watched my mom, whose hand had relaxed to her side and whose eyes had closed in peaceful sleep. She was ready to pass over. You may have all the world, give me Jesus. Was it really that simple? I wasn't trying to "have all the world." I wasn't tryin' to get rich or grab everything within sight. No. I was just tryin' to get by. Tryin' to navigate the challenges in my life. Tryin' to make a good place for my mother, for Estelle and DaShawn. And I thought God had my back, but . . . Give me Jesus? Was that all that mattered? How do you give up everything else? How do you give up your responsibilities—even for Jesus—without becoming irresponsible? It sounded almost like the pseudo spiritual pabulum that came from the TV preachers Mom listened to.

But I don't know.

I got up, wiped the tears from my eyes, and stepped over to plant a feather-light kiss on Mom's forehead before I left the hospital.

My cell phone rang just as I got to my car in the hospital parking garage. "Yeah, Bentley."

"Uh, Mr. Bentley?"

"That's me." Didn't sound like a telemarketer, so I gave the guy a few more seconds.

"This is Don Krakowski. I'm running a little late. There's more traffic comin' in on the Kennedy than I anticipated. We should be there in another twenty minutes. Hope that doesn't mess you up."

"No, no." I'd completely forgotten about Mattie Krakowski coming to find her lost box. "You're welcome when you get here."

As soon as I got home, I checked the first floor to make sure Rodney hadn't left the place an unspeakable mess. In spite of his other problems, he'd actually always been fairly neat, even as a kid. Today he was out job hunting . . . or something, and his room looked fine. The rest of the apartment was empty.

I ran upstairs. Oops, Corky! "You okay, girl?" She came up beside me, swinging her tail, and shouldered me in the leg like a safety trying to make an open-field tackle. But she didn't appear to need to go out. I gave her a pat and put some coffee on. While it was brewing, I went down to the basement to see if I could find that box. Corky trailed along just in case something exciting happened. Didn't find any boxes except our own and ran back upstairs. Whew! I was getting my exercise today.

When the doorbell rang, I closed Corky into our apartment and went down to greet the Krakowskis, only slightly out of breath. "Come on in." I held the door wide as an elderly white lady with a cane surveyed the entryway before entering it.

"Looks just the same, Donny. I thought you said they changed it all."

"No, Mom. I said they might've changed some things." He smiled and reached around his mother to shake my hand as she made it across the threshold.

"How you doin'? Got some fresh coffee I could bring down if your mom . . ." Duh! She was standing right there. "Excuse me, ma'am. Didn't mean to ignore you. If you'd rather not climb the stairs, I could bring some coffee down here."

But what are they gonna sit on? Rodney's bed and one chair? The old lady saved me. "Oh, I think I can manage the stairs if you don't rush me. It's just those basement steps that give me trouble." But instead of starting up the stairs, she turned left and opened the door to the first-floor apartment.

"Uh, no, Mom. That's someone else's apartment now. You don't live there anymore."

She turned and looked at her son with a bewildered look on her face.

"It's okay," I said. "We don't really have anyone in there right now. My son's using one of the bedrooms, but we've spent the last few weeks working on it."

Before I finished my explanation, Mattie took my it's okay literally and stepped through the door. "Oh, my! Oh, my! This is . . . this is different." She kept shuffling on into the living room. "I like it. It's so bright. Donny, can we put my TV back in the same place?" Then she turned to me. "I can still get Regis and Kelly, can't I?"

"Uh . . ."

"How about Oprah?"

"Well," I said, "I'm sure . . . though I . . ." I looked at Don for some help. ". . . I've heard Oprah's gonna—"

Don waved his hand frantically behind his mother's back to get me to stop.

I blew out a breath. "Yes. Oprah too."

I grinned at Don, and he nodded in relief.

We walked from one end of the apartment to the other with Mattie exclaiming over every room at what a nice job we'd done. To my surprise, she didn't ask whose things were in the bedroom. She peeked in and quickly pulled the door closed, her eyebrows arched high as though she didn't want to disturb anything.

Once we'd reached the sunroom, she turned her piercing blue eyes on me. "So did you find my box?"

"No, ma'am. Afraid we didn't. As you can see, there's nothing left in the apartment, and I didn't find anything in the basement either."

"To tell you the truth, I'd like to go down and look myself, if you don't mind."

I looked to Don and shrugged, leaving it to him to answer.

"Uh, Mom, why don't I go down and look. You tell me where you think you left it, and I'll go down and check. Okay?"

"Well, I know where it is. It's on those shelves your father built years ago."

We returned to the entryway where another door accessed the basement. Don went down the stairs while I stood there, not knowing what to say. Finally, I asked, "Is it nice where you're staying now?"

"No. Other people keep changing the channel on me to vampires and cop shows and things I don't like."

"That's too bad." The woman reminded me of my mom, facing life at the end with so little control over what happened to her. Must be hard.

"At least when my hip's strong enough and I move back in here, I won't have that problem."

My mouth dropped open. She wasn't just a little confused, she was expecting to move back in! She looked at me and cocked her head slightly to the side as if she couldn't raise it enough to look up at me straight on. "I'm here to tell you mister . . . mister . . . What was your name again?"

"Uh . . . Bentley, Harry Bentley."

"Well, I'm here to tell you, Mr. Harry Bentley, that I couldn't be more pleased with how nice you made my place look. Thank you."

"Mom? Mom!" Don called up from the basement. "There's no box like that down here. In fact, there aren't any shelves beside the stairs."

"Oh, fiddlesticks. Yes there are." She turned and shook her head at me. "That boy! Can't ever seem to do any errand I send him on."

"Well, there might've been some shelves here at some point," came Don's voice as he ascended the stairs. "I could see some marks and old nail holes, but they're gone now."

Mattie shuffled toward the stairs, but I stepped around her and put my arm across the doorway to the basement. "I don't think you oughta go down there, ma'am. After your fall and all—"

"Don't be ridiculous. I've been doing my exercises for weeks. I know how to do stairs. I turn around, hold onto both sides, and go down backwards."

"What?"

"Well, that's the way I do it. Here, move aside."

Don backed down the stairs a step or two. "She can do it. I've seen her. Just have to give her time."

Reluctantly, I removed my arm, glad we had liability insurance, and Don retreated, "spotting" her until she reached the bottom. By the time I got down there, she was frowning at the two small units not much larger than a pair of travel trunks that had replaced the enormous old octopus furnace. "It's all different." She pointed. "What are those?"

"New furnaces," I said. "One for each floor."

"They had to put in new furnaces, Mom. Remember, the old one broke? That's why you were going down the stairs that night when you fell."

"But why didn't they just fix the old one? These little things'll never heat the whole place."

"They'll do just fine, Mom. They're much more efficient."

"My, my, my!" Mrs. Krakowski began walking around the basement with small hesitant steps. "You got new laundry too. That's nice." Then, as though remembering why she'd come down, she gazed at the wall beside the stairs. "The shelves are gone."

I figured it was my turn to explain. "They had to take 'em out in order to put in new duct work for the furnaces."

"Does it still rattle and rumble when the furnace starts up?"

"No ma'am. It's quiet as can be. They run at different speeds depending on how cold it is."

"Hmmm. Well, where'd they put those shelves?" I shrugged. "I'm sorry, I really don't know."

She shook her head sadly and returned to the stairs. "Might as well go, Donny. But that box held my most important family pictures. Had pictures of you when you were just a baby in there. My grandma and grandpa too. Such a shame." She started climbing slowly, Don right behind her to steady her. "Guess I'm just gonna have to trust and obey."

I chuckled to myself. The lady was quite a character.

When we got to the entryway again, Don looked at me as though hoping it was okay to make the offer, and then said, "You wanna check upstairs, Mom?"

"No reason to. The box was never up there."

Don shrugged, thanked me for letting them come, and ushered his mother out the front door. I watched through the door window as he walked her out to the car and helped her in. In spite of her cane, the woman had made a remarkable recovery in such a short time—what was it? Just two and a half months? I felt really bad she'd lost something so valuable to her . . . and that she was fantasizing about coming back to live in her old apartment. Well, old people did have their delusions.

I went upstairs, poured some of the coffee I'd made for my guests into a travel mug, and took Corky out the back for a walk.

Trust and obey—what a strange thing for the old woman to say over losing something that meant so much to her. "Trust and obey, trust and obey." I said it over and over as we reached the perimeter of the cemetery at the end of the alley. The words had a familiar ring. Then I remembered the old gospel song by that name. That was it. She was talking about trusting God and obeying what he said. How'd the last line of the song go? "Trust and obey, for there's no other way to be happy in Jesus but to trust and obey."

I took a sip of coffee. Maybe that was the key to Grace Meredith's song. The only way to give up this world was to trust God's care in spite of all the zigzags. Maybe then, and only then, would Jesus become all that matters, the only way you could honestly say, "Just give me Jesus."

Was Mom in that zone? I looked through the fence at the gravestones, some plain, some tall and encrusted with lichen, some leaning a little. Did you have to be at death's door before you could say it and mean it?

Chapter 26

Hey, DaShawn." I eyed my grandson as he shoveled pancakes into his mouth Saturday morning. "What you doin' on today?"

He hunkered down in his seat as though making himself look small and weak might exempt him from any chores I had in mind. Made me want to laugh.

"I dunno," he finally mumbled.

"Well, if you don't know, guess no one else would either. How 'bout you, Rodney?"

Pick still stuck in his uncombed hair, he shrugged and shook his head, no less suspicious than DaShawn.

"Ha, ha!" Couldn't hold it back. "Relax, you guys. I been thinkin' we might see about puttin' up that backboard and hoop in the alley this mornin'. Whaddaya say?"

They both perked up, DaShawn sitting straighter in his chair. He glanced at his dad, and then turned to me with a bright grin on his face. "Well, I'm in, Pops. That'd be great."

"Good, good! But only if you're really up for it. Wouldn't want to overwork ya none."

Estelle put a second plate of pancakes on the table. "Don't forget you promised to fix my refrigerator door at Manna House."

I waved my hand dismissively. "Oh, I can get to that this afternoon while these guys knock themselves out shootin' hoops." I gave DaShawn a sly glance. "Then I'll come back and show 'em who's boss before dinner."

"Oh, you the boss, Pops. You da boss if you get that hoop up for me." The boy grabbed two more pancakes like he was storing up reserve fuel for the day.

181

After breakfast, we picked up the additional hardware we needed from Home Depot and, after a few minor complications, got the Spalding backboard and hoop mounted on the back of the garage before lunchtime. By then, DaShawn's friend Tavis had discovered what we were doing, as had his older brother, Destin.

I watched with satisfaction as a little two-on-two got organized, Rodney and DaShawn versus the two Jasper boys. Apparently, the morning's pancakes were lasting. Putting up the hoop definitely was worth the effort, not just for my grandson, but I could see it'd be good for other neighborhood kids as well.

"You wanna play, Pops? We can probably find someone else."

"Nah. I gotta take Corky for a walk and grab some lunch 'fore I head on over to Manna House."

Hustling up the back stairs, I asked Estelle if she thought I could take Corky with me to the shelter.

"Don't see why not. The Fairbank boys bring Dandy by sometimes for a visit. Of course, he's still the shelter's 'Hero Dog.'"

"Yeah, but Dandy's not a drug detector."

"Hmm. Hadn't thought of that. The shelter's supposed to be a drug-free facility, but . . . you can never tell. Maybe it'd be a good to have an occasional sweep."

"No, no, no. I was messin' with you. Corky's Amtrak. If she alerts to someone, I can just give her the 'free' signal, and they'll never know the difference. But I don't mind takin' her into unfamiliar situations. Helps keep her alert."

The hoop in the alley got a lot of play all weekend, attracting some of the other kids in the neighborhood, even young Danny and his two dads from the house a couple of doors down. There was lots of hootin' and hollerin' going on when Estelle and I came back from visiting Mom at the hospital Sunday afternoon, but everyone good-naturedly took a break as we drove into the garage.

Sure hoped the other neighbors wouldn't become upset over all the noise. Might have to set some rules about when things had to shut down in the evenings.

Rodney wasn't playing basketball. When I went down the front stairs to take some laundry to the basement, the front door to the first-floor apartment was open. "Rodney, you in there?"

"Yeah."

He sounded as dejected as a Bears' fan after a losing game. I walked in and found him on his bed in his room. "What's up?"

"Ah, Donita. Been on the phone with her for the last hour."

"That don't sound good." I didn't welcome hearing that name any more than a February snowstorm. "What's she want?"

"She says she's gettin' her life together. Started rehab, wants to see DaShawn."

"Not under my roof. That woman's poison."

"Yeah, I know . . . but she's still DaShawn's mom."

"You think he wants to see her?"

"Probably not, but there may come a day. You know, Dad, you didn't try very hard to keep our family together, though now you got a good one. I'll give you that. But I don't like the fact that mine fell apart, either. Sometimes I think that's my next step . . . to put it back together."

I looked at him and slowly shook my head. He was right about my failures, but I just didn't see any hope for him and Donita.

By Sunday evening, I started thinking about my workweek looming ahead. Since Captain Gilson seemed so eager for me to put in some extended time on the Southwest Chief—"The Drug Train"—maybe I'd substitute it for my overnight that week and postpone the Texas Eagle until another week. Tomorrow morning I'd go in early and catch the 7:30 up to Kalamazoo and back for a day run, patrol Union Station on Tuesday, and head out to Kansas City on the Southwest Chief on Wednesday afternoon. I could catch the eastbound Chief the next day and get back to Chicago on Thursday afternoon a little after three, presuming the Chief was running on time. It'd be a perfect week, and I could still take Friday off.

Everything came off without a hitch on Monday. I made a bust and still got home in plenty of time to have dinner with the whole

183

family. DaShawn was helping Estelle prepare dinner, so he got to bring the steaming bowl of green beans to the table as well as the Caesar salad.

"I made it myself, Dad." He ginned at Rodney as he plunked the salad bowl down in the middle of the table.

But when he returned for the hot chicken casserole from the oven, Estelle shooed him away. "Thanks anyway, buddy, but I'll get this one. Don't want you burning yourself on this hot dish—you might drop it."

Once everyone was at the table and we'd said a blessing, Estelle began serving up the hot chicken and rice. She handed Rodney's plate to him with a wink. "Might have some good news for you."

He inhaled deeply through his nose. "Mmm, smells like good news to me. Thanks. But, uh . . . were you meaning some other news?"

"Yeah. I was over visiting our neighbor across the street this afternoon—same woman we had to dinner a couple weeks ago—and her assistant, Samantha, was there helping her. Anyway, she's the one who arranges all of Grace's transportation—"

"She still gonna use the train?" I asked.

"Probably. But the news is . . ." She gave me a frown for interrupting. ". . . when I mentioned you were looking for a job, Rodney, Samantha all of a sudden blurts out that the guy at the end of our street here is looking for drivers. Might be worth checking it out."

"Wait a minute." I swallowed my mouthful of chicken. "Are you talkin' about that McMansion dude? He needs a personal driver?"

"That's not it. He's an attorney, but apparently he owns a limo company on the side—"

"That must be why those big ol' black stretches drive up our street sometimes." DaShawn hooted.

"Most likely. Samantha said the last time she tried to schedule one, she had problems because they were short of drivers. The person she talked to on the phone apologized and said they were looking to hire new ones. She just threw it out there as a possible answer to prayer since I'd asked them to pray for you."

Everyone was silent as Rodney chewed, staring at his plate. Finally, he looked up at her. "Yeah. Well, I'll look into it. Thank you. I'll definitely check it out."

Good! He made the right choice.

I took a deep breath and leaned back. "Hey, y'all. I got some news too. Made another bust today."

"Get outta here!" DaShawn jumped in as if he too had sensed the tension and was glad for relief. "Who was it this time?"

"Couple of ol' hippies, rich ones, if their car was any measure."

"What?"

"Well, if I tell ya, I'll have to . . . you know."

"Yeah, yeah. You'll have to kill us. Come on, Pops, we won't tell no one."

"Anyone." Estelle reached for the salt. "You won't tell anyone."

"Whatever. Come on, Pops."

"All right. But you can't be blabbin' it around, ya know."

"We won't. We won't."

Rodney eyed me with a smirk on his face. "Speak for yourself, son. This information might be worth somethin' on the street."

"Oh, yeah?" DaShawn came right back. "But your butt won't be worth nothin' if you sell it."

We all laughed. The boy was smart all right.

I took a couple more bites. "This is mighty good, Estelle. And your salad too, DaShawn." I paused and thought for a moment about how I could tell the story without revealing my cover to DaShawn or Rodney.

"Come on, Pops. Quit stallin'."

"Well, I went up to Kalamazoo today, and by the time we were nearly there, Corky and I had worked our way from the rear of the train through all the coaches except the first one, and we were nearly to the front of it when Corky suddenly sat down and identified this middle-aged couple who were sittin' there watching a movie on their laptop. I was still standing a little behind them, kinda lookin' over their shoulders, but they were so engrossed in their movie they didn't even notice us." I chuckled. "They were quite a pair, though. The woman wore a paisley tunic and had dreadlocks the color of a dirty gunnysack. And the guy had a gray beard and a nearly bald head—"

"Ha! Look who's talkin'," muttered Rodney.

"No, no, no." I stroked my short beard. "Mine's neatly groomed, isn't it, Estelle? And I shave my head so it has some class. But this guy . . . well, the most I can say for him is that he didn't do a comb-over, but let me tell you, those fly-away wisps of white hair looked like smoke streaming from a Gary steel mill."

"So what'd you do then, Pops?"

"Well, me and Corky—"

"Harry Bentley! How's this boy supposed to learn proper English with you saying me and Corky. It's Corky and I."

"Okay." I rolled my eyes. "Let's just say, I freed Corky with a hand signal, and we backed off without those two even noticing. Then we went down to the vestibule and were the first to detrain when it stopped a few minutes later in Kalamazoo."

I gave Estelle a wink. "Say babe, you got any more of that chicken and rice?"

She rolled her eyes and served me a small dab as DaShawn shoveled in his last couple of bites and passed her his plate. "Please."

"Now you're learning." She rewarded him with a much larger scoop and a smile. Oh well, my waist didn't need more.

"I didn't want to confront the couple near other passengers, so as soon as we got off the train, I headed for the station, which turned out to be nearly empty. Wanting to make sure the culprits saw my badge and service weapon straight off, I dropped my jacket, hat, and Corky's D-handle beside an old woman dozing on one of the benches and asked her to watch them for me. Her eyes got wide at the sight of my weapon, so I made sure she got a good look at my Amtrak Police shield as I clipped it onto my belt."

I was almost sorry I'd started this tale, but had to finish it now. "With Corky on her leash, we ran outside just as the couple who'd gone around the outside of the station crossed the street to their shiny BMW, which they'd parked in the Kalamazoo Gospel Mission's parking lot, no doubt without permission."

"How'd you know that?" Rodney asked.

"Since this ain't no courtroom, I can tell you. Pure conjecture. But as soon as they opened the trunk of their car, I confronted them. Corky sat down immediately, indicating that their luggage was dirty."

"Busted!" DaShawn punched the air above his head in triumph.

"Oh yeah, but they complained that I had no jurisdiction because they weren't on Amtrak property. Didn't make any difference. I insisted they open their bags, and there were the drugs— amphetamines and a baggy of weed. Oh, how they whined. 'Why aren't you out arresting people with guns or catching rapists? We aren't bothering anybody. Besides, we've got prescriptions for these.' But when they couldn't produce any documentation, I called 9-1-1—"

"Wait a minute," Rodney cut in. "What kind of documentation?"

I frowned. Was he looking for loopholes around the drug laws? "They didn't have a prescription for the pills or a medical marijuana ID card from the State of Michigan for the pot, so I decided to let the Kalamazoo police and a local judge sort out whether they were 'legal' or not. As far as I was concerned, those are controlled substances and against the law." I glared at Rodney.

Everyone was silent for a few moments, then DaShawn broke the tension. "So what happened to the old woman in the station?"

"Oh, I went back and thanked her for watching my stuff. Think she was in shock."

I didn't explain that her shock was topped off by watching me disappear into the men's room and emerge a few moments later as an ol' blind man with a guide dog. Who would have believed her story anyway?

I was just as eager the next morning to report my exploits to Captain Gilson, but on my way to work, just as I got on the outer drive, my cell rang. When I saw the caller ID said Saint Francis Hospital, my heart jumped. "Hello."

"Mr. Bentley, your just mother's had another stroke, and I think you need to get here right away. It doesn't look good. It doesn't look good at all."

"Is she conscious?"

"No sir. We may have to put her on a ventilator, so we need you to get here."

Ventilator! I pulled off the outer drive at Foster Avenue and headed back north as fast as I could go, calling Estelle as I drove. I knew if this was it, Estelle would want to be there with Mom.

We'd had so much hope Mom could come home soon! But now . . .

Chapter 27

IT WAS COOL ENOUGH in the Saint Francis parking garage that I didn't have to worry about leaving Corky in her kennel Besides, it had an automatic fan that would kick in if needed. "Stay, girl. You got plenty of water, and I'll be back to check on you soon as I can."

By the time I got up to Mom's room, Estelle was already there. She reached out and pulled me close as I approached the bedside. The beep, beep, beep of the monitor was the only assurance Mom was still alive. For reasons I couldn't quite identify, she actually looked like she was gone. Her face was vacant, gray, and seemed to sag.

"What'd they say?"

Estelle shook her head as she stared at my mother. "Hardly anything. Just that they had to resuscitate her and they're about to take her down for a CAT scan."

"Resuscitate? What about her DNR order?" Estelle shrugged. "Don't know."

"Has the doctor been in?"

She shook her head. "I just got here a couple minutes before you." A businesslike nurse bustled in and asked us to wait outside.

"We need to get Mrs. Bentley ready for transport." I stepped aside but asked, "Where's she goin'?"

"Down for a CAT scan."

"Last time they did an MRI. Why the change?"

Without looking at me, the nurse said, "You'll have to ask the doctor." But I had the impression she knew more than she was letting on.

"Has the doctor seen her?"

"Not this morning, but I'll let him know you're here. He'll probably meet with you after the CAT scan."

We stepped out into the hall and stood there in silence, staring . . . without seeing each other or the decorator prints on the wall or what was going on at the other end of the corridor. When the patient transporter finally arrived and wheeled Mom out and down the hall, we drifted aimlessly along behind like we were walking in a fog until we reached the nurse's station where Estelle leaned over the counter. "Would you let us know when Mrs. Bentley comes back up or when her doctor gets here? We'll be in the waiting room."

"Sure thing."

There was no one else in the waiting room, and Estelle sat down and bowed her head over folded hands. I picked up an old copy of Car and Driver and thumbed through it without finding anything of interest.

"You think they ordered that CAT scan 'cause it's cheaper? Maybe they've given up on her."

Estelle raised her head and gazed at me thoughtfully. "I really don't know, Harry." She bowed again over her clasped hands then abruptly looked up. "But ya know, hon, suspicion doesn't do much good at a time like this. I'd say, if you got that question, you should ask the doctor straight up, and put it to rest."

I tried to flush the suspicion out of my mind, but the questions still niggled around the fringes.

Half an hour later, the doctor came in and sat down to give us his report. He leaned forward, elbows on his knees, frowning as if he were trying to think of the best way to break hard news.

"I'm sorry, Mr. and Mrs. Bentley, this was a massive bleed, a subdural hematoma, which we usually see in head injuries. But sometimes it occurs spontaneously as a form of stroke. We might take some heroic measures to relieve the pressure, but I seriously doubt whether your mother will ever regain consciousness. And even if she does, the damage from this incident on top of her previous strokes would leave her so impaired that she would be . . ."

He didn't finish his sentence, but I heard the word he was thinking: vegetable.

It made me angry. If Mom regained consciousness, she wouldn't be a vegetable, no matter how impaired. "Why'd you give her a CAT scan instead of an MRI? Was it because it's cheaper?"

190

He looked taken aback. "Uh . . . uh, yes, in one sense a CAT scan is cheaper, but they are also better for some things. Better in a case like this with a very recent bleed. The MRI's told us how extensive the older damage was, but this bleed is ongoing, and a CAT scan shows it very precisely."

I glanced at Estelle. The gentle look on her face held no condemnation. I turned back to the doctor. "But you said there were some things you could do that might help. What?"

"Well, there's medication, of course, that might slow the bleed. But we're talking about a very delicate balance here. We don't want to create clots, which was probably the source of her first stroke. Beyond that we could drill one or more holes in her skull in hopes of relieving the pressure. However, this hemorrhage was so massive, I'm not sure we would succeed."

"And if you don't do anything?" I asked.

He looked away and then back as he took a breath. "The pressure will increase on her brainstem until she expires. Her respiration's already suppressed, probably as a result of the increased pressure."

I leaned back trying to absorb the horror of them drilling holes in my mother's head until the doctor broke into my nightmare with a further complication. "If that's the way you decide to go, we'd probably better get her on a ventilator as soon as possible. But you need to realize that mechanical ventilation does not insure her survival. And any meaningful recovery is highly unlikely."

"But not impossible?"

"Mr. Bentley, how do I answer that question? I am a Christian. This is a Catholic hospital. I have witnessed what I would call miracles. None of us wants to see our loved ones pass, but even the Bible says we are all appointed to die at some point."

My head fell forward so I was staring at my lap, but the doctor's confession of faith felt comforting. I glanced sideways at Estelle. She was looking steadily at me.

I finally realized the doctor was still waiting patiently.

"If this were your mother, what would you do?"

He drew in a deep breath, letting it out slowly in a silent whistle. "I would not put her on a ventilator. I would let her go."

I felt Estelle's hand reach for mine. I turned and looked into her dark eyes. They glistened until they overflowed in a small trickle down her cheek, her lips pursed tightly together. I was not alone as the room swam and swirled amid my own tears. "I think . . . I think that's our decision too, right, babe?"

She nodded slowly and pulled me closer.

Mom passed peacefully three hours later, and we spent the rest of the day contacting family and friends and making plans.

The first person I called was Rodney. After several moments of silence, he said, "I had wanted to come up and see her."

What could I say? You could've if you wanted to? Or, She was unconscious and wouldn't even have known you were there? But I got ahold of myself. "Yeah. That's too bad, son. Hey, we're gonna go get DaShawn out of school to tell him, but then we've got lots of other stuff to plan and do. Will you be home so he can stay with you?"

"I'll be here."

I'm sure DaShawn knew what was up as soon as he got the message to report to the office. His eyes were wide when he walked in and saw us standing there in front of the counter. He ran the last couple steps to give me an unembarrassed hug. Estelle wrapped us both in her warm arms.

During the ride back to the house, DaShawn asked lots of questions about what had actually taken his great-grandmother's life. Maybe this was his way of objectifying it all so it wouldn't hurt so much. The four of us had sandwiches for a late lunch, and then Estelle and I set out to take on the avalanche of decisions and plans we had to make.

After talking to Pastor Cobbs, we decided on a Saturday homegoing celebration since there weren't but a couple of family members who might come from a distance. The whole process was something I'd never done before.

It had been nearly twelve years since my father died, and I hadn't even gone down to Atlanta for his funeral. I was still pretty angry with him for abandoning Mom and me when I was just a kid. Had seen him only a couple of times since he left us, and both times weren't my choice—at the wedding of a cousin and once when he looked me up and wanted to borrow some money. I was a hotshot rookie cop at that point and told him I'd throw him in jail if he ever showed his face to me again. Didn't have any idea what I would've charged him with, but it was enough to scare him off for the rest of his life.

By the time he died, I was too busy in Special Ops at the CPD to break away. Sent flowers, though, and spent the evening after I got off duty at The Office, my favorite watering hole, toasting him with curses. It was my way of burying all memory of him. I was lucky to get home that night without crashing my car and picking up a second DUI.

But Mom's passing was different.

This time I wouldn't be going to The Office, but Estelle insisted I go to my men's Bible study. "You gotta share it with them, Harry, for your own good. Let 'em come alongside you, pray with you. I mean, those brothers are your closest friends. Don't lock 'em out at a time like this."

During the day we'd made arrangements with the House of Thompson in Evanston to take care of Mom's body and host the visitation Friday evening, and we talked some more with Pastor Cobbs to plan Mom's homegoing celebration for Saturday afternoon at SouledOut. He knew just what to do and contacted everyone necessary at the church. Estelle called Manna House and informed them she wouldn't be in for the rest of the week. And Captain Gilson told me to take off whatever time I needed.

Poor Corky. I don't think she had any idea why I cut short her evening walk as soon as she did her business and hustled back to the house. But I think she knew something was wrong.

The men in my Bible study were concerned about how I was doing. "I'm okay," I assured them, though I hadn't even had time to think about how I was doing.

But Ben Garfield, the older Jewish believer in our group, wouldn't let me off so easily. "Ha! Okay you're not when your own mother dies. Nobody is. So don't be telling me you are. What's wrong with you?" And then he went on to tell us about the death of his mother. To his credit, he kept his story shorter than usual. "Oy vey!" He rolled his eyes. "When you least expect it, the bekhi—the crying—it will come over you. It will not be denied."

I had no idea what he meant, but I figured he might be right about me not being as okay as I thought was, especially when Peter Douglass asked me what songs we were going to have at Mom's homegoing celebration.

I'd left all that to Pastor Cobbs and Estelle, but Peter's question sent me back to the day I'd played Grace Meredith's CD for my mother. It had been echoing in my head ever since. Suddenly, I had an idea. Would Grace sing it at the service? Didn't have much hope she could, though, since Estelle said she was busy preparing for her West Coast tour.

Still, I mentioned the idea to Estelle that night as we crawled into bed.

"Mmm. S'pose I could ask. We'd planned to get together tomorrow to pray, but with everything going on, I was gonna to call and cancel. But I'll mention it and see what she says. Not sure when . . . 'cause I gotta start cookin' for the repast."

I snaked my arm around her and pulled her close. "Oh, babe," I murmured in her ear, "that's a lot of work. Why don't you get someone else to do it?" I kissed her lightly on the neck.

She recoiled a couple of inches. "Like who, Harry? I'm the only professional cook around here."

"Yeah, but . . ." Had to be careful here. "We've had some pretty good eats at our church potlucks, don'tcha think?"

"Pot-blessings, Harry, pot-blessings. We don't leave the food to luck."

"That's what I'm sayin'. I mean, your Yada Yada sisters put on a pretty good spread. Seems to me Sister Avis makes some decent mac-and-cheese. And who's that Jamaican woman, Chanda? I really liked her rice and peas. And you can't say Adele Scruggs don't put her toe in those greens she cooks up. How 'bout Edesa's enchiladas? They're from south of the border if you ask me. And Florida Hickman's potato salad is off the chain. Even you liked—"

"Okay, okay. Made your point." She snuggled close again and yawned. "I'll call my sisters and see what they can come up with." She paused for a moment, then murmured, "Ya know, that's a good idea, Harry. Thanks. Takes a real burden off me. Don't know why I didn't think of that before."

I breathed in the warm smell of her, feeling comforted by her presence after the shock and stress of the day. "Now, I gotta say, no one makes fried chicken like you, Estelle, but maybe if you told 'em how . . ."

"Ha! That'd take more time than doin' it myself. We'll just order in the chicken from Popeyes and maybe some ribs from Hecky's. Gotta get some sleep now though, Harry."

I didn't get much sleep that night. A heavy weight pressed down on my spirit when I dozed off—then I'd wake up with a start, fighting the feeling that something terrible had happened, and it would flood in on me . . . my mom was gone. O God, I groaned inwardly. What now?

I was glad when morning arrived. Gotta keep busy. I spent most of Wednesday at the House of Thompson selecting a casket for Mom, signing papers, and then digging through dusty boxes in her old apartment to find her will.

Why we hadn't asked her for a copy months ago—years ago— I'll never know. Finally, I found it in a folder on paper yellowing at the edges. It was a short document, signed and dated properly as far as I could tell, and it left everything to me. But it named Rev. Winfred Johnson, her old pastor at Mount Zion Tabernacle on the South Side, as the executor. That church had been torn down in the urban renewal of the seventies, and I was sure Pastor Johnson had passed away long ago.

Nevertheless, the will was enough to convince our mutual bank to give me a summary of Mom's accounts so I'd know what to expect. She didn't have much. I'd be lucky if her assets covered her funeral expenses and other bills.

Made me wonder if that whole idea of her moving into the first floor of our two-flat would've worked financially. Just one more derailment. But maybe it wasn't God jerking me around this time. Maybe I should've done more investigating.

That evening when the family gathered around the table for dinner, Estelle served spaghetti from a bowl I'd never seen before, and a matching one on the table held salad. A few moments later, she set a basket of bread in front of us. "Sorry, it's not garlic bread." Seemed strange. She always made garlic bread with spaghetti, but maybe she didn't have time. "You make all this today?"

"No way." She sat down and slid her chair in. "I was runnin' all over plannin' the repast. We can give the Lord a special thanks for this meal, and you'll never guess who brought it by."

I waited, and it was obvious she wasn't gonna tell us until I prayed.

When I said amen, DaShawn spoke up. "So where'd it come from?"

"Tim and Scott." She pointed north.

I frowned. "The gay couple?"

"Don't know how they heard about Mother Bentley's passing, but they both came by to extend their condolences and brought us this meal. So I . . . well, I invited them to the homegoing celebration. I think they're gonna come and bring their little boy too."

I had no idea what to say, and sat there with the whole thing swirling in my head so fast that I didn't hear what Rodney said.

"Hallelujah!" Estelle burst out. "Praise the Lord! Now that's big-time answered prayer."

I looked around the table. "What?"

Estelle wiped her mouth. "I said, that's something else to praise the Lord for."

"What is?"

"Rodney's job."

I looked at my son. "You got a job?"

"That's what I said. Start tomorrow drivin' for Lincoln Limo Service. Ya know, the cat at the end of the block." He grinned at me with pride I hadn't seen in his eyes since he learned to ride a two-wheeler as a little boy.

Chapter 28

IGOT UP AND OUT EARLY THE NEXT MORNING to walk Corky. I needed the exercise as much as the dog did, especially to release the tension that had built up over the last twenty-four hours. Maybe Corky felt it too, because she jumped when the automatic garage door started to rise on the Molanders' garage just south of us. We stopped to let the sandy-colored Buick back out.

The driver's side window lowered with a soft hum, and Karl Molander leaned out. "Sorry to hear about your mother. Was she a believer?"

I nodded.

"You know, if you've put your trust in Jesus, you'll see her again."

I nodded again, though a little more slowly. "Thank you. That's a comforting thought."

The Buick began to roll back again as he finished his turn. "Well, gotta get to Dominick's before the crowds. Hate shopping when you have to wait in lines." The window hummed up, and he put the car in drive and headed down the alley, leaving a whiff of oil smoke in his exhaust.

Corky and I followed as she sniffed each trash bin and telephone pole. At least she didn't have to mark every one. The taillights on Molander's car came on just before he turned left onto Chase Avenue. How did he know about Mom's passing? How did the guys two doors north hear about it? Maybe this neighborhood was more connected than I realized . . . at least the grapevine seemed to be working.

Yet something about Molander's response irked me. Estelle said Grace Meredith was happy to sing at the homegoing, had even said she felt honored to be asked. Her singing would certainly add something special to the service. And the meal the guys up the street contributed last night—very thoughtful. But as true as Molander's comment was, it didn't address the empty feeling that tumbled over and over in my stomach, and it didn't cost him a thing.

Well, he hadn't offered to come to Mom's celebration, and I didn't intend to invite him.

I went early Friday evening to the House of Thompson to make sure everything was ready for the visitation. Estelle would follow later with Rodney and DaShawn.

From the vestibule I could see a small chapel on the left. It was empty except for a blue casket near the front. I'd ordered bronze for Mom. Then I noticed the directory board naming the deceased and their respective rooms. Wanda Bentley was in the Heritage Parlor. I made my way down a short hallway and found it on the right, a room with soft indirect lighting on the rose-colored walls, large potted plants, heavy drapes behind which I suspected were no windows, and a variety of overstuffed sofas and Queen Anne chairs casually arranged for quiet conversation. At the far end was the open bronze casket.

I signed my name as the first visitor in the guestbook that sat atop an imitation marble pillar. I glanced toward the casket, not ready to approach it yet.

This funeral home catered to the African American population on the North Shore. That's why I'd chosen it, but the soft, piped-in classical music didn't sound like Mom. I went out and tapped softly on the office door leading from the vestibule and stuck my head in. "Would it be possible to select some quiet gospel music for Wanda Bentley?"

By the time I got back to the Heritage Parlor, Mahalia Jackson was singing "Take My Hand, Precious Lord."

It was time to view my mom's body.

A small brass lamp similar to the kind illuminating wall paintings in art galleries was clipped to the raised lid of the casket and cast a mellow light on the satin lining within . . . and Mom. But it didn't enliven the gray pallor that had clouded her face in the hospital, and her cheeks seemed to sag even farther. She was recognizable but not herself. They'd fixed her hair just like the photograph I'd provided, but it wasn't quite right. Estelle had picked out the dress, and it looked nice, but I couldn't recall Mom ever wearing it. I reached out and touched her hands, one lying on top of the other across her stomach. They were hard and rough as if she'd been mixing concrete for the last few years. There was no life in them.

There was no life in her.

She was gone!

Tears slid down my cheeks. Scenes from my childhood began to flash through my mind as though I was watching one of those time capsule presentations on TV, flicking faster and faster. Mom walking me to kindergarten, cooking Sunday dinner over the small, hot stove in our eleventh-floor one-bedroom in the Robert Taylor homes, coming in after working the swing shift at Nabisco—her second job—and singing in the choir at Mount Zion Tabernacle, begging me to not stay out after the street lights came on even though she couldn't be there to check on me.

My throat tightened. "Thanks, Mom," I whispered. "I wasn't shot. I didn't end up in prison, and—except for the alcohol—I escaped drugs." I leaned down and kissed her rigid cheek. She'd given me everything she could.

Quiet sounds behind me let me know other people were arriving. I wiped my eyes, waiting to turn and greet them until I'd collected myself. It was Peter and Avis Douglass, Florida and Carl Hickman. And Jodi and Denny Baxter were signing the guestbook.

The sight of my old friends gathering around at this time of grief undid me as we exchanged hugs all around, no need for words. I wished I could've shown them the little slide show that had gone on in my head. To them she was just that sweet elderly lady I brought to church on Sundays.

Would the obituary give them a sense of who she'd been? Maybe. But as each of them hugged me, I knew they were primarily there to support me. What good friends.

I sensed Estelle's arrival and turned toward the doorway. There she stood, the picture of refined mourning, swathed in a royal purple and black caftan with her hair swept up on top of her head the way I liked it best, dangling gold earrings catching the light. In spite of the occasion, my heart jumped. How did I ever deserve her?

Both Rodney and DaShawn at her side wore dark suits. Rodney's, I noticed, had a black satin stripe down the leg and around his jacket cuff. Probably from his new limo job. At least he was here. That turned on my waterworks again. My son had a job, but he'd made it to his grandmother's visitation. Guess old Ben Garfield was right: the crying—or whatever that Yiddish word was—would not be denied. I didn't care anymore. I went over, and with my arms around my family, brought them to Mom's casket where we stood for several minutes in silence.

The riptide of feelings within me left me limp. At the same time I was grieving the loss of my mom, I was blessed with the best friends a guy could ever hope for and a family that was finally coming together in love.

"Can I touch her?" asked DaShawn, interrupting my reverie. "Yes." I reached out and brushed Mom's cheek with the back of my fingers to show him it was really okay. "But she won't feel the same." DaShawn touched her cheek. "Ooo. She's cold."

An idea came to me—maybe DaShawn could read her obituary tomorrow at the celebration. That would be special, her great-grandson. But then I looked at my son. "Rodney, tomorrow at the service, would you be willing to read Grandma's obituary?"

"Me? You mean that thing about her life?"

"Yeah, like her biography."

His eyebrows arched as he shrugged. "Yeah, guess so, if you want me to."

"Um-hmm," Estelle murmured, giving me a little smile. "We'd all be honored, Rodney."

"Sure then. How long is it?"

"Just a page. I'll get you a copy before we go home tonight."

More people began streaming in—old friends and our few remaining family members, even some people I didn't know. Where had they all come from? How had they heard about my mom's passing? I tried to thank them all, but I'm sure I missed a few.

I finally sat, exhausted, on one of the sofas.

The hectic pace continued the next day, and we appreciated it when the pastor's wife and another woman from church brought by a ham, a pot of green beans, and some scalloped potatoes. "You need to eat at a time like this," First Lady Rose said firmly when Estelle tried to protest, knowing we'd end up with a refrigerator overflowing with leftovers after the repast.

We arrived at the church early Saturday afternoon, but the sanctuary was already half full with SouledOut folks, other friends, and people whose names I didn't know. SouledOut might be a storefront church, but it was nothing like those little run-down places back in the hood where I grew up. Its whole front wall was glass, like all the other stores in the modern Howard Street Shopping Center. The only thing obscuring passersby from seeing the rows of chairs full of worshippers and the praise banners hanging on the wall were the words, SouledOut Community Church—All Are Welcome, painted in large red letters across the glass. It's one thing to invite everyone in the parking lot to watch us raise our hands and dance as we praise the Lord on a Sunday morning, but it felt awkward to celebrate a homegoing so publicly. And with a big black hearse parked out front there was no way shoppers wouldn't be curious about what was going on inside.

Soft, recorded music played as guests paraded slowly by Mom's casket, two large floral arrangements standing at either end. As family, we remained in back, milling with those who were still arriving and receiving people's condolences. We also had to dodge out of their way as they hung their coats on the rolling racks that sometimes gave our church the appearance of a resale shop.

When Pastor Cobbs signaled it was time to begin, we slipped around the back of the congregation and through the double doors into the hall leading to the bathrooms and offices. There we organized ourselves to come back in as a family and process slowly down the aisle to the front row.

The first thing I noticed when I came through those doors was that the guy who usually played the keyboard in our church's little praise band was sitting behind a classic Hammond organ, playing a beautifully slow and soulful rendition of "I'll Fly Away." Oh my, Mom must be loving this. But where had that organ come from?

Once we were all seated, the men from House of Thompson closed the lid of the casket and placed a framed photograph of Mom on top of it. Pastor Cobbs stood up from his seat on the low platform and, looking up with his eyes closed, began to softly clap in time to the music. Avis Douglass, sitting on the other side of the platform, stood up and joined him, then began to sing, softly at first until we rose and joined in. "I'll fly away; To a home on God's celestial shore." Soon the tempo picked up, the clapping spread, and our voices rose with joy.

Yes. In my mind's eye, I could see Mom doin' a little shufflin' dance.

More praise and worship followed, during which I caught Pastor Cobbs smiling and nodding frequently at the keyboardist on that old Hammond. And then it hit me, Pastor Cobbs had arranged for that organ to be here. A good Hammond isn't cheap, and there hadn't been anything in the church budget about getting an organ. Maybe he'd rented it. But whatever, there it was . . . for Mom's homegoing. Again the tears streamed down my face.

God was so good, always looking out for even the smallest things when the time was right.

Avis finally concluded our time of praise and worship with prayer, and we all took our seats. I couldn't recall what came next, so I opened the program, which had my favorite picture of Mom on the cover with Wanda M. Bentley, 1922—2010 below it. On the inside left panel was her biography, or obituary, as the printer had called it. On the right was the schedule for her "Homegoing Celebration." I scanned down. Next came the Remarks and Resolutions of Condolence, followed by the Reading of the Obituary. I glanced down the row, past Estelle. Rodney had his head down, studying the program. I smiled.

My attention returned to a woman reading a resolution . . .

". . . Whereas, Wanda Marie Bentley was a member in good standing of Mount Zion Tabernacle for twenty-three years; and Whereas, she faithfully sang . . ."

I had no idea who the woman was, dressed in her white "Mother's" uniform, but she sounded like she was from way back. I checked the program. It did not reveal Mom's middle name—not that it was any secret—but hardly anyone knew her middle name these days.

"... Now therefore, be it resolved, that the Daughters of Mount Zion express our deepest sympathy to Wanda's son"—she looked at me—"daughter-in-law, grandson, great-grandson, and the extended family over their loss. Be assured, she will be missed. Respectfully submitted, Claudine G. Jenkins, Acting President of the DMZ."

I took a deep breath as the woman returned to her seat and someone else came to the front to share a favorite memory of Mom. I'd mostly known her as my mother, always there, always believing in me. But her life had reached much farther than I had imagined.

Rodney read the obituary without a stumble, but he kept glancing at me between paragraphs as though looking for my approval. I nodded and smiled to encourage him. I wondered how often over the years my son had needed that affirmation and I hadn't been there to give it. I winced; this being a good father business took more than a single turnaround, and I was still spinning.

Grace Meredith's rendition of "Give Me Jesus" was great, better—if that was possible—than on her CD. And Pastor Cobbs's eulogy powerfully honored Mom's Christian testimony. If anything, it was a winsome salvation message, inviting anyone who didn't know Christ to find meaning and peace in relationship with him.

After the closing prayer, we followed the pallbearers as they rolled Mom's casket up the aisle and out the front doors of the church. But after Rodney's reading, my mind was distracted, wondering how I could repair what I'd messed up so long ago. Wasn't that what Mom would've wanted? Do right by your son, Harry. Bring him back into the family, embrace him, believe in him, show him God's love until he too wants to be in relationship with him.

Chapter 29

GUIDED BY THE TWO MEN from House of Thompson, the pallbearers slid Mom's casket into the back of the black hearse and closed the large door. The driver shook my hand. "Beautiful service, Mr. Bentley. Your mother would've been pleased."

"Oh, I'm sure she is pleased."

"Hmm, yes indeed." He checked his watch. "Let's see, you're gonna have the repast now. Take a couple of hours, so we could have everything ready at the cemetery by 6 p.m. Does that sound good to you?"

I nodded.

"And you said just family, right?"

"Well, family and the pastor and a few friends. But no more'n fifteen."

"Okay. We'll have the chairs set up and expect you at six. Sun doesn't set until about seven-thirty." He glanced up at the sky. "Only a few clouds, so we should have plenty of daylight. Graveside services don't take long."

Rodney was strolling in the parking lot talking loudly into his phone, waving his other hand in the air. When I caught his eye, I beckoned him back to the church so we could start the repast. "Who was that?" I asked when he finally came, a heavy expression on his face.

"Ah, Donita again. She's only allowed to make calls from rehab on the weekend, so . . ."

"So, what? What's she want with you, especially at a time like this?"

"Just forget it, Dad. You wouldn't understand."

I sighed as we went in through the door.

That evening, by the time the interment was over and we got home, the house felt as dark and empty as if Mom had been living with us. Made me cling to Estelle in a long comforting hug while Rodney and DaShawn disappeared to change their clothes. "I hope everything was okay today."

"Better than okay, hon. I'm sure your mom felt honored."

"That's what I told that guy from the funeral home."

"What do you mean?"

I chuckled. "Well, he said he was sure Mom would've been pleased, like she didn't exist anymore. But I said, I'm sure she is pleased. Because I believe she was lookin' down and knew all about it."

"Um-hmm. I believe she was too, but . . ." She pulled me tighter and nuzzled my neck. ". . . I'm trustin' the Good Lord also turns off the lights sometimes."

"Well, he better." We broke our clutch with a laugh. "Hey, got any leftovers from the repast? I was so busy talkin' to people, I hardly ate anything."

Sunday afternoon, I asked DaShawn and Rodney to come with me over to Mom's old apartment. We needed to sort through all her things and clear it out soon. When I'd been there earlier looking for her will, I'd realized there were a few things of value as well as several sentimental things we shouldn't leave in an unoccupied apartment. We packed up her good china, silverware, jewelry, boxes of important papers, and photo albums and loaded them into the RAV4. Also took her TV and some small appliances, though most were so old, they hardly mattered.

Back at our place, while Rodney and DaShawn were carrying most of the things into our basement, I got the stepladder to put the toaster oven, coffee maker, and other appliances that the cold wouldn't hurt up in our garage attic. But once I'd climbed the ladder, I saw a couple of boxes I didn't recognize sitting off to the side on the plywood that spanned the attic joists. I pulled one to me, blew off the dust, and opened it. Within were several old framed photographs of people I didn't recognize—white people. There was also an old cigar box of army medals and souvenirs. Below all that was a stack of papers, thick envelopes, and tattered documents. I flipped through them and was surprised to find that most of them were addressed to Wilhelm and Matilda Krakowski.

It was the old lady's box. Amazing! The other box was probably hers too, because I couldn't imagine Estelle wearing any of the three hats inside.

I left Mom's appliances up there, and took the boxes into the house. "Estelle! Look what I found."

"Wait. Don't put those dirty old boxes on my counter." But once I'd set them on a wooden kitchen chair, Estelle was eager to see what I'd found. "Well, Lord be praised. Wait till she hears about this. You think she put 'em up there herself and just forgot?"

"Can't imagine her climbing up there."

When Rodney came in, he solved the mystery right off. The boxes had been on the closet shelf in the room he was using downstairs. He'd taken them out to the garage when he was painting and didn't know anyone was looking for them.

"Well, we have to call her." Estelle flipped through the coupons, notes, and reminders pinned to the bulletin board. "Oh dear. I have no idea where that phone number is. Any of you see a little note paper I pinned by the phone with the Don Krakowski's name and number on it?"

"Gramma, there's so much stuff pinned on that board—"

"I'm just askin'."

I stared at DaShawn, realizing this may have been the first time he'd called Estelle Gramma.

"Harry, when you called to invite her to come for that visit, did you use the number on that paper?"

"Nope. Used Krakowski's card that I had carefully filed on my dresser top."

"In that mess? You brought it from our old place? And just dumped back on your dresser after we moved.

I grinned. "And it's still there!"

"Hmph! Well, go get it, then."

A couple minutes later I came back into the kitchen, waving the card in my hand. Estelle rolled her eyes and grabbed it from me to make the call.

"Yes, yes, we found your mother's boxes . . . oh, no problem," Estelle said into the phone as she eyed me. "We'll bring them out to her. How would next Saturday do? Just tell us her address."

I think Corky was just as glad to get back to work Monday morning as I was. We worked the station that day and the next, and I caught up on some paperwork. Made sure I thanked Gilson for being so flexible with the time to see to my mother's affairs.

"Don't worry." He grinned at me as though he expected me to know why. "We'll get it back from you."

Yeah, he would too. "Maybe I can do an overnight Thursday and Friday."

"Good. Let me know."

I got right back to him with a plan, and he approved it without a second look.

Tuesday evening while we were eating supper, I commented on how accommodating Gilson was being. Estelle asked if I'd seen Grace Meredith during the day.

"No. Why would I have seen her?"

"'Cause she and her assistant left today by train for—"

"Yeah, and I drove her," interrupted Rodney as he scooped more mashed potatoes onto his plate.

"You what?"

"In my limo. Her name and address came up on the board, so asked the dispatcher if I could make that run. Kinda cool."

"Yeah, yeah." I grinned at him. "Hope you gave her good service."

"The best."

"So where's she goin' this time?"

"Harry! Seattle, of course. She's headin' out there for that big West Coast tour she told us about. I went over and prayed with her yesterday afternoon when I got home from work." Estelle looked real thoughtful. "Ya know, I think the train thing's gonna work out for her. You were a real answer to prayer."

"Me?" I was a step behind in this conversation.

"Yeah. Takin' the train was your idea. Until you mentioned that option, I think she was about to pack it in and quit singing. But she has a real ministry. God's gonna use that girl."

"Well, that's good." I finally felt like I was catching up. "She's got a voice, all right. Sure appreciated her singing at Mom's homegoing." Huh, wish I'd remembered she was leavin' today. Would've liked to see her off. But I wasn't likely to have run into her, big as Union Station was.

I looked over at Rodney again. Had been wanting to invite him to our men's Bible study, but hadn't gotten around to it with all the distractions. Seemed like this might be a good evening for it given that things seemed to be going well on his job, but I thought I'd ease into the invitation. "So you drive any other interesting people around today?"

"Not during the day, just some business people goin' here there. But guess who I'm drivin' tonight. It's gonna be a late one."

DaShawn perked up. "Who?"

"Derrick Rose."

"Whoa! Da Bulls," he said with exaggerated Chicago-talk. "Is there a playoff game tonight?"

"No, but he's going to this fancy fundraiser, and I get to drive."

"Dad! Ya gotta get his autograph for me!" By now, DaShawn was bouncing all over his chair.

"No can do, my man. It's against the rules for Lincoln drivers to ask favors of any customer, especially celebrities."

"Aw, Dad. Couldn't you maybe slip him a blank card with a Jackson Five wrapped around it? Just say it's for your kid?"

"Ooo!" Rodney's eyes got big in feigned shock. "Now the boy wants me to bribe the man. You gonna have me back in the joint before I dry off."

"That's right, DaShawn," added Estelle. "Your dad's got himself a good job. He's not about to do anything to put it in jeopardy."

So much for inviting Rodney to the Bible study this evening. At least he held firm about following his company's rules. I'd go meet with my brothers myself and maybe debrief a little more about Mom's passing.

The week settled back into a welcome routine, and on Thursday evening I ended up taking the Cardinal train down to Indianapolis, planning to return the next morning. I should've stayed at the Omni, but instead, after giving Corky a walk, I ended up at a flea-bitten hotel that was probably slated for the wrecking ball any day. They gave me all kinds of grief about having a dog until I insisted a service dog was allowed anywhere open to the public. Couldn't resist quipping under my breath to the manager that Corky was in more danger of being contaminated by the hotel than vice versa. I think he heard me, or at least got the drift of my comment.

When I got to my room, I sat down on the edge of the bed and leaned forward, elbows on knees. For the first time in a long time, I felt an old familiar temptation. Being alone in a strange town made me want to go out and find a bar, tip back a few cold ones, and find someone to talk to. Corky ambled over and sat on her haunches right in front of me, staring up, mouth slightly open, panting gently, her liquid eyes asking, "What's next, boss?" So trusting. She would have come with me or stayed in the room, no judgment. It was all up to me . . . but so were the consequences. The last time I'd fallen off the wagon had been when I was losing my sight and couldn't handle the terror of it all. What was my excuse now? That I had no one but a dog to talk to? How ridiculous. And yet . . . I wasn't under a lot of stress. Maybe I could handle just one . . . or two.

The last time I'd stopped by The Office I'd told myself I wasn't stressed then, either. But I'd ended up staggering home and admitting to Estelle that I had relapsed. I'd had to confess the whole incident. I knew it hurt and scared her, but she just said, "Well, I think we need to pray. Mind if I pray for you right now?" It was as though she understood my fear and the temptation and didn't define me by my fall.

What trust! I couldn't break that trust.

"Corky, go lie down. Go on now. It's time we both went to bed."

At six the next morning, I caught the returning Cardinal back to Chicago. Man! Wasn't sure how many of those short nights I could take. And how close I'd come to falling off the wagon stuck to me like a bad dream that took hours to wash off in the light of day.

Otherwise, the trips both ways were uneventful. Corky didn't find any drugs on the trip home even though the behavior of one young woman made me suspicious. She appeared unusually busty and kept adjusting herself in a way that didn't look natural or move like silicon. Wouldn't have been the first time significant amounts of cocaine had been smuggled in a supposedly padded bra. But even though we walked by twice, Corky didn't alert. Don't know what I would've done if she had. I was still undercover and there were no female officers around.

The Cardinal was late getting into Chicago, so it was after lunch by the time I filed my report and stuck my head into Gilson's office to tell him I'd see him on Monday.

"Oh, Harry." Captain Gilson called me back as I started to leave. "Just got an e-mail from the DEA." He picked up a printout from his desk and scanned down it. "They're developing intel on what they think will be a major shipment of cocaine from LA to Chicago on the Southwest Chief. They don't know when it's gonna ship, but it could involve several kilos. So . . ." He looked up at me. ". . . just wanted to give you a heads up on that. If they can't do the interdiction before it moves, we may need you undercover to locate the mule."

I nodded. "Next week, you think?"

He shrugged. "They don't know. But you might need to get out there on short notice. Probably'll need to fly you out."

"Fly? What about Corky?"

"Oh, she can fly. Put her in one of those airline kennels."

Corky wouldn't like that. And Estelle would like me being gone several days even less. But I couldn't help feeling a twinge of excitement as I drove home. "Whaddya think, Corky girl?" I eyed my dog in the rearview mirror as we jockeyed through the traffic. "We might get to see some big action after all."

Chapter 30

GOING TO ELGIN WITH ESTELLE on Saturday morning with Mattie Krakowski's boxes wasn't much of a spring drive in the country. For one thing, there weren't many open fields left in the thirty miles between Chicago and Elgin. Urban sprawl, corporate campuses, and housing developments had eaten up most of the farmland except for a stretch near Poplar Creek. At least Cook County had protected its forest preserves.

The weather was also dreary, drizzling all morning and overcast all afternoon, as spring sputtered to get started.

We found Hammond Manor on the east side of Elgin, not far from Lords Park. It was a converted three-story Victorian. As we climbed the front steps, I began to wonder how an old woman with a broken hip would fare with all those stairs.

Inside, an attendant took us up in a grinding, slow elevator to the second floor and down the hall to the small room Mattie Krakowski shared with another woman. The other woman was lying in her bed, watching the TV suspended high on the opposing wall. Mattie sat in a wingback chair on the other side of her bed, the only other piece of furniture in the room.

"You have guests, Mattie."

The old woman pulled her attention from the TV and looked up at us brightly as we crossed the room to the foot of her bed, but she obviously couldn't place us.

The attendant was still standing in the open doorway. "Would you like me to bring in a couple of folding chairs?"

"That's okay," I said, putting Mattie's box on the floor. "We won't be staying long."

Estelle frowned at me, then turned to Mattie. "Do you remember us, Mrs. Krakowski? We're the people living in your building now."

"Oh yes." Recognition flooded over her wrinkled face, washing away her bewilderment. "You did such a nice job fixing up my apartment. Will I be able to move back in soon?"

Estelle glanced at me before answering. "I . . . I think you'll have to discuss your living arrangements with your son, Don . . . or do you call him Donny?"

"Hmm, sometimes Donny. But he hasn't been by this week. Usually comes on Sunday."

"Then maybe he'll be here tomorrow."

"Does that mean today's Saturday?" She had seemed fairly alert, but I guess I could excuse her not being able to distinguish one day from another in a place like this.

"Yes, it's Saturday," assured Estelle. "But Mattie, do you remember why Don brought you to visit us a couple of weeks ago?"

"Oh yes, to get my box of pictures and papers from the basement. But . . ." A sad frown clouded her face. ". . . we couldn't find it. Don't know what happened to it. It was down there the last time I looked."

"Well, we have some good news for you. We found it." Estelle beamed as she nodded to me. "Harry."

"Is this what you were looking for?" I picked up the box and put it on the floor in front of Mattie, then knelt down and pulled open the lid. "It got moved out to the garage attic before you came, and no one remembered it was up there. We just found it the other day." Mattie leaned forward to look and then clasped her hands to her withered cheeks. "Yes! Yes! . . . That's our wedding picture. Oh, my. Wilhelm and I were only nineteen." She chuckled. "Both our parents didn't think we'd last, but we did, fifty-one years."

I stood up and sat down on the edge of the bed while Estelle kneeled down and went through the pictures and keepsakes with the old woman. Mattie had a story for each one, and Estelle listened tirelessly. I watched them, regretting my previous impatience. Estelle was so good with elderly people. I felt a renewed pang of loss. Would've been so nice if Mom could've lived downstairs and enjoyed the support of my caring wife.

Mattie's stories rambled on and on. I began to wish we'd accepted that offer of folding chairs when a bell chimed somewhere out in the hall.

"Oh." Mattie sat up, eyes wide. "That's the lunch bell." She pointed to her roommate who'd been glued to the soap she was watching the entire time we'd been there. "She can't get out of bed, but I'm up and around now. Would you like to come downstairs and have lunch with me? I can have two guests a month, no extra charge." She made a sour face. "But the food's not very good."

Estelle stood up with a groan over stiff joints. "Maybe some other time, Mattie. It's been so nice seeing you. Glad you've got your box now. Oh, by the way, we have another box out in the car. Has some hats in it. We'll bring it in before we go."

"Hats? I don't remember any hats. Maybe they belonged to someone else."

"We'll bring 'em in anyway, and if you don't want them, maybe someone else here would enjoy them."

Couldn't imagine anyone wanting those flowery things, but I kept my mouth shut.

Mattie rose slowly from her chair, steadying herself a moment by hanging onto it until she grabbed her cane hanging on the back. She raised it, pointing toward the door. "Don't really need this any longer, but around here, they make me carry it for safety. When I get home, I'm gonna retire it."

We accompanied her down the grumbling elevator. I ran out and brought back the box of hats. Then we said our good-byes, and left to grab something to eat at a Subway before heading back into the city.

We'd been cruising east on I-90 for fifteen minutes, lost in our own thoughts until I said, "She sure is countin' on returnin' to her old place."

"Yeah, sounds like all her memories are tied up there. Kind of a sweet nostalgia."

"Kinda sad, if you ask me. She's living for this fantasy."

We rode on in silence for another mile or so when out of the corner of my eye I saw Estelle lean forward and turn to me. "Harry, maybe it doesn't have to be a fantasy."

"What? Whaddaya mean?"

"Well, we have to do something with that apartment. I don't know what her finances are, but what if she could move back in?"

"Estelle! She couldn't make her payments before, what makes you think she could afford rent now?"

Estelle leaned back. "I don't know. It just seemed like . . . like it might be a God thing, ya know. Like he might bring her home to spend her final days there."

"Yeah, but you're . . ." I stopped myself from accusing Estelle of getting caught up in the fantasy. I loved her for the soft heart she had for elderly people, and I didn't want to crush that. "I just don't think it's practical," I continued. "But you're right, we do need to put it on the market soon. With Mom's passin' and all, we just haven't had time."

"You're probably right." Her voice trailed off.

But the disappointment in her voice got to me. It was a crazy idea. It would've meant another jerk around in my life. The old lady had to move out because she couldn't make her mortgage, so now she was gonna move back in? Nah! Wasn't gonna happen. But . . . a thought whispered in the back of my mind . . . wouldn't that be just like God?

Arrgh! Just give me a straight path, okay God? Besides . . . "Besides, Estelle," I said much too forcefully, "what about Rodney?"

My wife gave me an odd look. "Rodney? What about him?"

"Where would he go?"

"I don't know. You weren't thinkin' . . . Harry, we never promised him anything. In fact, at one point you were real clear that he couldn't even come."

I sighed. "I know, but . . . where's he gonna go? He's doin' good. Got a job. I'm thinkin' maybe it's not right to kick him out on the street."

"Of course not, Harry. I'm not sayin' kick him out. But he's grown. Don't you think we should at least raise the question of what's next?"

"All right. We'll ask him, but I don't want it to come across like we're tryin' to get rid of him. Been thinkin' 'bout how I wasn't there for him all those years. And now, when he's tryin' to do good, maybe the best thing would be for him to stay in that apartment where he's close to DaShawn—gotta think about him too, ya know. And we'd be right there to lend support and give him . . . give him—"

"Some free meals," Estelle offered, and we both broke into a hearty laugh, relieving the tension that had arisen.

"Ha. Remember that ol' cigarette ad, 'I'd walk a mile for a Camel'? Well, you can bet Rodney'd walk a mile—or more—for a little of your cookin'. We all would!"

"Yeah, yeah, yeah. But seriously, Harry, with his job, he could get his own place."

"Or pay for the apartment downstairs."

"On what he makes?"

I shrugged. "Well, we were gonna give my mother a break on the rent, charge her just enough to help us meet our mortgage. Why not give Rodney a similar deal?"

Estelle waited a moment as an airliner zoomed low over us and touched down at O'Hare Airport. Then . . . "You're serious, aren't you? Well, I'd be open to that if it's the right thing to do. But what we need right now is a little guidance from the Lord."

"Now, that would be great." The cynicism in my voice surprised me. "What I mean is . . ."

"Well, what do you mean?"

"I don't know." Maybe I needed to exercise trust.

But before I could say more, Estelle said, "Well, can we pray about it?"

"Oh, sure. That'd be good . . . but would you pray?"

I didn't know whether she was peeved at me or just collecting her thoughts, but after several moments, she began in a soft voice. "Father God, we thank you for how good you've been to us. We thank you for the beautiful home you've given us. And we want to use it to your glory. We don't know whether that space downstairs should be Rodney's or someone else's. But most of all we want your will. We want it to be used for your glory. And, Lord, we thank you for the good things that are happening with Rodney, and we pray that they continue. Don't let him fall back into his old life. Plant his feet on the solid Rock, Jesus, and you are that Rock. Bring him to you. We're askin' this in the mighty name of Jesus, Amen."

Estelle's prayer touched me. Whether Rodney lived downstairs or in some other apartment, the good things happening in his life might not last without a relationship with Jesus. I knew that's what he needed, just like I'd needed it. Lately, I'd been blaming God for derailing all my plans. But Estelle's prayer reminded me that it wasn't all about me.

I felt a sudden swell of love for my wife. Estelle always seemed to raise me up to be more than I'd be otherwise. That's how it'd been from the time we first met. It's how I knew she was the one for me. She saw me as the man God intended me to be and made me want to be that man—for her, for my family, for God.

I slowed for the tollbooth, but when I got back up to speed and had merged into the traffic, I prayed too. "Yes, Lord. We both want what's best for Rodney. Please guide us . . . and I wanna thank you for my dear wife." I started to choke up, but managed one more. "Thank You."

Chapter 31

I'M ONE OF THOSE DON'T-ROCK-THE-BOAT GUYS. Even if something needs attention, I'm liable to avoid a socially awkward encounter if the status quo is more or less copacetic and likely to remain that way. But if something's hanging fire that might blow us out of the water, I'm all over it. That evening, as we sat around the supper table while Estelle served some leftover apple crisp she'd brought home from the shelter, I looked for an opportunity to settle our future.

"Hey Gramma," DaShawn said, "can I have some ice cream on my apple crisp?"

"All we have left is rocky road."

"Works for me."

Estelle put DaShawn's dish down in front of him. "Anyone else?" By the time Rodney and I had opted in, DaShawn had finished his and was getting up from the table.

"Uh, DaShawn, where you headed so fast?"

"Shoot some hoops with Tavis."

"Hang on a bit. We got some family business . . ." I stopped myself. Perhaps this discussion was best had with Rodney alone. "That's okay. Go have a good time."

"Thanks, Pops." He carried his dishes to the sink, rinsed them, and put them in the dishwasher. "See y'all later."

"So, what's this about?" Rodney asked as soon as DaShawn had rumbled down the back stairs.

I glanced at Estelle as she put her first bite of ice cream in her mouth. "Well, with Mom's passin', we've all been busy the last couple weeks, but with the downstairs apartment now finished— thanks to you—we need to make some decisions about its use." I eyed Rodney to gauge his reaction, but he continued to calmly scoop the last of his apple crisp from his bowl.

"Anyway, Estelle and I were talkin' earlier today as we drove back from Elgin, realizin' with your new job, it's only right to ask whether you'd be interested in renting the first-floor apartment. 'Course we don't know how much you're makin' or anything, but we're willin' to discuss it if that's something you'd want."

Rodney slid his chair back from the table with slow deliberateness, leaned back, and crossed his arms as though he were contemplating the origins of the universe. "Well, ya know, I been thinkin' on that myself. First off . . ." He looked me in the eye with genuine warmth. "I really appreciate you askin'. I appreciate being able to stay here while I got my feet back under me . . . and of course, your cookin', Estelle. And nothin's been more important to me than gettin' to know my son again. He's becomin' a fine young man—"

"And you've been very easy to have around," added Estelle, nodding her head.

"Thanks. But uh . . . I've been thinkin' about another option. Grandma's apartment's still there, and it's a little smaller, more my size, 'specially since I don't make all that much. Maybe I could take over her lease. Think the manager would go for that?"

I thought Rodney would jump at the chance to rent the downstairs apartment. "If it's the money, we'd be willing to talk—"

"Appreciate that, Dad, but there's also all of Grandma's stuff— not my style . . ." He frowned. ". . . and some of it's fallin' apart, but if we could clean out her old clothes and take back the dishes and stuff, I could get by. I obviously don't have the cash to furnish a crib right now. So that'd help me out big time. And if I didn't have to come up with a security deposit, that'd be even better."

I glanced at Estelle. If Rodney needed furnishings, we could certainly let him bring Mom's stuff over here—he must've known that—and waving the security deposit seemed only right within the family. Maybe he had a deeper motive for wanting a little distance.

I found my voice. "Just outta curiosity, Rodney, if we could work everything out for you to be here, would you still rather have Mom's old place?"

"Well, yeah. I think so. You've done so much for me. I wouldn't want to be beholdin'."

"But if we could work it all out . . . why would you go there?"

He squirmed. "Well, like I said, less money, hopefully no security deposit, and it's furnished—if you can call it that." He laughed sheepishly, and then his face sobered, and he looked at me with a steady gaze. "But . . . I guess there is one more thing. I know you don't like Donita. I don't really trust her, either, but she's tryin', and she's been after me every opportunity she gets to give her a chance."

Donita!

Estelle saved me from saying something I'd later regret by leaning forward with her elbows on the table. "So you think you'd have a better chance gettin' back together with her if you had a space that was more your own?"

"Yeah. Guess that's about it. Dad's made it real clear she's not to set foot in this place." He looked at me.

He better believe it, and I wasn't about to back down.

"And I respect that," Rodney hastened to add. "If anything's gonna happen, I'm the one who should be takin' the risk. I ain't fixin' to put that on y'all, and especially not on DaShawn."

That was the first sane thing he'd said on the subject.

His face hardened. "Whatever goes down, I don't want DaShawn in the middle of it. I know that at the very least we're gonna need some time—and space—to get a whole lot of things straightened out . . . and we may never succeed—"

"And you probably won't." My held breath exploded like a blownout tire. "You know that woman's poison. She's crazy. Tried to get me thrown in jail. I think you're a fool to give her another chance." Rodney's eyebrows went up and he looked down at the table as silence settled between us. Finally, he spoke. "That may be, Dad. But I'll never know if I don't try." He looked up at me with a squint. "This is something I learned from you, ya know . . . in a backwards sort of way. You took the other path. You didn't give my mom a second chance, and look where it got us. So I'm gonna try this path. I'm gonna give Donita a second chance. It may not turn out any better, but . . . but that's what your choice taught me." He spread both arms, offering himself as an example. "I gotta try."

My bad example was causing him to go the other way? I wanted to argue. I wanted to remind him that his mom had left me, but I knew he was right. I'd driven her away. But . . . I'd been in no shape to turn things around back then. I was . . . an alcoholic who'd refused help until everything fell apart.

But a second chance for Donita? His use of those words shamed me. If God had forgiven me and given me a second chance, why couldn't I forgive Donita? Part of me wanted to, but I hadn't heard anything to indicate she'd come to the end of herself. I picked at a hangnail on my thumb and bit my lip while the room remained stuffed with silence.

"All right," I finally said. "I hear ya. I suppose I should tell ya it doesn't matter, that you can bring Donita around here if you want, but I'm just not there yet. I—"

"You don't need to say that, Dad. I'm not askin' to bring her around here, not yet anyway. And like I said, I want to keep some distance between her and DaShawn. You see, truth is, I don't trust her either. I'm just sayin', I gotta try, and Grandma's place is the perfect distance from DaShawn. I'm not lettin' Donita move in, so I can have DaShawn over when she's not around, keep workin' on our father-son thing." He grinned in a charming way that defused the tension. "I'll make gettin' a nice flat screen one of my first upgrades, and he and I can have pizza and watch games together."

"Well, when you get sick and tired of all that pizza," offered Estelle, "you're always welcome to slide your feet under this table."

Rodney high-fived her. "And you better believe I'll be takin' you up on that offer more'n you probably want."

I sighed deeply. "Well, if that's what you wanna do, I think we can work out a deal with the manager on Mom's apartment. That guy owes me for gettin' rid of some loud partiers a few years ago so he didn't have to do an eviction on 'em. And one other thing." I stood up with a wry grin on my face. "My name's Harry, and I'm an alcoholic." I sat down. "Seriously though, AA was my first step to gettin' sober. God finished the job, but I needed the support I got in AA. Every addict does. And you might consider checkin' into Al-Anon too. They've got a good program to support families of addicts."

Sitting in church the next morning, I couldn't help thinking of this latest zigzag in my life. It had taken me as much by surprise as a tsunami. I had to admit, not every unexpected turn had turned out as bad as it'd seemed at first. I'd been concerned not to make my son feel like we were kicking him out. Well, apparently he didn't feel that way, but . . . getting back together with Donita? That still seemed foolish to me. Still, his motives were good, and there was a chance his efforts would take him to a place where he realized his need for God. That had certainly happened to me when I hit bottom after trying to quit drinking on my own.

Wasn't there a Bible verse somewhere that spoke of God's ways being higher than our ways? What if all these events that I'd experienced as detours and derailments were more like a chess game? Maybe God had to move me and those around me through several steps before we were set up to make the good play. Could I have accepted buying our house, agreeing for my son to stay with us, going back into law enforcement, losing my mom, and having Donita show up again as God's plan if he'd told me ahead of time? Huh! I'd wanted him to show me a straight track.

While we were singing during praise and worship—I confess I wasn't paying much attention—the thought hit me: What if this wasn't the final destination for Rodney or for me? What if the rest of my life continued to be a series of unpredictable zigzags?

As the service progressed, my mind drifted even farther afield. What was next with my job? I mean, we needed the money and all, and workin' for Amtrak fit my skill set, but surely God's purpose was greater than a monthly paycheck. Maybe I'd raise the question with the brothers on Tuesday night: Why does God have us workin' the jobs we work?

The booming voice of the short black man behind the pulpit cut through my thoughts. "Why are you goin' through what you're goin' through?" He waited a moment, and then said it again. "Why are you goin' through what you're goin' through? Most of us don't know."

Whoa! I packed up my little inner dialogue and gave him my attention.

"Turn to Second Corinthians, chapter one, and read with me starting at verse three." He waited a few moments. "Paul's speakin' here when he writes, 'God is our merciful Father and the source of all comfort. He comforts us in all our troubles so that we can comfort others. When they are troubled, we will be able to give them the same comfort God has given us. For the more we suffer for Christ, the more God will shower us with his comfort through Christ.'"

He read on through verse seven, and then went back to unpack them. "What you're goin' through is probably because God has something to teach you—but did you ever think it might also be for someone else? If you meant it this morning when we sang, 'If You can use anything, Lord, You can use me'"—I barely recalled singing the song—"then you gave the Lord permission to take you through a multitude of experiences that'll not only transform you, but equip you to minister to other people. You see, God doesn't waste anything!"

"That's right, Pastor, that's right." Voices all over the room shouted agreement.

"Don'tcha know, he's the great recycler. He doesn't waste a thing. That's what Paul is talking about here. He comforts us in all our troubles so we can comfort others. Too often we think everything's about us. Well, I've got news for you. It's not!"

Embarrassed laughter skittered through the congregation.

"God wants you to be able to understand and sympathize with what's happening to other people, so when you see them goin' through it, you can help them the same way God helped you."

Was Pastor Cobbs looking right at me?

"So how do we make it through what we're goin' through? The answer's in verse five. 'God will shower us with his comfort through Christ.' Did you get that? It comes through Christ. Usually when we're goin' through, all we can think of is, get me outta here, when we should be sayin', give me Jesus. Give me more of him. That's where the comfort is. That's the only place you'll find it. And that's the only sure comfort you can pass on to others."

Whatever Pastor Cobbs said after that was probably good, but God was talking to me. I'd started to get the message when listening to Grace Meredith sing, "Give me Jesus. You may have all the world, give me Jesus." That had helped me see I needed to focus on Jesus rather than the zigzags in my life. But I'd still been bewildered by how often I felt yanked around. And I still felt the need to understand what was going on and how it all worked together.

Maybe it was okay if I still didn't understand it all. If I could get my comfort from seeking Jesus rather than wrestling everything to the ground, then maybe I was being equipped to pass the same comfort on to other people. Give me Jesus.

Braving a light drizzle, I put on my rain jacket and took Corky for a long walk that afternoon, still thinking about what Pastor Cobbs had said. If Pastor Cobbs was right that God is the great recycler, then maybe I had more to offer Rodney in dealing with Donita's addiction than I realized . . . if I could get over my raw mistrust of the woman. But . . .

"Corky, get over here. Don't be digging in other people's trash. Come, now! I don't care if there's half a Big Mac in that sack. Get your nose out of it." I gave Corky's leash a tug and went back to my thoughts as we continued through the alleys.

Who was I to tell Rodney anything about what was right or wrong or how to live his life? I was the guy who'd let him down. Maybe I needed to start there, confessing the truth about who I was, not just by standing up and saying, My name's Harry, and I'm an alcoholic, but much more seriously. The real comfort God had given me over my failure as a parent was the second chance he'd given me. He let me be a father to DaShawn and gave me the opportunity to turn to God as my Father. Had I ever told Rodney about that?

My dogged efforts to understand every little thing happenin' to us hadn't brought much comfort. I needed to focus beyond myself, beyond where I was going to live, or what was happening to Mom, or why my son had returned. I needed to keep working on seeking Jesus and trusting that he was in control.

Maybe I simply needed to share with Rodney how God was comforting me now and not come across as someone who had all the answers.

When Corky and I got home again, Estelle was on the phone. She pressed the mute button. "It's your boss. He tried your cell, but you didn't pick up."

I reached for the home phone, realizing I'd probably forgotten to turn my iPhone back on after church. "Yeah, Bentley."

"Hey, Harry, just got word from the DEA. They think that big shipment is movin' in no more than a couple days. So, when you come in tomorrow, we need to do some planning. You might have to fly out to LA anytime this week. Just wanted to give you a heads up so you aren't out on some short run. According to the DEA, this is really big, so we gotta be on it."

I glanced sideways at Estelle. She wasn't going to be happy about this.

"Okay, Captain. I'll check in first thing."

Chapter 32

I DROPPED CORKY OFF AT THE AMTRAK KENNEL and went straight to Captain Gilson's office the next morning.

"Take a seat, Harry, and I'll try and bring you up to speed." Gilson scrolled through some e-mails on his computer. "Ah, here it is. Got this from the DEA last night saying the cocaine—that test shipment we talked about—was coming through in the next two or three days. I phoned them right back for details."

"Who we talkin' about here? Individuals or street gangs?"

"That was my first question too. Most of the Drug Train traffic comes from the gangs, some individuals. But this is different. This is the Sinaloa Cartel—"

"Sinaloa? Son of a . . . Wait! If the DEA has someone on the inside of the LA cell, that's huge. Why don't they just raid the place? Maybe they'll get lucky and cap their great leader"—I waved my arm expansively.—"Joaquin 'El Chapo' Guzman."

Gilson matched my gesture with a dismissive flick of his wrist. "El Chapo stays in Mexico. My guess is the DEA's a lot more interested in its Chicago operation than LA."

"Why's that?"

"LA's just one cell in the Southwest. There's San Diego, Phoenix, Albuquerque, San Antonio—lots of cities not that far from the border. But El Chapo himself has called Chicago his 'home port.' Given the fact that Sinaloa is the largest cartel in the world, Chicago becomes its most important transportation hub. We already know Sinaloa has been sending freight cars full of marijuana to Chicago. But they always diversify, and now it looks like they're opening up a new pipeline, like an octopus regenerating its arms."

I shook my head. "Octopus, huh? So what good will it do to snip a tentacle?"

Gilson shrugged. "Point is, this is a big deal. Potentially tens of millions. The DEA wants our help, and we sure don't want Sinaloa using our trains. I mean, they kill people, lots of 'em. They're known as the most violent cartel in the world. Can you imagine what would happen to our ridership if people heard Sinaloa was using Amtrak? We gotta nip this in the bud."

"All right. So, what's the drill?"

According to Gilson, the DEA liked my successful cover as a blind man, but they wouldn't be able to provide backup on the train. "Maybe it's better that way," the captain said. "We don't want one of our trains turned into a shooting gallery. We gotta nail this mule as quietly as possible."

"Okay, so give me his description."

"Uh . . ." Gilson grimaced. "That's the other thing. The DEA mole has no idea who it's gonna be. But since this is a test shipment, they expect it'll be a fairly large amount and carried by someone high in their organization. A real prize if we can bust him. Might be able to turn him and blow open their Chicago organization."

I blew out a long breath. "So, we have one of the most violent cartels in the world makin' a big run, and I have no idea who the bad guy is?"

Gilson clapped his hand and pointed a finger at me like a gun. "That's why you have Corky. She still behaving herself?"

"Yeah, she's good."

"Okay. Stick around the station today. Study mug shots, get to know the Sinaloa, do your homework. I'll keep you informed. But be sure to keep your phone on. Didn't like not being able to reach you yesterday."

"Sorry 'bout that. Won't let it happen again." I got up and started for the door. "Say, shouldn't I be able to expense my cell phone?"

"Actually, Amtrak will provide you with a phone if you want, but it'd be nothin' like that baby you've got."

"Then why would I want it?"

Gilson laughed. "You just catch the bad guys, Bentley, and I'll see what I can do about reimbursing your phone."

Monday I went through mug shots and read reports on the Sinaloa Cartel. They were even worse than the media portrayed them. The Mexican police and military were so afraid that they wore ski masks and bandannas as they stood behind sullen gang members in arrest photos. They feared reprisals. Given the bruises, puffy faces, and cut lips, it was obvious the police had worked over some of the arrestees. Still, all the cartel members looked brutish even in the photos they put up on the Internet to brag of their exploits. And they bragged. They even used a fleet of aircraft—including a 747—to fly drugs from South America to Mexico before shipping it to the States.

In the afternoon, I took Corky and worked the luggage room and cruised the station, but Tuesday morning I went back to studying photos. These thugs had a similar look—several were related—but I wanted to memorize their distinctive faces, especially since many had bribed their way out of prison and one of them could be my mule. But by afternoon, I was getting bored. Of course, I knew that was the nature of police work—hours of mind-numbing boredom interspersed with minutes of absolute chaos and terror.

I was looking forward to my Bible study that evening. Figured I could ask the guys for prayer without revealing too much of what I was up against. And I also hoped to take Rodney. But when I got home, he was out working.

"But," Estelle said, "he wanted to know if you'd called the manager of your mom's building yet. Told him I'd ask you."

I appreciated her gentle reminder. I called at work the next morning while I was again just waitin' around. After a little arm-twisting, the building manager agreed to put Rodney's name on the lease without raising the rent or charging him an additional security deposit.

By midmorning when Gilson hadn't yet called me, I took Corky into his office. "Hey, Captain, Corky here wants to know when she gets to go out to Disneyland."

He shrugged. "Nothing yet. In fact, when I called last night, they said it might be put off until the weekend."

Figured. Hurry up and wait. "So, can I take a short run today? I'm not doin' much good around here."

He laughed. "You're keeping Corky on her toes, aren't you? Actually, I'm not as worried about keeping you busy as I am in having you in position on that Southwest Chief when the mule decides to come this way. To be honest, I'm feeling nervous about the quality of the DEA's intel." He grabbed a notepad and a pencil. "At the very least, we'd have to have you at LAX by 4:30 p.m. to catch a cab to Union Station, pick up a ticket, and get on the 6:15 Chief." He looked up at me and grinned. "Even then, you'll be running."

I snorted. "Blind men don't run through busy train stations, especially when they don't know where they're going and have to ask for help." Gilson was off on one of his fantasies again, and I was determined to keep his feet on the ground or I'd be the one to disappear in a puff of pixy dust.

"Uh, right. Okay, add an hour. And use a Red Cap." He scribbled some more on his note pad. "That means you'd need to be at LAX by 3:30, so you'd have to catch a plane out of O'Hare about four and a half hours before that, though there's a two-hour time difference."

By the time we figured in the time it'd take to get to O'Hare, buy a ticket, check my weapon identifier code through the TSA, and the time it would take to get Corky checked in . . . "Oh, and you'll need time on the other end to take her for a walk."

"Okay, okay. Now you got me all confused."

"Don't worry. I'm keeping track. You'd have to leave here by 9:00 a.m." He took a deep breath and arched his eyebrows. "And that's presuming there are no delays."

I shook my head. "Sounds impossible to me."

"Hmm. Unless they give us a full twenty-four hours notice. So I'm thinkin'—"

"It don't make sense to wait for their call," I injected.

He grinned. "Exactly. I think we oughta send you out tomorrow morning to get a jump on this thing. You can get in position and be rested. If nothin' happens Friday or Saturday, you can take Corky to Disneyland."

I didn't feel like going tomorrow and just sitting out there in some motel, but waiting for the DEA's call sounded worse. "All right. Tomorrow it is."

✧   ✧   ✧   ✧

Rodney was delighted that evening when I gave him the news about the apartment. I shrugged. "Looks like you can move in whenever you want."

"Thanks, Dad. I'll go by the manager's office tomorrow and sign the papers." He turned to Estelle. "Think you could come with me in the afternoon to clear out some of Grandma's stuff? I'll give you a nice ride in a limo."

"You can do that?"

"Not if I get a call. But the boss allows minimal personal use of the car provided I pay mileage."

"Can I help you move? I can be home from school before four." DaShawn hadn't said much at the news of his dad moving out, and Rodney hadn't explained about Donita. Made me wonder whether that would cause DaShawn to think his dad wanted to get away from him or didn't care about him. So I was relieved at Rodney's response.

"You bet, son. And if I can get that apartment set up, how 'bout goin' to a Cubs game with me Saturday afternoon? They're playin' the Arizona Diamondbacks. Should be a good game."

"Can we go in the limo?"

"No way. We'll take the 'L'."

While I was helping clean up the kitchen after supper, Estelle said, "I called Leroy today, and he didn't sound too good. I think we should go see him."

"That'd be a good idea. With the house and Mom's passin', it's been weeks."

"More like months. Makes me feel bad."

"When were you wantin' to go?"

"Saturday?"

"Sure, you should go. But I can't come."

"Whaddaya mean?"

I told her about my trip. She got real quiet. Finally, her big eyes all sad lookin', she said, "I know it's your job, Harry, but I don't like it when you're away overnight. So, what's 'a few days' mean?"

"Oh, I think you should still go see Leroy, 'cause—"

"That's not what I asked. How long're you actually gonna be gone?"

I explained this depended on the DEA, but avoided mentioning the cartel and the danger of going up against them. No need to scare her. "But once I'm on the train, it'll take two nights, about forty-one hours . . . if it's on time."

"So . . . you'll be home Saturday?"

I winced. "But probably not in time to go with you. See, we don't exactly know. I might have to wait in California a day or two before headin' back. It all depends on when the drug runner decides to make his move."

"Well then, what's your best guess for when you'll get home?" I shrugged. "DEA is guessing the run'll be this weekend."

"So you'll leave there Friday and get home Sunday?"

"Maybe, but it could be later . . . look, babe, I'll phone you regular and keep you informed."

"You better phone me . . . every day. But how do the train conductors and crews manage these long runs? Do they have families?"

"Oh, yeah. Lot of 'em do." I was beginning to sense this wasn't about me accompanying her to visit Leroy. "For the crew, it's two days out, sometimes a layover, and two days back—five days."

She sighed and her eyebrows went up. "Well, you know that's not the way I like it." We stood there, staring at each other, not knowing what to say.

"But then they get five days off," I finally offered.

A mischievous grin slowly melted her features. "Five days, huh?" She whipped the end of a dishtowel around me, grabbed the other end and reeled me into a tight clinch. "So, what're we gonna do with your comp time? Should be a whole week when you add the weekend." I could see her mind spinning. "Want me to take the time off work? We could go on a short cruise. They're always advertising those last minute specials."

I grinned back at her. With the swirl our lives had been in lately, we needed a rest, a real rest. But a cruise? "Ah gee, babe. I'd just be getting home from one long trip, might not be very eager for another. How 'bout a few nights in nice hotel downtown? We could take in a play, listen to some jazz, go to the Art Museum. There's lots of stuff we could do. Wanna ride a Segway again?"

"Not on your life, Harry Bentley. You got me on one of those two-wheeled things once, and that's enough."

I chuckled. "Well, it got you to say yes to marryin' me. Thought I'd try for a rerun."

"No way! Like you said, I'm a married woman. Don't need any more of those kinda thrills."

"Okay, okay. But don't schedule anything until I actually get back. With this kind of an operation, you never know until it's over."

Chapter 33

ICALLED HOME THURSDAY EVENING just to say I'd arrived safely and had checked into the Great Wall of China Motel. "It's not got much in the way of amenities," I told Estelle. "I think they call it the Great Wall because the whole thing's made out of concrete blocks. But it's clean and only a few blocks from Union Station. Oh, and bein' right here in Chinatown, there's some great-looking restaurants around."

"Well, tell me if you like their breakfasts."

"Why? What's the matter with breakfast?"

"Oh nothin', but I prefer a Danish and coffee, myself." I heard her take a deep breath. "So when're you comin' home, Harry?"

"Just got here, babe. Still waitin' for the green light, ya know. But I'll call you as soon as I know."

We chitchatted a while longer, but I could tell she was already feeling lonely. I was too.

I wanted to try one of the restaurants I'd seen in the area, but didn't know whether to take Corky or leave her in the room. She was legally welcome anywhere, but I didn't think I wanted to spend my whole time in LA fighting for the rights of handicapped people.

Finally, I decided. "You stay, Corky. I'll bring you back something nice. Then we'll go for a walk." Found a nice restaurant, and ordered seafood bean curd soup, moo shu chicken, and spicy stir-fried greens with garlic and shitake mushrooms. It was awesome and far more than I could eat. But it wasn't much fun having a fancy meal alone.

The next day I had lots of time on my hands, so I decided to try reading the Bible. It's something I genuinely wanted to do at home, but I often got distracted. Here, I had plenty of time with no interruptions, but I still couldn't engage. What a sorry Christian I made. It was God's Word, after all. Ha! Reminded me of the disciples who couldn't watch and pray in the garden on the night of Jesus' betrayal. I looked up that story in Matthew 26. It wasn't very comforting to read how disappointed Jesus was when he came back and found the disciples sleeping, but apparently he understood. "The spirit is willing, but the body is weak."

I sure didn't feel honored to be in the company of the disciples in this regard, but to realize Jesus understood meant a whole lot. I dropped my head in my hands. "O Lord, I'm sorry. I have heard your voice on other occasions, and I can say, 'give me Jesus,' and really mean it, but . . . I'm still not connecting. So I'm askin', please be with me in the next few days even though I don't know how to be with you."

Corky nudged me with her nose as if saying amen.

When I called Estelle Saturday night, I still didn't have any news.

"Harry! Feels like it's dragging on forever. Is there only one train a day? Does that mean you won't be back until Tuesday?"

"Afraid so. I'm really sorry, babe. But if I'm still here by Monday, I'm gonna insist Gilson pull the plug on this operation."

"Monday? Well, he better pull the plug by then! And you can tell him for me, it doesn't sound like they know enough to even put you on that train. They oughta fly you home . . . Oh, here's DaShawn. He wants to say something to you."

There was noise as the phone changing hands. "Hey, Pops. You shoulda seen that game today. Cubs pulled it out after being down three to the Diamondbacks."

"Really?"

"Yeah. Soriano homered. Then Derrek Lee delivered a two-run single. Cubs won seven to five."

"Wish I could've gone with you and Rodney. How you guys doin'?"

"Oh, we're cool."

"Is he all moved in to Great-Grandma's place?"

"Yeah, an' he said I can sleep over sometimes on the sofa."

Things were changing back home and I was two thousand miles away.

"Hey, let me speak to your gramma again."

Once she was on the line, I said, "Just wanted to catch up a little more. Did you go down to see Leroy today?"

"Yeah. He seems to be doing okay." I could hear the longing in her voice. "All his burns are healed, but in some places the skin's still so thin. The nurse was encouraging though. Said he might be able to move out of the nursing home by midsummer. But I don't know, Harry, all the meds he's on keep him in kind of a fog."

"We'll find somethin' for him, babe. God'll help us." And as we ended our call, I believed it too.

Sunday morning Corky woke me from a sound sleep whining to go out. I pulled on my pants and got her outside in time, but her stools were as loose as soup, and she needed to go out four times in the next couple hours. The leftovers I'd brought back to the motel must've made her sick. Thankfully, by noon she seemed okay.

Then my phone rang. "Bentley. It's a go for tonight's train! Get yourself in position, and keep me informed. You might even snag the guy in the station."

"Any description on the perp yet?"

"Nada, nothin' at all."

"All right. I'll call you once I'm on board."

I hung up and called Estelle right away. She was one happy lady. "But pray for me, babe. Gonna need it to find this guy."

After packing, I took Corky for a good long walk. Much to my relief, she seemed fully recovered. Back at the motel, I left her in the room long enough to check out, making sure the security latch on my door was flipped over so it wouldn't close all the way and lock me out. When I returned, I slipped Corky into her harness with the words, "Guide Dog," on its side. "Well, old girl, here we go." I rubbed my hand over my head to make sure it didn't need a shave, then put on my plaid flat hat and mirrored shades. We exited the room as a blind man with his seeing-eye dog. Behind me, my small, black suitcase rolled clickety-clack, clickety-clack over the joints in the sidewalk.

No one paid us much attention as we walked the mile along North Broadway toward Union Station. The smell of fried prawns and crab rangoon sizzling in hot oil gave way to exhaust fumes from the busy street, finally masked by the sweet scent of the bougainvillea growing in sidewalk planters. A few clouds were collecting overhead, but I'd had enough days in the California sun to last me for a while, so I didn't mind.

It was tempting to gaze up at those tall, spindly palm trees or study the beautiful mosaic of blue-and-white glazed tiles lining the arch of the station's main entrance, but I couldn't appear to be a man enjoying the sights. Still, I couldn't help but notice the Spanish architecture of stucco walls and high-beamed ceilings inside the station. It rivaled the magnificence of the towering Corinthian columns, solid limestone, and marble of Chicago's station.

Travelers crisscrossed every which way, heading to and from trains, buying tickets, and picking up food and magazines from concessions, looking for arriving passengers. To my surprise, cops were everywhere . . . not Amtrak police but TSA agents, Los Angeles County Sheriff's deputies, and teams of private security guards, patrolling in units of two to four men. They appeared outfitted for battle—bulletproof vests, web belts crammed with extra clips, cuffs, riot batons, cans of Mace, radios, and some serious weapons.

I made my way cautiously through the main waiting room. Finally, I took a seat in one of the large leather chairs with high backs and sturdy wooden armrests. They were custom-built antiques, adjoining one another like theater seats, and so big I felt like a little boy sitting in a grandpa's chair.

Corky stiffened, and I glanced down to see if she was alerting. But it wasn't about drugs. A K-9 unit was coming our way—two deputies and a German shepherd half again as large as Corky. As they got closer, I half considered letting them know that I was on the job too, but they veered away before I said anything. Across the hall, I saw another K-9 unit, this one with a black lab like Corky. What was going on? Had the DEA turned out the troops to catch this same Sinaloa mule I was after? It looked like they were expecting a war.

Then a greasy-haired kid came by on his skateboard, and Corky alerted immediately. And no wonder—the kid cupped a lighted joint between his thumb and forefinger. I could smell the smoke from ten feet away. I watched as the boy swerved through the crowd, heading right for the K-9 unit with the German shepherd. But when he got near them, the German shepherd barely glanced at the kid. And the deputy merely gave him a hand signal to get off his board. No riding in the station.

They weren't here for crowd control or to bust druggies.

I got up and walked with Corky to the restroom, passing another cluster of four deputies while meeting another pair coming my way. Standing to the side of the restroom door, like a valet at a hotel, was an older man dressed like a farmer, or maybe a shepherd with a staff. The staff, which was at least a foot taller than he was, was an ornate cross with the words "Jesus Saves" carved on it. He wasn't talking to anyone or even looking them in the eye. Just standing there holding up his sign. Guess that was something.

About forty-five minutes before my train was to depart, I started speaking randomly to anyone close by, acting as though all I could do was hear or sense their presence. "Excuse me. I need to catch the Southwest Chief to Chicago, could you help me find a Red Cap, someone who could take me to my train?"

"I'd love to help," said a woman hurrying past, "but I'm about to miss my own train." But when she'd gone about twenty feet beyond me, she began calling to a guy emptying a trash can. "Sir, sir, could you help that man back there?" She pointed my way. "He's trying to find a Red Cap."

"I'm no red—" The janitor saw me and waved to the woman that he was on the case. Within five minutes, a Red Cap helped Corky and me get on board an electric cart, driving us through the station and down a long corridor to my train. I felt guilty using the service some truly handicapped person might need.

As I rode along—the cart emitting its annoying beep, beep, beep to warn people it was coming—I realized I didn't see any more cops, not one, whereas a half hour earlier, I'd counted over twenty.

Obviously, something had been going on. Those dogs hadn't been sniffing for drugs. Probably searching for explosives. Made me feel insecure to have no idea what had just gone down. But apparently, the crisis had passed without incident.

Captain Gilson's secretary, Phyllis, had booked me in an accessible bedroom on the lower level of a Superliner sleeping car, in keeping with my cover. Mine happened to be right behind the engines and baggage car.

Since I was the first person to board, my car attendant went out of his way to help me get settled. Eyeing Corky as she curled up on the floor beside me, he raised his voice as if blindness equaled hearing impairment. "Now over here is your basic washbasin—hot and cold running water. Just press the levers. And on the side, the yellow-lighted button—oh, sorry—anyway, you can feel an emergency call button on the side here. Press it anytime you need me. Then comes the toilet. There's a curtain behind it if you want to draw it for privacy, but—"

"Carl—is that what you said your name was?—I'm not totally blind. I can see light and dark. In fact, I can see that you're standin' over there by the door."

"Oh, yes sir. Sorry."

Corky groaned and stretched out on her side while the attendant frowned at her. "Your dog okay?"

"She's fine."

"Hmm. Well, if you need anything . . . Actually, there are little braille labels on everything. And the shower is just down the hall, second door on your left. You'll find plenty of towels in there on the shelf."

"Thanks. I'm sure I can manage. I've ridden the train many times, and I've been able to find my way around. Just one thing, how far back is the dining car?"

"Oh, you don't have to worry about that, sir. I'm glad to bring you your meals—"

"How far?"

"Third car back. This is car four thirty-one, and there're two more sleepers behind us, then the dining car. After that comes the observation . . . I mean, the lounge car. The snack bar and café are on its lower level. All the rest are coaches, four I think." He hesitated. "Well, if you don't want me to bring you your meal this evening, do you want me make a reservation for you?"

"That'd be great. How 'bout seven? Now . . . don't want to hold you up any longer. You probably have more passengers comin' along soon. But I appreciate your help, Carl. I really do."

"No problem. I'll put you in for seven, then. But what'll you do with your dog when—"

"Don't worry about her."

"Okay, but if you need anything, anything at all." He backed out of the compartment, starting to give me a wave and then stopping.

I shook my head and turned to my window as hundreds of first class and coach passengers began to stream along the platform. Carl was out there by the door, ready to welcome the other first class passengers assigned to 431. With the tinted windows of my compartment it wouldn't be easy for people to see in, but I still kept my shades on as I watched them dragging luggage and hanging onto children, trying to figure out where they were supposed to go.

I studied each face. Who was my mule? Who was the man who carried hundreds of thousands of dollars in cocaine or meth or heroin? The dozens of mug shots and photos I'd studied of cartel members flicked through my mind, creating a morphing composite of a heavy-faced, stockily built Hispanic man with short, unkempt black hair and wary eyes, mustache almost always, sometimes a short-cropped, jawline beard.

Suddenly, Estelle's question came to mind: "You sure it'll be a man?"

No . . . no, I wasn't sure. I needed to keep my mind open. I started watching the women too.

And then I saw her . . . the woman who lived across the street—the singer, Grace Meredith. She was walking up to Carl, holding out her ticket!

Chapter 34

Iwatched as Carl handed the tickets back to Grace Meredith and an attractive young black woman standing with her—probably Grace's assistant. To my relief, he pointed the two women on down the train to another car. The women set off, each pulling a large and a small piece of luggage while juggling other items like a couple of porters. Why hadn't they hired a Red Cap?

I released the breath I'd been holding. At least they weren't getting on my car . . . but they were on this same train! How could that be? I'd forgotten about Grace's West Coast tour. It must be over, and they were headed back to Chicago.

I couldn't hide in my room. I had a job to do, and it meant sweeping the whole train until I found the mule and the drugs. Surely Grace Meredith would spot me and break my cover. My flat hat and shades and blind man act wouldn't be enough to prevent recognition.

At the very least, I had to know where they were riding. Maybe I could avoid her. I jumped up. "Come on, Corky. You need one more walk." I grabbed the handle of her harness.

Out in the hall, a passenger was standing in the vestibule wrestling with his luggage, so I feigned not being able to see as I felt my way along the wall and stopped in the open doorway. Carl checked another passenger's ticket. "Coaches are down that way, ma'am."

Stepping onto the platform beside him, I looked blankly over his shoulder just in time to see Grace Meredith and her friend step aboard the sleeper, two cars down. Whew! Thank you, Jesus, I sighed.

"Oh, Mr. Bentley, is everything okay?"

"Yeah. But . . . I was just wondering whether I could give my dog one last walk before we pull out."

239

"Well, the relief area's not very close." He looked around. "But I suppose I could take her over to those open tracks if she just has to pee, but . . ."

I almost snorted. Carl was trying to help, but he obviously didn't have much experience with service dogs. "When's the first rest stop?" I asked.

"Uh . . . the first scheduled break's Flagstaff, Arizona, but that's not until four thirty in the morning."

I'd seen what I'd come out to see. "Don't worry about it, Carl. We're prepared." I leaned closer, intentionally awkward. "I brought pee pads. We'll be fine." I turned and followed Corky's lead aboard the train.

Back in my compartment, I closed the door and paced back and forth. Then I sat down and called Gilson.

"Hey, Harry. How's it goin'? You got him yet?"

"Oh, yeah. Grand jury's convening as we speak. Should have this wrapped up in about twenty minutes."

"Funny. What's happening?"

"A bit of a complication. There's a woman on this train who knows me."

"She made you yet?"

"No. Hasn't seen me, but I've seen her. It's my neighbor from across the street back on the block. She's a traveling singer on her way home from a concert tour, I think."

He swore, then remained quiet a moment. "Guess you'll have to find a way to fill her in on what you're doing and swear her to secrecy. Can you trust her?"

"I s'pose. But I don't like complications."

"Harry, there's always complications. You know that."

"But I don't like 'em showin' up this early."

"Suck it up, man. When's the train leave?"

I checked my watch and looked out the window. "We're startin' to move right now."

"Okay. Just get the bad guy, and keep me informed."

Within minutes we were creeping along the bank of the Los Angeles River. The channel looked like a below-grade expressway with a water slick in the bottom and gang graffiti plastered along the concrete banks. Too bad trains had to enter and exit cities through their ugliest corridors. Except for rural towns, almost all trains passed through depressing slums, abandoned factories, and cluttered freight yards before they got to a station. And while those classic old stations might be impressive, they didn't erase the unpleasant memories of what you went through to get to them.

I unsnapped Corky's handle and gave her a scratch, then punched Estelle's number into my phone. "We're on our way, babe. But do you remember when the woman from across the street's supposed to get home from her singing tour?"

"Grace? Sometime this week, I think. Not sure she told me the exact day."

"Well, she's on this train along with her assistant."

"Really? Oh, Harry, that's great. You'll have someone to talk to. I've been thinkin' how lonely it must be for you out on a job like this where you aren't havin' meetings or goin' to conferences like most people who have to travel on their jobs."

"Not so great, Estelle. I'm workin' undercover, remember. Can't risk her giving me away and blowin' the whole case."

"Oh, she wouldn't do that."

"Not intentionally. But you know how some people are. They just can't keep from talkin' when something unusual is going on. That's why I called you. You've gotten to know her better than I. You think she can keep her mouth shut about something?"

There was a silence on the other end of the line. "I'm sure she can, Harry. She's had more practice keeping a secret than any one person should've."

Huh. Wondered what she meant by that. "Well, that's good. Still, I hate to bring her into it. But I'll probably have to. Pray for us. I'm gonna need it."

"Of course, Harry." There was a moment of silence, and I was about to give Estelle my love and say good-bye when she started to pray. "Father God, we come to you right now, asking for wisdom for Harry and discretion for Grace . . ."

My wife continued praying fervently that all would go according to plan and that we'd remain healthy while mingling with so many people in a small space and eating food that might not agree with us. Finally, she said, "In the mighty name of Jesus, amen." I had to smile. That was so like Estelle, speaking to the Lord without any formal hesitation, reminding me the Lord was just that close.

I thanked Estelle while secretly thinking "remaining healthy" might involve far more than she realized. Busting the Sinaloa Cartel was far more serious than trying to scare a few college students straight or nabbing a kid with a suitcase full of grass. The Sinaloa Cartel had filled mass graves in Mexico with their enemies.

And I was about to make myself one of them.

The sun had set, silhouetting the palm trees and hills against the iridescent blues, pinks, and oranges of a cloudless sky, when the dining steward's voice came over the PA inviting those holding seven o'clock reservations to come to the dining car.

I snapped Corky's handle back on her harness. "Okay, girl, here we go." She jumped up at the word go, tail wagging.

This was my first time staying in the lower-level accessible bedroom. It made sense, not only because of the length of the trip and the chance for me to have a few moments when I didn't have to act blind, but because there was a good chance such a high-level mule would travel first class. Once car attendants got to know their passengers, it wouldn't have been easy for me to roam through their sleeping cars unless I too was in first class. I had no intention of breaking my cover, not even to Amtrak staff to explain my mission. But first class created its own challenges. The compartments had doors that closed and curtains that pulled.

When I got to car four thirty-three, the one I'd seen Grace Meredith enter, I proceeded carefully. I didn't want to face her until I was ready, but I wanted to know what compartment she was in. The little roomettes seemed too small for two unrelated people to travel in comfortably, so I focused on the five bedrooms. There was a family bedroom on the lower level—on the other end of the car from the accessible bedroom—but it had four beds.

The door to Room E was closed and the curtain pulled sufficiently so I couldn't see in. I listened. No sounds from within.

Room D was open and empty. I checked behind me to be sure no one was coming and stepped in. No luggage, no personal items on the sink, and the pillows and Amtrak schedules on the seats seemed undisturbed.

The curtain over the door window to Room C was open enough for me to see the legs of a heavy man elevated on the footrest of his seat. His trousers were badly wrinkled, and the heels to his shoes worn down at an angle.

I slowed to listen to faint music from Room B. Grace was a musician, perhaps . . . Then the sound of dialog and a laugh track confirmed that someone inside was watching a movie. Sounded like a kids' movie. I looked down at Corky. She gazed back, wagging her tail, as if to say, "You said go, this isn't go, so when are we going?"

One more room. I was almost there, when the door slid open and a middle-aged white couple came out and looked at me, an embarrassed expression spreading over their faces. "Hello. Do you want past?"

"No, that's okay. You go ahead."

I waited for a few moments while they went on toward the dining car.

Three rooms eliminated. But I still wasn't sure whether Grace and her friend were in Room E or Room B. I kept going. The pneumatic door whooshed open, and I stepped from the third sleeping car across the clattering, windy connecting section, pressing the plate that opened the door to the dining car. Waiting just in front of me was the couple from Room A. The woman looked back anxiously at Corky, but I stared straight ahead as if I hadn't noticed.

Within a few moments, the dining steward beckoned for the couple to proceed and be seated at a table a third of the way down the car. Then he summoned me with a wave and turned to walk on past the galley area toward the other end of the car.

I was looking forward to this meal. Amtrak's food was good, and one of the most enjoyable parts of a train journey was meeting new people with whom you shared a table. So far no one had objected to Corky sitting under the table on past trips, but there were always a few awkward moments while they figured out how to talk to a blind person. Awkward or not, I was eager for a little conversation, not having spoken to anyone except by phone for three days.

But the steward had only beckoned, so I held my place until he turned and realized I wasn't following him, and then he saw Corky standing by me. He finally figured out my shades weren't merely because I was trying to be cool. Coming back, he spoke in muted tones. "If you'll follow me, sir, I have a seat for you at the other end of the car. Feel free to grab the backs of the seats to steady yourself as you go."

I followed, trying not to appear too confident of where we were going. But we had no sooner passed the galley area in the center of the car, when a tentative voice called out from the first table on the left, "Mr. Bentley?" and then with more urgency, "Mr. Bentley, is that you?"

Grace Meredith was sitting in that first booth with her back to the galley divider. She'd only seen me as I passed. I kept walking without acknowledging her. Several feet beyond, the steward said, "Your table is here on the right, sir. I'll be back in a moment to go over the menu with you."

"Uh . . ." I stopped in the aisle. "I want to go on through to the lounge car. Don't need a table right now."

"I'm so sorry. I thought you were here for dinner. Go right ahead." He stepped aside, leaning a little into the empty booth to give me room to pass.

A whoosh and another whoosh of the sliding doors, and I was safe. It was tempting to look back through the door windows to see what Grace was doing, but I couldn't risk it.

Sitting down in one of the lounge chairs, Corky at my side, I went over what had just happened as my heart rate returned to normal. That was close, but not something I could've foreseen. And I had learned something valuable: Grace Meredith was in Room E.

Chapter 35

M Y STOMACH GROWLED WITH HUNGER. So much for a good meal in the dining car. I made my way down the winding stairs to the café in the lower level of the lounge car. It wasn't easy going up and down those stairs with a guide dog. They just weren't wide enough for side by side. But we'd worked it out so she'd lead going up and follow coming down while I held onto the railing.

"Yo, brotha, what can I do for you?" I recognized the voice from the PA that announced the Amtrak services and rules—especially, absolutely no smoking—when we first got underway.

"Well, whatcha got?"

"Bunch of stuff you wouldn't want. But we got dogs and burgers, barbecue chicken sandwich, pizza—"

"No pizza. I'm from Chicago and learned my lesson the hard way tryin' to eat pizza from anyplace else. How 'bout a cheeseburger and fries?" I could see the menu on the wall behind the attendant, and it didn't include fries.

"Sorry. No fries. Chips come with it, though."

In a few moments I was at a table by myself with a cheeseburger, chips, and a Pepsi, thinking about my next move. My first priority was making sure Grace Meredith wouldn't blow my cover. But I couldn't do that until I could speak to her alone. She and her assistant would probably be at their table for close to an hour. I could quickly finish my burger and walk to the rear of the train and back by then. In spite of my theory that the mule might be in first class, I needed to check the coaches.

I finished my meal with an Almond Joy bar, went back upstairs, and turned toward the rear of the train, walking slowly to give Corky a chance to catch the scent of any drugs.

"Okay, girl," I said as we pressed through the junction doors. "Now the coach cars."

Searching the lower areas in the coach cars was always awkward because I couldn't walk straight through. When I got to the last seat, I had to turn around and come back, feigning the confusion of a lost blind man. Often passengers offered to help me find my way, and I'd have to thank them but disengage as soon as possible.

I saw several passengers who fit my profile . . . kinda. But three of them had families. One was sleeping next to his girlfriend all cuddled up to him. In each instance, I reminded myself that the real mule didn't have to fit any profile. But Corky didn't respond to any of those people, and none of them exhibited any other suspicious behaviors.

We got all the way to the back of the train and turned around and came back without Corky alerting on any passenger.

In the lounge car, I took one of the observation seats near the front. I could see into the dining car from there. Grace and her assistant were still at their table. I relaxed, swaying with the rhythmic movement of the train, probably causing some people to wonder why a blind man was taking up an observation seat. I didn't care, and it was almost dark outside anyway.

My attention drifted back to my walk through the coach cars. We weren't looking for marijuana. Cocaine or heroin could be carried in a much smaller container and stowed, perhaps, in the overhead luggage rack. If it were sealed tightly enough, maybe Corky would miss it. What then?

Suddenly, I noticed the two women getting up from their table. I ducked my head, but it was unlikely they'd notice me in a completely different car. Sneaking a peek, I caught my breath. I could see the young black woman coming my way.

I swiveled my chair away from the door as it whooshed open, hunching down as much as possible. Corky lay on the other side of my chair. If she didn't move, they might not notice her on the dimly lit floor. I kept my eyes on the reflections in the dark window. Grace's assistant passed, but Grace didn't appear, and her assistant continued heading down the aisle of the lounge car. I glanced her way as she sat down in one of the sofa-like seats, her back toward me. Where was Grace? I turned. She wasn't anywhere in the lounge car. I looked again at the assistant. She was opening a paperback book, making herself comfortable.

Thank you, Jesus. He was answering Estelle's prayer.

Rising quietly, I took Corky's harness handle, left the lounge car, and passed through the dining car, wishing for a moment that I could've had one of those juicy steaks other passengers were enjoying.

Moving into the first sleeper, I tapped lightly on the door of Room E.

"Yes, who is it?"

I just tapped again, not wanting to announce myself to neighbors who might overhear.

The curtain over the door window moved aside, and Grace stepped back with a start, then cautiously slid the door open.

Making sure that no one was in the hallway, I removed my shades. "Can I come in, Miss Meredith?"

"It was you!" It was somewhere between accusation and relief. Her dark eyes remained wide as she looked me up and down.

I put my finger to my lips and raised my eyebrows to renew my request to come in.

"Of course! Come on in. What in the world are you doing here?"

Corky and I stepped in, and I slid the door closed behind us. "Sorry to bother you."

"No problem. Here . . ." She quickly zipped a brush and small cosmetic bag into the teal-blue piece of luggage that was open on the sofa and put it on the floor. "Sorry. Have a seat." With a nervous gesture, she brushed her long, dark hair away from her face and sat down in the opposing seat.

I released Corky, who immediately began nosing around the room.

"Didn't mean to ignore you in the dining car, Miss Grace, but you almost gave away my cover." A bewildered look flashed over her face, so I hurried on. "You know I do security for Amtrak. Right now I'm riding some of the trains as an Amtrak detective, and this is my cover. I need to ask you not to speak to me or acknowledge me in any way. Or your friend either. She . . . doesn't know who I am, does she?"

Grace shook her head. "She knows your wife, but I don't think she's ever seen you. And she thinks I was totally off base thinking I knew someone on the train."

I nodded. "Good. Keep it that way. Wish I could stay and talk, but I should move on. I'm two cars ahead in the handicapped compartment."

Corky, who'd been investigating everything in the room, came up to her. "You mind?" I asked.

"Not at all. Such a sweet dog." She reached out her hand, and Corky licked it.

I stood up. "Yeah. Corky's my partner. But please don't interact with her out in the train." I put my shades back on. "Well, I'll be seeing you around." I emphasized the word seeing with a grin. "Just don't be offended if I don't speak to you during the rest of the trip."

"Of course."

"Come on, Corky." We left, and I slid the heavy door shut behind me.

Whew! Over one hurdle . . . I hoped.

As I started to leave the car, I recalled my speculations that the mule might travel first class. Corky hadn't picked up any scent as we'd passed through the upper levels of all three first-class sleepers, but we hadn't checked the lower levels except for my car. "Let's go back, Corky."

We returned to the center of Grace's car and clambered down the circular stairs. The door to the accessible bedroom was open. I stepped in there first. It was clearly unoccupied. We were headed to the other end to check the lower roomettes and the family room when Corky sat down so firmly she nearly jerked her harness handle from my hand. "What is it, girl?"

She was alerting into the common luggage area, a space nearly as large as a roomette with seven or eight large suitcases lined up on edge on the floor and as many more stacked like bricks on the two sturdy shelves above.

"Which one, Corky?" I whispered, glancing around. If there was anyone else on the lower level, they were behind closed doors in their roomettes or in the toilets. With a quick glance, I saw that none of the little amber "occupied" lights glowed above the shower and toilet doors, and one door even flapped open and shut a few inches with the sway of the train.

Corky pointed to a large teal-blue rolling case. I pulled it out—it must have weighed close to fifty pounds—and Corky followed it with her nose. And then I saw the name on the tag: "Grace Meredith, 7333 Beecham St., Chicago, Illinois."

I straightened up, dumbfounded. Grace? How could that be?

There was no question what Corky thought. I tried to redirect her back to the bags remaining in the compartment. She obliged for a moment, sniffing here and there, but gave it up to return to the big blue travel bag.

A knot formed in my stomach. I had to confirm whether this suitcase was dirty, but no way did I want to find out that Grace Meredith was the mule. O God . . . please no! How could she be?

Okay, okay. Calm down, Harry. First things first. Check it out all the way.

I looked again to be sure I was alone and then rolled the heavy bag into the empty shower room. "Come on, Corky. Get in here." I slid the curtain back and pushed Corky into the still-dry shower stall while I sat on the small changing bench, staring at the case. It was definitely the mate to the smaller case that had been open on Grace's sofa.

Hearing someone outside, I slid the lock closed with a click and waited. Whoever it was entered one of the three toilets. I heard water running.

There was nothing to do but open Grace's suitcase. I unzipped it and began running my hands through layers of dressy clothes, a coat, three pair of high heels—the obvious attire of a concert performer—and a couple of books, then felt the heat of embarrassment creep up my neck as I checked a bag of underwear, probably headed for the laundry. Nothing there . . . or there . . . nothing in the shoes. I checked all the zippered pockets. Nothing.

"You gotta help me, Corky. If it's in here, I can't find it."

Stepping gingerly out of the shower as if she understood my problem exactly, Corky began sniffing at the backside of the suitcase. Then she sat down in the alert position again.

"Back here? There's no pouch back here." I rubbed my hands up and down the flat back of the case and could feel several lumps within. Was that just clothes and shoes pressing through? But the lumps seemed too smooth and even.

I snapped my fingers and pointed into the shower stall. "Get back in here, girl. There's not enough room out here." She obeyed, head drooping as if she thought I was disappointed with her.

I stood up, took off my hat and wiped my shaved head. I was sweating. I couldn't stay forever in this shower. Was I going to have to empty the whole bag? And then it struck me. The telescopic handle retracted into a thin pocket down the back of the case. It had to be protected from the clothes or the handle could snag items and become tangled, unable to extend or retract. The divider protecting the handle created a virtual false bottom in the case.

Forcing my hand down through the opening designed for the handle, I found there was room for my whole arm to go in. I reached deeper and felt several smooth tubes, like flattened sausages. I pulled one out through the hole. Fifteen inches long and weighing perhaps two pounds, it certainly wasn't sausage encased in that black, shrink-wrap plastic. I made a tiny hole in one end with my pocketknife. A lab would have to confirm it, but from all my years of experience, I'd bet my career it was pure cocaine.

I blew out a long breath. "We got 'em, Corky. Good dog."

Feeling inside the back of Grace's suitcase again, I counted five more tubes. At a kilo each, the haul could have a street value over a million and a half. Those DEA guys were right. This bust was worth all the trouble we'd gone to, especially if the cartel was just opening up this pipeline.

But Grace . . .? I carefully slid the tube I'd examined back into her suitcase and adjusted its position so it wouldn't be noticeable to any casual viewer. Surely she wasn't involved in a scheme like this!

Chapter 36

I SAT IN MY COMPARTMENT, head in my hands, unwilling—unable—to believe Grace Meredith was a drug runner for the Sinaloa Cartel. Corky hadn't detected anything suspicious about her or in her compartment, not even that piece of matching luggage. But the scent had been strong coming from the big suitcase, and Grace had been handling her luggage less than two hours ago. Surely it would've contaminated her enough for Corky to detect something. No, she couldn't be the mule.

Despite my attempts at profiling, I had calculated that a mule might be sophisticated, professional—someone who appeared above suspicion. Well, who would attract less attention moving drugs around the country than an upstanding, white, contemporary Christian singer? No one would suspect her, and she traveled regularly. I coughed a laugh at myself. She had a better cover than I did! I considered myself good at detecting guilt in a person's eyes, their body language, and evasive comments, but she hadn't exhibited any of those signs.

No, it didn't make sense! She couldn't be the mule. But . . . how had the drugs gotten into her luggage?

I needed to cast the net wider. Maybe it was her assistant. I pulled a pen and small notebook out of my jacket pocket and made a list of everyone who might've had a chance to hide drugs in her luggage. Grace was at the top of my list, but I added her assistant—Sam, I think her name was. Who else? Uh . . . the limo driver in LA would've handled the bags. Could he have slipped something into Grace's bag? Maybe if he'd moved fast while they were getting seated and he was loading the luggage in the back. But he'd have to know where she was going before picking her up. And if they could arrange for another driver to pick her up on the

251

other end, the mule wouldn't even have to be on the train. Let an innocent citizen do their dirty work.

Another possibility was an Amtrak employee. They handled people's luggage all the time without question.

But I kept coming back to the obvious. A wily drug runner had hidden the drugs in Grace's luggage for the duration of the trip to be retrieved at the other end. He'd gambled—probably accurately—that her cosmetics, overnight items, travel clothes, and everything she'd need for the trip would all be in the smaller suitcase so she'd have little reason to get into her big case down there on the lower level. But how and when would he retrieve the drugs? And how could I catch him?

My mind churned. Perhaps just before she detrained. The train attendant would be distracted helping people, collecting pillows, emptying trash, cleaning and straightening up the train for the next run. The mule could come down to the luggage compartment and retrieve his packets without suspicion. No harder than a pickpocket lifting a wallet.

The more I reviewed my theory, the more certain I became that I'd figured out the method. But the biggest question still eluded me: Who was the mule? I had to catch him with the drugs or I'd do no more than confiscate a delivery. I had bigger plans.

I looked down at Corky. "We gotta move, girl." She jumped up, ready for anything. "We need to be where I can watch that luggage, night and day. We gotta switch to the handicapped compartment in car four thirty-three."

There was a knock at my door. I sat down and put my shades back on. "Yes?"

Carl poked his head in. "Mr. Bentley, I was wondering if you wanted me to make up your bed now."

I almost looked at my watch. Only at the last moment did I feel the top as if it were a Braille watch—I'd have to get a real one before someone caught me and blew my cover.

"No thanks, Carl. But I have a different favor to ask of you. I need to move to another car."

"Is something wrong, sir?"

"Well . . ." The train whistle accommodated by blowing at just that moment, something it did three times before every crossing. "You hear that?"

"Hear what, sir?"

"The whistle. You're probably so used to it that you don't even notice. But with my . . ." I raised my hands to my shades. "I've become very sensitive to sounds. I'm just sayin' . . . I don't think I could possibly go to sleep this close to the engine with the whistle blaring like that all night. Would it be possible to transfer me to the last sleeper car?"

"The last?"

"Yeah, car four thirty-three's the last sleeper, right?"

"That's right, but I don't know, Mr. Bentley. I don't have any authority to do that." I knew he didn't, but I just waited for him to figure out something. "Even if there's an open room, it might be reserved for someone getting on later. It's all computerized." Again, I waited, leaning forward expectantly. "But . . . well, I guess I could check with the conductor. He's the only one who could make such a switch."

"That'd be great." I reached for my wallet and pulled out a ten for his trouble.

"Oh, thank you very much, Mr. Bentley," he said as I handed him the bill. "I'll get right on it." He started to leave and then turned back. "Say, if you don't mind me askin', how'd you know what to give me?"

I laughed. "I don't mind, Carl. I know in what order I put the bills in my wallet. I gave you a ten . . . right?"

"Ah, yes, a ten. You're right, it's a ten, and thank you again, sir."

That ten must have greased the wheels, because forty-five minutes later I was settled in my new handicapped-accessible compartment waiting for my mule to come to his bait, almost giddy with my progress on the case.

When Sylvia, the African American attendant in my new car, came in to make up my berth, I said, "The top one, please."

"Are you sure? We usually only make up the top berth for a passenger's assistant. It's safer if you're not trying to climb up there."

"Yeah, I know. But I don't have an assistant, and I'm not gonna fall. Thing is, I'm not ready to go to bed yet, so I'd like my seat down here to remain functional."

"Okay. But don't blame me if you have trouble getting up there."

"I won't."

As soon as she left, I fed Corky and got her settled on the floor. After turning out my lights, I jammed a magazine in the track of the door to keep it open about four inches and went to my seat to see if I had a clear line of sight to the common luggage area. Perfect. No one would be able to mess with Grace Meredith's suitcase without me seeing them.

A few people came down the stairs to use the toilets or shower, but no one bothered Grace's luggage as the train ventured into the Mojave Desert. Lights from the Marine Corps supply depot flicked past my window as we got going again after a brief stop in Barstow. It'd be two and a half hours before the next stop in Needles, and I was getting sleepy.

This was not going to work. I couldn't stay on watch for the next forty hours. I needed help.

I called Gilson's cell phone, and when he answered, I tried to explain my predicament. All he heard was the good news that I'd found the drugs. "That's absolutely phenomenal, Bentley! I'm gonna put you in for a commendation."

"Thanks, Captain." Maybe this time I'd get some credit. "But we gotta catch this guy with the drugs or we got no case."

"You're losing perspective here, Bentley. You've got the drugs, you know who the luggage belongs to. Let's set up an arrest in Albuquerque. We got a cracker-jack detective there. I think I told you about Brian Conway, covers the whole southwest. He's as good as they get . . . like you. Look, you won't get there until noon tomorrow. That'll give him plenty of time to coordinate with the DEA. We can arrange a targeted interdiction that won't scare any of the passengers. It'll be—"

"Captain, it's not her!"

"Whaddaya mean?"

It took me thirty minutes to convince him that I couldn't arrest Grace Meredith without more evidence. He still thought she was my mule, but he finally agreed to continue surveillance.

"And that's what I need your help with. You keep telling me about the guy in Albuquerque. You think he could get me some high-tech hardware by the time we get there tomorrow? I need to set up some kind of an alarm system. Can't stay awake for the next forty hours like an owl watching a gopher hole."

"Hey, you're the one who wants to drag this out."

"Come on, Captain, work with me here."

He finally gave me the cell phone number for Detective Brian Conway.

I called Conway as soon as I got off the phone with Gilson and told him exactly what I needed—a wireless motion detector I could set up in the luggage compartment that would send a radio signal to a receiver in my room if someone reached in. The receiver needed to have an audible alarm to wake me up. Conway promised to see what he could do and meet me in Albuquerque.

"But if you're undercover," he asked, "how'll I recognize you?"

"Ha! I'm the blind guy with a guide dog. You got an animal relief area, don't ya?"

"Blind detective, huh? That's a new one. Yeah, we got a relief area, little grassy yard on the north end of the main building. Meet you there."

I sighed with relief when I'd hung up. If I could set it up correctly, I could get some sleep. In the meantime, all I had to do was to remain awake for the next twelve or thirteen hours.

Did I dare call Estelle this late at night? She was two hours ahead, one-thirty in the morning her time. I punched her number.

"Hey, babe. Everything's okay, just wanted to—"

"What's the matter? You safe?"

"Yeah. I'm fine. I'm really sorry to be callin' in the middle of the night, but you know how sometimes you can't go to sleep and just need to talk to me?"

"Sure, sure . . . What's this about? What's happening, Harry?"

"Well, I just need to talk. You mind?"

I told her about finding the drugs but didn't tell her they were in Grace Meredith's suitcase. Just said I had reason to think the owner of the suitcase wasn't the real mule so I needed to continue surveillance until I caught the perp red-handed. "But I'm fallin' asleep on the job, so I just needed to talk for a while . . . could use some prayer about this too."

After we hung up, I felt much better, but Gilson's doubts about Grace Meredith's innocence troubled me.

Chapter 37

As my nighttime vigil progressed, I couldn't help dozing off for a minute or two here and there. Worried that I might miss my mule, the memory of the Naperville bust for which I got no credit stirred in my foggy mind. This fish was much, much bigger, but if I didn't stay awake, it would be my fault we didn't catch him. I looked down at Corky. "It's just you and me, girl. And we can't let 'em get away.

I went for some low-tech reassurance. All had been quiet out in the hallway for hours, so I told Corky to stay and went out to the luggage compartment. Reaching in across Grace's suitcase, I set a small paper cup on the back edge, leaning against the wall. If anyone moved her luggage, the cup would fall off. Appearing to be nothing more than a piece of trash, I doubted the mule would even notice it.

Comforted by my partial trap, I dozed a bit more. When we stopped for a few minutes at Flagstaff, Arizona, at four thirty in the morning, I took Corky out to relieve herself in the dog run. It was a risk leaving my post, but I hoped the cool air would wake me up.

By morning, the cup was still in place.

Shortly after six, I heard movement upstairs. Probably Sylvia making fresh coffee. Soon, the passengers would be up and about, and it'd be even less likely for the mule to touch his cargo.

I cocked my ear. Someone was coming down the stairs. I put on my shades and stood just inside the partially open door as Grace Meredith, dressed in a dark green lounging outfit, stepped off the stairs and turned my way without even glancing at her luggage. She was carrying toiletries and clothes and after she passed through the vestibule, she reached for the handle of the shower-room door.

Perfect. A chance to get more background information from her.

I slid my door open farther. "Hello? Who's there?"—deciding to stay in character. Her eyes got big, and it took her a few seconds to respond. She blushed, maybe embarrassed at being caught with a bedhead and not yet dressed for the day. I smiled and gave a little wave to assure her everything was okay.

"It's Grace Meredith from Room E," she said, playing along with my cover.

"Uh, miss, would you mind getting me a cup of coffee? I'd ask the attendant but I don't know where she is."

She smiled, seemingly enjoying her role-playing. "Of course. Give me a minute."

She walked back down the little hallway and put her things on the luggage compartment shelf before bustling up the stairs. When she returned a couple minutes later with a cup in each hand, I motioned her into my compartment and closed the door.

I took off my shades and we sat down in the opposing seats underneath my unused bunk—how was I going to explain that to Sylvia?

"You caught me by surprise," she said quietly, sipping her hot coffee. "I thought you were in a different car."

I shrugged. "Asked if I could move. The train whistle was just too loud in that first sleeper."

I needed to explore my other theories, especially how she engaged her limo drivers. Was there any chance the cartel had known enough about her trip to mark her for their carrier? I decided to begin on ground that was a little closer to home. "My son said he gave you a ride to the train. Did you ask for him?"

She tentatively shook her head. "I think he saw my name on that day's list of pickups and asked for the assignment. Nice of him. Said he'd pick us up when we got back too."

Hadn't expected that. If limo drivers were involved, then the cartel would likely need a dirty driver in Chicago to retrieve the drugs. But . . . my son?

Grace was still talking. "I really appreciate Estelle, Mr. Bentley. Your wife . . ." Grace hesitated. "She has really helped me face some things spiritually."

I chuckled and gazed out the train window, arrested by the dazzling brilliance of the sun shining on the towering red cliffs as we crossed the Arizona-New Mexico border. "Yeah. That sounds like Estelle. She's a rock, that woman." As solid and beautiful as the sculpted cliff I was gazing at. But my thoughts spun to the news that Rodney had arranged to pick Grace up in Chicago.

"Mr. Bentley," Grace said suddenly, bringing me back to the conversation at hand. "How'd you know Estelle was the one—you know, the person you were supposed to marry? The two of you seem to have a very special relationship."

I didn't have to think long on Grace's question. I smiled and looked back at her, the vision of Estelle's strong character fresh in my mind. "Because when I'm with Estelle, she makes me feel like a complete person. Like I can be who God wants me to be. She believes in me, even when I don't believe in myself."

I almost missed the tears glistening in Grace's eyes as she finished her coffee and stood up. "I should probably get my shower. Thanks, Mr. Bentley."

I rose and let her out, more certain than ever that Grace was innocent. No conspirator in a high-rolling drug deal could talk so personally about love and life with a police officer if she were guilty.

But as I slid the door nearly closed, I felt like my legs had been knocked out from under me. Had I been so off in reading Rodney? The idea of my own son arranging to pick up Grace in Chicago made me quake.

I postponed Sylvia's curiosity about my unslept-in bed by folding it up out of sight by myself, and when she appeared at my door, I asked if she would bring my breakfast on a tray. So much for the joys of socializing with other passengers. I had a suitcase to watch.

Even though it was daylight, extra cups of coffee barely kept me awake for the next couple hours, and I was never more pleased to roll into a train station than when we arrived in Albuquerque. Did I dare leave my watch for the full thirty minutes we'd be there while the train was refueled and serviced?

It was a gamble, but I figured if the mule was going to detrain here, he would've retrieved his fortune earlier, when people wouldn't be coming and going through the vestibule at unpredictable moments.

"Ah, come on, Corky. I'll give you a good walk."

As I waited in the vestibule while other people detrained for a break at Albuquerque, I could hear Sylvia directing passengers to concession stands nearby that sold Native American art and crafts.

"Hello there, Mr. Bentley. Comin' out for a little fresh air? Watch your step, now. There's a stepstool first. Then you'll be on solid ground."

"Yes. Thank you." I stepped down as she positioned herself to help me if I needed it, and took a deep breath of the cool air, turning my face upwards. In spite of a few scattered clouds, the warm sunshine felt good. "Can you tell me where to walk my dog?"

"Certainly, and I'll bet she's really ready for one too." She smiled approvingly at Corky. "Just cross the tracks and go straight ahead to a concrete wall, turn right and follow it until it ends. The yard'll be down some steps on your left."

Asphalt fill at various intervals along the empty tracks indicated where pedestrians and vehicles were supposed to cross, but in a display of my "blindness," I intentionally headed to the side of one those crossings where I'd have to step down onto the railroad ties, over the rails and ballast, and up on the other side.

"No, no, Mr. Bentley. Not there. You're liable to fall." Sylvia came running up and grabbed my elbow. "Here, let me walk you."

I thought I'd performed a good demonstration for her and all the other passengers milling around on the platforms. But as Sylvia led me to the animal relief yard, I wondered if I'd made a mistake. Wouldn't a real guide dog have directed his master away from the open tracks and over the intended crossing?

Hopefully, no one put two and two together. It seemed to have worked for the moment.

I had just unsnapped Corky's D-handle to let her run freely in the yard when a voice behind me said, "Harry Bentley?"

I turned to see a stocky white man of about fifty leaning casually in the arched doorway of the adjoining building. I drifted his way. He was as bald as I was but sported only a stubbly gray mustache. When he pulled back the edge of his Arizona Cardinals' warm-up jacket, I saw a gold Amtrak Police shield pinned to his chest and his sidearm holstered on his belt.

"Detective Conway?"

He nodded and lifted a tan, Home Depot plastic bag toward me.

"Home Depot, huh?" I chuckled. "That's pretty clever." I looked around to make sure no one could overhear us. "No one would guess you were delivering high-tech spy equipment to me in a Home Depot bag."

He shrugged. "They wouldn't have to, 'cause that's where this came from."

"What? What's in there?"

"You asked for a motion detector. And 'Spies-R-Us'..." He snarled the name and made a sinister face with one closed eye like a pirate. "...wasn't open yet.' So... had to make do with Home Depot."

"But couldn't you... what about the FBI? Surely they could've—"

"This'll work, Bentley. Believe me, I've tested it."

"What is it?"

"It's a wireless, remote motion detector, intended for home use, but . . . The receiver plugs into a 110-volt outlet in your compartment. But the detector itself uses double-A batteries— already put 'em in. I also cut off the back mounting bracket so you can stick the thing flat against the wall with the 3M Command Strips I included, sticky on both sides. They should hold it. When the detector broadcasts a radio signal, your receiver will beep. You can adjust its volume loud or soft... or turn it off. Simple as that."

"That's it?"

"What else you want? An eight-hundred-dollar price tag? This'll do the job, and it only cost forty bucks."

I looked around to be sure again that no one was observing us, then took the bag. "Thanks. Hope you're right."

Committed as I was to this mission, I felt like throwing up my hands. I'd been expecting to play Agent 007 with real high-tech spy tools. What a comedown. Probably just ego, though. I knew simple was always better. If Conway's gadget worked, wasn't it even cooler to catch the mule with a home device anyone could buy?

As Corky and I climbed the steps back up to the track platform, I slyly checked my watch. We had more than fifteen minutes before the train pulled out, so I wandered down to the concession stands where many of the other passengers were looking at the Native American souvenirs and crafts. At the first table, I noticed some nice placemats with Anasazi designs—the little Kokopelli guy with his flute, leaping antelope, various geometric designs, a scorpion, and a lizard.

"What do you have that my wife might like?" I asked the guy behind the table. He looked Native American—leathery skin, straight black hair pulled back into a ponytail.

He named several items, including the placemats.

"Where are the mats you mentioned? Can I feel 'em?" They were, of course, right in front of me. He described each of them as I picked them up to inspect them more closely with my hands. "Nice sturdy woven mats," I commented, about to purchase a set for Estelle. But when I turned one over, a little tag on the corner read, "Made in China."

I nearly snorted. But without indicating that I'd seen anything, I said, "Thanks. Think I'll keep looking."

Never did get anything for Estelle, but once we were underway again, I tested the motion detector several times in my room. Conway was right. It worked like a watchdog, causing my receiver to beep every time anything passed its field of view. One thing worried me, though. Anyone walking down the hallway or going up the stairs would also trigger it. Using an extra sticky strip, I taped on a cardboard shield to restrict the field of view. I only wanted it to watch the small area where the suitcases were stowed.

We were twenty minutes out of Albuquerque before I ventured out of my compartment to install the detector in the upper corner of the bottom luggage compartment. An average-sized person would have to kneel down to see it up under the edge.

But would it trigger on the motion I was concerned about?

For a test, I put my shaving kit on top of Grace's suitcase as though I'd left it there by accident, then returned to my room to wait with the door open. I turned the receiver down to its lowest volume so only I'd be able to hear when it triggered. I didn't have to wait long until a woman came down the stairs to use the restrooms. "Excuse me . . ." I almost said ma'am. "I think I left my shaving kit out there in the luggage compartment. Do you see a small leather case about so big in there?"

When she reached in and pulled it out, my receiver emitted a faint beeping that I could barely hear. Thank God, it was working.

She held up my bag. "You mean this?"

"I'm sorry." I got up and went to the door. "I'll need to check it." I reached my hand out. When she handed it to me, I felt around it a bit and said, "Yep. That's it. Thank you so much. You have no idea what a relief that is." She had no idea at all. After thirty hours of trying to keep my eyes open—I could finally get some sleep.

I slid my door shut, pulled the curtains, and flopped into my seat. Putting my feet up on the opposing seat's cushion, I was asleep within five minutes.

A jerk of the train woke me. We were starting to move again after some stop. I stood up and went over to use my toilet, but for some reason, I first pulled back the curtain to see where we were. The late afternoon sun shining out of the west made me squint. Nearly silhouetted on the top of a hill rising above the buildings of a classic western small town was the town's name in billboard-sized letters: RATON. To its left, a huge American flag fluttered on a tall pole. What a beautiful sight.

But as the train gained speed, sliding past a large gravel parking lot between our train and the town, I did a double take. Grace Meredith and her assistant were climbing aboard a shiny new Greyhound bus while the driver threw her luggage into the compartment beneath. The big teal-blue bag I'd been watching so carefully for so many hours landed with a jolt that I felt all the way to the bottom of my stomach.

Chapter 38

I dove for my compartment door and slid it open, running out into the hallway without my shades or any attempt to behave like a blind man. I had to get off the train. That large suitcase with $1.5 million of cocaine in it was escaping . . . as was my chance to catch the mule. I couldn't let that happen.

Sylvia was in the vestibule, stowing the yellow stepstool when I came around the corner to the side door like a wild driver in a destruction derby. "Mr. Bentley! What in the world's the matter? You ill? What are you doing? No, you can't open that!" She yanked my hand from the door handle.

She was a lot stronger than I expected, but I broke free and pulled at the handle again. The door wouldn't budge. This time she threw her body between me and the door like a Chicago Bears linebacker. "Mr. Bentley, stop!" she yelled. "This is an outside door! If you open it and fall out while we're going forty miles an hour, you'd kill yourself. Now get a grip, man!"

The door hadn't budged. I'd forgotten about the big safety "dog latch" at the top corner. But Sylvia was right. We were going far too fast to jump from the train without serious injury. I'd be the one making the six o'clock news if I jumped the train.

I stopped pulling at the door. In spite of myself, I knew I hadn't fully blown my cover with Sylvia. In the melee, she'd been telling me this was an outside door, still assuming I couldn't see.

"Sorry, sorry." I stared blankly over her head as we relaxed. "Must've gotten disoriented . . . panicked." I reached out and touched the walls on either side and backed off. I needed to think, maybe call the state police to stop that Greyhound Bus. "I'm really sorry, Miss Sylvia. I'll just go back, now. Don't worry about me. I'm okay. And thank you. Thank you."

She was shaken, but let me go without asking questions. She'd have a story to tell the other attendants after this.

As I returned to my compartment, I noticed an envelope on the floor just inside the door. I picked it up and slid the door closed, then returned to my seat to figure out what to do. I opened the envelope absently and pulled out a handwritten note.

> Dear Mr. Bentley,
>
> Sorry I didn't have a chance to tell you this personally, but I got a call from my agent in Denver inviting us to stop by Bongo's offices. Seemed like a good opportunity to catch up and work on future plans, but we had to get off the Chief in Raton, New Mexico, and take a bus up to Denver.
>
> We'll spend a day there and catch the California Zephyr home. Get in to Chicago just a day late. Hope all is —

A crashing erupted out in the hallway, and I could hear hushed, angry voices. Passengers were going to think this sleeper had turned into a madhouse. This time I remembered my shades before opening my door a few inches. Sylvia wasn't in sight, but a couple of passengers by the luggage compartment were arguing with each other. A young girl, maybe seventeen, with long black hair, was waving her hands and putting her finger to her lips in an attempt to quiet a tall, older guy with spiked blond hair. He was grimacing and swearing in a barely restrained voice, slugging the suitcases on the upper shelves, and kicking those down below.

"I can't believe it! It's gone!" He turned and almost backhanded the girl, but she cowered and slid to the floor. He grabbed her wrist and yanked her back up to her feet as she began to whimper. "Shut up," he snarled. "Someone'll hear."

Just then the door of one of the compartments beyond slid open, and a woman peeked out with a horrified look on her face.

"What you lookin' at? Get back in there and mind your business."

The row suspended as if in midair until the woman retreated. Then the man said in a hoarse whisper. "I thought you talked to her."

"No, no, you don't understand. She said she was going to Chicago. You gotta believe—"

"But she didn't go, did she, and now it's gone!' he hissed. "They're gonna kill me, but not before I kill you." He raised his hand again.

"No, Max! Please no. Somebody's gonna hear us." She put her finger to her lips again. "Come on, come on. We'll figure something out. I got her number."

"What?" He lowered his threatening hand. "She gave me her phone number."

"In Chicago? You sure?"

"Yeah. We can still find her there. Number's up in my purse."

"You dumb slut." He raised his hand for another blow.

"No, no! Please!" The girl put her arms up to block the blow, and I slid my door all the way open and stepped out, ready to intervene. "Everything okay out here?"

"Yeah, yeah. No problem."

They stood frozen, and then the girl's eyes dropped to the floor as if she were embarrassed.

"Come on." The guy grabbed the girl's arm and pushed her ahead of him up the stairs.

When they were gone, I went out and looked in the luggage compartment, even though I knew the blue suitcase was gone.

I'd found my mule.

I returned to my compartment and checked the train schedule. There was almost an hour before our next stop in Trinidad, Colorado, and the mule couldn't jump from a fast-moving train any easier than I could. Even if he decided to chase his drugs, I had a little time to figure out what to do. Should I follow the drugs or stick with the mule? Surely Trinidad would have a little airport. Maybe I could charter a private plane and catch up with Grace. She'd mentioned the name of her agency in her note, so I could probably find it in Denver, but then I'd have to tell her why I'd tracked her down.

Still, the situation was near the tipping point where it might be necessary to do that for her safety. Yet the mule didn't know where she was going—Colorado Springs, Denver, or someplace else—only that she was from Chicago. It wouldn't benefit him to chase after that Greyhound even if he had a way to do it.

I needed more information from Grace. I picked up her note again and noticed a P.S. at the end. "If you can, please keep an eye on a young couple in the first coach behind the lounge car. He's tall, blond, late twenties, name is Max. Ramona's just a teenager, has dark hair. Something doesn't feel right. She seems scared. He seems too controlling."

That confirmed what I'd just seen in the hallway—and reinforced my belief that Grace was innocent. Grace had included her cell phone number in her note and encouraged me to call her. But first, I needed to confirm where my mule and that girl were sitting.

I looked down at Corky. "Come on, girl. We're hot on the trail."

When I got to the coach car, the girl was talking on a cell phone, while the guy leaned in close, clenching his fist, making hand signals, and mouthing words he apparently wanted her to say. They were so engrossed in their efforts that they didn't even glance my way. I continued on up the aisle until I got to the midpoint in the car, then asked a passenger what car I was in. When she told me, I turned around as though I'd been lost and made my way slowly back, approaching the couple from behind.

The girl was off the phone, but the guy was still lecturing her in a hushed voice while tears ran down her cheeks. Grace had certainly been right about their relationship. He was more than a bully. He was terrorizing her like a controlling pimp.

Once I passed them and entered the lounge car, I sank into an empty seat and reviewed all I'd seen. The girl might be Hispanic, was rather pretty in spite of looking so frightened. But the guy . . . he was Caucasian with blue eyes, clean shaven with a lantern jaw and spiky blond hair. What was a white dude doing working for the Sinaloa Cartel? I hardly needed to ask—money!

Once back in my compartment, I dialed Grace. Cell phone coverage was spottier in the mountains, and at first she sounded like she couldn't hear me, but after a few moments, her voice stopped breaking up. She said she was sorry she hadn't said good-bye, but they'd changed their plans at the last minute, getting their tickets changed in Albuquerque.

I assured her it was okay, then casually asked her about the couple she'd mentioned in her note.

"Well, maybe it's nothing, but the girl was all friendly when we talked in the LA station. But as soon—"

"Wait a minute. You met her before?"

"Yeah, in the station before we got on the train. She asked if she could sit down beside me in the waiting room, and we got talking. She wanted to know where I was from, and it went from there. But when I saw her on the train with her 'man,' as she called him, she was completely different. That's why I asked you to look out for her. Seemed like he was . . . I don't know, very manipulative. So, if you—"

"Excuse me for interrupting, but back in the station, did you have your luggage with you?"

"Oh, sure. We hadn't gotten on the train yet, in fact, Ramona—that's her name—asked if we were going to check it."

"Really?" I was getting a picture of the girl scouting a likely carrier for the drugs. "She actually asked if you were going to check your bags?"

"Yeah, just making conversation. She was really friendly, but like I said, I didn't like how that guy treated her, all cozy one minute, then snapping at her, making her sit down when she wanted to get up, stuff like that."

"Can you describe them a little bit more?"

The description fit, and then Grace said she'd had a big accident spilling some coffee and mustard on the girl's fancy jacket when they were talking in the café.

"So you talked to her again?"

"Yeah, but I felt so bad about ruining her jacket that I insisted on taking it with me to get it cleaned on my own and return it to her in Chicago."

"She give you an address?"

"No. She didn't want to give me an address."

"Phone number?"

"No. Said she didn't have a phone, but she would call me. So I gave her my phone number. She just called me a few minutes ago. Guess she saw us get off the train, she sounded upset. I assured her we'd be back just one day later, coming in from Denver, and I'd —"

"She called you?" This might be a break. "Uh, what number did she call from?"

"Oh, I don't think she wants me to call her back—Sam thinks the phone belongs to the guy, and she doesn't want him to know about the jacket."

Hmm. Probably was the guy's phone. Not allowing the girl to communicate on her own was a way for him to maintain more control over her. Grace had good cause to be concerned. "Grace, is that number still in your phone? Might be useful to have it just in case . . . you know, the concern you raised. Might be nothing we can do, but if something did happen, perhaps we could use it to get in touch with her."

Grace found the number and gave it to me.

Bingo! A Chicago area code. We said good-bye, then Grace added, "Tell your wife hello for me, will you?"

I held my phone in my hand for a moment after hanging up. The implications of what I'd learned were two-edged. It wasn't possible to reach down into the handle cavity of most roller luggage bags. My little bag had a shield past which I couldn't get my hand. So to find their "mark," the perps needed to not only know who was traveling to Chicago, but that the brand of luggage they carried would suit their purposes. They were not mere opportunists. This job had been well planned.

On the brighter side, it appeared the drugs hadn't been hidden in Grace's bag until after she got on the train. I sighed with relief as I mentally moved Rodney and his limo company to the bottom of my suspect list.

Time to call Gilson. At first he was upset that I'd lost contact with the drugs, but when I assured him that I'd identified the mule, and that he was still on the train, the captain calmed down.

"Better yet," I said, "I think I have the perp's cell phone number."

"So you want to call him up for a chat?"

"Ha! Ha! Look, just get a court order for the cell phone company to give us the information on who it's registered to and any GPS tracking they have on it."

"A guy like him has probably disabled the tracking."

"Maybe, but unless it's a prepaid throw-away, there'll be a billing and registration address."

"Okay, I'll check it out. Meantime, you stick like glue to that mule. Ride him all the way into town. What about telling your neighbor what's going on? She could be in danger."

"Don't like involving civilians in a sting operation. Too many chances for mistakes."

"She's already involved."

"You're right about that. But she doesn't know it, and civilians act more natural if they don't know what's going on."

I said it more confidently than I felt. Ignorance wouldn't keep Grace and Sam safe—not the young girl, either, who was obviously the mule's pawn.

Chapter 39

"YOU AIN'T GONNA TRY AND JUMP THE TRAIN AGAIN, are you, Mr. Bentley?"

"No ma'am. Sorry 'bout that back there." We were slowing for the stop at Trinidad, and Corky and I had come into the vestibule where Sylvia was preparing to open the door. "If you don't mind, though, Corky and I need to step outside for a minute."

"This ain't no smoke stop, Mr. Bentley—just stop and go."

"I won't be long." I'd be able to see whether Ramona and Max got off or not. If they got off, I might have to break cover and run after them. I couldn't let them get away, especially if the mule was deciding to follow Grace.

Sylvia was eying Corky. "Does she really need to go? She don't act like it."

I leaned slyly toward Sylvia. "I think it's me," I said in a conspiratorial voice.

She chuckled. "All right. Trinidad's nothin' but an Amshak anyway, just a square trailer and a port-a-potty for a station. Make sure she goes on the gravel next to somethin' where no one'll step on it."

No one got off the train at Trinidad, and Sylvia was soon urging me to get back on, coming to hold my elbow and walk me back to the sleeper. "Did she go? I didn't see her."

"We're good, Sylvia. Thank you."

I returned to my room and looked at the schedule again. La Junta was an hour and a half down the track, but it'd be a ten-minute stop. No need for shenanigans with Sylvia. If Max and Ramona hadn't detrained by then, I could be pretty sure they'd decided to continue all the way through to Chicago. Was "pretty sure" good enough? The whole operation was at stake, not to mention the potential safety of Grace and Sam. Maybe I should move up to the mule's coach where I could watch him, though I dreaded the idea of another vigil.

Then it hit me . . . why hadn't my motion detector worked? I pulled the receiver from the plug and looked at it . . . and moaned. When I'd tested it by asking the woman to retrieve my shaving kit, I'd turned the alarm down to its lowest level. The beep, beep, beep had been barely audible in my compartment above the noise of the train, but I'd been listening for it. But I hadn't turned it back up before going to sleep! As tired as I'd been, it could've beeped all afternoon at that level without waking me up.

Felt like kicking myself, but there wasn't much I could've done had I known Grace was removing her luggage. Man, derailed again.

I breathed a desperate prayer. "Come on, God. You gotta help me catch this guy and make a good collar of it."

All I could do now was wait. I sat there thinking about all that had happened on this trip. "Thank you, Jesus!" I wanted to say, "Thank you that Rodney doesn't have anything to do with it." Of course, I couldn't scratch him completely off my suspect list. An organization as sophisticated as the Sinaloa Cartel might well have a backup plan, and the next most logical person to handle that bag alone would be a limo driver. "But I do thank you, Lord, for protecting me from making any premature, disastrous moves."

My thoughts drifted to all the things over the last couple months that had felt so confusing but now seemed to be working out. Such a labyrinth! But I was beginning to feel back on track even though there were still some loose ends. "O God," I prayed. "There're still so many things about tomorrow I don't understand . . ." That phrase rang a bell. Where had I heard it before? I said it over and over until its rhythm triggered the memory of an old Barrett Sisters' record my mom used to play . . . "But I know who holds tomorrow, And . . . I know who holds my hand."

Maybe that was the key to walking through the mazes of life. I'd been angry at God over all the turns and switchbacks when I shoulda been sayin', Give me Jesus. Shoulda been trusting that He was holding my hand and would work it all out.

I needed to trust God with Rodney and to work it out renting the apartment too. At least we weren't in as desperate a situation as poor Mattie Krakowski.

Wait. Mattie Krakowski. What was it Estelle had said? Maybe it doesn't have to be a fantasy. Hadn't made any sense to me then, not with her finances, but . . . we hadn't checked it out. We didn't really know why the bank had foreclosed on her.

Something else that Estelle said . . . Just seemed like it might be a God thing. Like He might bring her back to her home place to spend her final days. Exactly what we'd wanted to do with Mom.

I checked my watch. Still had an hour till we got to La Junta. I dialed Estelle. "Hey, babe. How you doin'?"

"Harry! Is everything okay?"

"Sure, it's all copacetic here."

"Oh, Harry, when you gonna quit usin' that five-dollar word?"

"Ha, ha. Only when it ain't so. Hey, Estelle, been thinking about the first-floor apartment. Have we gotten any more calls on the ad?"

"A couple. But nobody's come by to actually see the place. Sorry, Harry."

"Well, maybe that's okay. Remember when we were comin' back from Elgin after visitin' Mattie? You said maybe it didn't have to be a fantasy about her movin' back into her old place. Well, I been thinkin' . . ."

By the time I finished, Estelle was chuckling. "Can't believe I'm hearin' this. Been thinkin' the same thing myself. But you seemed so sure she couldn't afford it, I didn't want to be buggin' you. But God kept droppin' the idea into my spirit."

"Well, maybe she can't. But we don't really know, do we? Why don't you call her son, Don, see what he thinks?"

Couldn't believe how happy Estelle sounded. "Okay. I'll call this evening. You still gettin' in tomorrow afternoon?"

"Far as I know, but then . . ." None of this was going to be over until Grace arrived two days from now with the drugs in her suitcase.

"What, Harry? But then, what?"

"Nothin', babe. Lord willin', I'll be there on time." Lord willing—it was a qualifier my mom used to attach to all kinds of plans, never understood why. Now I was getting the idea.

273

"Well, you better get back here on time, 'cause I been missin' you too much."

"Me too, babe. Love ya."

"Love ya more."

I hung up with the tune of that old gospel song still going through my head. There were plenty of things about tomorrow that I still didn't understand, but I know who holds my hand.

"Sir, are these your seats?" It was the attendant in the coach car where I'd moved on my own so I could still watch my mule.

"Oh, I'm sorry. Were you sitting here?"

"No. I'm William, the attendant for this car."

"Well, hello, William. Thanks so much for checking on me. No, these aren't my seats. I have an accessible compartment in first class, but it's on the lower level, you know, and I just wanted to be up here a while. Gets kind of lonely down there by myself."

"Well, there's always the lounge car. You're welcome there."

"I know, but . . . is there a problem sitting here? The seats seemed vacant."

"They are, but—"

"Great. I won't be any trouble at all, and the little boy across the aisle seems to be very interested in my dog. Isn't that right, son?"

"She's a nice doggy," said the boy, standing backwards and playing with Legos on his seat.

William sighed. "Well, okay. But if I need these seats, I'm gonna have to ask you to move. Agreed?"

"Yes, sir. Whatever you say."

Between stops, I had a nice dinner, confident that the mule would remain on the train. At one point I went down to my compartment and called Estelle again. Told her I'd identified my perp, but that I was going to wait until we got to Chicago where I'd have plenty of backup before attempting an arrest. That seemed like good news to her.

Once the lights were dimmed in the coach, William stopped by again. "Don't you want to go to your compartment?"

Playing the sleeping passenger, I said, "No, no, no. Don't bother me. This is just fine." In Kansas City, where we had an extended stop, I detrained to give Corky a walk while I kept an eye on Max, who smoked two or more cigarettes in the twenty minutes we were there.

Sylvia called to me as Corky and I passed her on the platform. "Where you been, Mr. Bentley? I was afraid you might've succeeded in jumpin' the train and was about to put out a search call for you."

"Ha, ha. Don't worry 'bout me, ma'am. I found some folks up in coach who are real interesting. But here," I thrust a twenty-dollar bill toward her. "If I should happen to miss you in Chicago, you've been very kind, and I appreciate it."

Corky and I stood in the vestibule as our train rocked and swayed, weaving its way slowly through the Chicago train yard toward Union Station the next afternoon. Other passengers of car 431 were coming down the stairs, picking up their luggage and crowding into the tight space, eager to detrain. I'd intentionally left my bag in my compartment to be picked up later. Dragging it along might hinder my efforts to tail Max-the-mule and his girl, Ramona.

When we'd last spoken by phone, Captain Gilson had told me the cell phone company was balking on coughing up Max's address. If a judge didn't move quickly to issue a warrant, the information might come in too late for us to make any use of it, so I needed to follow him, find out where he lived, maybe even identify the cartel's Chicago headquarters.

"I'll have your vehicle waiting in the taxi lane," Gilson had said. "That's my best guess of how he's gonna get outta here. But I can't spare much backup. Mayor Daley's scheduled to make a speech in the Great Hall for an awards ceremony just shortly after your arrival. I can give you two men, but everyone else is needed on security for the mayor."

"That should be CPD's job."

"Well, it is, but this is our house. We know every nook and cranny of the place, so they want all of us on duty. Sorry, Harry.

You'll just have to make do. Besides, show time is tomorrow when your girl comes in, right? We can't do anything today if this guy isn't carrying."

He was right, but we still didn't have a fix on the mule, and I wanted to find out where he was headed. I gave Gilson a full description of the suspects, and he promised to pass along the information to my backups and have them waiting when we arrived. Communication, however, might be difficult. We'd have to rely on cell phones.

The train wheezed to a stop. The door opened. As I stepped onto the platform, Sylvia steadied my elbow. "There ya go, Mr. Bentley. Hope you had a real good trip, and you be sure to choose Amtrak again, now, won'cha?"

"Yes, ma'am. And thank ya, Sylvia. You've been great. We'll be back. Come along now, Corky. Gotta go." But the day might come when Sylvia and other Amtrak personnel began to recognize me. Then what would I do?

I briefly merged into the stream of people surging toward doors into the station, then ducked behind one of the large concrete pillars that supported the roof above the platform.

My cell phone sounded. "Yeah, Bentley."

"I'm in position, just inside the doors." It was a female Amtrak officer.

"Good. They haven't passed me yet, but keep this line open. Is your partner patched in?"

"I'm alone. Captain needed Johnson at the last minute for the mayor's thing."

I swore under my breath. What was Gilson doing to me? He'd been so excited about this operation, and now it felt like he was pulling the rug out from under me. I intended to give him a piece of my mind . . . but that would have to wait.

"Subjects in sight," I said. "He's tall, maybe six feet, wearing all black, looks like an open-necked sport shirt. You heard that he's got blond, spiky hair, right?"

"Roger that."

"Okay. I'm steppin' in behind them now, keepin' about five yards back. Crowd's kinda tight here. We're almost to your door.

The girl's got long dark hair hanging over her right eye. She's wearing a white-and-green plaid shirt, tight jeans, and brown boots. He's holdin' her arm—"

"Got 'em. You want me to fall in behind you?"

I saw my partner. She was in uniform, but uniformed Amtrak officers cruised the station all the time. In fact, it might appear unusual to the mule if he didn't see one or two.

"Sure. Fall in behind. Just don't give me away."

The station was exceptionally crowded, perhaps because of the mayor's visit, but it made it hard to keep within a good distance of our subjects. Then, suddenly, the girl peeled off to the right.

"Follow her. Follow her," I said into my phone.

"Roger that."

"Just don't lose her!"

I continued following Max up the escalator and out the doors toward the line of cabs waiting along Canal Street. And there was my SUV at the end of the line, probably making some cabbies angry for taking a space. They'd have to suck it up. I ran for my vehicle as I spoke into the phone. "You still on her?"

"She went into the women's restroom, but I can't find which stall."

"Brown boots. Brown boots. Look for brown boots."

"There aren't any."

"Well, keep lookin'. Suspect's takin' a Norshore Cab. Can't see the number, but I'm getting' in my vehicle now. . . . Corky, up in there. Good girl. . . . I'll be in pursuit in a second. Keep this line open."

"Wilco."

I roared out into traffic, trying to catch up with the cab that was about to cross Adams Street four cars ahead of me. It scooted through the intersection, but all the rest of the traffic stopped, even though I could see that the light was still green. I laid on the horn and looked for a gap between the cars to squeeze through.

No chance. Two motorcycle cops were blocking the intersection, and then I saw why. Two more motorcycles led the mayor's limousine slowly through the intersection, where it stopped, followed by a large black security SUV, which still blocked my way while the mule in his turquoise-and-white cab sped north.

Chapter 40

I FELT BAD DRIVING WITH CORKY to work the next morning. Estelle had been so glad to have me home the night before. She'd invited Rodney over for dinner, so all four of us were together, but I wasn't much company. I still felt distracted by the unfinished business at work. Rodney seemed totally relaxed except for a phone call he got during dinner. He'd jumped up from the table and gone into the living room, muttering into his cell. "No! Not now. I told you never . . ." I couldn't hear what followed. Might've been Donita, but he didn't say when he returned a minute later.

Estelle mentioned that she'd talked to Don Krakowski, and that everything was working out for Mattie to move in, but all I said was, "Oh, that's good."

"Good! Harry, he's bringing a bunch of her furniture by this Saturday to set up the place, and all you can say is, 'Oh, that's good'?"

"Well, isn't that what we wanted?"

Estelle sighed like a deflating balloon and shook her head, but later as we got ready for bed, she asked what was wrong.

"Sorry, babe. Guess I'm just not home yet."

"You're sitting right there on the end of the bed, and you look like a real warm bod to me." She grinned. "Real good, in fact."

I sighed. "It's the case. I don't have it wrapped up, and my mind is still spinnin'."

"You found the drugs and identified the guy who was carrying them, what else is there?"

"We haven't made an arrest yet. And figuring out how to do that is what's preoccupying me, so make sure you don't say anything about the case until it gets settled." I looked at her, not knowing what else to say. "Maybe you could pray for me."

Without asking for any more details, she sat beside me on the bed, put her hand on my shoulder, and prayed a simple prayer of God's blessing. I went to sleep, grateful that she trusted I'd be back "home" with her as soon as I could.

The first thing I did when I got to the station was check Corky into the kennel. She didn't seem too happy to be left after spending so many days with me. I think that dog really loves working. Once I got to my office, I called Grace Meredith, hoping her cell phone had a good signal. The Zephyr was probably somewhere in Iowa.

"Just checking to see if everything's working out for you after such a long trip."

"Ah, Mr. Bentley. You're too sweet. Thanks. Yes, we're doing fine, though I'm actually glad we laid over in Denver for a night's rest in a regular bed."

I laughed. "Yeah. Sleeping on a train berth's not quite the same. Hey, how you gettin' home once you get in? You need a lift?"

"Thanks, that won't be necessary. I felt bad canceling on your son yesterday so I called him personally to apologize. He was very gracious. Even insisted we let him pick us up this afternoon. So we've got our ride. Wouldn't dare cancel on him again."

"Well, you enjoy the rest of your trip. Hey, if you see me around the station when you get in, you can wave as long as I'm not undercover."

"I'll be sure to. Thanks, Mr. Bentley."

Rodney had insisted on picking them up? That set off alarm bells in my head. But I still had to meet with Captain Gilson. I didn't want to lose our perp again. I didn't name Rodney, but Gilson immediately zeroed on the limo being the probable retrieval point.

"It's a no-brainer, Bentley. Once she detrains, that's the only time when the luggage will be out of her possession. Think about it." He started in like he was giving stage directions. "She walks up to the limo. The driver greets her, opens the door. She and her assistant get in and sit back in those soft seats, exhausted, facing forward while the driver goes around to the back to stow their luggage. He raises the trunk lid, so even if they happen to turn around—which they're too tired to do—they won't see a thing."

"Yeah, yeah. I can see it might happen that way." I didn't like the clues that implicated Rodney, but even more I didn't like Gilson's insistence on positioning most of the Amtrak police outside the station to target the limo. "Nevertheless, Captain, I'd feel better if we weren't locked in to one option. We need to be ready for anything."

Gilson tossed up both hands. "Okay, okay. We'll keep a few officers in the station. But we position a couple of our own vehicles on Adams to pull across the intersection and block all traffic on Canal just like the mayor's motorcade did to you yesterday. Only this time we use it to trap the limo."

Well, it'd probably work, but . . .

I started to leave his office when Gilson said, "Oh, one more thing. Got good news for you. Warrant went through for the phone records. Cell's registered to a Marcel Wagner up in Logan Square. Building's a restaurant that's been closed for remodeling for the last two years. Got a couple of apartments above it. DEA and CPD are coordinating a raid as we speak."

"No, no, no! Can't do that until we nab this mule with the dope! Anything goes wrong with the raid and our perp disappears. I want this guy. Call 'em and tell 'em to hold off until we give the green light."

Gilson shook his head. "Neither agency likes anyone else tellin' them what they can or can't do."

"But you gotta tell 'em."

He shrugged. "I'll try."

Everyone was in position by 2:40 even though the 2:50 train was running a little late. Except for a couple of momentary false alarms, no one had sighted our perp. Perhaps Gilson was right. It was going to happen at the limo and Max might not even be in the vicinity. O Lord. Please don't let Rodney be involved in this mess.

I waited alone, out of sight behind a pillar on the platform for Track 28 as the two huge diesels pulling the Zephyr crept slowly past at three o'clock, the bell clanging and air hissing from the brakes like steam from an old steam engine. A baggage car, three sleepers and the dining car slipped by before the train came to a complete stop. Perfect. I still had a good view of the sleeper cars, but Grace and Sam weren't likely to look my way as they headed for the doors into the station.

They'd be hard to miss. Not too many young women—one black, one white—traveled together like that. They stepped off the train, making sure they had all their luggage while I took note that the big blue roller bag was with them. I waited until they said good-bye to their attendant and were underway. Twice that morning I'd reloaded and checked my pistol, but as I merged into the flow of tired passengers and began following Grace and Sam, I felt once more for the P250 beneath my sport jacket. Too bad Corky wasn't with me. She was better protection than any weapon. It seemed unfair to deny her a role in the knockout punch for this operation. Sorry, girl.

Grace and Sam went through the doors into the station just as Max and Ramona had done yesterday. Glad I wasn't having to communicate by cell phone this time, I lifted the radio mike to my lips. "We're coming in." Only three uniforms were stationed along the probable path Grace and Sam would take. Two here on the concourse level, and one at the top of the escalators before they'd exit onto the street. Most of the other officers were out on the street in plain clothes. Only a couple there were in uniform.

I searched the crowd for Max as Grace and Sam turned into the wide corridor heading for the main lobby. He was tall enough that I should be able to spot him, but the farther we went without seeing him, the more I began to admit that Gilson might be right. I couldn't imagine Max making his move in this throng. People moved and jostled one another like red blood cells pulsing through an artery.

Ahead of me, I thought I saw Grace and Sam pause near the base of the escalators. Was that them? Yes. What were they doing? The girl. The one from the train, Ramona, they were talking to her. Ramona was putting on a tan jacket. I pushed forward as I toggled my mike. "This could be it! Bottom of the escalators in the main lobby. No, wait. They're moving around to the back of the escalators, toward the fountain."

I emerged from the corridor as the throng between me and the fountain came to a complete standstill, congested by the lines of passengers waiting at the Amtrak ticket counter. Partially hidden by a large pillar, I hesitated. And then the girl's head slumped from view followed by Grace and Sam dropping out of sight as well. I elbowed my way forward as people huddled like a football team, looking down as if the women had disappeared into a sinkhole.

A small break in the crowd gave me a glimpse of Ramona on the floor, where it appeared she'd fallen. Grace and Sam were stooping beside her trying to help. I pushed closer, only a dozen feet and twenty bodies away. I looked around for Max. He had to be somewhere close. I spoke into my mike. "Watch for the male suspect. He may be on the move." Why wasn't I getting any response from my backup?

I looked for spiky, blond hair, but what caught my eye on the far side of the fountain was a brief glimpse of Grace's big teal-blue suitcase being pulled by a man with a black hoodie over his head and a gray backpack slung on one shoulder. He walked briskly out of the lobby toward the Great Hall but not so fast as to draw attention. I cut back around the other side of the escalators where the crowd was not so dense, hot on the perp's trail and in time to see him turn north by the Metra ticketing area. "Any APD officer, please respond!" I barked into my mike. "Suspect will soon pass the door of our offices. Please respond." I ran a Walter Payton through the passengers to catch up, hoping help would've emerged from our offices by the time I turned the corner.

Max was heading for the doors out to the old taxi pickup area that dumped onto Clinton Street. But we now used that "tunnel" as parking for our police vehicles, including my SUV. I clicked my mike again. "Any officer in the motor pool area, apprehend male suspect pulling a blue luggage bag." Still no answer. As I rounded the corner, I saw Max again. Instead of going through the doors to the motor pool, he was turning right down the slight ramp to the north set of tracks. Okay, he was heading for a Metra train. With 120,000 commuters per day, access to those trains wasn't restricted. You jumped on board and showed your ticket or pass to the conductor, usually after the train left the station.

Max was no more than thirty yards ahead of me when he ducked left through the automatic doors and onto the platform between

Tracks 13 and 15. I sprinted—as fast as a guy my age could—past all the other doors to the platform Max had taken.

Where was he? A few passengers still straggled toward me after getting off the train on Track 13 to my left, but no one was boarding the outbound train on Track 15 . . . because it was starting to move. I groaned. Was Max getting away a second time?

I jogged along beside it, peering up into the windows, hoping to spot him. In a matter of moments, the train outpaced me, and then pulled away completely. I came to a stop at the end of the platform, bent over, hands on knees as I sucked air like a winded racehorse.

I triggered my mike. "Find out . . . which Metra train . . . just departed . . . on Track 15. Have local police . . . and the DEA intercept it . . . at its first stop. Apprehend suspect."

When I got a confirmation, I turned and staggered dejectedly back along the platform. I'd failed. Max had gotten away again. And the chance that suburban police could coordinate a successful bust on such short notice was slim at best.

One more commuter stepped from the recently arrived train on Track 13 and turned in front of me toward the station. Then I noticed the gray backpack he held in his hand. Faded jeans, a Chicago White Sox jersey and cap over . . . blond hair.

I unholstered my SIG as I hustled to catch up. "Max Wagner?" He turned a shocked face to me, and I could see he was about to bolt. "Don't try it." I showed him my weapon and pulled back my jacket so he could see my badge.

He stopped and rolled his eyes like a teenager. "What is it now?"

"Mind if I have a look in your backpack?"

"You got a warrant?"

"I can get one as soon as I need to. Up against the train. I'm sure you know the position."

He turned, but not fast enough to suit me. I slammed him against the train and frisked him. Unarmed, but I still cuffed him as I called for backup and told someone to have Creston bring Corky and meet us in the office.

✧　✧　✧　✧

Max wasn't giving up anything as I put him in the interview room, and he still hadn't given me permission to examine his backpack. Where was Corky when I needed her?

I'd dispatched two uniforms to search the last two cars of the Metra train Max had gotten off, but I'd pretty much figured out that he'd jumped on board with Grace's suitcase, retrieved his drugs and ditched his hoodie, and then detrained like a north suburban sports fan on his way to watch the White Sox play the Royals that evening. He'd almost gotten away with it, but I'd bet my house his backpack held those six sausage-shaped rolls of cocaine.

When I left the interview room, Gilson was standing outside watching Max through the two-way mirror.

"Good work, Bentley."

"Thanks." I nodded, feeling a little smug. "And you can greenlight the raid now too."

"I'll make the call."

I was heading back through the offices when I noticed Grace and her assistant sitting at a desk in one of the office cubicles filling out forms. How much did Grace know? She'd certainly had an unpleasant experience of her luggage being stolen, but I didn't really want her to know she'd been carrying $1.5 million worth of cocaine all the way across the country, not if I could help it.

As I got to the door that led into the rest of the station, it flew open, and Creston burst in. "I'm sorry, Bentley. Your dog won't come."

I held my finger to my lips and pushed him back out. "What's up? What took you so long?"

He shook his head. "I can't get Corky to budge. She's been sitting in front of a utility closet door for the last—" Creston threw up his hands in desperation. "—five minutes, and I can't get her to move."

"Where's she now?"

"Still there! Just around the corner and down the hall. Come on. I'll show you."

When we got to the door, Creston was right. Corky was sitting in her alert position, with her nose up to the door.

I loosened my SIG in its holster. "Corky, free."

She bounced up, wagging her tail and grinning at me like she'd won a bag of treats and expected me pay up right then.

"What's in there?" I asked Creston.

"I don't know. Just a utility closet, far as I know."

"Stand back." I swung the door open. "Well, look who we have here."

Chapter 41

How Corky knew the girl was in the closet, I may never know. Ramona didn't have any drugs on her, and we hadn't given Corky her scent to track, but somehow she knew.

It wasn't the tears and pleading that got to me as I walked the girl back to the Amtrak Police offices. Anyone can wail and moan when they're caught. But the poor girl shivered like she'd spent the day in a Chicago blizzard. Trembling is involuntary. She was truly terrified. It was clear she'd been a decoy to distract Grace and Sam while Max made off with Grace's luggage, but Grace had probably been right. The guy had manipulated her into being his pawn, and I wished I could do something for her. We had only one interview room, so I locked her in the lunchroom with instructions to Phyllis, whose desk was just outside the door, to make sure she didn't get out.

When I returned to the interview room, Captain Gilson suggested we videotape Corky's response to Wagner's backpack to make sure no procedural questions came up during prosecution. We didn't have to encourage Corky in the least. She went right over and sat down, pointing her nose at Wagner's backpack in the classic alert stance. I grinned at Max. "Well, there you have it, my man, just as if you were displaying all that blow in plain sight. Now may we search your pack? Oh, don't bother answering, 'cause we don't need your permission anymore."

All six packets were inside. We arrested Wagner and read him his rights. "But relax, it'll be a while before the CPD arrives to take you to Cook County Jail. They're busy at a restaurant up in Logan Square gettin' acquainted with a few of your friends."

With a snarl of his lip, Max swore at me. "You think we don't have the best lawyers money can buy? You'll never make this stick."

I just smiled at him. It would stick.

I left and wound my way through the cubicles until I looked over the divider where Grace and Sam were speaking to an Amtrak agent. "Ah. You're still here."

"Mr. Bentley!" Grace turned. She looked relieved to see a familiar face.

I nodded toward the report form she'd filled out. "You lose something?"

Grace grimaced. "My suitcase was stolen."

I grinned. "Well, I've got good news for you. We caught the perp red-handed and got your suitcase back."

Both Grace and Sam gasped. "What?" Grace stared at me like I'd performed a miracle. "How . . . oh, my. I can't believe it."

"That's the good news." I said. "The bad news is, uh, Amtrak police need to keep your suitcase for a little while until they've completed all the paperwork. A list of the contents would be helpful to make sure everything's still there. I'll see that you get it back as soon as they release it. Hopefully it won't be too long."

"Oh, Harry! Thank you!" Grace got up and gave me a big hug. "I'm going to tell Estelle to cook you one of her famous dinners tonight. You deserve it!"

"Uh, make that Detective Bentley here at the station." I laughed to assure her I was joking, then gazed at her, wondering if I should tell her the whole story now that the danger was over. No, she still seemed too upset. "Okay, ladies, gotta go. C'mon, Corky." But as I left, I winked at Grace. "Told you Amtrak security was on the job—even when you didn't know it."

After such a busy day, Corky seemed particularly eager to head home, but with all the paperwork, it was after seven before we got out of there. Riding home up the Outer Drive as the setting sun streamed through scattered clouds in the west, streaking the sky pink and amber, I did feel accomplished. We'd made a good collar on Marcel (Max) Wagner with close to $1.5 million of cocaine in his possession, though the purity awaited lab confirmation. In the meantime, the

CPD—backed by the DEA—raided what they believed to be the Sinaloa Cartel's Chicago headquarters, arresting eight people and confiscating another $1.7 million in marijuana, cocaine, heroin, and meth. In the haul they also grabbed eleven weapons, including two sawed-off shotguns, and eighty thousand dollars in cash.

I glanced back into Corky's carrier. "Not bad for a long train trip, was it, ol' girl. Too bad we never got to Disneyland, though. Maybe next time." Corky whined and adjusted her position, her mouth hanging open as she panted happily.

I still felt bad about Grace. I'd convinced her to travel by train, and though I'd managed to keep her oblivious of the hurricane of crime and danger that had swirled around her, she'd been robbed right in our own Union Station. I'd called Estelle earlier not only to tell her I'd be late getting home but also to ask her to check on Grace. I hoped she was okay.

By the time I got home, it was nearly eight and Estelle had dinner waiting for me. Bless her! She'd even waited to eat with me, the table set beautifully with candles and Mom's china.

"DaShawn already ate. He's over at the Jaspers, supposedly doing homework." She lit the four candles. "But if you ask me, DaShawn's gettin' sweet on that girl."

"Who, Tabitha? I thought his only interest was playin' hoops with Tavis."

"Hmm." She set a steaming casserole with a flaky crust between us and moved our bowls of colorful salad aside to make room for a basket of fresh garlic bread. "I don't know. The hormones are surging by thirteen. But we don't have to worry about tonight. Rodney's pickin' him up from the Jaspers at nine when he finishes his run, for a sleepover."

"Sleepover on a school night?"

Estelle shrugged and gave me a sly smile. "Why not?" She flipped off the dining room light and sat down across from me. "Oh—" She held up a finger. "—before I forget, when I checked on Grace this afternoon like you asked me to—took her some of this supper—she seemed real concerned about a young girl she'd met on the train. Said she disappeared. She mentioned something about a mean boyfriend."

"Ah yes. The girl with the stained jacket." I nodded. "She definitely disappeared. I'll have to tell you all about it."

"Well, I want to hear everything, soon as you give thanks for the food."

I reached out and took Estelle's hand. "For food in a world where many walk in hunger, for faith in a world where many walk in fear"—Like Grace Meredith, I thought—"and for friends in a world where many walk alone, we give you thanks, Lord." I paused a moment without letting go of Estelle's hand. "And Lord, thank you for the best wife you could've ever given me, and for bringin' me home safe to be with her this evening. Amen."

When I opened my eyes, Estelle was grinning. "Shepherd's pie?" She spooned a generous helping of meat and colorful vegetables onto my plate, the flaky crust sitting askew on the top. "What's this about bringing you home safe? Was there ever any doubt?"

I had no interest in scaring my wife, but we don't keep secrets from each other, so with the operation concluded, I told Estelle the whole story, including how Grace had been carrying a load of cocaine without knowing it.

"Harry Bentley! I can't believe you let her do that!"

"Didn't have much choice. In fact, at first I wasn't able to exclude her from consideration as the carrier—"

"You mean you suspected her? How could you? All you had to do was call me, and I could've told you that was impossible. That poor girl. I can't believe it!" She rolled her eyes and shook her head like I was a lost cause.

"Well, it wasn't as if I singled her out. I had to look at everyone who had any contact with that luggage." I watched Estelle continue shaking her head, totally unconvinced. "Give me a break, Estelle. I had to look at everyone. My list of suspects even included Rodney; he—"

"You also suspected your own son? Harry—"

I tried to explain the theory of a limo driver having enough time with the bags to accomplish the drug plant and retrieval. ". . . and then when I heard Rodney had not only arranged to pick up Grace yesterday but insisted on driving her today, I had to consider the poss—"

"This is too much! That boy was just being neighborly. He brought her home this evening after waiting all afternoon for her.

Probably lost a couple fares while he waited. He'd be here eating with us right now except he had to work tonight. Suspecting your own son? That's scary, Harry Bentley." She crossed her arms and glared. "Who's next? You gonna suspect me?"

Estelle was steaming mad. And an evening that began with high hopes for a romantic rendezvous—candles, special dinner with the love of my life, just the two of us alone—had turned into a scolding. Couldn't blame Estelle, though. I'd quaked in fear every time I thought Rodney might be involved. But what else could I have done? I wanted to explain, defend myself, prove that I'd done the right thing.

Instead . . . I hung my head and just sat with it a few moments. Thankfully, Estelle's fury seemed to burn itself out.

Finally, I looked up at her. The flickering candlelight blurred in my eyes as the woman I loved, the woman I wanted to respect me more than anything else in the world, sat perfectly still, her eyes closed as if in prayer.

"I'm sorry, babe," I said. "I'm truly sorry. Can you forgive me?"

Her eyes opened, and I could see tears. "Yes, Harry. I forgive you," she said in that velvet-soft voice of hers. "And will you forgive me too? I didn't mean to go off on you like that. I know you have a hard job, sometimes requiring choices that hurt more than I can imagine or understand. But thank you for being the kind of man who hasn't hardened himself to the pain of those decisions. That truly would be scary. But you don't scare me, Harry Bentley, and I'm sorry for saying so."

I got up, went around the table to take Estelle's hand as she stood up too, and we embraced for a long, comforting hug.

"Let me get the candles." Estelle untangled herself and whoofed out two of them, handing the other two to me still lit. "Bring 'em with you. We can leave the dishes till tomorrow."

After all the twists and turns, I was finally home.

Epilogue

TWILIGHT TURNED THE TREES BLACK and the houses on Beecham Street dark shades of blue and gray under overcast skies, making the warm lights in the windows all the more homey and inviting. Twenty-some neighbors—nearly half of the people on the block—milled around, taking care not to step on the glimmering luminaries marking the walk up to the two-flat.

"Hey, Pops, can Tavis and I put out more of these paper sacks with candles in 'em?"

"Don't we have enough already?"

"We need a couple more up on the steps, you know, so it's like leadin' her right into her house."

I looked at the first-floor unit, all lit up with bright lamps and clean curtains in the windows. It already looked welcoming, but . . . "I guess so. Be careful with those candles."

There was just enough nip in the air that everyone welcomed the cups of hot chocolate Estelle brought around on a tray. I was delivering half sheets of paper to each neighbor.

"Tim, Scott," I said to the neighbors from the bungalow two doors north as I handed them a sheet. "Good to see ya."

"Wouldn't have missed it for the world," said Tim.

"Where's Danny?" I asked. "Haven't seen him around this evening."

Scott thumbed over his shoulder toward the west. "He's visiting my mom in Glenview. She's about the only one in either of our families that . . . you know." He shrugged and glanced at Tim.

"Sorry about that." I couldn't help wondering what I'd do if it were my family. "Well, like I said, thanks for joining us."

I moved on. "You might not be familiar with this," I said as I handed a song sheet to the Jalilis, "but it's easy to pick up."

Farid looked at the words for a moment. "Well, we never sang these words back in Iran, but I think we've heard people sing it New Year's Eve in the States. Right?"

"You got it. Estelle changed a few of the words, but . . . Glad you can join us."

"Dad." Rodney snagged me as I passed. "Don't know if you've met my boss yet. This is Lincoln Paddock. Lives at the end of the block." I felt embarrassed as I extended my hand. We'd been in the neighborhood over two months, and I hadn't yet met the lawyer and owner of Lincoln Limo. He was slim, handsome, mid-forties and wore a black suit with no tie. We talked for a few minutes, and then I went looking for Grace Meredith who was standing at the edge of the gathering. A man I didn't recognize stood beside her with his arm loosely around her waist. I hadn't spoken to Grace since I'd returned her suitcase a week before.

"Grace! So glad to see you. Here are the words for the song. Estelle said you're gonna lead us, right?"

She nodded as she glanced over the sheet.

"So how's it goin'? You finally recoverin' from your West Coast tour?"

"Yes, doing fine." The flickering light from the luminaries gave her face a vibrant glow. She gestured toward the dark-haired man beside her. "This is Jeff Newman . . . Jeff, this is Mr. Bentley—"

"Just Harry." I extended my hand to the newcomer. "Good to meet ya."

"Jeff's my . . ." Grace stole a nervous glance at the man. ". . . he's my agent."

"Oh, so you're the one who sends this young lady all over the country."

Jeff returned a near-schoolboy grin, with a quick look at Grace. "Well, Grace is very special. We all love her at Bongo."

"Bongo? As in . . .?" I mimed patting a pair of small drums.

"Yep, that's the name of our agency. Bongo Booking."

"And Harry's the man who saved . . . who encouraged me to take the train. He works for Amtrak."

"Really, now. Well, she seemed to have a good trip."

"Better'n good." Grace flashed Jeff a shy grin that made me think they were becoming an "item."

"Speaking of your trip," I said, "Estelle mentioned you're still worried about that young girl you met on the train."

"Oh, yes, Ramona. Your wife really encouraged me to pray for her every day, and I've been doing it too. Did you ever find her?"

"As a matter of fact, we did. That's what I wanted to tell you. I think we were able to pry her away from that man who'd been . . . hassling her. Turned out she was basically homeless, except for him. I was able to get her into the Manna House Shelter just yesterday—same place Estelle works. So she's in a good place now, at least temporarily. They have programs to help someone like her get back on her feet, maybe even get her back home to her family in LA."

"Oh, I'm so glad! I was really worried about her. Guess my prayer times with Estelle will hit a new level of praise now."

I chuckled. "Estelle will be all for that. And Jeff," I turned to Grace's . . . uh, friend, "it's good to meet you. You take care of this young lady, now. We're tryin' to learn how to be good neighbors around here, so we'll be checkin' up."

Jeff smiled easily. "You've got nothing to worry about, Mr. Bentley."

"Harry. Just Harry'll do." I moved on to speak to the Jaspers, aware that helping Ramona hadn't been as easy as I'd explained to Grace. We'd had to arrest her as an accomplice to the robbery and drug transportation and because she was seventeen, Ramona was too old for the Juvenile Detention Center and spent over a week in Cook County Jail—very sobering, I'm sure. But I was able to convince the State's Attorney to drop the charges against her if she'd enter a facility that could help her. The word to Ramona was that if she were ever picked up again, she'd be prosecuted. So she was pretty happy to go to Manna House.

"Here they come! Here they come!" The word spread through the group, and we all turned to watch a car glide slowly up the street, its headlights shining in our eyes. It passed our house and turned around in the cul-de-sac to return and park on our side of the street. The headlights went off, and Don Krakowski got out, came around to the passenger side, and opened the door for a wide-eyed old lady. The son helped Mattie Krakowski stand up, which she was able to do without a cane. And then a clear soprano voice led out. Following Grace's lead, a motley crew of Beecham Street neighbors began to sing.

> *Should old acquaintance be forgot,*
> *and never brought to mind?*
> *Should old acquaintance be forgot,*
> *oh, not this friend of mine.*
> *For our dear friend of days gone by,*
> *has been away too long.*
> *We'll take a cup of kindness yet,*
> *and toast her with a song.*
>
> *And here's a hand our trusty friend*
> *that we once failed to give!*
> *Grant us the chance to make it right,*
> *in peace among us live.*
> *For our dear friend of days gone by,*
> *has been away too long.*
> *We'll take a cup of kindness yet,*
> *and toast her with a song.*

I looked over at our new renter. Tears were streaming down her wrinkled face.

THE END

Book Club Discussion Questions for
Derailed

1. Aside from affordability and the physical adequacy of the dwelling, what other factors mattered most to you in the past when you considered a move (church, schools, shopping convenience, proximity to family, beautiful surroundings, parking, ethnic diversity, threat of natural disasters, threat of violence, etc.)? Did any of those factors change in their importance after you moved to the new place? How and why?

2. Like Harry and Estelle Bentley, has concern for extended family members (elderly parents or adult children or grandchildren) played a major role in your life decisions such as where and how you live? Describe.

3. Have you ever believed God was leading you in one direction only to later conclude that you'd been "derailed"? How did you deal with that? In what ways did it affect your future willingness to seek and follow God's leading?

4. After moving to Beecham Street, Estelle baked cinnamon roles to share with their neighbors—kind of a reverse Welcome Wagon approach to getting acquainted. She cites Proverbs 18:24, which in the King James Version says, "A man that hath friends must show himself friendly." While other translations phrase this verse differently, what do you think of the idea?

5. Harry and Estelle consider letting Rodney rent the first floor apartment to give him a "second chance." But later when Corky finds a joint in Rodney's jacket, he declares his innocence and says, "I was hopin' for a second chance, Dad! But I see I ain't gonna get one around here." Are there conditions

for giving someone a second chance? What might they be? Has God ever given you a second chance? According to 1 Corinthians 13:7, what is God's attitude toward second chances?

6. Harry thinks some of Captain Gilson's ideas about his job as an undercover detective are over the top, unworkable, and perhaps dangerous. Describe a situation where someone in authority over you had unreasonable expectations for you. How did you deal with the situation? What do you think about Harry's response?

7. What do you think of Harry's decision to conceal what he found in Grace's luggage from her? What might have happen if he had confronted her? What do you think about his keeping the whole story from her right through the end?

8. Do you think an undercover K-9 detective posing as a blind man with a service dog could have worked around you without blowing their cover? Why or why not? How do you feel when you are in public places and observe teams of law-enforcement officers milling through the crowd?

9. As Harry listens to Grace sing, "You may have all the world, give me Jesus," he wonders, Was that all that mattered? How do you give up everything else? How do you give up your responsibilities—even for Jesus—without becoming irresponsible? How would you answer him?

10. What do you think of Harry's continuing suspicion of Rodney and the possibility that he be involved in drug trafficking? Was he being wisely cautious or unduly suspicious?

11. Harry often felt God derailed his life by failing to give him direct instructions concerning what he should do—and yet later realized God was leading him to a greater purpose. Can you think of a sequence of seeming reversals in your life by which God took you from point A to point B, not by a straight route, but by the only path you would have followed? In what ways has that deepened your trust in God in situations you don't understand?

Acknowledgements

I first of all want to thank our agent, **Lee Hough** of ALIVE Communications, who believed in this series and especially the phenomenon of Parallel Novels from the outset.

Special appreciation also goes to **Steve Parolini**, our most excellent editor, who definitely made this a better read than what I wrote!

While Neta and I have always loved to travel by train, not even our 5,500-mile research trip on Amtrak—duplicating Grace and Harry's West Coast trips—provided all the information we needed. So, special thanks to **Marc Magliari**, media relations manager for Amtrak; **Captain Gary Jones**, overseeing Amtrak Police from Chicago to points west; **John Clayborne**, Amtrak detective out of Albuquerque, New Mexico; **Sergeant Lisa Mueller**, Chicago Police Canine Training Center; **Officer Juan Martinez**, Chicago Police Department (retired) and his fantastic K-9 partner, **Rocky**.

Neta and Dave

Chapter 1

Michelle woke briefly when Jared's alarm went off at five, but she didn't move. She needed the extra hour of sleep before she had to get up. But it seemed like only minutes before her own alarm went off at six. Uhhhh. If only she could sleep in . . .

Forcing herself to throw back the covers and get up, she almost stumbled out into the hall to go to the bathroom, but remembered in time that they'd made love last night and she was still naked. Slipping on her robe and slippers, she headed for the basement. They'd put in a second bathroom a few years ago when trying to make do with just one for a family of five became a major headache. Even though it was further away, she preferred the newer bathroom for her morning shower—no tub, just a big shower with a glass front and glass sliding door, two sinks, and a large mirror with vanity lights. She wasn't as likely to wake the kids before six-thirty either.

Michelle let the hot water run over her head, waking up her brain. Today was Jared's craziest day, working the control tower from six till two, then again from ten tonight till six Friday morning. But at least he'd be home for supper. And the weekend was coming up. Maybe they could even get a night out. And Memorial Day weekend was coming up too . . . if they planned ahead, maybe they could take a couple days away as a family. Wouldn't that be great?

But she couldn't just stand in the shower. She had to get dressed, get the kids up, throw lunches together, set out breakfast—cold cereal on weekdays—and get out the door herself if she wanted to get to the office by eight.

Even though the day was overcast, the temperature had climbed into the seventies by noon. Made her glad she'd packed a sandwich and could eat her lunch in a park near her next client visit. She dreaded this one. DCFS had received at least five calls from neighbors in an apartment building about a baby crying for hours, what sounded like drunken fights, people coming and going who weren't on the lease. DCFS had passed it on to Bridges Family Services and her supervisor had dropped it on her desk.

"Just check it out. Might not be anything we can do. Use your judgment."

Right. Not serious enough for DCFS to intervene. And the parents themselves weren't asking for help. One of those dysfunctional families that so often fell through the cracks. But . . . she'd "check it out."

Michelle parked her car on a nearby residential street and found a bench where she could eat her lunch. The park was fairly empty for such a warm day. But it was only late May. Kids were still in school. Most adults were at work. Still, a cluster of young men loitered near the playground equipment, smoking, drinking beer, talking loudly. Walking around like ducks in their low-slung pants. Doing nothing. Why weren't they in school—or at work? She shook her head. O Lord . . .

Sometimes the dysfunction in the city threatened to overwhelm her.

But once her sandwich, apple, and snack-size bag of Fritos were gone, she couldn't put it off any longer. She walked back to her car . . . darn it! A parking ticket! She snatched it off her windshield. What in the world for? There weren't any parking meters . . . and then she saw the fire hydrant on the other side of the car. Oh great. Just great. How could she have been so stupid? She squinted at the fine print on the yellow ticket. A hundred dollars?!

Now she felt like crying.

By the time she found the address of the apartment building she was supposed to visit—after encountering half a dozen one-way streets—her mood was as sour as spoiled sauerkraut. Standing in the foyer of the apartment building and staring at the names above the two rows of mailboxes—several of which hung open or otherwise looked busted—she finally located the name and apartment number she'd been given. Blackwell 3B. Two other names had been scrawled beside it. Owens . . . Smith. She pushed the button. Heard nothing. She pushed again.

Just then a man barged out the inner door, startled to see her in the foyer, but just kept going out. Seemed in a big hurry. Michelle caught the inner door before it wheezed shut. Okaay. Not exactly legit, but she'd make one more try at contacting the Blackwells.

No elevator—but she wouldn't trust one in these old apartment buildings anyway. The stairwell smelled musty, stale. She walked up the stairs to the first floor landing . . . then second . . . finally third, feeling out of breath. Was she that out of shape? Locating 3B she rapped loudly on the door and listened. A baby was crying somewhere, but she wasn't sure from which apartment. She knocked again, even louder.

The lock clicked. The handle turned and the door opened a few inches. But nobody was there . . . until she looked down and saw the cute face of a girl about seven. Nappy hair caught up in three pigtails, one on either side, one high in back. Michelle smiled. "Hi, sweetie. Is your mommy home?"

The nutmeg brown face nodded. "But she sleeping."

The sound of the baby crying was louder now. From this apartment.

"What's your name?"

"Candy."

"Is anyone else home?" A solemn nod. "Otto."

"Who's Otto?"

"Mommy's friend."

Hmm. "Can I speak to Otto?"

A shrug. The door opened wider and Michelle followed the little girl into the dim interior. The apartment smelled like urine and cheap alcohol. She tried to breathe through her mouth. The little girl pointed into the kitchen. Standing in the doorway,

Michelle felt like gagging. Otto was slumped over the table, his face smashed in his plate of food, passed out, dead drunk.

Michelle turned and followed the sound of the crying baby into a dark living room, old sheets covering the windows. A child about nine months old stood hanging onto the side of a netted playpen, wailing half-heartedly. The baby was wearing a shirt and a dirty diaper—full from the way it hung. And smelled.

She turned to the little girl. "Can you go wake up your mommy?" Candy shook her head. "She tol' me she'd spank me good if I woke her up. Said she gots ta sleep, 'cause she gots ta work tonight." Yeah, I bet. Michelle was unsure what to do. She felt like an intruder, even though she was there on official business and the child had let her in. The one thing she could do she didn't want to do. Oh, suck it up, Michelle. "Candy, do you know where the baby's clean diapers are?"

Candy nodded, disappeared, and came back with a disposable. "We only gots one."

One. Michelle was on the verge of either laughing hysterically or crying hysterically. The situation was heartbreaking! But she picked up the baby, found the bathroom, wrung out a used washcloth hanging on the tub, and tried to clean the baby's bottom—him, it turned out, when she peeled off the offending diaper. An ugly rash covered his entire genital area. She wished she had some zinc oxide ointment to soothe it.

It took several rinses of the rag to wash the baby, but finally the clean diaper was on. The baby had stopped crying and just stared at her. She picked him up and held him, noticing his large beautiful eyes as she returned to the living room. "What's your brother's name?"

"Pookey."

"Pookey! Is that his real name?"

Candy shrugged. "That's what Mommy calls him. Just Pookey."

"Who are you?" A harsh voice hurtled into the room from the doorway. Startled, Michelle turned quickly. "Whatchu doin' wit my baby? Give 'im to me!" A woman in a rumpled nightshirt stormed across the room and snatched the baby from Michelle's arms. "Whatchu doin' in my house? Git out! Git out!" The baby let out a wail.

Michelle didn't move. "I'm from Bridges Family Services. My name is—"

"I don't care what yer name is. Git out!"

"Ms. Blackwell, DCFS has received calls about possible neglect, and we need—"

"I said, Git out! Or I'm callin' the po-lice."

You do that. Might be the best thing. But the woman's face was twisted with fury and Michelle wasn't sure what she might do. "All right. But we do need to talk about these children." She held out her card to the woman. "Please, give me a call. Our agency can help. We have resources—"

Parked on his mother's hip, Pookey started to cry again as the woman marched to the door and yanked it open. "I said, git out. Now!"

Michelle gave the card to Candy. "Don't lose it," she whispered . . . and a few moments later found herself in the hall with the door slammed behind her.

But as she started down the stairs, she heard the door open again and the mother's harsh voice sailing after her. "How'd ya get in th' buildin' anyway? How'd ya get up here?"

Michelle just kept going and called back, "Goodbye, Ms. Blackwell! We'll be in touch!" By the time she got to the ground floor and headed for her car, she was muttering to herself. Could she make a case for neglect? Turn it over to the state attorney's office? Probably not. She didn't have enough information. But she wished she could get those kids out of that awful situation.

She hardly noticed it had started to rain.

Order PENNY WISE from wwww.daveneta.com
or ask for it at your local bookstore.
It's distributed by Ingram.

CPSIA information can be obtained
at www.ICGtesting.com
Printed in the USA
FFOW03n1111151215
19369FF

9 780982 054482